MAYFLOWER MAID

BY
SUE ALLAN

BABASH-RYAN PUBLISHERS

ISBN 1-904706-15-0
Babash-Ryan Ltd Publishers

*This book is dedicated to the Separatists, whose story this is,
and to all those who stand up to unrighteous dominion.*

CHAPTER ONE

PLYMOUTH COLONY 1623

The delicate porcelain-skinned woman lay thrashing like some tormented doll on the makeshift bed as insatiable fever devoured her body. Like a tillerless boat cast adrift in a tempest, she pitched, tossed and rolled in a desperate bid to ride out the waves of the lethal storm.

"So?" asked her ashen-faced husband despairingly as he searched his companion's face for some glimmer of hope, "is my dear Dorothy going to die too then, Samuel?"

"In truth I do not know, Francis," the doctor replied with brutal honesty. "That she should have survived at all, after nursing so many though such sickness as this these past turbulent years and not have succumbed herself, bears testament to her inner strength and tenacity. However," he added sombrely, "I am fearful for her life, and I would be doing you a disservice to say otherwise. I would have hoped for the crisis to have passed long before now, but instead, I fear she is growing weaker. Her spirit is strong, I have no doubt of that, but her body simply cannot take much more of this punishment! Francis, you should prepare yourself for the worst," the physician said, placing a kindly hand on the poor man's shoulder. "Dear God! I had hoped to have seen the end of these wretched infections and fevers."

Francis reached over the mattress and placed a fresh damp cloth on his beloved's forehead and did his best to cool her fevered brow. Finally, she slumped back upon the pillows and fell into a fitful sleep once more. Samuel sighed deeply and wiped his thin grey hair from his heavily-furrowed brow as they climbed down from the cramped loft-space and stepped across the tiny room to sit beside the open window. "I tell you Francis," he said, casting his eye across the vista of this newly settled Plymouth, "in my estimation, for every acre of land that we now have under cultivation, we have planted one of our dear congregation beneath this poor virgin soil. So many feel it is a bitter crop we have sown; dead seeds with no harvest to come. So many have passed over now, so many good, strong souls amongst them."

The two men slumped down wearily on the chairs. Samuel turned and looked Francis straight in his pale, attentive blue eyes.

"Forgive me," he implored, "but at times like this even I, of all people, question the Good Lord's intention. After so many years of persecution; of being hounded from place to place by our own kinsmen and exiled to Leyden, we harboured such hopes when we embarked upon this endeavor. Husbands, wives, children; all hoped for a better life in a new world free from the bigots and conformists we had struggled to shake from our sleeves. This was to be our new Eden and a fresh beginning for Christ's Gospel. The return to a purity of worship as He has shown us - as He had intended. Why then, has He led us all the way here to the Americas? Why have we, who followed Him in good faith, been sacrificed to pestilence and disease for so little profit?"

This outburst from Samuel Fuller was indeed unexpected. For from a person who was both surgeon- physician and respected man of God, such words shook simple carpenter Francis Eaton.

Francis had lost his first wife, Sarah, within weeks of the Mayflower landing, to the initial general fever that had struck the pilgrims down with such ferocity, and Samuel himself had suffered the loss of his brother and sister–in–law during that same outbreak.

"There has been neither rhyme nor reason as to whom it has taken and whom it has spared," Samuel said wearily. "I am of above forty years and still live while those barely half my age are cut down and gone, and now serve as but bone-meal for the hungry sod." The doctor paused for a moment in deep reflection, and then continued, "They say in the Old World that to grow a strong vine, first you should lay down a dead donkey in the planting pit so that in its decay it might feed and nourish the roots of the new plant, thus bringing forth strong sturdy shoots and an abundance of sound fruit. I hope to God this proves so."

Francis added his own sentiment.

"I pray that we who remain survive and multiply to justify the lives that have been laid down to grow this new dominion of the Lord."

"Amen, Francis. We need to secure a foothold to heaven here. Right here! if we are to build a true stairway to God's Kingdom."

Now, cruelly, one of those who had survived thus far, Francis's second wife of less than three years, lay dangerously close to death, clasped tight in the grip of fever. Fresh cries from her sunken form drew their attention away from this discourse and hurrying back up the ladder, they crouched anxiously by her side. Her long loose tresses, damply curled by perspiration but still perfect in their form, tumbled over onto the pillows on which she was supported. Her pearly visage, pale apart from scarlet flushed cheeks, remained unstrained yet her lips contorted in wild torment as a disarray of words came forth in gasps. Yet, all the while those large brown eyes usually so full of humility and compassion, as had been well witnessed by both men now at her bedside, had long remained firmly shut. So, as she had selflessly ministered to their loved ones as they each in turn had lain dying, now these grateful menfolk were tending to her in return.

"There, there," Samuel soothed, taking the cloth from his patient's forehead and replacing it gently with a new one that had been set to soak in a bowl nearby, "try to rest, Dorothy."

"Dorothy?" Her words were faint yet clearly audible. "My name is not Dorothy," she insisted, "not Dorothy!"

Her husband looked on in alarm, not knowing what to make of his wife's words.

"Of course it is, my beloved," Francis said. Then taking up his dear wife's hand and tenderly reassuring her, he repeated his words, "Of course it is. You are Dorothy. You are my own dear wife - Dorothy Eaton."

"It is delirium, Francis. It is nought but the fever talking," Samuel Fuller said knowingly, trying his best to comfort his distraught companion.

With this, the woman rose up a little from the pillows and her eyes finally fluttered open. Fleetingly they fixed, staring beyond that simple cabin interior to some distant point that may even have transcended life itself. Labored, yet clearly audible, she gasped but five words:

"Bessie - my name is Bessie!" before gently falling back and into a deep, peaceful repose.

***

LINCOLNSHIRE, ENGLAND - SOME TWENTY YEARS EARLIER

Bessie woke. Her hands and face were freezing. Outside, somewhere in the blackness a young cockerel screeched its immature greeting to the fast approaching dawn. The girl rubbed life back into her cold stiff limbs and willed her aching bones up from her meagre straw-filled mattress. Across the room, from behind a makeshift partition of Hessian, she could hear the snorting of her stepfather as he slumbered deeply. Snatching up her brown, coarse woollen overdress, Bessie crept quietly over the rough bare floorboards, away from her sleeping family towards the open hatchway and deftly descended the wooden steps. Once safely below, in the only other part of their humble stone cottage, the girl made for the warming glow of the dying embers of last night's fire. She reached over to the large willow basket by the hearth, took out a fresh log and quietly placed it in the fireplace. As she fumbled in the flickering light to dress herself the log spat and crackled as the fire once more sprang into life, sending shadows dancing wildly across the scantly furnished room. Sitting on the low wooden stool, as close to the grate as she dare, Bessie spread apart her legs, raised the linen petticoats, which she had slept in, and thankfully warmed her legs as she laced up her badly worn shoes. Gazing into the flickering flames Bessie wished she could remain basking in their warmth but she knew she could not afford to. Besides, if she tarried there too long it would only serve to make her feel the cold more keenly once she ventured outside, as she knew she now must.

Bessie drew up her unruly mane of chestnut brown hair, covered it with her white cap, which she tied in an untidy bow at her chin before throwing her black shawl around her elegant but half-bare shoulders. She took a taper from the clay pot up on the mantle and plunged it briefly into the fire until it too was aflame, quickly using this to light her waiting candle before snuffing it out again with her thin spittle-wet fingers. Picking up the wooden pail and lid, Bessie made for the door.

As she stepped outside into the gloom the cockerel crowed once more, joined this time by a scant chorus of cheeping from birds perched in nearby trees and hedgerows. Then, suddenly, something scuttled across her feet before disappearing away into the darkness and although it had been too quick for Bessie to get a good look, she guessed it had been a rat. There were always rats around; the chickens attracted them.

It had been a cold still night and the air pinched at Bessie's bare hands and cheeks. The sky was deep, deep blue and the stars still sparkled like jewels above her head although beyond the row of farm cottages a precursive splash of crimson was heralding the rising sun. In this half-light the scrubby sheep pasture had been transfigured with glistening hoarfrost into a vista of breath-taking beauty. Beyond this, the church stood silent, silhouetted against the sky on the hill gently rising up before her. Bessie thought of her Father lying alone beneath the frozen sod in the poor corner of the graveyard and a solitary tear trickle down her face before she could stifle it. She felt a chill run though her and pulled her shawl up close to her neck for warmth and protection. Taking care on the cobbled path not to lose her footing on the ice, she made her way to the ramshackle cowshed just across the yard. Once there she slipped the bar from the rickety door, went in, set down the candle on the ledge and quickly shut herself in again in an effort the keep out the cold. Inside it was warm to some degree from the body heat of its sole occupant, an aging brown cow and she could hear the rustle of straw as a gentle lowing greeted her. Bessie could easily see her breath and that of the beast as it broke out into the cold gloom of the shed. She patted the tethered cow tenderly and spoke to it as she drew up beside it with the wooden milking stool and bucket, snuggling up close and resting her cheek against the cow's side as she positioned herself ready for milking; the entire time still speaking to the animal as if in pleasant conversation with a dear friend. The girl blew on her fingers and rubbed them together for a moment to warm them, then gently she grasped hold of the cow's warm teats with her hands and set about the rhythmic release of the milk. Her bovine companion swished her tail and mooed as if with relief and gratitude for this easing of her previous discomfort.

"Poor creature," Bessie thought to herself, glancing up and noticing how increasingly pinched in the old cow was looking in the haunches, "that last calf really took it out of you, didn't it?"

Bessie was right. Since the birth of her last offspring, a sickly bull calf, the cow had swiftly fallen into decline. Even more so since it was taken from her and subjected to an intense but fruitless effort to fatten it enough for slaughter. When the time came, it had made a miserable carcass of more bone than meat. Then again, Old Tom, once herdsman up at the Manor house, had warned Bessie's stepfather not to allow the poor beast to be serviced by the bull again.

"Not at her age, Nathan. It's asking for nought but trouble!" he had warned. But Bessie's stepfather had not heeded the stockman's words and now the milk too was dwindling with each passing week. Bessie's mother prayed the cow would pick up in the spring with the fresh new grass. Otherwise, she fretted over how they would manage with no spare cheese or milk to sell; they barely scraped a living as it was and she could see no possible way of affording a replacement.

Bessie covered the milk pail, untied the cow and turned her out of the shed. She took up the pitchfork leaning against the wall and cleared away the soiled straw, replacing it with fresh in readiness for the creature's return that evening. It was Sunday and Bessie planned to go out that day, God willing, and she didn't want to put this task off until later in case she arrived home late. She knew to her past cost that she could plan to go to her aunt's house, but whether or not her stepfather would actually allow her to when it was time for her to depart, was never a certain thing. His mood swung wildly from hour to hour and there was little love lost between him and his estranged half-sister.

Bessie picked up the candle and carried the milk pail back to the cottage and set it down on the cold slab just inside the tiny pantry. As she bent down, she felt coarse hands on her thighs trying to raise up her skirts. She quickly straightened up and stubbly skin scratched forcefully against her soft cheek and hot foul breath pervaded her senses. She rounded quickly on the transgressor and pushed him away. It was her stepfather and it wasn't the first time he had tried this of late.

"What this?" he sneered lasciviously, "no kiss for your

Father?"

"You're not my Father!" the girl snapped back in a hushed voice, her large brown eyes blazing with anger. Just then, Bessie's mother appeared on the steps, making her way down from above. Bessie felt her face flush. She was certain her mother must have caught some of what had passed or at least partly seen what had happened, yet if she had, she made no remark to her daughter at all. Deeply embarrassed the girl quickly gathered up her overskirt, filled it with corn from the sack by the door and went out to feed the hens. In her wake, from behind the closed cottage door, she could hear the raised voice of her mother followed by a shriek, then abrupt silence. Bessie sighed and made her way across the yard to the henhouse near the beck. It had already become quite light in just that short space of time and the sky was a beautiful bright blue etched with pink as the sun steadily rose. Above the naked sycamores the moon was still there, just a slender crescent of pale luminosity high above wispy transient clouds. Birds were still singing, but not so many now as the daily race for survival had begun; a race to find enough sustenance to see them through another Lincolnshire winter's day.

A different sort of dawn chorus now resounded through the air; the raucous racket of chickens growing impatient for their enforced nocturnal confinement to come to an end. Bessie unlatched the door with one hand as her other held fast to her skirtful of chicken feed. A commotion of chickens tumbled out in all directions, flapping and clucking and scratching at the earth. Bessie broadcast the corn in small handfuls among the greedy throng until it was spent, then taking up a stout piece of wood the girl smashed away the layer of ice that had formed on the water trough overnight. She quickly checked inside the hen house for any early laid eggs amongst the straw and was rewarded by four warm beauties, which she carefully picked up and popped in her pocket to take back to the cottage. Eggs were at a premium this time of year as most of the hens were out of lay. Last season's youngsters needed building up for point of lay in spring but the old boilers could now be dispensed with over the winter months, they were needed for the pot. There were still a few roosters in the fattening pen too, which Mother would tend to later.

On her way out Bessie noticed something lying in the straw. It was an old speckled hen, still warm but dead, its beady eyes staring blankly. Bessie picked up the fowl by its scaly yellow claws and carried it dangling at her side with head bobbing and soft lifeless wings flapping against her skirts with every step.

Bessie went back indoors to gelid silence. Her stepfather, Nathan, did not notice her return. He was seated with his back to the door by the fire, with a platter of bread, cheese and cold meat. He was devouring his breakfast like some frenzied wild beast mauling a carcass, his teeth snapping and mouth slobbering over every mouthful, his short fat fingers forcing ever more food into his already crowded mouth. In betwixt he swilled down gulps of small beer from his battered pewter tankard, wiping his mouth from time to time on the sheen of dirt on the back of his sleeve. With thighs so corpulent that they spilled over the edges of his seat, obscuring it completely and calves easily the girth of a child, he did not cut a pleasing figure. To Bessie her stepfather was nothing but a greedy, ugly, demanding cuckoo in what was once a happy nest. She regarded him with utmost despite and loathing but on no account dared to show her true feelings. He was truly an ill-bred oaf of a man, devoid of a crumb of decent manners and so unlike her dear late father. When he had suddenly died of a spring fever four years earlier, mother was facing destitution and eviction from her tied cottage until Nathan stepped in and offered marriage to keep the roof above her head. It was an ill match but one made of necessity if mother and child were to survive, for there was no one else to take them on.

Nathan had been wed before but his wife had died in childbirth. He was by an accident of birth a poor but distanced member of the Tourneys, one the county's richest and most powerful families. Although Nathan was the laziest of all the farmhands in the village he got away with it solely because of this tie and the landlord farmer's fear of causing offence to the greater family by dispensing with his services.

Mother was busy in the pantry putting together a basket of provisions for Bessie to take to her aunt after church. Bessie slid in beside her, put down the eggs and furtively showed her the chicken. A swift, covert collaboration between Mother and daughter took place before the older woman glanced up and remarked loudly.

"Go wash your face girl! You can't be going off to church with your cheek smeared with goodness knows what. And your hair! There's straw in it!" she exclaimed.

"Yes!" her stepfather interjected from his cosy, warm nook. "How do you ever expect to get a husband looking like that? You are sixteen girl and it is about time you were wed!"

Bessie said nothing. She went out into the yard and drew up a bucket of water from the well, letting the pail rest a moment on the stone lip to give the ripples time to settle. Then she peered over, checked her reflection and washed away the offending mark. She returned to the cottage and picking up her brush, removed her cap and brushed out her wild locks till they were tangle free, smooth and silky. She looked beautiful as she was but her mother insisted on braiding her hair tightly and pulling it up severely under a fresh white cap.

"That's better," her mother smiled lovingly. "They do say loose hair means a loose woman! It may be alright for the farmyard but not for church on a Sabbath."

Her stepfather turned around from his fireside chair and looked the girl up and down.

"Yes, better," he agreed grudgingly. "At least you won't

be letting me down when Elias Wilkins comes a-calling to walk you to church presently.!"

"Elias?" Bessie exclaimed with despair.

"Yes my girl! Elias! And if I were you, I'd look kindly upon him because he has intimated to me that he would have you to wife."

"Wife?" Bessie cried out in horror. "I'll not marry him…ever! He's…"

"Too good for you?"

"Too old and repulsive!" Bessie retaliated.

"Granted he may not be the youngest or most handsome man in the world but he's not too badly off and ready to take on a wife at the right price," Nathan replied casually.

"Price? You would barter me away?"

"No, but I would expect some sort of compensation for losing your labour here helping your dear mother about the place. Only reasonable is it not? Besides, he's also offering me a fine milker into the consideration and you know we sore have need of one. That cow out there dies then how do you think I can afford to keep you?"

"Well I will not have him! Not if he were the last man in the village!"

Nathan's wife's eyes flashed in alarm, warning to her daughter to desist.

"Listen, girlie!" Her stepfather learned right forward from his chair. His steely grey eyes widened and his crooked top lip quivered as he countered coolly, "And just whom do you think you are to make such a decision? There aren't that many single men left in this parish and yet a surfeit of marriageable girls from which to choose. Think on! There are better than you for him to choose from! Take young Humility Brown, for example, now there's a fine young heifer for a young man to espouse. Good wide hips for child bearing and plump firm dumplings for a man to enjoy while he's having his meat!"

"Nathan!" Bessie's mother exclaimed appalled by her

husband's crudeness.

"What?" Nathan protested loudly, turning like an angry dog on his wife. "I am only saying how it is and this flibbertigibbet should be heeding my words unless she wants to end up like that aunt of hers!"

"Well the girl has told you her views on the matter, Husband, and that's an end to it! You know full well there's no point trying to force her into anything either, for the rector made it quite plain when he took up the encumbrance of this parish that he would not marry any dissenting brides in his church. Not while he's rector!"

Nathan's eyes narrowed but he said nothing. Instead, he sat by the fire smouldering. He was dangerous when in such a frame of mind and the women became wary with good cause. Nathan did not take kindly to being disobeyed and both women in turn felt fearful lest they had crossed that fine divide over which they stepped on pain of retribution. Such an intense atmosphere followed that it might be portioned with a knife.

Bessie's mother continued to pack up the basket for taking to Nathan's half-sister hoping that he would not throw a fit of temper and forbid the visit out of hand. Her daughter helped. It was such a meagre offering that they had cobbled together but as much as they could afford to spare and more than Bessie's aunt could hope for.

A loud rapping at the cottage door suddenly breached the impasse. Bessie's mother answered it with the girl peering over her shoulder from the shadows to see who it was.

" Now then, Mistress Birch," came a typical local greeting. It was Elias Wilkins, his ruddy face unusually clean for his custom and his dank hair obviously wetted down for the occasion, leaving it looking like a starling's plumage.

"Ah!" he exclaimed catching sight of the girl, "now then, Bessie! My but you're looking lovely this morning!" Elias smiled broadly before adding, "I've come to walk you to church."

"Now then, Mister Wilkins," Bessie's mother repaid his greeting politely, "would you care to step inside out of the cold?"

Bessie smiled weakly before returning quickly to finish with the basket. She took a large piece of cheesecloth and covered over the contents securely. Her Mother fetched the girl's best shawl and hat and helped her daughter on with them, saying, "Why don't you two young people go on ahead? We will catch you up shortly."

The thought of Nathan going to church made Bessie angry. He only attended because it was compulsory and showed he was not of a separatist persuasion. The man mocked the clergy at every turn and broke the commandments without hesitation if it suited him better than to obey. And yet it was he who so often sat by the fire with the Bible teetering on his fat knees, sanctimoniously lecturing his women on their 'duties' towards him as Master in this Christian home. He, who like them could neither read nor write, yet opened the good book at every turn to smite them into subjugation by imperiously quoting verses at them to impose and enforce his dominion over their miserable lives.

Bessie picked the basket up by the handle and made to leave.

"Wait a minute, girl!" Nathan sprang to his feet and snatched off the cloth from over the basket. He peered inside and seized the modest cheese round from inside.

"There, take the rest but leave the cheese! Can't afford to go giving to that daughter of my father's what we need for ourselves!"

Neither woman made comment or opposed Nathan in his action. Instead, Bessie silently recovered the basket and left the cottage in the company of Elias. She was thankful at least that it appeared her stepfather was allowing her visit to go ahead after all that had been said that morning.

Elias and Bessie walked up towards St. Peter's church along the little lane. Across the sheep field to their left as they make their way up the hill Bessie watched as a mist rose up and began to blot out the roll of The Wolds beyond. Conversation was slight and strained on both parts: he not quite sure what to say next in response to her one word answers to his questions and she, in turn dreading having to respond to him at all. Then Elias clumsily reached out for her slender hand and grasped it in his own.

"Stop," she squealed pulling it away from his tenacious grip, "you're crushing my fingers."

With that, they continued their short walk up the lane in silence and on reaching the church separated to merge into the congregation.

The sermon that day seemed unending. Inside, the five hundred year old church was as cold as it was out, even though the congregation stood huddled together like a flock of sheep in a blizzard for warmth. Try as she might not to, Bessie's eyes and thoughts repeatedly wandered away from the rector's words and she found her eyes falling towards poor old Tom, for he had finally gone to the wall. It was so sad, she thought, to witness a once strong man, such as he had been, and a friend to her father confined to the stone seats at the edge of the church for want of being able to stand unaided, for any but a short length of time these days.

Most like he's not much longer for this world, she thought to herself with pity.

When the service did come to an end and the flock dispersed from its shepherd, Bessie slipped quietly away towards the high road at the top end of the settlement to make the long walk to her aunt's house. She stopped at the end of the lichen-spotted graveyard wall and under its concealment hoisted up her skirts to reveal the chicken secreted under them. She untied the cord at her waist and placed the bird inside her basket. As she peered back towards the church she glimpsed the unmistakable form of Nathan deep in conversation with another man whom she had trouble making out clearly, but who she took to be Elias, in the lea of the Norman arched south porch of the church. Of course, there was no way that she could have been privy to their discourse. But if she had been, she might have chosen to forsake her journey that day for the relative safety of her hearth and home.

"She will not have a bar of me Nathan," Elias was saying mournfully to Bessie's guardian. "'Tis a lost cause I tell you!"

"Nay, nay, Elias!" Nathan urged the thwarted suitor. "She might simply have refused you out of hand because her head has no idea of what's good for her! I tell you, do as I have suggested and she will be wed and under your roof before Easter. Do exactly as I said, mind," the older man warned, "and have no fear of it for there will be no other consequence than to gain yourself a wife!"

"No consequence, Nathan? Are you deadly certain on that?"

"Yes," he replied without hesitation, "deadly certain! Bessie is playing hard to get, that is all. She wants you; she's been saving herself just for you. I tell you, she just a-feared! She will be thankful to you once she has lost her maidenhead. It is just the silly fear of it that drives these girls to resist, that's all. Fear of the unknown! The fight goes out of them after that first time. I promise you! All will come right!"

Chapter Two

The walk, though long, was pleasant enough. It was already approaching noon but the sun had failed to burn off the mist that had steadily risen up from the fields since daybreak. All that betrayed its presence were occasional pale fingers of watery sunlight clawing at the half obscured shapes mystically rising up in the mid-distance, as if frantically scratching away at the murkiness before being quickly gloved again. This gloom seemed firmly set to cling to the remainder of the day. The highroad was deserted and Bessie did not pass a soul on her way along it out of the village, but then again this was the Sabbath. Apart from carrying out tasks that were necessary for the welfare of the animals, those who usually laboured in the fields flanking the road did not today. In any case, at this time of year, with its short dark days, except for tending the sheep and livestock there was little work to be done on the land apart from repairs to fences and hedges. Come spring though this would all change dramatically. Then there would not be enough hands or hours in the day to do all the tasks that were needed. Especially come lambing and ploughing time.

Today Bessie had chosen to avoid the cart ruts in which she had easily made previous journeys during the unusually dry summer and autumn of that year. After the hard frost of last night and the thaw of the milder morning, they were soft and muddy and Bessie did not want to clag up her feet. Instead, the young girl favoured the drier, banked verge beside the road. As a precaution she hitched up her skirts and tied them in a knot at her left thigh to save the hems from dragging in the dirt or getting wet brushing against the long, damp sedge as she passed by.

Bessie's aunt lived down a long, narrow, snaking lane that skirted thick woodland. She had never married and the reason behind that unfortunate condition had never been a subject of conversation at Bessie's home. Not in her hearing at least. Aunt Annie seemed a handsome woman to Bessie's way of thinking, so she could not understand her single status or how she managed to eke out a living. True her home was little more than a hovel; nothing more than a large room with a chimneybreast at one end and a large bed at the other secreted behind a flimsy cloth partition. There was an old oak table, a chest and two wooden chairs and home made rush matting upon the floor. It may have been sparse but it always held a warm welcome for the girl.

As she arrived there that day Bessie carefully checked, as previously advised, to make certain there were no men's boots discarded by the front door recess, nor a horse secretly tethered amongst the scrubby trees to the rear. If so, then on calling at the house, Bessie had been instructed to wait patiently nearby until Annie's visitor had departed before knocking at the door and entering. As there was no sign of company, Bessie tapped then went straight in.

Annie was delighted to see her step-niece. She leaned over to the cauldron set above the crackling fire and ladled out a dish of hot but thin broth to warm the poor girl through. Her aunt seemed delighted with the basket of food and especially once she spied the chicken. She took the fowl straightaway to her seat by the fireside and set about plucking the feathers as the two chatted happily about everything and anything. Anything, that is, but Nathan. Neither chose to speak that man's name, ever.

Once having brought her aunt up to date on gossip from the parish, Bessie foreshortened this visitation. She had noticed how the mist had thickened during her walk there, finally making it difficult to judge even what time it was and as she needed to be home again before twilight to open the shed and see to the cow again for evening milking, she made her stay brief.

As was her custom, Bessie chose to take the straighter,

quicker low road home. This would bring her out at the bottom end of her village near the little bridge over the beck where the sheep were dipped.

As Bessie fondly kissed her aunt goodbye and set off, a keen chill set in. The unseen sun was dying with the day and taking what little warmth there had been with it. Soon it would slip beyond the invisible horizon and darkness would swiftly follow. Bessie could hardly see any distance at all as the swirling mist began to close in and envelope the remaining landscape around her. It was unnervingly still and quiet. Not a bird, not a sound broke the silence. As she approached skeletal trees, they took on an eerie appearance, first emerging then quickly disappearing back into the impenetrable grey as she passed them by.

Then, as the timeless minutes slipped by, almost subliminally Bessie began to sense that something was following her. The hair prickled up across the nape of her slender neck as she became aware of an intermittent crackling sound that was coming from somewhere close by. She stopped, rigid with fear, craning her ears to hear and standing perfectly still for a moment or two. Nothing. She heard nothing. Cautiously she slowly started on her way again but within a few hesitant paces, she had heard it once more. This time it was closer and coming from somewhere beneath the trees off to her right. However, it did not take very long for the girl to realise that this was not the sound of branches gently snapping under stealthy feet as she had envisaged but only condensation dripping from the bare branches all about and onto the dead bracken. Reassured, she walked on until without warning a large, startled cock pheasant bolted out from the bushes making her gasp in fright before it disappeared into the murk ahead. With her heart still thumping from fright, Bessie's lungs exploded with a sigh, followed by a girlish giggle at her own stupidity for letting her imagination run away with her like that.

Once over her excitement, Bessie was aware that she urgently needed to pass water and would be unable to hold it for very much longer. Although utterly certain by now that she was alone on the lane, modesty still led her to leave the track for the cover of bushes close by. She placed her basket on the ground, lifted her skirts and squatted down amid some soft grass and let her relief flood from her.

As she stood again, shaking her skirts down she half registered something, large and dark, looming up swiftly behind her. Before she could even scream, the breath was knocked out of her as she was grabbled from behind and flung heavily to the ground onto her back. It was Elias. Throwing himself astride her body, he subdued her with his muscular frame and forcibly kissed her full on the mouth, his chipped, jagged teeth catching her gentle fleshy lips and drawing blood. She tried to push him away; to tell him to stop but he bore down upon her heavily, his mouth pressing so hard to hers that she could not utter a sound. Bessie felt herself gag as he attempted to probe between her lips with his large, slobbering tongue to explore inside her mouth. She clamped her jaws firmly shut in resistance. He pulled back momentarily and laughed heartily.

"You know you want this, silly goose. You know you want this!"

"Get off me, you pig!" Bessie swore at him and attempted to lash out, but he caught hold of her delicate wrists and forced them down behind her head upon the trampled bracken.

"Get off me! Get off me, you brute!" she screamed at him.

"Now, now then, Bessie. I'm tired of cooling my heels. I know it's just a game to you. Girls like to play. To spin it out enough to drive a man crazy but it has gone too far now and taken far too long. So I need to take matters into my own hands," he said calmly

Elias held both her wrists, tightly, in the span of his huge right hand as he manoeuvred his other one down and attempted to loosen the strapping on Bessie's snug-fitting bodice. At first, the knotted lace proved an obstacle to Elias working single-handed but soon he managed to fumble it undone. Given slack, the woollen garment now easily gave way to reveal Bessie's flimsy under blouse and Elias quickly tugged it down to release her firm, youthful breasts from their bondage. Her blushed pink nipples, like rose buds, looked inviting and ready for plucking and lowering his head and with his temple pressed against her chin, he lunged his tongue into into her cleavage. Then he opened his mouth wide and almost completely engulfed each breast, in turn, sucking and nipping at the warm soft flesh.

"Oh Bessie!" he sighed breathlessly, raising his head to look up as he still mouthed her. "What fine, smooth duckies you have for a man to pleasure himself with!"

"Stop this!" she pleaded. "For the love of God!" she protested, but to no avail.

The taste of her was in his mouth and her sweet heady scent was on the air. This hound was bold. Excited. Intent on the quarry and closing in for the kill.

"Now Bessie don't be afeared," he said. "I know how you girls are, for your first time, but it will be all right. Believe me. I know this for a fact. Once I've shown you the way and made a woman out of you, then you will be thankful to me for this!"

Bessie felt his calloused hand now move purposefully down and across her body. He grasped a fistful of her dress and yanked up her skirt and petticoats. She shuddered at the icy contact of his cold hand against her warm, bare, thigh. Valiantly she struggled to halt him. She tried to hold her knees together but he simply wrenched them apart and secured them that way with his left shin rammed against the inside of her right leg so she might stay opened for his advances. The metallic clink of a buckle being released sent further alarm surging through the girl as Elias unfastened his britches. Then she felt his fingers clawing and prodding, searching for her most private place.

"Please stop this! Please!" Bessie begged, but it was as if Elias had not registered one, solitary word that she cried. Instead he went on probing. Then she felt him there, trying to dig his way into her opening, stabbing at her with his fingertips but unable to breach the resisting flesh. With that he huffed, and his hand emerged from under the veil of her skirts, up to his reddened face and to his mouth. He violently hawked up a mass of spittle and carefully coated his stubby digits. Then he continued his foray below and she felt their slimy trail as he massaged her open, inching her apart and sliding his fingers in. She tensed her body and shut her eyes tightly, trying the blot out the horror.

"Come on, my beauty," Elias urged her, "it will be all right. Just trust me. We are going to make a baby for the springtime. You'll see," he told her. "You will thank me for this."

A horrified Bessie suddenly saw an image flash into her mind. In it, she was a little girl again and she could see her father clearly. He was going on his way into the fields to work. She could hear the words he spoke to her then as clearly as if it were yesterday.

"Old Tom is coming soon, Bessie," he informed his daughter. "Tell him I've got the cow in the field already and lead him up there to show him when he comes."

"I will Father," she had replied diligently.

Tom duly arrived leading a huge black bull with a gleaming ring in its nose and Bessie took the man to the field as directed by her father. As promised, the young heifer was tethered securely to a post happily eating the lush spring grass and unaware of their approach. Batchelor Tom loosed the bull but did not bid the child specifically to depart. Therefore, innocently, she had stayed and witnessed the proceedings. The huge bull stood passively for a moment, pawing gently at the ground and flexing his haunches. Then he stopped. Lifting his enormous broad head up high, his nostrils flared as he started snorting something in from the air. Bessie stared, mesmerized, as the beast's penis then suddenly flopped into view from between his hind legs. She watched intently as this rod-like 'thing' unexpectedly began to elongate and quickly swell to impossible proportions. She wanted to look away but curiosity rooted her gaze to the beast as he trotted purposefully towards the cow, his swollen appendage jigging to and fro beneath him. Little Bessie felt terrified and confused as the imperious bulk of this beast reared up onto the diminutive heifer's back and and she stared in disbelief as the 'rod' disappeared deep into the bellowing cow's body. Bessie shuddered at the heifer's mournful lowing and the perceived a look of gloating evil in the bull's black, glazed eyes as he pounded, relentlessly, against the rump of the cow.

"Stop him! Stop him, he's hurting her," Bessie cried out.

"It's all right child," Tom replied laughing." She's not in any harm! They are only making babies."

Making babies. The dreadful realization dawned upon Bessie. Elias was about to do to her as that bull had done to the cow. In dread anticipation she gasped, panicked and struggled all the more as she was made aware that the hitherto unseen member of her assailant was now pressing solidly against the lips of her entrance. It felt hot and hard. So very hard. Then the head of the hardness penetrated her, cautiously and shallow at first and Bessie prayed that this was as far as this thing would ingress. But then she cried out in fear as she felt her insides trying to stretch and adapt to accommodate it as it started to drive upwards, slowly inching in.

She was terrified; certain in her mind that her whole body was about to split apart at any moment. Elias paused, but only momentarily. Then, with a huge grunt and one almighty thrust, he forced himself up inside her as far as he could. Then she felt it, something snapped inside and released, her body then betrayed her and yielded to the enemy.

"Aaawww!" Elias groaned. "He was right! You were untouched and saving yourself for me. And now I've taken your maidenhead, it's my duty to finish your instruction," he said breathlessly as he started to thrust deeper and deeper, faster and faster, building up into a frenzied rhythmic assault.

"Aaawww!" he groaned and grunted, over and over. "Oh, my beauty! I am having you!"

Bessie stopped struggling. It was useless. He was too powerful and too far advanced along his course of action to be stopped. Instead, she now tried desperately to be somewhere else. To retreat. To hide huddled in some dark, safe corner of her mind where he could not penetrate. Nevertheless, he was everywhere. In every one of her senses. His moaning filled her ears and the foul smell of his sweaty body assailed her nose as it writhed in congress with her unwilling own. Perspiration dripped from his brow and fell down upon her face, the taste of his salt was in her mouth and his touch was burning her flesh. The pounding of her own heart beating coursed through her head. Unrelenting, the rhythm of her torment went on and on. She prayed. Prayed to make it go away.

"Make it end! Make it be over, for pity's sake!" she pleaded with her God.

All Bessie could now think of was that black bull in the field as it rammed, again and again, against the rear of the cow. That glazed faraway look, back then, in that beast's eyes was the same as that now planted on Elias's face.

Suddenly Bessie heard bellowing. The pitiful bellowing of that young heifer so long, long ago but then realized it was now she who was bellowing like a wounded beast. Bellowing and shouting to make him stop. Make him stop! But he would not. He just moaned and groaned as he continued to pump away at her. Still he thrust at her with an ever-increasing vigour until, abruptly, he cried out. Cried out such a cry. Like a whipped dog as his face contorted in some terrible anguish. With a pained breathlessness, he gasped one long, ardent gasp. She felt his whole body flex as with one final, spiteful thrust he skewered her like a piece of meat for the spit. Bessie felt such a pulsating, deep within her that she instinctively knew it was done. His seed was now lodged inside her. There was nothing left she could do.

For a fleeting moment Elias was finally silent. Then his mouth fell open as did his eyes and he grinned. Such a self-satisfied grin. He pulled out of her, loosening his hold on her as he rolled onto the ground beside her, waiting a moment to catch his breath.

"There, my lovely! Didn't I say I'd make a woman of you and now I have. Come three or four months from now and you've got a belly full of arms and legs to show for it, I will come and claim you and the child and then you will have to marry me!"

Sobbing uncontrollably, Bessie struggled to cover her nakedness from his sight. She screamed at him hysterically.

"Never! Never will I marry with you! Never!" she raged bitterly.

"Oh but you will girl," Elias retorted, rising to his feet and swiftly refastening his britches,

"You won't have no say in the matter!" he sneered.

Bessie watched him disappear into the mist as he made off across the fields towards the village. As he did so, she could just determine another figure, that of a man, rise up from nearby and slap Elias on the back. The muffled sound of their laughter barely carrying on the hushed, still air. Then the shock set in.

Bessie remained upon the ground distraught. Uncertain of whether she was still capable of standing. She shook uncontrollably. Her legs felt shaky and strangely weak. She hurt too. She hurt badly between her legs. Believing her assailant to be long gone, she raised up her skirts to inspect the injury. As she glanced downwards at her linen petticoat, she immediately noticed with consternation that it was streaked with bright, fresh blood. She ran her finger gently across her swollen opening. It throbbed with pain and was sticky to the touch. She withdrew her fingers from below and looked. Again a streak of red. She was bleeding from the assault.

Still weeping Bessie struggled to her feet and tried to stand. Feeling faint and woozy, she sat down again, quickly. Suddenly she felt nauseous and was indeed violently sick.

Bitter tears still flooded down her cheeks as she tried to compose herself, burning a trail of despair across her face. Bessie tried to stop them but could not, all she could think about was the attack. In her mind, it was still going on. On and on. Replaying over and over in her head. Every second was now indelibly etched into her mind and soul forever. Only now did it strike her. Of all the terrible things Elias had uttered while he raped her, just three words now suddenly hit her like a lightning bolt.

"He was right," Elias had said. "He was right when he said that you were untouched…"

Oh God! An anguished thought flashed across her mind. The he to whom Elias referred could only have been Nathan!

Her own stepfather might even have put her attacker up to this deed in order to force marriage upon her, and might even have been secreted away nearby to bear witness to the despicable event itself!

This revelation stunned Bessie to the core. That the two most reviled men in her life might have conspired together to bring about her downfall not only enraged her but also strengthened her resolve to expose their vile evilness. She vowed to herself that as soon as she got home she would confront Nathan. Confront him and unmask the true depths of wickedness to her Mother

Bessie eventually managed to get to her feet and pick up her belongings. Although unsteadily at first, she began to make her way homeward. She felt so physically altered by the assault she fretted that if anyone met her along the lane and saw her gait they would know, instantly, that she had lost her virginity. It made her feel dirty and shameful. Elias's taunts about her having to marry him now gnawed at her as she walked. She knew he was right. Who wants an impure bride deflowered by another man? Worse still, who would want a woman carrying another man's child? The shame and humiliation would be unbearable. The truth was that, spoiled as she now was, no one would have her. No one apart from Elias, of course. Once an unmarried woman with child began to show, village and church morality would demand to know who fathered it and force the culprit to make her an 'honest' woman; to wipe out the sinful union and legitimise the otherwise bastard offspring. If not, then while the man might recover his honour, the unfortunate woman never could; she would be an outcast for life. Therefore pressure for her to marry Elias would be intolerable. Her fate seemed firmly sealed, yet still she was determined to face the wicked pair with the truth.

Twilight was approaching as Bessie crossed the little bridge over the beck just beyond the yard, the smell of wood smoke cloying the heavy air. As she neared home, she could see the cottage windows already shuttered against the coming night. Unnoticed, Bessie slipped by the house and over to the well. She drew up a pail of water and took it with her into the shelter of the empty cowshed. Taking up the remnant of cloth from her basket, she submerged it in the cold water then, partially wringing it out she lifted her skirts and began to wipe between her legs. A desperate need surged through her to wash away every hint of Elias from her body. The smell of his foul presence clung to her skin and she had to drive away every trace of his filth before she could go in and tell her mother what had happened.

Bessie had her back turned towards the half open door. Completely absorbed in her task the girl was not immediately alert to the fact that it was being pulled shut and barred from the inside. By the time she was, it was too late. Startled she snatched at her skirts and covered her modesty then turned to find Nathan standing, motionless, behind her. An air of menace hung about him. Emboldened, the girl looked him in the eye.

"You know what's happened, don't you?" Bessie was atremble but adamant in her determination to confront her stepfather.

"Do I?" he said coldly, "tell me, then. What has happened?"

"You know full well!" she said accusingly. "You put Elias up to it didn't you?"

Nathan said nothing.

"I am going to tell!" Bessie warned him, "I am going indoors, right now, and I am going to tell my Mother what the two of you did."

"Are you now?" he replied calmly. "In that case you better pick up the basket and bring it with you," he said, making as if to unbar the door.

In her disturbed state of mind, unthinkingly Bessie turned around to do as he had bid. With that, Nathan lurched towards her and pushed her, face down, over the straw pile and smothered her cries with the palm of his hard hand.

"Going to tell on me are you, young Bess!" he snarled close in her ear. "Tell on the man who puts bread in your belly and a roof above your head? Well tell on this!" he said and proceeded to rape his stepdaughter.

"Tell on me, will you? To your mother?" he taunted her relentlessly as he carried out his onslaught.

Bessie struggled and tried to bite and kick her way free, which only served to amuse Nathan all the more. In the end, she submitted. Her fight was all but drained from her anyway.

"And how do you think she will feel? Eh? When you tell her that you have had knowledge of her own husband?" he panted, as he leaned into the girl and spitefully took his pleasure. "When I tell her that you have been leading me on to it? You stupid little bitch, she will disown you! And do you know how people treat wanton trollops like you?" he gasped. "Trollops who have seduced their own fathers!"

He continued his abuse, shooting it through with ridicule and insults, until he was done. Then he withdrew, got hold of the whimpering girl by her hair and dragged her across the floor of the shed and dropped her near the bucket.

"For god's sake clean yourself up!" he said breathlessly. "You look a mess! And don't go getting the foolish notion in your head that you are going to tell anyone else either! Elias will swear you often arranged to meet him alone in the lane. That it was not the first time either and that he was not the only man to plough your field!" He laughed callously. "Do you want to end your days like that aunt of yours? Wife to no man but mistress to any! You are going to marry with Elias in the spring, so you better get used to the idea! Meanwhile remember, I'm only helping nature along for your own good!"

Destroyed, Bessie sat amongst the straw weeping in utter despair and disbelief trying to comprehend the horror of those past few hours.

Of the two attacks, Nathan's cruelty cut the deepest swathe. It was clear to Bessie that it had been no accident that he had happened upon her alone on her return. It had probably been planned in his mind all along. How he had revelled in the act of humiliating and humbling her. Now he was indoors undoubtedly waiting for her to walk in and to see what she would do next. She could just picture him as she had witnessed him so many times before, with an unnatural smile upon his face and an uneasy air about him: like the calm before the storm breaks; biding his time to see which way she jumped. Most likely he had an evil plan ready to bring into play to discredit her at every possible turn. She was done for. Defeated. Her life choices had been snatched from out of her grasp, apart from one she discovered in that depth of despair. One even Nathan might not have considered.

A sudden equanimity flooded over the girl. Bessie dried her eyes on her cuff and calmly reached up to the peg on the wall and removed an ill-used hank of rope. Carefully she laid it out on the floor and stared at it intently, as she ran her trembling fingers along its rough, fibrous length. Then she took up one end and tied a slipknot in it, just as she had learnt to do to make a halter for leading the animals. Diligently she double-checked the loop would slip smoothly and hold tight. She rose to her feet and regarded the wooden rafters above her head. There was a large, old hammered metal hook in the crossbeam just as she had recalled.

Bessie fetched the rickety wooden milking stool, climbed awkwardly up on it and fastened the free end of the rope securely to the hook. Then self-composed she took up the other end and placed her head through the noose and slid the knot tight about her slender neck. For a moment or two, she teetered on the brink of the seat of the stool. Then, after quietly saying a prayer for forgiveness, she launched herself forward, at the same time kicking away the stool. She dropped. Hanging, with the rope strangling her windpipe, her eyeballs felt as though they were about to explode as she gurgled and she felt as if her face would burst from the congestion. She kicked and struggled for life then, but after only a few agonizing seconds, she fell, landing heavily with a thud upon the floor below. The rope had snapped. Death itself was rejecting her.

Half-choked, the girl's natural reflexes took over as she quickly loosened the noose and gulped down air. Then she cried and cried till she could cry no more.

She thought about her plight long and hard, weighing up whether or not she dare tell her mother what had happened. She felt so ashamed and dirty. What if Nathan was right and her Mother turned against her? Bessie had seen the look of suspicion in her eye already. What if he persuaded her that her own daughter was in some way to blame? That she had tempted him beyond his ability to resist? Conversely, what if her Mother did believe Bessie's account? What then? What if her Mother confronted Nathan herself? He already beat and abused her, no matter how she already conspired to hide that fact from her daughter. Bessie knew though. Knew what he did. And what if the authorities became involved? If Nathan and Elias were accused, found guilty and hung for her rape? She and her mother would certainly be forced out of the tithed cottage and made destitute. All the grisly details of the events with her stepfather would become common knowledge. The fuel of such a scandal would burn in local memory forever. Who would want to marry her then? Who would dare try to make an honest woman of her? She knew the answer. There would always be an irremovable stigma attached to her and any child born of this shameful affair would carry the burden of bastardhood.

What would happen to Bessie if Nathan remained true to his threat and countered hers with a claim that it was she who had set out to lure him into adulterous, almost incestuous intercourse with her? She might very well be taken and hung for her part, after bringing the baby to term that is. Bessie raised her hand up to her neck. Only now that she had so narrowly missed hanging herself she realized what a dreadful way it must be to die.

A low, persistent lowing brought her to her senses. The cow had come home for milking, nudged open the door and now nuzzled the young girl's shoulder. Its large brown eyes seemed to sense the sorrow in her and she found a first glimmer of comfort in them. Then she remembered. The first time that Tom had come with the bull, the heifer did not come with calf. The mating had been full, Tom had assured her father, but the seed simply had not taken that time. "Maybe," she told herself, "it will be the same with me. Maybe I have not fallen with child, then come spring I will not be forced to marry Elias after all. Maybe I could get away. Go and live with my aunt, perhaps."

Bessie tethered the cow as normal. Then she washed her face again and ordered her dishevelled clothing. Wrapping her shawl up high around her neck to hide the redness from the rope burn, she snatched up the basket, left the shed and forced herself to walk across the yard to the cottage. Summoning up all her strength and willpower she entered.

"What on earth has happened to you?" her Mother asked as she came through the door. "You are covered in mud and straw!"

"The cow has just come home, Mother," Bessie replied, avoiding her gaze, "and she is caked in it. I must have brushed against her as I let her into the shed."

Bessie put down her basket and quickly fetched the milk pail.

"I will just go and milk her," she said. "I won't be long."

She was relieved to be out of Nathan's sight once more. She dare not look at him, but she could feel him gloating as he sat by the fireside not even bothering to acknowledge her.

CHAPTER THREE

Bessie avoided Nathan as much as she could after the attack. In fact she had caught a bad chill, and for several days after had been ordered to stay abed by her mother. This was a blessing. It presented her with time to recover from her ordeal and to think. To search each and every avenue of action open to her; to contemplate where each, in turn, might lead.

Several Sundays passed by without Bessie attending church. She felt defiled and dirty, unfit to drag herself before her maker through fear. Fear that her loss of virtue might somehow be visible – clearly manifest and marking her out as a sinner amongst that pure, god-fearing congregation gathered there. Bessie had worried herself sick over this.

Her mother, who had become increasingly distant during that time, served only to make matters worse. Not that they were ever that close to begin with. Young Bessie had been her late Father's pride and joy and although she loved her other parent dearly and honoured her, as any good daughter should, there was never that special bond between them. Since her remarriage to Nathan, the two had drifted apart. Following the rape, their relationship had teetered along the brink of outright estrangement. The haggard, greying, sallow–faced Mother, looking older by far than her thirty–two years, had taken to regarding her pretty, fresh-faced daughter with protracted, silent looks brimming with suspicion. Pushing the girl to an emotional arm's length just at the time when she desperately needed a loving mother's embrace most.

Three weeks after the outrage Bessie had tentatively returned to church services, although she kept herself to herself and apart from the rest of the congregation. This situation persisted beyond Christmas and well into the turning of the year.

However, one bright dry Sunday, after service, Bessie

stayed behind to tarry a while in the solitude of the churchyard. Lost deep in her troubled thoughts, she meandered down the narrow yew edged pathway, picking her way past the ancient graves. Then quite unbidden her soft footsteps stopped. She had reached the weatherworn tombstone of Molly Grimes.

The girl pondered over the slim recumbent effigy of its medieval occupant. The sight of this ancient lady; serene, with eyes closed tightly and slender hands joined together in eternal prayer, only focused her mind more keenly on her present wretched dilemma. It would soon be spring, and the yearly ritual of Molly Grimes' bequest would be played out. This noble lady had left a tidy sum to the Parish and in return, the maidens of the village were expected to take part in a gruelling run to a natural spring, several miles away. There they were to fetch a pail of its untainted water and return with it, unspilt, to scrub clean this stone effigy's feet in an act of remembrance. Only a virgin was permitted to run and Bessie knew in her heart that when that time came, she could not act against her good conscience and take part. Not even to protect her secret.

Bessie roused herself away at last and across to her father's bare patch of grass with its simple wooden marker. She ran there and crouched down beside it in silent remembrance trying to recall the warmth of her father's kiss upon her cheek; how his strong arms had enfolded her in a tender embrace and how his words were spoken to her so softly. Bessie wished she could stay there, simply running her hands through her father's soft sphagnum moss shroud, watching the sunlight dance through each feathery strand and never having to return to the reality of her now-woeful home life again. If only she could die and be with him again.

Suddenly Bessie's thoughts scattered like sleek, scavenging rabbits on a newly sewn field, spooked into flight by a slinking red fox. A long, dark shadow cast itself ominously across the ground before her. It was the shadow of a man approaching from behind. Bessie quickly turned and scrambled to her feet.

"Oh!" she gasped. "You gave me a fright, Sir!"

"I'm sorry, Bessie," the black-cloaked, mild-mannered vicar smiled apologetically," I did not mean to startle you."

Bessie smiled back nervously not quite knowing how to respond or where to look. She felt awkward. Her face flushed with embarrassment at her perceived over reaction. Then, all at once she felt a rush of deep foreboding as to why she had drawn the vicar's attention for he had rarely spoken to her before.

"Is there anything the matter, child?" he enquired gently, "for if you are troubled, God is always here to listen through his servant."

Bessie avoided his eyes and replied,

"Troubled? No! Not I, Sir. Whatever gave you that notion?"

He sighed and looked on her with a perturbed expression.

"Walk with me a while," he said, "and I will explain my concern"

Bessie meekly obeyed and like a lamb followed her shepherd back up along the narrow churchyard path.

"Your absence of late," he explained, striding purposefully, "has not gone unnoticed."

"Unnoticed?" she blurted out, fearful that she had already, somehow, become the butt of local gossip. "By whom?"

"By me, of course!" the vicar replied half turning his face with a knowing smile. "I may seem distant, up there in the pulpit but when one of my flock is missing, I am like a diligent shepherd. I notice!" he said coming to a sudden halt. "Then," he added, as he turned about and his eyes calmly met hers, "I wonder why."

Bessie's face drained pale.

"Why, then Bessie?" he demanded with friendly concern. "Why did you miss church for three Sabbaths?"

"I had been abed, ill, Sir!" she blurted out in hesitant, self defence.

"And is this the only reason?"

"Yes, Sir," Bessie answered. Her gaze fell but could find no easy place to come to rest.

"And you are quite recovered now?"

"Yes, Sir!" Bessie began to shake like a small child confronted by her parent with the evidence some blatant misdemeanour.

"Then," he pressed, "why have you not been taking the sacrament with the rest of the congregation?"

A tear trickled down Bessie's pallid cheek betraying the true state of her deeply troubled mind. She quickly wiped it away on her sleeve hoping the clergyman had not seen. He had though and tried to comfort her.

"If you feel you are no longer in a state of good grace," he said softly, "you can talk it over with me, Bessie, in the strictest confidence. No one need know but you and I and the Lord. I am here to help you find your path to redemption."

Bessie's head began to spin. She was terrified of telling anyone what had happened to her. Yet the burden of it all had grown so heavy she longed to lay it down. She broke apart where she stood. She told him of the attack by Elias and the scheme of it all betwixt him and Nathan. However, in deep shame, she shied away from telling of the second attack by her stepfather.

"This," the Vicar said, deeply touched by her plight, "is a most unholy state of affairs. That your own guardian should pressurize you and abuse his stewardship of you is enough! But that this Elias should force himself upon you! It is not only a grave sin but an unlawful act also. Bid me so," he pleaded, "and I will report this beast to the authorities?"

"No! No!" Bessie was adamant.

"Then," he asked, "am I to take it that you intend to proceed into marriage with this man?"

"No!" Bessie replied equally adamant in her decision, "I

shall never marry him!"

"But what if you are with child? Are you indeed with child?"

"I don't know," said Bessie, crying in desperation. "I don't know how to tell and I dare not ask my mother!"

"If you are, then it is your duty to look to the well-being of the child," he told her. "The child is as innocent in this affair as are you are! Yet..." he explained gently to the girl, "it would be your duty to that child to marry the father and afford it its rightful legitimacy. Better by far, for you and the child, than the alternative. Though now it may seem distasteful to consider matrimony with this brute, the consequences of bringing a child into this world otherwise, are shame and despising for you both, for the remainder of your lives. As distasteful as it would be for me," he added with a deep sigh, "to conduct a marriage service over you both, knowing full well the details of your betrothal, I believe it would be for the best I'm afraid to say."

Bessie's heart sank. The thought of taking Elias to husband sickened her.

"However," the vicar said, offering a few crumbs of hope, "if you are not with child and brought before me, in time, for marriage and, as I suspect against your will, I will publicly refuse to read the banns. If necessary, I will even help you find a place of safety away from this village, if that is your wish!"

Bessie smiled with faint relief. She suddenly felt as if a great weight had been lifted from her by sharing her dreadful secret, yet at the same time, utterly crushed by the prospect of pregnancy.

"In the meantime though," the vicar continued, "it is best you find out your true condition. I am afraid that is an area where I cannot help. However, if you come with me now, I know someone who can."

Bessie willingly agreed and walked with him once more. It was but a short distance to the vicarage. It was an old thatched, timber-framed house, enclosed by an ageing moss-clad limestone wall. A fitting residence for a vicar of this parish, yet inside modestly furnished for this poor encumbant and true man of the cloth.

The vicar showed Bessie into his tiny study and she waited patiently while he fetched Mistress Fletcher, his housekeeper. She was an abrupt woman with a surly shock of black hair and disposition to match. A late-aged widow woman, taken on to help around the house during the vicar's late wife's last short illness, she had stayed on to attend to the needs of the bereaved widower following her mistress's demise. After the briefest of introductions, the vicar took his leave and left the two to talk.

"So?" Mistress Fletcher wasted no time in broaching the subject, "the Master tells me you might have trouble!"

Bessie averted her gaze and responded timidly that she feared this was indeed so.

"Well then girl, tell me this!" the woman demanded. "Since this congress with the man, have you shed any blood?"

Bessie thought for a moment before replying that she had.

"Then you isn't with child then, girl. Simple as that!" she assured Bessie firmly. "So long as you sheds blood after yous with a man then yous not with child! Yous been lucky this time, girl! Might'nt be so lucky next time, so take heed!"

With no more ado, Mistress Fletcher simply turned about and left Bessie to find her own way out.

It was a blessed relief, but Bessie knew it might only be a matter of time before Elias or Nathan tried further advances. She had to somehow strive for time until she could get to her aunt again and ask for her assistance in quitting the village for good. It was the only way she could see of ever being safe from those two men.

***

The morning sun fell like a warm, tender kiss on Bessie's

winter-bleached skin as she drove the cow towards the beck and over the wood and stone bridge towards the orchard. The beast lumbered awkwardly across the algae-greened planking boards as it struggled to keep a footing. With a large willow pannier tied to her back Bessie too found keeping her balance on the slippery surface difficult. Below, the swirling brackish stream, swollen with rain and recent snowmelt, rushed swiftly by, away towards the River Ancholme.

Once safely across on the other bank, Bessie studied the gnarled, wind-ravaged, ebony frames of the stooped apple trees cowering in the bright sunlight. Their naked branches already showed signs of buds and new life. Beneath them, struggling up from under a blanket of dead leaves, the nodding heads of Snow Glories were already in full flower and shafts of plump, green Lenten lily leaves were well in advance.

"T'won't be long till spring," Bessie spoke aloud to herself, "and this awful winter behind me."

Bessie imagined the Maytime blossom and how pretty the orchard would look then. Meanwhile a gaggle of geese, greedily cropping the lush new shoots of grass, hissed and pecked at the heels of the cow as it rudely intruded upon their pasture, but soon settled down again to graze alongside their new four-legged companion.

Bessie left the cow and made her way up Pretty Lane towards the fields in search of her stepfather. Her mother had given her a cloth-wrapped lunch to deliver to her husband as he worked in the gang ploughing Long Acre field. Bessie wondered at the new rash of rich, dark, molehills skirting the edge of the sheep field. These rarely seen little creatures had been industrious of late and had obviously fared none the worse for the recent cold. Soon the tiny white feet of inquisitive spring lambs would tread down their marker piles of brown earth and flatten this transient scar on the landscape. Beyond the sheep field lay the first swathes of already ploughed land, its dark, yawning furrows awakening to the warm sunshine and waiting for the seed of new life to be planted deep within them.

Beside the fields the leafless trees, stark against this morning's bright blue sky were clothed in a fine moss that grew up their trunks and stretched out along their spidery branches, soft and velvety like the emerald gown the Lady of the Manor had worn to church on Christmas morning. Other trees along the way were clad in clasps of glossy ivy. One such, a fine oak that Bessie had passed by, had been choked into final submission by this plant's death grip and felled to the ground during recent gales. From the plentiful sycamore trees, strange bundles dangled down resembling a legion of brown-winged, over-wintering moths huddled together for protection from the elements. They were seeds, still undispersed and hanging by the hundred. It was the abundance of this species that lent its name to this part of the parish - The Siggimoor.

Judd Lowe, coming up from the opposite direction, met Bessie in the lane. He had a broken harness in his arms and was heading back towards the Manor Farmstead.

"Ah! Looking for Nathan?" he exclaimed with a welcoming smile as he approached, "not that he's done a hand's turn today to even break into a sweat! Let alone work up an honest appetite."

Bessie could not help but giggle to hear such candour.

"Why your poor mother had to marry with such a lazy so and so . . ." Judd stopped a moment in his progress and shook his head.

"Oh if only I had been a free man. I'd have happily wed her and kept you both in far better fettle than he has!" he sighed tossing his head. "Ay, but there's no justice in this life, girl! No sooner had she wed than my own wife ups and dies!"

Judd studied Bessie carefully.

"You look pale, lass!" he said genuinely concerned. "On

your way back pop by my cottage, step inside, if you will, and in the larder, to the left," he explained, "you will come across a fine ham wrapped in a cloth. Take up a knife from the board beside it and cut yourself a good half, girl! Take it back home to your mother and tell her who give it you! And," he stressed, "that it's for you and her, mind, not for him! Be sure to tell her that, Bessie! For you twain," he said as he started back along the lane, "not that great fat hog!"

"Thank you kindly, Mister Lowe," Bessie called out after him.

Judd half turned and smiled in acknowledgement. He was always kindly and Bessie liked him a lot.

She continued on her walk with light happy steps, cocking her head to listen to the birds fussing noisily, engaged in early courtship amongst the thorny sloe bushes. Ahead, away in the distance, the sunlight played upon the gently rolling wolds. In the clear air these hills now stood out in all their glory, no longer the blur of so many a winter's day past. Above, amidst the brilliant blue, just a scattering of white clouds ambled by. Yet, when they fleetingly veiled the sun, the light breeze that tousled Bessie's hair and blew it across her eyes, still bit with an all too familiar chill. Winter was in its death throes but not dead yet.

Not much further along Bessie found Nathan in Long Acre field. Elias was close by, also working the gang that day. Her stepfather immediately grabbed the cloth bundle from her, snatched up the bread and began at once to tear at it as she started to walk away. Elias stared at her but said nothing until she was almost out of earshot. Then she half heard a lewd remark pass between the two men.

She paid no heed and continued her way back down the route she had come. She did, however, make one slight detour to venture into light woodland beyond Black Thorn spinney. She liked this spot. She remembered going there to dig for pignuts with her father when she was little. Bessie un-harnessed the cumbersome basket and set about filling it with sticks and small branches for the fire at home. When it was full as much as she could carry, she hauled it back up onto her shoulders and headed off once more.

Stopping by Judd's cottage on her way home, she put down her load in the porch, unlatched the door and let herself inside. She was pleasantly surprised. It was meticulously neat and clean. Everything had a place and everything was in its place. The young woman marvelled at how organized he was for a single man. Judd appeared to live simply but comfortably. Bessie went to the larder, finding it well stocked with produce from the cottage garden and Judd's smallholding of livestock and fowl.

As Bessie looked about she recalled Judd's words as they had met in the lane. He was right, of course, Nathan was a lazy man. She and her mother lived in penury because of that man's laziness. He could provide for them if only he had a mind to. Bessie's own Father had! Right up until the day he died. He often worked their tiny plot after a hard day labouring for the master. He grew fruit and vegetables for the table aplenty; they had a cow, a couple of sows and even a few lambs each year to provide meat for the table. They weren't rich but there was always food in the larder and a stock of split logs ready for the hearth. Nowadays mother did her best to tend to their land but the digging was hard for her, suffering as she did, from the bone ache that half crippled her in the cold months. Nathan rarely helped her, his obesity and laziness had hobbled them into poverty.

Bessie laid hands on the ham just where Judd had directed and portioned it as he had told her to. She placed one half in the basket, neatly rewrapping the remainder carefully in deference to her benefactor, then returned home and ate a much-needed hearty meal with her mother before they secreted away the remaining meat.

That evening Bessie prepared to milk the cow as usual. She stepped out from the cottage across the yard, but this time she was hotly pursued by Nathan, having made the excuse to her mother that he thought Bessie looked pale and that he would 'go help her bring in the animal.'

The cow was not in the yard. The shed door was swung open so Bessie ventured inside to check for her. Nathan crept in behind. The young woman turned and defiantly stared him out as he approached in silence. Blank, emotionless eyes stared back at her. Brazenly he leaned into her, edged his hand under her apron and pushed hard against her body with the palm of his hand. Bessie had the presence of mind to quickly respond. Instead of recoiling from her stepfather's touch, she slackened her muscles, causing her belly to bulge outwards deceptively. Nathan felt the contour, smiled knowingly to himself and with that, let his stepdaughter be. Bessie was thankful to have thwarted her stepfather's unwanted attention, but she knew she would not be able to keep up this pretence up for long. Sooner or later Elias and Nathan must surely call her bluff and before that time came she must piece together a plan of escape. A plan which she would need help with, and the only person she knew and trusted, apart from the vicar, was her aunt. Nathan, however, had curtailed her visits there. Maybe now, believing she was trapped by pregnancy and seemingly resigned to her destiny, he might be willing to relent, she thought.

Early next morning Bessie went out to search for the cow. She eventually came across it lying on the bank of the beck far beyond the orchard. The poor animal's russet-brown hide shimmered in the immature sunlight with a thousand beads of dew. Her broad head, with long rough tongue lolling stiffly from the corner of the mouth, lay awkwardly to one side. Large, brown eyes stared, unseeingly, open wide and oblivious to the black flies scurrying over them. The cow was dead, her scrawny carcass icy to the touch with rigor mortis well set in.

Nathan insisted on having the creature hauled back to

the homestead instead of burying it in a pit as suggested by his neighbours who had come to help. Although she was little more than skin and bone, he had insisted on butchering the beast and the family making the best they could of the meat over the coming weeks. Bessie all but heaved after every meal. Especially as Nathan had ordered them to partake of the remnants of the beast long after the flesh had turned rancid.

***

It was Humility Brown's wedding day. She had landed herself a fine catch indeed by hooking the second son of the owner of Home Farm. Not that the course of their true love had run smoothly. Indeed, it had run into tempestuous waters and eddied against the groom's family's intentions for their lad before reaching the calmer reaches of relatively mild misgiving regarding the outcome of this day.

The young master had been set sweet on young Humility from the off and had apparently been dipping his wick into her wax for quite some time until the inevitable happened and she caught with child. Then the truth of their carefully kept secret liaisons was well and truly out. The Browns turned up at the big house one day demanding that the young man marry their daughter. Instead, the master tried to rebut them with the promise of a settlement on the unborn child and an allowance for the mother. The Browns held out though for nothing less than matrimony.

Then the old master set about trying to cast aspersions on Humility's character by saying she and her family had set out, all along, to trap his son and that the expected child was in fact not even his. To his credit, however, the young master steadfastly stood by his sweetheart and made public his claim of fathering the baby. So it was that their fate was finally sealed and begrudgingly, peasant-stock Humility was accepted into the nobler landed family.

After the churching was over there was to be a big party

held in the Old Tithe Barn for the couple to attend, briefly, before a more befitting reception up at the big house for the Groom's relatives to mark the occasion. The celebration would provide welcome relief from the unrelenting round of lambing and spring ploughing and sewing, which had all but exhausted the farm workers - man, woman and child alike. However, if anyone knew how to celebrate, be it dancing, singing and making merry, then it was these same common folk.

A generous donation of grain was given over to the locals, several weeks beforehand, for the home-brewing of ale for the village festivities. Then on the day, a hog roast, brawn, mutton pies, cheese tarts, creamy milk possets and copious amounts of other fine food were laid out upon two gigantic trestles, with a huge shoulder-high willow basket of bread standing alongside. Makeshift dining tables of planking were set out around the edges of the barn with log cuts fetched up for seating. Garlands of greenery and strips of bright cloth were strung low from the rough-hewn oak crossbeams above. Such dancing and merriment reverberated around the old building that evening as had never been seen in the village before.

As the festivities opened with a honey-mead toast to health and future happiness, the newlyweds sat beaming at the top table, with the Browns and the vicar. While the bride and groom alone picked at token portions, the wooden trenchers and glossy black earthenware mugs of their guests ran over with food and drink.

After a respectable interval, the bride and groom rose from the table and took to the floor to join in a boisterous dance. The woven garland of wilting spring flowers adorning Humility's flailing, flame red braids scattered its petals as the couple pranced and jigged their way across the barn, accompanied by raucous clapping and feet stamping in time with the impromptu music. Humility's new blue gown barely skirted her now generous girth as she kicked up her petticoats with indelicate steps. After this, the new wife bade a farewell to her friends and family and left with her husband to live her new life apart from them. The party in the barn, however, continued unabated despite having lost its guest of honour.

Late on and by far the worse for ale, Elias rose to his feet and grabbed Bessie roughly by the arm. He dragged her out of her seat and over to the centre of the floor, where the revellers had just finished a dance. Slurring his words badly, he starting shouting to call those gathered there to attention. To Bessie's horror, Elias then began to announce his forthcoming marriage to her.

"No! No!" Bessie yelled out defiantly "I shan't marry you!"

A stunned silence crushed Elias. For a moment it seemed to Bessie as if the whole world had stopped turning and been struck dumb. Then, poorly muted groans and mutterings rippled around the room. Elias turned this way and that, not quite knowing in his stupefied state, what to say or do. One thing was for certain in his mind though. Bessie had utterly humiliated him. Humiliated him in front of the whole village. He turned on her.

"But I've had you, you bitch!" he taunted. "You are carrying my child! You have to marry me!"

"I am not!" Bessie made a stand despite the accusing eyes burning in her direction." And I do not!"

Elias could not believe his own ears. After all the assurances he had received from Nathan. From that moment on, sheer spite seethed forth from Elias's lips.

"She's a liar! I've had her…and often!" he sneered. "And I wasn't the first! In fact, she's made quite a habit of seducing men along the top lane amongst the bushes. I could name names but I don't want to cause no heartaches here for some of them men are happily settled. She is nothing but a whore! Like that aunt of hers. Nothing but a barren young whore! I didn't really want her anyhow!"

Utter pandemonium broke out. Angry faces met Bessie's

and fists raised in anger against her with jeers of "Shame on you!" being mouthed over and over at her. Even her own mother turned her back on the girl leaving her to the mercy of the baying pack.

Nathan railed too. Shouting to the throng, that Bessie was now disowned by him and branded a whore. For not only had he lost the coveted cow he expected from his future son in law, but also he was desperate to renounce the girl squarely. He had to discredit her totally now, in case she dared try to come back at him over the child that he was certain, in his mind at least, she was indeed carrying.

Bessie ran out into the moonless night with no destination in mind other than to distance herself from the angry scene within. She ran up the village, sobbing and falling repeatedly, in the blackness on the deeply-rutted road. Her eyes burnt with bitter tears, as the insults did in her ears. She wanted to lie down and die.

Suddenly a horse came galloping up behind her and in fright she cowered down low. In the darkness, the rider barely missed striking her with his mount as he caught her up.

"Thank God I've found you child!" he said.

Bessie at once recognized his voice. It was the vicar.

"Come up here," he said, grasping her by the arm and swinging her up onto his horse. "I am taking you home with me tonight! On the morrow I will find you sanctuary away from this rabble!"

Bessie lay on the makeshift bed in the vicar's study and cried herself to sleep. She awoke just before daybreak and lay thinking. Today she would be leaving. Leaving behind her mother, her village and everything she knew of life. Today she was leaving for a place she did not know, to live out her life amongst strangers. The prospect seemed terrifyingly unreal yet she knew it was one she must make the best of. She had chosen this path the moment she had decided to reject Elias. That was a decision she knew in her heart she had made for the best. There could be no going back. The two men who had wrenched her innocence from her had also cruelly now succeeded in destroying her character too. There was no way she could stay in the village now that she had been branded a harlot. Not unless she was willing to live out the remainder of her life with everyone believing that she was. But she was not! All she could pray for now was that her new life would treat her more fairly.

After a hearty breakfast, the vicar saddled up his grey mare and brought it around to the front of the vicarage. Bessie, on the other hand, had hardly eaten a scrap. She felt sick to the pit of her stomach. Yes, she wanted to get away from the village and the dreadful pressures from Nathan and Elias for her to wed, but she had not foreseen it would be like this; the numbness in her limbs, the heavy aching in her heart and the deep, deep resentment of being made out the villainess of the sorry piece. To be hounded out of her home by shame and malice. It was all so unfair and there was no way she could right this wrong, which only intensified her anguish.

The vicar had readily picked up on this and had decided that, without further word or ceremony, he and Bessie should slip out of the village and away.

At first he rode, as befitted his position, and Bessie walked close behind carrying a small bundle of provisions swiftly cobbled together by Mistress Fletcher. Once out onto the road and beyond the village precinct, he gallantly took it in turns to walk while Bessie rode on their journey across the pleasant rolling countryside. From the village of Caenby the road climbed steadily until they reached the breezy ridge at Harp's Well. There they tarried a while to break their journey and rest.

From up on high the view down into the valley beyond was magnificent; the sky was so big, yawning across a panorama of woodland and farmsteads stretching out off into the horizon. Just in sight above the interrupted tree line, a blurry ridge of high land rose up once more.

"Look, there!" the vicar pointed something out to Bessie, who strained to see. "Just before those hills is where we are heading for. That's the Trent Valley and Gainsborough Town is there, right on the river."

Their journey now resumed, and as luck would have it, they came across a wagoner on his way to Gainsborough to deliver his wares to the Mart Yard Market. Bessie was much obliged to be able to hitch a ride on the cart the remainder of the way to town while the vicar rode alongside.

The Old Hall was a magnificent ancient building that lay on the northern edge of the small town on the Lincolnshire side of the tidal River Trent. Under Sir William Hickman's ownership it had undergone and continued to undergo much modernization and renovation, which removed it from its origins as a medieval Hall house.

The north held a view as old as the Hall itself of an expanse of lush fields and fruit orchards and to the eye of an ancient inhabitant, this aspect would appear not to have changed very much.

From the south, however, much had been visibly altered of late. Between the east and west ranges of the house a wall had been built, creating an enclosed courtyard for security and privacy, for within this wall was a new gateway that opened up onto his newly developed Mart Yard. To have a market place in such close proximity to the mansion itself, reflected the continuing relationship between this latest Lord of the Manor and the profits of the town.

The River itself lay immediately to the west, and it was at this point in its course that sea-going vessels could still reach upstream and meet with inland barge traders. The town being a trading port led to its prosperity. Lord Hickman, a London merchant, had recently bought the Hall from the near bankrupt Burgh family and used his new manorial position to dominate the political and commercial life of the township.

The vicar had hoped to speak with Sir William himself, or at the very least make representation to the Steward of the house to whom he was personally known. As it transpired, neither was at the Hall at that time, Sir William and his entourage being away. The Steward's rather rotund sister, a certain aptly named Mistress Goode remained to preside over the day to day running of the household and the skeleton staff left to maintain it.

The vicar sought an interview alone, at first, with this housekeeper so he might put forward his case for seeking an opening for his companion as a servant there. He did not, however, go into the exact details of Bessie's predicament, choosing instead to say only that she had been 'the innocent pawn in some unsavoury dealings' and now needed a place of sanctuary to rebuild her life anonymously. Mistress Goode agreed to consider his request and asked to see the girl for herself.

Bessie shifted uneasily from foot to foot and avoided the old woman's gaze. Mistress Goode looked the girl up and down intently.

"Let me see your hands, child!" she said.

Bessie immediately held them out palm down thinking Mistress Goode wanted to inspect the cleanliness of her nails, which she did.

"Other side now, if you please."

Bessie was afraid to, as her undersides were calloused and rough from hard toil about her home. She need not have been though. This was exactly what her prospective overseer had hoped for.

"Not a stranger to hard work, I see. Good!" She turned to the vicar, "I can always use a hard worker. I will take her off you!"

"Thank you, mistress. I am certain you will have no need

to regret this," the Vicar smiled. "May I make a recommendation, though?"

"Go ahead, Sir! Pray speak your mind. I am all ears."

"The circumstance of young Bessie's departure from her home was, as I have already explained you, due to matters of a delicate nature. In this event, I think a change of name might prove prudent to protect her true identity and ensure the girl's future stability here away from the traumas she has suffered."

"Yes. I can see the wisdom in that," Mistress Goode conceded. "And 'Bessie' is also his lordship's familiar address for Lady Elizabeth, so a change of name seems in order .Yet what shall it be?"

Mistress Goode looked towards the girl but Bessie had not an answer to hand. However, the vicar filled the void with a suggestion of his own.

"What about 'Dorothy'? It was my late wife's name and she was a good Christian woman."

'Dorothy'. Bessie smiled in agreement. It was a pleasing name and she felt it the least she could do to repay the vicar's kindness.

"Dorothy it is then!" Mistress Goode smiled. Then she went to the door and shouted out to summon a maidservant to her aid. "Comfort! Comfort! Come here, girl!"

A very tall, thin girl with wispy straw-coloured strands of hair escaping from under a large floppy linen cap came scurrying to answer Mistresses Goode's command. Dorothy could not help noticing that she had the greenest eyes she had ever seen.

"Yes, Mistresses Goode?" Comfort enquired respectfully.

"This is Dorothy. She is to be a new maid of all work serving here alongside you."

Comfort smiled easily in greeting.

"Does your mother still have space for a lodger, Comfort?"

"Yes, Mistress. She does."

"Then kindly take Dorothy with you to your mother

under my recommendation. Let her know I will arrange to make an advance on the lodgings tomorrow - myself."

"Yes, Mistress Goode. Thank you Mistress Goode."

"'Tis late in the day and almost time for you to leave," the housekeeper added, "Comfort, take Dorothy with you now, and in the morning have her at your side to find her way about and learn her duties from you.

Dorothy made her grateful farewell to her saviour and Mistress Goode. Comfort led the way out of the Old Hall grounds and down towards the main town. Comfort's mother, Hope, lived in a room above the large inn down by the river. She took in washing and mending and helped out in the inn to eke out her living. She was a widow woman. Plain and weasely looking with small beady eyes set deeply in her head. She had the same wispy straw-like hair and pale complexion as her daughter but seemed a little more robustly built. Her looks may have been coarse and her language and manner skirting around roughness, but she was as kindly a person as Bessie could ever have hoped to meet. Biding in together with mother and daughter soon became as natural as if it had always been so. Bessie might have lost her family, but Dorothy had found hers.

CHAPTER 4

Several weeks later news filtered through to the Old Hall that the absent Lord Hickman and his entourage were on their way back from their extended visit to York. Soon the echoing silence of the empty Hall would be replaced once more with the industrious bustle of everyday life in a wealthy merchant's household.

On the anticipated day of the Hickmans' arrival, Mistress Goode called Dorothy and Comfort to her and told them to busy themselves ferrying kindling and logs from the wood store to the house. The private family apartments had been closed for over a month now and the linen on the beds would need turning down and all the fires lighting to drive away the dampness that had no doubt taken up residence within the fabric of the rooms during their absence. After that, there was endless dusting to do.

As the two maids tumbled out of the doors with their large, closely woven willow baskets, they laughed in shock with their first breaths of cold, still air. They watched in amusement as their warm breath leached out from their gasping mouths as they made their way, giggling, to the wood store beyond the stables. There had been a sharp frost the night before, but the birds were singing loudly and the sky was clear blue and dazzling bright. The early sun felt good against their pale young complexions, although their noses, bare cheeks and fingers quickly chilled, reddened and tingled.

Beside the stone garden wall, golden lantern lilies, already in full flower to trumpet the arrival of spring were now drooping, a little sadly, above the hard dark soil below. Heavy rainfall from the afternoon before had made the yard as slippery as glass but not enough to deter the two giggling maids as they repeatedly slid on their way betwixt house and log store. From the gables of the Old Hall roof, long thin icicles sparkled like Damoclean diamond daggers above their bare heads. Dorothy paused to stare up at them in wonderment before catching Comfort up.

Inside the servants' entrance, Mistress Goode was stooped from the waist, wisely spreading out a layer of fresh straw upon the threshold so that the girls might be certain to wipe their feet clean before proceeding upstairs to the family's apartments.

She straightened up and scolded them. "You silly young'uns! You will catch your deaths! Where are your caps?"

Just then, Dorothy's face flinched a little.

"You look pained, Dorothy! Are you alright child?" The old lady enquired with a worried look etched across her kindly, round face.

"T'is nothing, thank you Mistress Goode," Dorothy replied politely. "I am certain t'is no more than a stitch in my side from hurrying across yon yard"

Satisfied nothing was seriously amiss with Dorothy, Mistress Goode's attentive gaze fell down towards the other girl's feet.

"And look at your woollen hose, Comfort!" she said, regarding the young servant's wrinkled ankles. "You need tie them garters better than that or they will be about tripping you on the stair and breaking your silly neck!"

Comfort immediately put down her basket and turned her back. Thoughtfully shielded by her friend, Comfort quickly lifted her somber grey skirts, pulled up the woollen leggings and retied the red linen strips tightly above her bony red knees.

"Much better! Now be off, the both of you!" Mistress Goode laughed and muttered to herself as she made her way back towards the kitchen as the girls scurried upstairs.

After setting each of the endless fires and stacking the logs the two warmed themselves awhile before starting outside again.

Each time they did, though, it seemed to be getting

increasingly cold. As the morning wore on, small white clouds arrived to dot the bright blue canopy above. Then heavier, darker ones followed on to blot out the warmth of the sun before a real bone-chilling coldness set in before eleven. As the sky increasingly darkened, Dorothy noticed the ivy cleaved to the bare trunks of surrounding trees begin to gently sway. The glossy, broad, green leaves curled upwards and fluttered as the previously slight breeze began to strengthen from the east and catch them in its wake.

"Oh!" exclaimed Comfort, looking up at the gathering grey, "we are in for a thunderstorm!"

Dorothy too had noticed how threatening the sky had become.

A passing groom, carrying a battered hay bag to the stables, had heard Comfort's remarks and shaking his head knowingly commented, "Nay, duck! T'is too cold for rain. They look mighty like snow clouds to me!"

In the master bedchamber, at the top of the stairs in the East range, the girls prepared the final fire. This was Dorothy's favourite room. The deeply carved dark-wood bed was decked with green taffeta curtains. Upon its high, inviting mattress lay a long feather bolster topped with plump, goose down pillows. Fine, white Dutch linen sheets were turned down over an embroidered counterpane, to match the drapes, and finished off with a valance edged with a deep silk fringe.

"Oh, it looks so comfortable," Dorothy sighed. "I wonder what it feels like to wake up in a bed like that every morning?"

"Go on!" Comfort giggled, "try it out for size!"

"Oh, no! I couldn't!" Dorothy was taken aback by the audacity of the suggestion.

"Go on with you. One little lie down won't do any harm. Besides," she added, "who will know?"

Dorothy was tempted but resisted at first. Comfort did not, though she was mindful to remove her shoes first before she boldly climbed up upon the bed and stretched out.

"Oh, it's lovely," she sighed, "come on! Just once!"

Dorothy gave in, kicked off her boots and joined her friend briefly on the bed. Comfort was right. It was sumptuous!

For a few fanciful moments, Dorothy lay there, looking about the chamber from a mistress's perspective for once. This room was so restful. Two pretty tapestries hung on the wall and there were three chairs with lavish embroidery too. Close by was a little table and a cupboard. Over the polished wooden floor lay a long green carpet with an embroidered border and silk fringe that was just perfect to greet bare feet in the morning, Dorothy thought. How different it all was from her humble roots.

Suddenly Comfort lurched backwards and banged against the head of the bed. The two girls were stupefied to find a hidden door in the centre of the carving had sprung open. A string of pearls spilled out onto the lace-edged pillows from within a secret hidey-hole. For a second or two the girls froze, just staring down in amazement before hurriedly picking the necklace up and frantically popping it back where it had appeared from. Then they scurried off the bed and diligently settled back to the task in hand.

Soon this fire too was lit and crackling lustily, so the girls made their rounds polishing furniture with bees wax, checking the other fires and mentally preparing themselves for the tedious replenishment of the logs, which stretched before them for the remainder of the day until the regular boy returned with his Lordship that afternoon.

The heady aroma of stewing quinces, like the scent of musk roses tinged with sweet honey, permeated the air and wafted up the staircase to meet the hungry girls as they descended towards the kitchen to collect their midday meal. Inside, cooks were busy preparing all manner of food for a welcoming feast for Lord Hickman. Over the roasting fire there was a boar and a generous hunk of beef on a spit being turned by a rather bored looking young scullion. The girls were offered a small dish of hot cooking juices and chunks of fresh bread to dip into it as a warming treat. It was so welcome after their morning's labour. The sight of so many victuals being prepared and the workings of such a large kitchen fascinated Dorothy. Even more so when she realized that there were only men employed in this work, when at home in her village she had only ever seen women cook. She watched intently as she gratefully ate her meal sitting on a small bench by a wall out of the way. Glancing up, Dorothy could see the flaps move in the large louvre in the centre of the towering ceiling, helping to ventilate the kitchen of steam and fumes.

Across the kitchen, in the second of the brick fireplaces, a hefty ham infused with spices was bubbling away over the fire in a large, blackened cauldron. To its side, a little further away from the heat, a large, equally blackened pot of robust-looking pottage was gently simmering. Every now and then, a warming bowlful was ladled out and handed to one or other of the household servants as each in turn partook of a hasty midday repast.

Further along the head baker was cautiously breaching the hot, dough-sealed door of one of the brick-built, beehive roofed, bread ovens. Once opened he lurched back and forth, deftly fetching the well-risen, brown loaves out on a long, poplar-wood peel and placing them carefully on the side to cool. Dorothy watched him intently as he checked the temperature of the second oven by throwing a handful of flour into it. On seeing it burst into flame, he quickly pushed the next batch of loaves in before sealing the metal door tight with raw dough.

In the corner, a pasty-looking man was preoccupied trying to catch hold of a wildly swinging sack of flour being lowered down on a pulley from the storeroom above. His face, hair and shoulders were powdery white. Meanwhile, in the dough room, a young assistant was furiously kneading a sticky mound on the generously-floured surface of a wooden brake, whilst yet another lad knocked back the plump dough and shaped it into a further batch of loaves for the next baking.

After they had eaten their bread, Mistress Goode came over to the two maids and set them each a bowl of warmed milk, with a hint of nutmeg and sweetened with honey, to ward off the chill.

Suddenly Master Best, with watery eyes and glowing red nose breezed into the kitchen with a brace of geese, three brown rabbits and a hare to take to the game room in the northern corner of the kitchen building.

"My, but it's a lazy wind out there!" he exclaimed breathlessly. "Just passes straight through instead of going around you!"

The girls laughed for it was true. The fat, head cook stopped Best momentarily, relieved him of one of rabbits, which he proceeded to lay out on the main worktable and skinned, ready for stew.

By now, it was time for the two young women to get back to their own work. Soon snow began to fall. Just a flurry at first and no one thought it would really settle or amount to much at this time of year. A light dusting whispered downwards barely covering the ground, then abruptly ceased. The girls carried on fetching wood into the house and tending the fires.

Yet, at around three, from out of the green room window, Dorothy noticed the sky turning ghostly. Silvery shafts of sunlight glanced briefly across the town roofs far beyond, before the sky suddenly filled with the swirling white of snow falling thick and fast and blowing in every direction. As the girls made their way out of the Hall to return home to town for the night, Mistress Goode stopped them at the door.

"Look out there, my dears! "she told them. "A real blizzard has blown up. I think it's best if you don't dare venture out just now, but tarry here, safe, for the night. I am certain

Comfort's mother will gather where you are since the storm happened upon us so unexpectedly. So don't be afeard about alarming the poor woman!"

Mistress Goode instructed the maids that it was best to let the fires upstairs burn out of their own accord, as His Lordship would not be coming home now. Most likely, the snow had reached York well before it had hit Gainsborough, so it was expected that Sir William would stop over wherever he was, in comfort, until a thaw set in.

'Oh!" Mistress Goode had a late thought cross her mind. "Let out all the fires, that is, except for the one in the end chamber at the top of the back stairs. That may well be kept burning and drying the room until curfew," she said. "Only with the ladies' maids gone and their empty quarters in the attic freezing, coupled with those rascal kitchen boys already sleeping in down here, safer all round if you stop up there and take advantage of the warmth by sleeping on the landing tonight."

Mistress Goode summoned up her best deadpan housekeeper's face and added, "I can trust you, not to touch anything. Can't I?"

The girls nodded.

"I will be abed in my quarters," she warned raising one eyebrow, "nicely placed to keep an eye on you all! I'll not be tolerating any 'funny going-ons'!" she added.

A lad was duly sent up the ladder to the storeroom to fetch the bedding down and after supper, the two friends settled in for the night in front of the open chamber door. Although the fire itself had been snuffed out by the heavy metal curfew at eight, the embers still radiated gentle warmth well into the night.

Comfort snuffed out the candle, the girls had no need of it anyway to see clear across the landing. It was so light, so unnaturally light, for outside the deeply banked virgin snow reflected the brilliance of the almost-full moon, robbing the night of its mantle of darkness.

Dorothy slept fitfully and soon began to feel unwell. She had occasionally complained of a stomach ache throughout the day to Comfort but had dutifully carried on with her chores nonetheless. Dorothy sat up and rubbed her abdomen with the flat of her hands making firm, circular movements in a bid to ease the tormenting cramps, then she tried to settle down once more for the night.

However, the nagging pain got worse, with the cramps increasing in strength and duration. Comfort awoke to find her distraught companion crying.

"Try passing water," Comfort suggested, "that sometimes helps me when I have the guts ache."

Dorothy struggled up and made her way to the gare de robe. She was all but bent double with the pain that kept seizing her in wave after wave. She hoisted up her skirts, sat over the cold, stone opening and urinated, then tried to pass a stool but it hurt so much. Outside, she could hear the wind howling like a mad dog mocking her agony.

Dorothy made to get up again but was alarmed to find blood smeared upon the inside of her thighs. She looked down between her legs. There was something there. Unnaturally dusky, tiny yet perfectly formed, a limb hung limply down from inside her body. Dorothy's scream of horror brought Comfort running to her aide. Spurred on by her companion's hysteria, Comfort quickly swept aside any notion of taboo and briefly examined her friend below.

"Oh My Lord!" she shrieked in panic, "you are having a baby! I can see a tiny leg!"

Her friend helped Dorothy back to the chamber and left her sitting on the mattress, trembling, with her knees drawn up tightly under her chin. After reassuring words, Comfort ran to fetch Mistress Goode.

No sooner had she gone than Dorothy felt something slither effortlessly from out of her body. She parted her knees and looked down upon the scant bedding. There lay a tiny, perfectly formed infant complete in every detail. Dorothy went into shock. From then on in it was as if all this horror was happening to someone else in some other place far removed from her. She felt strangely detached from the events that followed. A wide-eyed open-mouthed onlooker at some macabre travelling play. None of it seemed real. Not even the tiny baby itself. It looked so alien. Not like a real baby at all, but more like the rabbit carcass she had seen lying, skinned, earlier in the day on the great kitchen table; its skin so strangely translucent that most of its tiny blood vessels and organs could be clearly made out beneath it. Its tiny eyelids were closed fast and yet its pitiful face seemed peacefully serene. Dorothy picked it up for a moment and cradled it gently in her hands. She half hoped it would cry at any moment and gulp in sweet life-giving breath, but it remained still and motionless. She carefully laid it down again and waited. Waited an eternity there alone. Alone, bathed in pale moonlight amongst the shadow of the night, looking down at the body of her dead child and the haunting recollection of its creation.

Eventually Comfort returned with a lantern. A breathless Mistress Goode dressed only in a flimsy shift, nightcap and a woollen shawl, clinging lopsidedly, across her plump round shoulders followed close behind her.

Mistress Goode struggled down beside Dorothy and examined the girl. Then she turned and shook the stupefied Comfort, who was standing beside her, transfixed by the ghastly sight.

"Quick, Comfort, go down to the kitchen and wake up one of the boys. Get them to light the main fire and to set me a large pan of water to heat, but don't breathe a word of all this, mind!"

Comfort grimly nodded in acknowledgement.

"Then while it heats up," Mistress Goode added, "go to my room and fetch more rags from the chest at the foot of my bed and bring them here once the water is hot. Quickly girl!"

Comfort relit her candle from the lamp, then immediately did as she had been instructed. However there was really no great urgency for the water, for there was nothing to be done now that could not wait for a little while. It was a kindly ruse, mixed with wisdom, on the old woman's part to distract a now deeply troubled Comfort with this errand. It also gave the housekeeper time to be with Dorothy, alone.

Mistress Goode swiftly wrapped the tiny body in a blanket and moved it to one side out of sight. Then she turned her attention towards the mother. This was a serious situation indeed, especially in a strict, respectable household. To come knowingly pregnant into the household would have proved a shameful deception and betrayal of her mistress's trust, a misdemeanor worthy of instant ejection. Yet Mistress Goode had formed such a good impression of the girl she felt she needed to hear Dorothy out before dismissing her out of hand.

"Oh Dorothy!" The old lady frowned hard, causing her forehead to furrow so deeply that her bushy, grey, eyebrows almost met the edge of her white mop cap. "I'm deeply disappointed in you!" she said firmly. "I thought I knew a good girl when I saw one! How did this all come about?"

Dorothy came to her senses and began to sob uncontrollably. She gradually blurted out the whole sorry tale about Elias and Nathan and how they had both raped her. The old woman was deeply moved by the poor girl's plight. She flung her arms about Dorothy and drew her close in comfort.

"Well, then my girl," she said gravely, "this must be a judgment from the Almighty himself. For He has chosen in His infinite mercy not to burden you with such an affliction, as you are the innocent in so dark and wicked a deed! This way the sin has been taken from you. This way you have a second chance. You can redeem yourself and live a good life in service here in this Christian household rather than live on the street branded as a harlot! You are a good girl at heart, I know Dorothy. And I feel certain in my soul that you will not be caught so cruel again!"

Mistress Goode took up the bloodied bundle and started away with it.

"But my baby! Where are you going with my baby?"

"To the kitchens, girl. I will cast it on the fire and no one need ever know the little bones are anything other than chicken."

"Onto the fire?" Dorothy was horrified. "No!" she cried, "why can't I give it a proper Christian burial?"

"Because you can't, girl. If you are to stay here not a word of this is to get out. You understand? Besides, it has not been baptized and so it is damned to Hell. This creature," she said holding the shrouded infant out, "is the embodiment of your sin. Besides, what's never drawn breath has never lived. It's for the best, dear, you will see. It will all work out for the best. I will go make you a brew of lavender and meadowsweet flower tea to ease you. I will send Comfort up with the linen to staunch the discharge. Meanwhile you keep still and try to rest."

***

The freezing weather lasted the best part of a week before a gentle thaw came and melted the snow away. During this time, Dorothy rested up under the watchful eye of Mistress Goode. During all that time neither a note of self-pity nor a word of complaint passed her lips, instead Dorothy unfailingly met her overseer with nothing less than brave, grateful smiles.

Mistresses Goode, however, was not blind to the hastily dried, red-ringed eyes and tear-stained cheeks. Nor deaf to the swiftly stifled sobs as she approached to check her young charge. The housekeeper could see for herself that Dorothy was grieving for the tiny, dead baby. The usually suppressed motherly instinct of this older, childless woman desperately wanted to scoop the girl up into her arms, to hug her close and tell her that it was all going to be all right, to tell her to go ahead and cry with all her might and let the sadness tumble out. The crying and the overwhelming feeling of intense emptiness, that she undoubtedly was feeling deep inside, would pass away in time. Dorothy would put this all behind her.

Mistresses Goode held back though. It was not her place and Dorothy was not her child. She was wary lest this proved a step too close to an intimacy with a member of staff that could badly backfire in the future. After all, she did not know the girl that well yet. Therefore, Mistress Goode remained caring but distant. Yet, privately she pained for the wretched girl's plight.

Gradually Dorothy returned to her duties about the Hall. She went about her daily tasks diligently paying great attention to whatever was asked of her. She appeared happy enough to the casual eye, though Mistresses Goode could see the change within the girl, there was a deep-seated sadness that still lay beneath the surface of every smile that she so readily proffered to others. The more Mistress Goode came to know Dorothy, the more determined she became to find a way to help ease the loss of her child; but how? She did not yet know.

CHAPTER FIVE

Behind her back, the disingenuous amongst respectable Gainsborough society had privately dubbed her 'the crow'. Slight in frame, capped and richly gowned in widow black, Rose Hickman's fine pointed features indeed gave her a bird-like appearance. Yet, Lady Rose was still a formidable woman. Still the matriarch of this prosperous Hickman family. Still the brains and the will behind this profitable Gainsborough enterprise. However, her increasing frailty and old-lady stoop could lure the unwary into a dangerously false sense of security. Only the most foolhardy of souls though, dared go on from this precarious presumption to underestimate her true strength and power

The local gentry did not care for her and they did not like her son either. As far as they were concerned, the Hickmans were exploitative southern merchants who had newly bought their way into local society with the purchase of Gainsborough Old Hall from the long established and well-respected Burgh family. In truth, the fact that these fine gentlemen really could not stomach was that the Hickmans had applied all their business acumen to exactly the same manorial rights as the Burghs had enjoyed over the town and its small port. However, they had succeeded, and quite spectacularly too, in turning a bankrupt estate into a very profitable concern indeed. Although Lady Rose was the daughter of a knight of the realm, and a true Lady by birth, she had insisted on marrying her merchant lover against her family's true wishes; a man below their expectation of a 'titled' husband. Undeterred, Lady Rose's greatest ambition had become that of creating a new ennobled family of her own. A lofty ambition indeed and a goal that had eventually taken more than fifty years to achieve with the recent knighthood of her son, William, as reward for his early allegiance to King James.

With the completion of renovation and remodelling of

the woefully outdated, yet still impressive, old medieval hall house now completed, the 'master' accommodation was relocated to the newly refurbished East wing. Ageing Lady Rose quickly seized this opportunity to take over the once prestigious Solar as her own 'private' apartment. It suited her well. Finding walking unaided increasingly difficult, she ensconced herself in the Solar, though it was not by any means a sign of a slow withdrawal from active life. Indeed the choice of this room was logical and carefully calculated to allow her just the opposite. The Solar was a substantial, richly furnished chamber, more than large enough for the old lady to have her great bed tucked discreetly away in the corner behind her almost forever open door, leaving an ample area near the fireplace for day-to-day use or to entertain.

The 'Great Hall' of this house itself was no longer used as originally intended. There were no longer the long the rounds of pretentious, self-propagandising feasts, nor was there the possibility of the owner having to accommodate the monarch and their travelling court in a great flourish of extravagance, as under the late Elizabeth Tudor. Queen Elizabeth's appointed heir and successor, King James Stuart of Scotland, was no Tudor, just as Sir William was only a nobleman by title and not birth. As a result, the customary legions of household staff were no longer necessary. Instead the house was now run exactly as one might expect a family of merchants to run one - as efficiently as any good business. Sir William's steward meticulously kept all accounts, all expenditure was scrutinized and waste eliminated, which included any staff deemed 'surplus' or 'lacking'.

So as a result of these measures, coupled with the fact that the Hickmans now preferred to dine in private in their newly created, wood-panelled dining room, most of the furnishings in the area of the Great Hall had been removed completely and the huge log fire was no longer lit. Therefore, for the greater part, this hall mostly remained a lofty, unheated empty space. Like some large internal courtyard simply to be traversed by visiting merchants on their way up and down the main stairway, to conduct business with Sir William in the Great Chamber above.

The steward and his sister, Mistress Goode, had faithfully served the Hickman family for many decades. Between them they oversaw the day-to-day running of the household, but as for its organization, that was still very much Rose's direct concern.

It was for this reason that Rose Hickman's choice of domain became evident. Often these same visitors chatted as they walked, unthinkingly passing remarks freely amongst themselves, going over proposed transaction oblivious to the fact that they might be overheard. If Rose was not to be found sitting in her heavily carved, cushioned chair by the landing window, then she was almost invariably to be caught peeking though the 'squint' hidden behind the ornately embroidered wall hangings in the Solar.

From this tiny, glassless window Rose was able to look down into the hall itself and covertly hear and observe all the visitors coming and going below. Like a crow, Rose Hickman's sharp, beady eyes rarely missed a thing, never failing in picking up the slightest nuance of stance or the merest unguarded gesture or word that might give the untruthful away. Therefore, far from being removed and cut off from life, day after day, from either of these two vantage points it continued to play out for the old lady's hungry eyes to endlessly feast upon.

Merchants, visiting for the first time to do business at The Old Hall often seemed mildly amused to find this old lady swiftly joining Sir William in The Great Chamber. Then, on further occasions, they soon realized that she was always there, sitting quietly in her chair, seemingly on the very periphery of every important meeting between her entrepreneur son and would-be partners, as they discussed this or that new venture. Rose would sit patiently by;

waiting, watching, and listening in silence. Rarely was she openly seen to interfere in any of Sir William's dealings, yet unbeknown to the untrained eye he relied implicitly on her judgment in all matters. Especially more so if it involved determining who might, or who might not be trusted when he was about to be expected to invest money with them. One glance from Sir William towards his mother, before the final drawing up of a contract, could make or break a deal in the 'unblinking' of an eye. Rose Hickman's steely glare was a tacit accusation.

One particular morning, Mistress Goode had summoned Dorothy unexpectedly. As the errand boy had come up to the chamber to fetch her away from her cleaning, Comfort had glanced towards her friend with deep concern and foreboding.

"You are to go to the Solar, Mistress Dorothy," was all the lad could say, "and wait upon the pleasure of the Lady Rose."

Dorothy had not yet the occasion to meet Rose Hickman.

"Lady Rose?" Dorothy uttered nervously, "what on earth can she want with me?"

Then her heart sank. Her Ladyship must somehow have found about her miscarriage. Perhaps Dorothy was about to be dismissed.

Comfort read her friend's face in that instant. She raced across the room and hugged Dorothy close.

"Wuzzan't me, Dorothy," she said, "I would never tell on you! Perhaps she wants to see you on another matter."

Comfort tried to reassure her, but Dorothy's face paled and she suddenly felt her stomach knot in anxiety. Her friend tenderly straightened Dorothy's cap and tidied the tangle of stray hairs up and back under it with her chapped red fingers.

Dorothy tried to force a brave smile but her heart was in her throat. Comfort took the cleaning rags from her as she fumbled to slip off her grimy apron and neatly fold it before handing it over for safekeeping.

As Dorothy timidly made her way up the back stairs to the east wing, all she could think about was that night and what was going to become of her now. Where would she go if she were turned out from the Old Hall? How was she going to survive?

Skirting along the main corridor wall like a frightened mouse, Dorothy soon noticed the sickly sweet, unmistakable aroma of Virginia tobacco permeating the air as she approached the Great Chamber. The heavy oak door was open and as she passed by Dorothy glimpsed the slight frame of middle-aged Sir William stooped over a large pile of papers spread out across a deeply polished table. With a sterling silver pipe hovering on his lips, the Master appeared to be studying one particular document intently. Shortly he glanced up, and upon catching sight of the girl, smiled briefly before getting back down to his work. Dorothy quickly bobbed in a half-curtsey before scurrying passed. She reached the landing just as Mistress Goode finished puffing her way to the top of the main stairs. The red–faced housekeeper paused briefly to catch her breath before intercepting Dorothy.

"Good!" she said, checking the lass over. "You look presentable." With that, she smiled, such a kindly smile, that it gave hope to Dorothy that all was going to be well.

"In we go then!" the housekeeper said.

Standing before her in the grandeur of the Solar, the young maid was utterly absorbed by Rose Hickman. Dorothy had never imagined anyone living into their seventies, let alone encountering one in person. The younger woman was spellbound by Her Ladyship's papery white translucent skin that crinkled like fine kid leather with every facial expression. She was intrigued by the way the old lady's blue veins lay raised up upon her spindly, brown speckled hands and wrists and her very pronounced stoop as she shuffled forward from her chair, supporting herself on her ivory-tipped stick to take a closer look at the girl.

"Mistress Goode! Draw up a seat so I might have young Dorothy sit and talk with me a while," the old lady cawed.

Mistress Goode fetched a chair forward, and then politely enquired: "Shall I go fetch you your mid-morning herbal, My Lady?"

"Yes, Goode," Rose replied, "but there is no great urgency about it."

Mistress Goode withdrew to make her way to the kitchens.

Dorothy suddenly felt dreadfully uneasy perched upon the grand carved chair in front of the now silent Lady Rose. It was almost as if she were on trial and yet she still had no clear idea why she had been summoned for this interview.

Nonetheless, Lady Rose seemed to have fixed her gaze her lowly servant, not with the cold eye of an inquisitor but with more of the manner of one who angles for the truth. Not with a whip and chain but more subtly with a hook and line.

"I know all about your recent problems," Lady Rose said calmly as she looked Dorothy straight in the eye.

Dorothy immediately lowered her gaze in shame. Her lips quivered and her hands, now wringing in her lap, began to shake as the first of her tears welled up and snail-trailed down towards her chin.

This was it she thought in silent grief. She was going to be dismissed.

Lady Rose nudged her cane forward and tapped Dorothy's leg reassuringly as she handed across her own lace handkerchief to the young woman.

"There, there, girl! Look at me!" she said in an effort to alleviate Dorothy's obvious distress. "I am not about to peck your eyes out!"

Dorothy stifled a nervous, involuntary giggle as she wiped her face.

"It seems a little unfair that I know of your secret," Lady

Rose smiled. "Perhaps I should even the score a little by telling you some of mine..."

Dorothy was astounded. She smiled faintly herself. Her curiosity had been aroused.

"Don't you think I understand what it is like to be young and to suffer under the unrighteous dominion of another?'"

Dorothy's eyes widened in bewilderment.

"Oh! I don't mean exactly as you have," Her Ladyship continued, "but I do understand".

Rose sighed a little and leaned back heavily on her plump goose feather cushions.

"I know this much," the old lady added, "if you defy a bully head on, they will knock you to the ground instantly without a second's thought. But if you are wise and stand up to that bully by degrees, inch by inch undermining their power and control by stealth, then in time, they simply cease to wield that power over you anymore. For you have stolen it back and once they come to realize that, the bully inevitably begins to cave in!"

Dorothy's face looked mildly puzzled once more. After all, she had been led to believe by the other staff that Lady Rose's marriage to her late husband, Anthony, had been a very happy one.

"In my case I do not mean a man," Lady Rose saw the need to explain. "I am talking about a past Queen."

"Good Queen Elizabeth?" Dorothy frowned.

"No Child!" Rose corrected her. "I mean her half-sister, Queen Mary!"

It had been an easy mistake on the young woman's part, for who had she ever known who remembered any other queen than the late Elizabeth, who had reigned longer than most of her elders had lived?

"Queen Mary?" Dorothy repeated.

Lady Rose smiled wryly. It was the smile of someone, who having achieved great age reluctantly had come to realise that their own past life was now consigned to history by the latest generation. This only served to make the old lady even more determined to make certain that her account of events was the one that would be planted and nurtured in this young maid's mind.

"May my Lord bear witness that there was many a time I prayed to Him to take the wretched Queen Mary out of this life, or else to please take me!"

Dorothy listened patiently. Clearly not out of deference to Her Ladyship's position as mistress, nor to curry any false favour with her, for it was blindingly obvious to Lady Rose that the young woman had a natural thirst for knowledge that had been ill served up until then. It was also a rare treat for the old lady to be in the company of one so young and vital. The Lord had chosen to bless Sir William late with long-awaited offspring through his second wife. Rose may well have also been resigned to the fact that there could be little possibility of her surviving long enough to see her beloved granddaughter, Frances, grow up or to be able to sit and chat, like she and Dorothy were doing now. Maybe that was why Lady Rose was so generous, that morning in sitting and indulging this lowly maid with her company.

"I am proud to have been born a Protestant, in a Protestant England under its Protestant King Henry," Lady Hickman boasted. "When both he and his poor son passed on, that woeful Queen ascended our throne with her mind set on but one thing; to vilify her 'heretic' father for divorcing her mother and to return England to its former Catholic faith. And," Rose added scornfully, "had she but a dram of her Father's kingship flowing through her Spaniard-tainted veins then maybe she might have succeeded, given time, through persuasion alone, in doing that. Instead, this Bloody Queen burnt dissenters into subjugation, giving new meaning to the respectful term, 'Our Dread Sovereign'! For there never was a time of such oppression over so many good souls by such a tyrant as she! God grants us free will, so how dare man contrive to shackle it!"

Dorothy soon realised, as Lady Hickman railed on that Her Ladyship had not been, at that time, about to be ordered against her conscience to desert her own deep held belief in religious freedom. Not by anyone, let alone a Queen. Not only that, but it soon transpired that as a young couple at that time, the Hickmans had been granting refuge to many a protestant in their London home directly against the edicts of Queen Mary. Not only had the Hickmans offered sanctuary, but with their money and trading connections, they had also provided the ways and the means for these persecuted people to illegally flee to the continent and safety. As a result, life was about to become very dangerous for them.

"Mary's wretched spies were everywhere!" Lady Rose said. "In time they began to shadow us all about the City; they followed our friends and made detailed reports on anyone that called at our house..."

Lady Rose fell silent for a moment and her eyes glazed. It was as if she had wandered off, mid flow, into some other place, long ago and far away. Dorothy did not know what, if anything, she should do about this sudden impasse so she just sat, quietly, until Lady Rose sparked back into the conversation again of her own accord.

"Anthony and I were betrayed," she resumed her tale. "We were seized and thrown into the stinking Fleet Prison...confined apart...never knowing from one day to the next if the authorities had gathered enough evidence to have us tortured and burnt at the stake. To make matters worse, I was pregnant."

"Oh," Dorothy let out a little gasp of heartfelt concern.

"It's alright child!" Lady Rose leaned forward and winked wickedly, "they had nothing, so eventually they had to let us go. Still, I feared it would be but a short reprieve until our persecution began once more, so I begged and persuaded my husband to flee the country for Holland."

"You didn't you go with him?" Dorothy could not resist the question.

"I was heavy with child and afraid of losing him to the rough journey by sea," she replied, "so I decided to tarry here until he could be safely delivered. But even then," she added resentfully, "although weak and vulnerable and still 'lying in' after my confinement, this wicked Mary would not let me be!"

Lady Rose went on to tell Dorothy how a Catholic priest was dispensed to inform her that she must immediately present herself and the baby, to the local church for its baptism. A Catholic baptism! Rose had been outraged but quickly saw it for what it was - a wicked ruse upon their part. It was a finely sprung trap, which they hoped they could harry the new mother into. The authorities were probably anticipating that in the heat of anger Rose would defy the order out of hand. For had she risen to the bait, then they would have had her. If Her Ladyship had been seen to openly refuse Catholic baptism for her child, then it would be on the pain of her own death. Some small recompense for Queen Mary after having had Anthony Hickman escape from her clutches. Yet to have her baby baptized into the Catholic faith would be anathema to Rose Hickman's conscience and a denial of her deeply held Protestant beliefs. It was a lethal quandary. However, Rose was determined not to have her faith compromised or her hopes for safely reuniting her family in Antwerp dashed. Quick-thinking and wily as ever, Rose had managed to prevent her child from receiving a full Catholic baptism, by sleight of hand, as she prepared to leave with the Priest. She managed, with great daring and courage to substitute the sugar she was obliged to provide for the ritual with salt. The effect of this thus nullified the ceremony. It was a sweet revenge and no one ever found out. Thus Rose was left able to maintain, jubilantly, for the rest of her life that she was never was present at any of the Popish masses, nor a willing party to any other idolatrous service.

Satisfied now that Rose Hickman had given in to the authorities at last, she dropped from their attention. It was a big mistake for Rose was about to execute her escape plan to join her husband abroad. Unbeknown to her persecutors, Rose had secretly arranged for all her furniture to be spirited away and stored in friends' houses, all apart from her feather bed, which she had thrown into the bottom of the rotting hulk she managed to secure with much bribery. In this, she made her escape to Holland with her child. The perilous journey vindicated her previous decision not to risk her pregnancy on a similar crossing earlier. For on this voyage she lay confined to her bed, clutching her baby in the rat infested hold of that ship for five agonizing days as it tossed and pitched in the fiercest of gales. It was a miracle that the ship did not sink and that they did not drown.

After Queen Mary's death and Elizabeth's accession, the Hickmans returned to their previous London life and prospered. However, for all its struggle against the wave of Catholic persecution, the Anglican Church left in its wake remained an essentially catholic one with all the idols and elaborate ritual still in place. Worse than this, the sovereign seemed steadfastly opposed to any attempt to re-establish the state church to a purer, un-idolatrous form as many now were calling for. Then again, why indeed should she? For she followed her father King Henry's lead knowing full well that with the monarch as head of the Church in England, the sovereign held power over both body and soul. Every loyal subject conceded that their liege king or queen should hold dominion over their body, yet some now dared argue what mere mortal could lay claim to another man's soul? Surely, this could only be a matter between a man and his God?

The Hickmans were among those who wanted reform and so quietly, over the coming years, they covertly assisted others in pursuit of this aim. Now Dorothy understood the tight-lipped loyalty amongst the household servants in their dealings with those beyond the Old Hall in the town. And why there was such secrecy around the group who regularly 'congregated' on Sundays in the Great Hall or the grounds outside? These 'visitors' were of the Separatist persuasion. Groups from around Gainsborough facing persecution for wanting religious freedom. Although not a separatist herself, Rose was extremely sympathetic to their cause and believed vehemently in their right to follow their conscience when it came to their faith. So, it seemed that yet another Hickman homestead was playing refuge to those suffering religious persecution. Under Rose's kindly protection the Old Hall had become their sanctuary, and the great yawning hall within it a safe place for them to meet and worship. It was also a dangerous involvement for all parties concerned.

Something suddenly caught the old lady's attention, for Lady Rose unexpectedly stood herself up, albeit a little unsteadily. She leaned forward, precariously, as she raised up her cane to hook the heavy curtain away from the squint. Dorothy sprang forward from her chair to support her Mistress. Lady Rose turned her face towards her briefly and smiled appreciatively, before craning through the squint to see what was going on in the Great Hall below. Voices were rising. Sir William's trusted steward was at the far end waving papers in the face of someone who was probably a merchant's runner or a ship's messenger from the nearby wharf.

"Ah! T'is something and nothing!" Lady Rose exclaimed, somewhat disappointedly.

With that, she let the curtain drape again and then gently dropped back into her seat guided by her maid. Dorothy dutifully settled the cushions behind Lady Rose's back and had just resumed her own seat when Mistress Goode returned with daintily etched silver half-tankard and a slipware jar upon a hammered pewter charger. The housekeeper proffered the tray to Her Ladyship, who in return swivelled the turned wooden honey catcher inside the pottery pot. Then Lady Rose carefully extracted it, guiding it swiftly across to her chamomile tea, clearly delighting in the sight of the cloying honey forming sticky golden strands that then ran down into the steaming brew. It was a simple enough pleasure to pacify this elderly lady's sweet tooth.

"I have so enjoyed my little talk with you, my dear," Rose said in between tiny sips of her hot drink. "It has gone far to substantiate all the good reports I have received of you so far!" She smiled, examining Dorothy once more with those rook's eyes of hers. "I can see for myself now that you are indeed a steady, sensible girl. Exactly what I am looking for! Yes!" she exclaimed, blinking several times, as she cast her gaze towards the housekeeper, " I agree with your recommendation, Mistress Goode. I think she may do very well indeed!"

Very well? Dorothy thought to herself, do very well, for what?

It soon became clear that the loss of Dorothy's own child had coincided with the happy confirmation of yet another pregnancy for Lady Elizabeth. There would soon be pressing need for an extra nursemaid and so with forethought and compassion, Mistress Goode had put forward young Dorothy for consideration.

"This time I shall have a grandson to carry on the Hickman name," Lady Rose said, contentedly turning towards her faithful housekeeper. "This time I am certain of it, Mistress Goode. God will answer my prayers."

Chapter 6

The lady Frances was a delightful child with sapphire-bright blue eyes. A wayward mop of wheat blonde curls tumbled over her chubby red-flushed cheeks as the toddler squealed, insistently, for the exhausted looking nursery maid to swing her, upside down, just one more time. The memories of that first meeting with the blessed child would live with Dorothy to the end of her days.

"Mistress Speake," Mistress Goode made the introductions. "This is Dorothy!" Dorothy politely bobbed to the nursemaid who seemed well pleased to be shown such respect. She smiled back at the young maid in approval.

"She has been sent to help you," the housekeeper continued. "Part time for the present, but with a view that should she prove competent, she gradually trains up to take over the care of young Lady Frances here so you might be less burdened when the new baby arrives."

"I am certain we will rub along nicely, Dorothy," Mistress Speake replied, looking gratified beyond words to at last be getting some help. She was a nice enough woman as Dorothy came to realize but as it turned out, was rarely to be seen with a smile on her harassed looking face. A nice enough woman but Dorothy later surmised, perhaps a bit inadequate to care for such a boisterous young child.

The nursery was at the very top of the east range and had been especially created, on Rose Hickman's instructions, above the master bedchamber. Rose had strong, if unconventional, ideas about the rearing of her grandchildren. For one, she was strictly opposed to the accepted custom of nobler offspring being wet-nursed instead of being suckled by their natural mother. Rose was of the unusual opinion that to do so was inviting disease. In any case, Rose argued, it had never harmed her to breastfeed a child!

Young Lady Elizabeth, though, tried to resist Rose's view of child rearing, preferring instead to go along with the thinking of her own mother and the accepted wisdom of the time: that to have the child wet-nursed was actually a good thing it as it allowed the Mother to recover quicker by not having an infant at her breast, sapping her valuable strength. Unfortunately, Rose's opinions appeared to have been vindicated, Elizabeth and William's first born, Anne, was lost when the wet nurse procured from the town died from a mystery illness, taking the life of her vulnerable young charge with her. From that pregnancy onwards it was decided that each new baby was to be suckled by Lady Elizabeth herself. They would be brought downstairs from the nursery in the night and into Her Ladyship's changing room so as not to infringe upon Sir William's much needed sleep. They could expect to enjoy the close comfort of their Mother's breast at least until weaned. Then, like little Lady Frances, at barely a year of age, turned over to the care of nursemaids to complete their day-to-day upbringing.

Lady Rose also had strong opinions not only on the nurturing of this new generation of Hickman progeny but also their 'naturing', as she called it. She believed characters could be moulded at will and was determined to set her grandchildren on the path of good education, training and conditioning, just so they might become the perfect brood of entrepreneurs; even though she knew, at her late stage in life, she could never hope to see it completed. Yet, she did know that once she had instigated the mode of their instruction that she could then rely on her dear William to see it through to her desired conclusion.

Being herself a self-made product of a new order of enlightened women, Rose was determined that young Lady Frances would be educated too. However, she was not about to have this all undone by surrounding the child with frivolous influences. To this end, she was determined to carefully groom the Lady Frances' closest future companion too. Which, of course, would be Her Ladyship's personal maid. After months of scrutiny, as the young Dorothy settled into her new duties, Rose Hickman was fast considering her as the ideal candidate.

The role of nursemaid suited Dorothy's gentle temperament and she soon built up a strong rapport with the little Lady Frances. This closeness began to heal the grief Dorothy held over her own lost baby, but it also gave way to deeper questions that slowly emerged from the darkest recesses of her troubled mind. She would look upon her angelic little charge busy at play and wonder. Wonder, what would her own child have been like, she had not even registered whether it was born a boy or a girl. Most of all, she asked herself repeatedly, was she right in the decision she made not to marry Elias. Was she to blame ultimately for the little mite's death? These considerations clawed at her thoughts like long, dark fingers of shadow cast over the brightest of days.

***

Late spring melted into a long, balmy summer that often found Dorothy's days consumed by entertaining little lady Frances in the grounds of the Old Hall. She would usually sit enclosed in a wicker-walled pen under the shade of a large willow and play until the child was aired and tired out. Then she would rock her to sleep in the crook of her arm, to a dulcet mingling of turtledove coos and cuckoo calls adrift on the wings of the wind. Here she could let her imagination run away with itself, and pretend that she was really a mother and that the Lady Frances was her own dear baby. She adored the little girl and Lady Frances willingly returned that love in equal measure. Such a bond was forged between child and nursemaid that it almost fashioned this fancy into truth.

It was on one such afternoon, with the brilliant sunlight filtering softly through a languishing weep of willow branches that Dorothy first saw him; a young man, walking in the gardens in the company of one of the other regular Sunday visitors to the Hall. As soon as she chanced to glance up and catch sight of his angular face, Dorothy felt a sudden, exquisite jolt; as if she had been shot through by some unseen bolt of lightning. From that moment on, she could not take her eyes off him.

He was a handsome gentleman in his mid twenties. A scholarly, younger son of a modestly landed family from nearby. Modestly landed, yet rich enough to have bestowed a Cambridge university education upon him in the hope that he might forge a career in the Church. It later transpired, however, that his parents had been much aggrieved by their son as he had been 'requested' to give up his studies after repeated disagreements with his tutors over matters of Theology. Sadly for him, he had also already been married and widowed within the past year.

Dorothy admired the cut of his clothes as he stood, deep in conversation with another, slightly older but equally good-looking man. She watched as the two began to saunter along the length of Lady Elizabeth's flowerbed, which was in glorious full bloom and a riot of clashing colours, ablaze in the sunlight. In his dark green coat and breeches, topped with a red cap perched upon a head that constantly nodded back and forth, as he walked and listened intently to his companion, Dorothy thought him as beautiful as any flower.

Comfort arrived with some much-needed refreshments for the nursemaid and her young charge who was slumbering, blissfully, in the folds of Dorothy's skirts.

"Who is that?" Dorothy whispered.

"Oh. That's John Smyth," Comfort replied. "He was clergy but got sacked by the Bishop of Lincoln, that's all I know and that his Lordship allows him to lead his own Gainsborough followers in worship here in private."

"No. Not him," Dorothy sighed, "the younger man, in green!"

"Oh!" Comfort exclaimed, "I'm sure I don't know!" She strained herself right forward and scrutinized the man as closely as she could from that distance for a moment or two. "Just one of John Smyth's Separatist congregation, I suppose."

With that, she returned to her duties inside.

So Dorothy watched the object of her fascination walk away, without knowing his name or if she would ever cast her lovelorn eyes on him again. For the time being he would remain unnamed and unknown. It would not be until much later, with the hot summer spent and the misty autumn arrived, that Dorothy would learn his identity. Unbeknown to Dorothy though, he had also noticed her.

***

Sir William and Lady Elizabeth stood in the nursery looking gravely on. It was obvious the child was seriously unwell, for a day or so beforehand, Frances had caught an autumnal cold.

"It was no more than a snuffle really," Mistress Speake tried to explain to the doctor as she grappled with the writhing child, now barely in her grasp. "Nothing to raise any fears in me," she added, "she wasn't off her food or anything like that. Just snuffles!"

However, in the small hours of the morning and in a state of some distress, the child had awoken Mistress Speake from her bed in the nursery.

Suddenly now, the little girl started making strange beastly half–barking, half-crowing noises like a blocked hunter's horn. Her tiny face reddened with every breath she struggled for. A tear-stained face, gripped with terror as if unable to comprehend from whence came the sounds now emanating from her own mouth.

The Doctor asked the nursemaid to pull up the little girl's shift, which she did with some difficulty, so he might get a closer look at the child's torso.

"There is no rash that I can determine, nor sign of any obvious injury," he said ponderously.

However, he had taken notice of how the child's skin clearly tugged in between her ribs as she struggled to breathe air in. He noted how she would gasp and then cry with her lips turning dusky and with a distinct tinge of blue. Blue lips - so often the ominous precursor of death. The doctor made to touch her. As he did so, the child instantly threw herself backwards hard against Mistress Speake's chest; arching her back in frustration, desperately trying to avoid his stranger's touch as she turned her face away and screamed "No!" in choked fury.

"Sissy! Keep stilly you naughty girl!" Mistress Speake scolded the child.

Ignoring her inarticulate pleas, the physician laid his hand on her clammy skin anyway. She felt hot to the touch. So very hot. He advanced his bony index finger, lifting the toddler's arm while he thrust it under her armpit as if to double check. If anything, it felt even hotter there. In his learned opinion, the child was running a dangerously high fever.

Just then, Dorothy arrived from her night-time lodgings in town. She was shaken to see the toddler in so much distress. Immediately Frances looked up. On seeing her surrogate mother, she rallied. The tot thrust out her arms towards Dorothy as if begging to be scooped up into her tender care. As she did so she was struggling for every breath almost as hard as she was to break away from Mistress Speake's weary grasp.

A voice suddenly snapped a command.

"Let the child go, Speake! If it comforts Lady Frances to be with Dorothy at least grant her that!" Framed by the open door way, Rose Hickman stood leaning heavily on her stick. Mistress Speake grudgingly relinquished the toddler, who clambered weakly into Dorothy's loving embrace and began immediately to calm down.

"Mother!" William exclaimed, "you should not be here! What if this illness is contagious? And the stairway up here is so narrow; you should never have attempted to climb them unaided."

"I may be old, William," she retorted, "but I am not yet ready to be considered an invalid! As for this illness being contagious, I very much doubt that it is. Dangerous, yes. But not contagious. I am certain she has Kroepm. I remember it from Antwerp and a neighbour whose child had the same symptoms."

"Yes, M'Lady," said the physician bowing respectfully. "I am in complete accord! It is indeed the croup and with a sore fever. The most dangerous type," he sighed knowingly and looking towards the parents and handed out his earnest advice.

"You must wrap the infant warmly in blankets to sweat out the fever and I prescribe a physic to purge the child's innards, and a sleeping draught so she might be made to conserve her energies."

"A physic, "Rose snapped. "It is not her innards that ail her! It is the humours in the air attacking her lungs! And as for a sleeping draft, the child is struggling for air as it is. Sap her of consciousness and she may forego to breathe altogether!"

The doctor bit back his urge to argue.

"I have seen the treatment on the continent," Rose continued, "and we will follow the Dutch physician's example! Your mistreatments have cost us one child already! Your services are no longer required, Sir. I bid you good day," she said, dismissing the man out of hand.

Sir William seemed quite unperturbed by his mother's handling of the situation but clearly his young wife was deeply distressed.

"And the child, Mother?" The heavily pregnant Lady Elizabeth could hardly bear to watch her daughter's distress a moment longer, "The child in Antwerp? Did it survive?"

"No," came Rose's blunt reply. "The child succumbed but my granddaughter shall not!"

Lady Elizabeth let out a loud gasp. With that, a now deeply concerned William, fearing for the sake of his other, yet unborn child, led his wife away. A precious unborn child, made even more so now because he might be about to lose Frances.

"Speake!" Rose commanded, "arrange for the child's belongings to be moved. With Lady Elizabeth's bed chamber directly below and her so near to confinement, the poor woman will get no rest. In any case," she added unexpectedly, "it is far too dangerous for a brazier up here.

"A brazier, M'Lady?"

"Yes. Speake. Help me downstairs first then bid Mistress Goode to arrange for a small cooking brazier and burning slab to be brought up and placed over the gare de robe in the tower bedroom. Quickly then! And water!" she stressed. "I need lots of water!"

Lady Hickman turned towards the young nursemaid comforting the ailing child.

"Young Dorothy here and I shall attend the child ourselves. Meanwhile you best attend upon Lady Elizabeth until this business has run its course."

The tower was at the opposite end of the eastern range within easy reach of the Solar landing. It housed four bedchambers, placed one above the other, each boasting its own gare de robe. These rooms also enjoyed private, alternative access, apart from the main house, by means of an integrated narrow, stone spiral staircase, leading from ground level up to the turret above. From the castle-like battlement the view was spectacular across the river Trent to Nottinghamshire in one direction and over to the Wolds in the other.

Dorothy carried the little girl gently to the large canopied bed and eased her down upon it, propping her up with its many fat pillows. Then, still holding her chubby warm hand in hers, slipped to the floor and knelt beside Frances, comforting her as she continued to struggle for breath. Lady Rose pulled up the blankets around her granddaughter and tucked then in tightly around her little body.

"T'is this fever that really concerns me," she sighed. "These poor little mites have no reserves built up within to fight them off. All we can do is to pray for it to pass!"

"My Lady, " Dorothy was afraid to speak out of place, yet she was so concerned that the child might perish that she summoned up all her courage to speak out against her Mistress's wishes. "My Lady, I think you are wrong to cover the child thus!"

Rose Hickman was not used to being questioned, let alone by a servant. However, she was not a woman who had ever been too proud or arrogant not to at least hear out the other person's point of view.

"You do, Dorothy?" she said calmly, and then smiled for she realized the strength of character it took to question authority. "Then tell me why and what you propose instead."

"With all respect, My Lady," she said hesitantly, "when I was just a little child and the summer heat too much for me to bear, my father would stand me gently in a half barrel and pour fresh drawn cool well water over me," Dorothy explained. "I remember how good it felt and how cool I was after."

The old lady thought for a moment. There was logic and sound thinking behind what Dorothy had said. After all, had not Rose too got a similar memory to support her theory? One from her escape to Holland when the cold North Sea water seeped into the hold of the ship. How she had felt its chill about her ankles as she ventured down from her bed.

There was no time for Rose to respond to Dorothy. Just then, the portable brazier arrived, supported by poles and complete with glowing charcoals. Her Ladyship's attention was immediately drawn to that and away from the conversation in hand. Dorothy feared this abruptness might also be a mark of her mistress's displeasure.

Lady Rose busily supervised the installation of the burner above the opening of the crude toilet. Comfort followed closely with a cauldron and huge ladle commandeered from the cooks, while two hefty kitchen boys with sooty faces and calves like tree trunks carried in a large butt of water.

Turning upon her stick and bringing her attention back to Dorothy, Rose explained, "I am going to get them to set some water to boil." Then she smiled and with less fraught tone added, "Meanwhile, strip the child down to her napkin and sponge her with a cloth soaked in some of that water. Let's see if it will help."

Dorothy willingly obeyed and presently the child's skin began to feel cooler.

A cauldron was set to boil and soon the tiny room was filled with a fug of thick steam.

"Please bring the child, Dorothy," Rose called across from the partition, "and let her breathe in the hot steamy air in there and see if it aids her breathing."

Dorothy did as she was directed, though she failed to see what good this could possibly do.

At first, as Dorothy carried her across the chamber, the little Lady cried and screamed clinging tightly on to her bodice and pinching her hard with her frightened fingers. Then, once inside the heavily-curtained-off cubicle and in the thick of the steam, as if by magic, she stopped. Frances's breathing began to ease dramatically. Within half an hour, she was so much improved that she was able to sip the infusion of lungwort and chamomile prepared by Mistress Goode. A few minutes more and she was taken out once more and allowed to lie on the bed, snuggled tightly against her nursemaid. Then, effortlessly, she fell into a gentle sleep.

"Is she cured, My Lady?" Dorothy whispered.

"I do not think so. Not yet," came the hushed reply. "Make the most of this respite and rest there with her as much as you can. You may be grateful for it later on," she warned. "I will send word to Comfort that you will be sleeping in at this post until the child is better – hopefully. I will make certain Mistress Goode looks in on you regularly and sees to both of your needs. Mind I am sent for if needed but for now I too should rest and conserve my energy for later. There has been far too much excitement today already for my blood!"

With that, the old lady quietly withdrew, leaving the two in peaceful solitude.

Dorothy and the child slept for several hours until Dorothy was aware that Lady Frances was no longer beside her. She opened her eyes with a start, only for them to be met by the sight of the smiling infant playing happily with her rag doll at the foot of the bed. Her cheeks were still flushed and her forehead still felt a touch warm, but Dorothy was relieved Lady Frances was so much better.

Comfort arrived at around noon with a salver of coddled eggs for Lady Frances and some pottage for her friend.

"Comfort, will you let Mistress Goode know little Frances is much better than earlier?"

"Yes I will, if I see her that is!" Comfort replied with a teasing glint in her eye.

"Why? Where is she?" Dorothy knew her friend was itching to pass on some gossip.

"With Her ladyship! In her chamber," Comfort said excitedly. "Lady Elizabeth has gone into labour so they are all with her, waiting to help with the delivery. So it's just as well that Lady Frances is improved because they are all going to be very busy and for quite some time, if her other labours are anything to go by!" Having imparted her news, Comfort breezed out.

Dorothy attended to her own duties, managing to coax her little charge into eating some of the egg and even a spoon or two of her own midday repast. The little girl was still very hoarse and occasionally coughed like a dog's bark, but no longer gave rise to concern in her attendant. Indeed, the afternoon was spent at gentle play and again the little girl managed some food later on in the day.

Come nightfall, and within an hour or so of the two settling down to sleep once more together in the large half-tester bed, the little girl suddenly woke Dorothy with a fright. She was dreadfully croupy again and robbed of her breath. Worse still, she was hot again. The fever had returned.

Dorothy jumped out of bed and went to the chamber door. She called and called out for help but nobody came to her aid. Instead, she heard a terrible commotion some way off at the far end of the East range. She looked back towards the little girl and not daring to leave her alone, scooped her up and carried her, crying, the few steps further out into to the corridor proper and called out again. This time Comfort came to her aid running along the corridor with a lantern.

"It's Lady Frances!" Dorothy cried, showing her friend the child. "She's taken bad again!"

Lighting the bedside candle from her lamp as Dorothy propped the child up on the bed, Comfort could see for herself. "Don't worry, I'll go tell the Mistress. Then I will come right back!"

Comfort lifted her skirts and sped back from whence she came.

Dorothy hurried to the water butt; wet the cloth as before and with the little girl now perched on her knees, began damping down her body once more.

An animated Comfort soon returned.

"Mistress Goode cannot be spared nor can Lady Rose come!" she explained breathlessly. "It's Lady Elizabeth's baby! It's breached! Mistress Goode is trying to help turn it around from inside and her Ladyship is screaming the place down…Lady Rose says she dare not leave and that Mistress

Speake is ill abed... and that you are to do as before and minister to Lady Frances as you see fit!" Comfort took a deep breath, then continued, "I am already sleeping in tonight, outside in the corridor so will be on hand to run your errands. Fetch and carry, whatever you need of me. Oh! and My Lady told me to tell you that she trusts you implicitly to do whatever is needed!"

Dorothy was astounded by this show of faith in her and determined to prove it well founded.

"Send a boy up here, Comfort," she said with a new air of authority, "and get him to relight the brazier."

"But Dorothy, it's nearly curfew! You know it's against the law to have a fire burning at night."

"Needs must, Comfort! There's no other way! I must make steam for this little one to breathe!" she said, cradling the distraught child in her arms. "Go do as I ask. I will shoulder any blame!"

Comfort did as she was told.

"It will be alright, my precious," Dorothy whispered, kissing the little girl's hair, "I'm going to make you all better my love. It's all going to be alright."

Dorothy was right. The steam once more made the little girl's breathing ease. Again the procedure had worked its magic, although, coupled with the sponging down, it had to be repeated several times over before morning broke. Thus, the pattern of treatment was set that was to last several more days until a cure was affected and the child restored completely.

About a week later, Dorothy found herself wondering how much longer she should remain in the tower with her young charge. When a suitable opportunity arose, she set the question to her mistress.

"Shall I return Lady Frances's belongings to the nursery?"

"No," Lady Rose replied. "I think perhaps it suits my purposes better that lady Frances remain here at this end of the range close to my own quarters. She is growing fast and I think it is time I started teaching her to shape letters. I intend her to have an education and now would be a good time to start. I want you to become her personal nursemaid and sleep in with her in the tower chamber from now on. Is that agreeable to you, my child?"

Dorothy was deeply flattered. "Yes, My Lady. Thank you My Lady."

"Good! Then it is settled. Besides the nursery will be a noisy place from now on! My new grandson, Willoughby has a good pair of lungs and a lusty appetite, so Lady Elizabeth reports!"

Dorothy curtsied to her mistress and made to leave but her lady had one more thing yet to say.

"Without your diligent service, Dorothy, my granddaughter might not have fared as well as she did. You have my undying gratitude." The old lady reached out and taking Dorothy's hand added, "You showed fortitude and great sensitivity and proved yourself a valuable asset to this household. I, for one, will never forget this and if ever you need my help, it is yours!"

CHAPTER SEVEN.

The vivid colours of Lady Elizabeth's flower border were all but gone, cut down by frost and decay into brittle standings of dead stalks and a droop of brown-petalled flower heads weeping for summer spent. Here and there, a spider's gossamer thread woven in amongst the stalks of the dead plants was gilded by the soft sunlight and strung with diamante droplets of morning dew. Yet, amongst the grim debris of the reaper passing by, the odd, tattered, die-hard rose still bloomed defiantly, as if refusing to relinquish this last vestige of the season mourned.

In accordance with Rose Hickman's instructions, Dorothy dutifully tramped amongst the ruins of the gardens to provide Lady Frances with an hour's 'airing' after morning prayers each day. The little girl looked so dainty these days, dressed up in all her finery; a perfectly scaled down model of her Mother, the Lady Elizabeth, from her heavy blue brocade dress with its sheaves of petticoats beneath, right down to her tiny leather shoes. Yet her nursemaid regarded her with a pitiful eye. She knew only too well the tears and the struggle required to coax the poor little mite into layer upon layer of laced and buttoned clothing, how impeded the child was by it all as she tried to walk along, weighed down by its encumbrance. Playtime in the privacy of the nursery, where she could run about in a simple shift, was like a treasured breath of sweet release for the little girl. Time for playing though, was becoming less and less as education under Lady Rose's stern instruction began to take precedence over recreation.

"Pssst!"

Dorothy span around towards the house with surprise. It was Comfort trying to get her attention.

"Pssst! Dorothy! Quickly!" she hissed from the cover of the servant's doorway. "He's here!" Checking back and forth, that no one was watching her, Comfort pointed, rather animatedly, back inside.

Dorothy shrugged and quietly called back, "Who is here?" She was certain that Mistress Goode would appear at any moment and scold Comfort soundly. Dorothy did not want to be seen to be a party to any of her friend's silly goings on. She had responsibility now and did not want to disappoint Lady Rose.

"It's that man!" Comfort would not be deterred. In fact she hissed back even more determined than ever as she beckoned Dorothy to come to her.

Dorothy could not think who Comfort could possibly mean but never the less, it was cold and still misty outside and Lady Frances was clearly bored, so she decided it was a reasonable time to curtail the child's exercise and go indoors to warm up. She took the young girl's kid-gloved hand and gently led her towards Comfort, who could hardly contain herself as Dorothy drew near.

"What is it, Comfort?"

"It's him," she squealed. "You remember? The man you liked from the garden that day. His name is Master Thomas something or other. I heard someone call him by his name. He's right here in the Great Hall, with the others, waiting for Mister Smyth. It's all right!" she explained, "they haven't settled down to their meeting or anything yet. They are all just milling around in there like a lot of loose chaff looking for somewhere to settle. Go look for yourself!"

"I can't, Comfort, as well you know!" Dorothy rebuked the maid. "I can't just go wandering into the Great Hall. I have no reason to be there!"

"Well you would if the tower door were accidentally locked from inside!" she giggled. "Then you'd have to take young Lady Frances back upstairs through the Hall then!"

"But it isn't locked…is it?"

Comfort grinned broadly; her cat-like green eyes glinting with mischief. Then she scurried off, giggling, leaving Dorothy with no other course of action than the one she had already suggested.

Dorothy led Lady Frances to the ancient stone archway beside the Great Hall's large, medieval bay window. She drew a deep breath and tried to compose herself. Then she opened the heavy oak door and stepped through. Entering the Great Hall, she felt nervous and conspicuous. Her modest gaze naturally wanted to be drawn down to the ox-blood red-tiled floor and she headed for the stairway at the far side. Yet, at the same time she desperately wanted to glance up to see if the man really was there as Comfort had told her. She felt awkward, clumsy and out of place amongst these gentle folk. After all, she really had no right to be there had it not been for Lady Frances. With a momentary lapse in concentration, Dorothy stepped awkwardly, caught the hem of her skirts with her shoe and tripped. As she did, friendly arms reached out to steady her. Thankful, she looked up. Dark eyes greeted her own. Horror of horrors, it was him. Thomas. He had saved her. Dorothy felt her face flush hot through from her cheeks to her bone.

"Oh!" her tongue betrayed her as she fumbled though her words. "Thank you kindly, Sir"

"My pleasure," he assured her, lingering to smile a little longer than was strictly necessary. "More haste less speed," he added playfully.

Her heart racing, Dorothy felt compelled to hurry on out of sight, with smiling young Lady Frances clinging tightly to her hand.

"Dorothy!" Mistress Goode caught her at the top of the stairs, "what are you doing coming up this way?"

"The door," she explained hesitantly. "The door at the bottom of the tower…I couldn't get it open! I think it must be locked or jammed!"

"Oh! Very well then!" Mistress Goode said, "I will get Comfort to go check it after I've sent her up with some warm cinnamon milk for Her Ladyship. That is if I can find her," she added with a sigh of resignation.

***

Rose Hickman sat patiently each morning in the Solar with her granddaughter, laboriously tracing and retracing letters of the alphabet, slowly bestowing the gift of reading to the child. Little could she have realized that as she did so, she was also opening up her maidservant's mind to the world, for as Dorothy sat waiting in attendance on the child, she too was learning to unravel the mystery of the written word. Unheard of for a lowborn country girl.

As young Lady Frances grew and began, falteringly, to sound out the form of words on her lips as her small, hesitant finger stumbled along the lines of print in Rose Hickman's English translation of the Bible, Dorothy was already to the bottom of the page and desperate to read on for herself. Rose saw and was pleased to indulge the young woman. She often allowed her a great privilege by letting her take the book away for an hour or two to read by herself as Lady Frances took her afternoon nap.

To read aloud to an illiterate is to pass on some small measure of knowledge, but to teach that illiterate to read is like giving a blind deaf-mute, eyes, ears and a voice with which to question. So it was with Dorothy. Each time she dutifully returned the Bible to Lady Rose, the questions came. Questions that unraveled into long, firelit discussions, spinning out into the dark winter evenings as the two sat knitting together. Once Lady Frances was safely in her bed, it was a much-needed diversion for the young woman after a daily round of duty and welcome company for her elderly mistress. Dorothy was like the whetstone to Rose Hickman's knife-like intellect. The young woman's natural inquisitiveness keeping honed the mind of this increasingly frail-bodied old lady. Dorothy gave her Ladyship a great deal of satisfaction in that her unexpected protégé soon converted to her own belief that the Church must be returned to its ancient purity; to recover its primitive order, liberty and beauty without hindrance from either the monarch or Rome.

In Dorothy, Rose saw a glimpse of her younger, more vital self; a spark from out of the same flame that had burnt steadfastly throughout the long years of her own eventful life, a flame she was only too glad to fan in this young woman's soul. Thus, Dorothy became enlightened far above her humble standing. The problem with fire though, is that once lit it may burn its own path far beyond the initial fuel and out of anyone's control.

In the years since Rose's generation of puritan believers, who wanted to reform the existing church, there had now grown up a new crop of Protestants fruited with bolder ideas. These wanted complete religious tolerance to worship God in their own simplified way. They demanded the right to read and discuss the doctrines in the Bible amongst themselves. They now had a Bible printed in English instead of the Popish Latin. Anyone in the country was in theory at liberty to read it, but as for discussion? The mainly corrupt, rich, power-broking bishops of the day were not going to allow that. They would not allow anything that might lead to the questioning of their office, and ultimately undermine their positions of immense power and influence over the common man. Instead, they seemed hell-bent on trying to shackle and gag such dissenters, especially Separatists.

Although her personal beliefs were not as radical as theirs, one such Separatist congregation was the one Rose Hickman permitted to meet in the Old Hall away from prying eyes. She often watched them from the squint in her room. She listened to their discussions with interest and admired their conviction and enthusiasm, an enthusiasm that soon rubbed off on Dorothy, as she too was encouraged to take a turn at this glassless window. So, when she asked permission to join with the congregation for worship, how could Rose then refuse?

On weekdays, Dorothy took part in her early morning prayers with Lady Frances and other Hickman family members in their private chapel. On Sundays though, after this daily devotion, she was excused duties so she might later join the Separatist congregation who travelled in from the town and surrounding district to meet. To Dorothy's dismay though, she was soon to learn that the handsome Thomas was not a member of John Smyth's sect as she had first thought. She was naturally disappointed, of course, but the discovery in no way detracted from her newfound faith in the movement.

John Smyth was a born leader and as charismatic as he was handsome. With his thick, full beard, dark wavy hair and soulful eyes, he attracted followers in the way the over-ripe pears in the Old Hall's orchard did wasps. They swarmed from all over to hear him preach, won over by his honeyed voice delivering honest words. Yet, for these sins, he was fast becoming a wanted man.

***

The skies were as leaden as the empty beer tankard that now dangled, absentmindedly, from William Brewster's index finger as he talked at length with John Smyth in the gardens of the Old Hall. Grey, flat clouds, slung ominously low in the summer sky, shimmered overhead like hammered pewter; strangely all the more dangerous-looking for their eerie beauty. A light rumble or two shuddered above the conversation yet no one seemed in any hurry to leave the remnants of this hot sultry day for the shadowy nooks within the Great Hall; even though they could smell rain on the air and feel the electrifying tension of an imminent tempest.

William Brewster and his nearby Scrooby sect had joined the Gainsborough Separatists in outdoor worship earlier that day. Two separate groups of state church dissenters, joined by mutual love and fellowship and their belief in the freedom of worship. However, even the Old Hall could not hope to shelter this Gainsborough congregation indefinitely from the ever-threatening clouds of persecution fast gathering from the direction of the established church. The Separatists would need to scurry further afield to find a secure refuge for their faith. Holland beckoned, like an old mother calling in her children from play before the storm hits.

Brewster stood some time in deep discussion with his Gainsborough counterpart. Inn keeper William had already begun to feel pressure being brought to bear against him. Like many of the Gainsborough group, he had been cited for non-attendance at church and was being 'investigated' by the bishop's agents.

The strain had become increasing unbearable for John Smyth too of late. Firstly, there was the loss of his living as a preacher for daring to speak out in favour of reform. Then followed persistent persecution from the Bishop of Lincoln for forming his own congregation of like-thinking Christians. He had been hauled up before the Lincoln court and fined, and fined again. All to no avail. This Separatist was as likely to give up his stand, as the Bishop was to stomach Smyth's idealistic views. In this game of nerves, stalemate seemed to have been reached. The current impasse only served to heighten the tension being felt amongst Smyth's following rumours which spread rapidly and which suggested that new powers were being sought from the King to facilitate the taking and silencing of these and all other dissenters. Dissenters of the Church could conveniently be described as dissenters of the King, the Head of the Church. In short, it could be interpreted as tantamount to treason; and the remedy for treason was death. There seemed now only one sensible path for Smyth to take, and to take quickly.

Today had been a coming together to mark a parting of the ways, for the two factions to bid farewell to one another.

John Smyth and his followers were leaving, packing up lock stock and barrel to head for safety overseas. All, that is, except for Dorothy. She wanted to go, being torn, in fact between her duty to her conscience and her duty to Lady Frances and the Hickmans. The latter won.

Even the Hickmans were out amongst the throng in the garden that afternoon. Lady Rose included, having been littered outside on her chair by two burly stable hands as if she were as light as a manger of thin hay. Holding court beneath the shade of a tree, she lacked for nothing the whole afternoon, least of all company as all came, in turn, to pay her their respects.

Dorothy had just roused Lady Frances from her afternoon nap. She brushed out the little girl's beautiful golden curls and freshened her tiny eyes of their sleepy dust and patiently dressed the child in her finest beaded, saffron gown and cap, wide lace collar with a tiny string of pearls strung around her neck ready for the gathering outside to adore her. For once, her little Ladyship co-operated fully.

As Dorothy strolled with her along the garden path, she heard Lady Rose's unmistakable voice ring out.

"Dorothy! Here!"

Thinking no more than that she was being summoned to show off this highly cherished granddaughter, she led the little girl over to the clique gathered around her mistress. As Dorothy and the child approached both she and Lady Frances curtsied, elegantly, in perfected and carefully rehearsed unison. However, as it transpired it was Dorothy that Rose wanted to introduce.

"I would like you to meet the new tutor," Lady Hickman said. "I have just agreed to take him on to help educate Lady Frances and, of course, Willoughby when he is old enough."

Until then, Dorothy had been so focused upon her chage's performance that she had failed to notice who else might be standing by.

Lady Rose leaned around to the person standing beside her chair then, smiling broadly, with her bony outstretched hand she made the introduction.

"This is Master Thomas," she said, "you will be seeing quite a lot of each other from now on!"

Dorothy hardly dared believe her ears or trust her eyes as she bobbed a curtsey to the man.

"Mistress Dorothy," he said removing his cap with a flourish as he bowed politely, "'tis a great pleasure to make your acquaintance at last!" Thomas ginned such a grin. It was as if his smile had stopped Dorothy's heart dead, mid-beat, like a butterfly caught in his fist. For a moment, she felt quite faint, desperately trying to contain any outward hint of excitement about the prospect of being close to this young man almost daily from now on.

Primarily Master Thomas was engaged to teach the basics of mathematics, music and drawing to the up and coming Hickman brood. However, as time passed by and a tired Frances needed to nap after morning tutelage, Thomas would turn his attention to coaching his older more attentive pupil instead. He soon found great pleasure to be gained from pressing into fruitful service not only the sum of all his privileged university learning, but also the experience of times well spent in the capital city, London. He attempted to instil into Dorothy the essence of his own knowledge of modern life, including the popular entertainments of the day; especially of the playhouses and the most popular playwright of the day- one William Shakespeare.

On dreary wet afternoons, as Dorothy sat by the landing window at her mending or sewing, or candle dipping with her mistress, if Thomas were free, he would come and recite, aloud, a Marlow or Shakespeare play to them. Many a favourite line Dorothy learnt by rote. All under the keen ear and watchful gaze of Lady Rose, who neither condemned nor condoned this intelligent intercourse, although many another employer would have nipped this flowering in the bud. Instead, she regarded these two young people with knowing smiles as she watched their relationship unfold scene by scene, in silence.

Time hurried by in a blur of activity and learning. Autumn days shortened into scant, shadowy winter days, with long dark nights to sleep and dream through. Winter snows drifted into spring showers that heralded cuckoos and on into yet another summer. What a summer it was. Such evenings that seemed as if they would never end.

At the end of the day, when Lady Frances was abed, Dorothy was free to take a turn outside and pass a little time in the company of Master Thomas. They would walk along the pathways, brushing along the lavender bushes that billowed out across them, sending their scent to fill the air, their heady perfume clinging to clothing and intoxicating the senses. Musk rose petals scattered on the breeze, and hover flies darted across the bright faces of the dog daisies; steamy evenings after mid-summer showers bringing the swifts spiraling above the lawn at breakneck speed, to snatch at the rising cloud of midges. They watched rainbows magically come and fade away and suns that refused to set until late. Then one special evening, friendship spilled over into something more.

As they had strolled in the garden, Dorothy looked on with horror as Thomas snatched a long stalk of Golden Rod from Her Ladyship's prized border and with a flourish, playfully decapitated the yellow flower.

"What on earth are you doing?" she cried out, as deftly Thomas stripped back all the leaves bar two, which he left intact at the very tip of the arrow-straight shaft.

"I, my Queen of the Twilight," he said quite seriously, "am going to beckon forth a bat from on high to stoop, here, before your beauty!"

"What? You are quite mad!" Dorothy exclaimed. However, she soon realised that her friend was not only serious in this pursuit but also adamant of success.

"Then I will wager you a kiss that I can!" Thomas countered.

Dorothy reluctantly accepted the bet. She marvelled and giggled, all at once and in such disbelief when he said, that just for her he would demonstrate his prowess as a 'bat-baiter'. She then kept perfectly still, crouched on the sideline, watching anxiously as Thomas stood, statue still, camouflaged amongst a flowering shrubbery. She struggled to contain her laughter, her hand clasped across her mouth, regarding Thomas and seeing in her mind's eye how he had described Master Shakespeare's actor playing the fairy queen, Titania, wand in hand held high aloft. As if reading her thoughts, Thomas swiftly broke into a whispered quote from that same play: "Lord, what fools these mortals be!"

Dorothy stifled a chortle as Thomas gestured her to keep quiet and set about making the stalk gently shake and quiver the top two remaining leaves into life, giving them the semblance of tiny, fluttering wings.

Dorothy watched anxiously for maybe four or five minutes as Thomas patiently continued his ruse. Then, just as all hope seemed to have evaporated away, suddenly a dark, shadowy shape swooped down from out of the gloom to snatch at the tips of the taunting leaves. Within moments the bat returned to dart so close as to make contact, before disappearing once more in the blinking of an eye. She smiled in amazement and wondered at this mysterious creature of the night being so skilfully tricked.

"See, I told you, Oh Doubtful One!" Thomas laughed. "He thought it was a juicy moth for his supper!" With that, the young man threw down his lure and pushed his way out of the bushes. Drawing close to his companion he added: "That, I believe, is a kiss you owe me if you are to honour our wager!"

Dorothy remained coy, slow to proffer up the pre-agreed reward.

Thomas drew close and wrapping one arm about her

shoulders, he leaned in, lifted her chin with his fingers and gently stole the sweetest kiss.

"I love you Dorothy, Mistress of my heart," he whispered breathlessly. "I love you, I love you, I love you!"

"Shh!" Dorothy broke away. "Someone might hear!"

"I don't care! I want the whole world to know. I love you!" he shouted.

Dorothy hid her face in her hands and ran towards the servants' door. This was wrong. This was exactly what she had been warned about by the other servants, cautioned about the sinful perils awaiting maids who become involved with those above their station. She knew it was also far less than her mistress, Lady Rose, might expect of her in return for so much privilege and yet, it felt so right.

"It's late. I really must be in my quarters now with Lady Frances!" Dorothy gasped back, without turning.

Thomas caught up and stopped her fast in his arms. Half-heartedly she struggled.

"I do love you Dorothy! Marry me?" he implored.

"Marry?"

Dorothy's whirl of thoughts blurred into one; how could this be? How could this gently-raised man be in love with one as lowly as she?

"Why the surprise? Isn't that what people do when they have got to know each other well?" Thomas asked.

She looked him in the eye, coldly serious for the moment, then replied,

"I cannot."

"Why not?"

"Because my place is here and I have a duty to my lady."

"And what about a duty to yourself?" he countered. "A duty to be happy. Maybe to make me happy too?"

Her gaze fell. She had no reply. Surely he must have understood the gravity of her situation though.

"I can't be happy without you My Love!" he entreated. "The time is fast coming when I fear our congregation will have to make hard decisions. It is doubtful whether we can even safely remain here much longer! When that time comes, I too may have to flee the country like John Smyth and his followers."

Dorothy sighed in resignation at the reminder of their dreadful predicament.

"You must go too if you are true to the cause. And true to me!" he added. "I want us to marry then, Dorothy. I want you to be my wife."

This was all too much, all too sudden for her to take in.

"Give me time," she pleaded.

"Time may not be in my gift to give, Dorothy," he said gently. Pausing thoughtfully for a moment he then added gravely, "Answer me this then, if you will. If word comes that we must flee, will you come to Holland with us or watch me walk away for good?"

The thought of leaving England had played in her mind before. She had felt guilty watching her Gainsborough brethren being forced away but that was before…before she had Thomas. Now, the reality that he too might have to go away for ever, struck home with a devastating coldness and the ring of unbearable finality.

"No Thomas. I couldn't bear to be without you."

"Then come with me my love, and marry me there in our own way, at the hands of our brethren as God intended!"

Dorothy paused for reflection; resigned to the fact that this was, indeed, the path she desperately wanted to follow.

"But what about my mistress? She would never consent."

"When the time comes, I will approach her. Have no fear."

With that, the two embraced passionately.

High above from the Solar, Lady Rose had been watching from her window. She looked down at Dorothy and regarded this hand-reared fledgling of hers testing its wings. The only problem with having such a caged bird as this was that the owner had always to live with the knowledge that although they had hand-fed every scrap that made the cherished creature grow, and lavished care and love upon it, should the door of the cage slip ajar, just once, then that bird would be off and away into the blue. No matter how much one might desire it to stay, a bird cannot fight its nature unless you were to clip its wings Unnatural subjugation had always been a concept abhorrent to Rose Hickman. No, if Dorothy were to desire to fly away with this man, then so be it. The old lady would not stand in her way.

CHAPTER EIGHT

There was no other choice. The net was fast closing in around the frightened congregation. If they were to remain loyal to their convictions then they would have to flee the country just as the Gainsborough sect had done the year before. It was a terrifying prospect, especially for the women and children who for the most part had never ventured out of their own villages before. The question was how were they to make their exodus without arousing suspicion. How could so many people be on the move at one time, with all their possessions, tools, livestock and pets in tow and travel without drawing attention to themselves? Moreover, when would they make their bid for religious freedom? It had to be soon because it was already fast approaching winter, yet Mary Brewster was heavily pregnant and there could be no question of leaving without her. Every new day bought nearer the expectation of the bishop's men's arrival to arrest William Brewster and the other key members of the group. All they could do in the meantime was to plan a route of escape, pack all of their belongings, put their affairs in order and pray Mary to give birth quickly so they could be on their way. That is what happened exactly.

***

Dawn was barely breaking. Half asleep, Dorothy fancied she was on a ship being rocked by waves and with the rush of wind on her face. Suddenly she woke with a start to find Mistress Goode, in her nightclothes, looming over her. She had the fingertips of one hand pressed up against her pale lips as she shook Dorothy awake with the other.

"Shush! Dorothy! Wake up!" she said quietly, half glancing towards the blissfully sleeping child tucked up in the other side of the bed. "Get your things together, my child! Master Thomas is here. You have to leave!"

"Leave? Leave when?" Dorothy was still not quite to her

senses.

"Now! There is no time to spare!" the old lady explained in a hushed but excited voice. "The congregation is leaving! Thomas has come to fetch you away with them."

Dorothy slipped carefully out of the sheets, hastily dressed and silently gathered her things. When she had, she tiptoed to the bedside where the little, angelic Lady Frances slumbered on unaware of the frantic happenings around her. For Dorothy, leaving this beloved child would be the greatest wrench of all. Leaning over, she softly stroked away the tousled wisps of golden hair and planted the gentlest of kisses on the little girl's forehead and murmured a sad farewell.

The Housekeeper quietly shut the door to the chamber and the two women paused for a moment outside.

"It will be all right," Mistress Goode softly reassured Dorothy, "I will stay here with her till morning and explain things to the child. She won't be alone when she wakes. I will see to that."

Then Mistress Goode thrust a small leather pouch into Dorothy's unsuspecting hand. She could feel it contained money.

"We all knew this day was coming," Mistress Goode explained, "and Lady Rose insisted I kept a full and current account of your accrued yearly earnings, ready in coin by me at all times. She knew if things came to a head like this suddenly, then you would have need of money and wanted to be certain you did not go without. You are loved in this household, young Dorothy!" The old lady's voice wavered.

There would be no time for Dorothy to say her goodbyes to the rest of her friends in the household. Only Mistress Goode was able to hug her and to bid her 'God speed' and beg His blessing to keep her safe.

With barely time to glance back and with tears in her eyes, Dorothy left the Old Hall, by the servants' door and made her away across the courtyard to where a brooding Thomas was waiting with a large chestnut stallion.

Dorothy sensed impending danger.

"Hurry Dorothy!" her fiancé said in a state of high excitement as he secured her bundle to the horse. He swiftly mounted and then swung Dorothy up and across into his saddle. "We must get to Littleborough to meet up with the others."

Holding tightly, they rode through the gateway and galloped away, the sun fast rising at their backs.

"What's happened, Thomas?" she asked pensively.

"Dreadful news, my darling! The worst we could expect," he said agitatedly. "A Post dispatch rider, a man loyal to William Brewster, arrived like a storm the middle of the night and thundered upon his door. He had ridden through the dark, non-stop from Tuxford. Killed his beast in the process!"

"Tuxford? But that's not far at all?" Dorothy exclaimed.

"Only twelve miles but far enough if you are in command of a prison wagon that has broken an axle and can go no further till repaired!"

"A prison cart?" Dorothy gasped.

"Yes. Sent from the Sheriff's bailiffs at Southwell."

"Southwell?"

"Southwell, Lincoln, York, and the King's Court," Thomas added," are now all of one accord! The guards are apparently holed up in an alehouse, whiling away their time while they wait for the cart to be repaired. Brewster's man overheard the drunken braggarts boasting that they were on their way to Scrooby to net a pretty kettle of fish for the Bishop's pleasure. He knew full well who they meant, so rode flat out from there to raise the alarm."

"These fish? Did they mean our congregation?"

"Exactly!" Thomas replied

Dorothy felt a wave of fear surge through her as the gravity of Thomas's words sank into her brain.

"Oh no! What will become of us?"

"Well, if we remain hereabouts then they will arrest every dissenter they catch. It is almost certain that Brewster is their main target. If they get a hold of him then the Bishop will certainly stretch his neck. That is if they do not decide to burn him to death instead. There can be no question about that."

"Burn him? Burn kindly William Brewster?" The thought was abhorrent to her. What had he ever done to harm another human being, she thought to herself? Kind, caring, William Brewster, whose only crime was to want the tolerance he lavished on others, granted back to him in small measure so that he might follow his faith, according to his conscience.

"Because he preaches sedition! He preaches against the unrighteous dominion of greedy Bishops who are not men of Christ. Else, how could they bear to sit by, gorging themselves inside their palaces as their flock goes hungry in hovels? They are only Bishops because the King has appointed them. Preach against them and you preach treason! They would execute Brewster!" Thomas stressed," and Clyfton and Robinson too as they have both already been sacked as Church ministers. And maybe some of us other men also, as collaborators and to set an example!"

Dread shuddered through Dorothy at such a thought.

"But where will we go?" she asked.

"To the coast. To Boston," he replied. "To pick up a ship to Holland".

"Boston? But that's over sixty miles away!" Dorothy blurted out in disbelief. "What about Mary Brewster? She's expecting a baby any day now?"

"Thank God, she's had it!" Thomas exclaimed. "A little girl. Two days ago! They have baptized her 'Fear'."

An apt name indeed, Dorothy thought to herself. They must be terrified out of their wits to even be contemplating going on the run when that poor woman should be lying in bed for a fortnight yet.

"What if she haemorrhages? What if she gets birthing fever?" Dorothy was deeply concerned. "She could very well die!"

Thomas agreed but the situation was very grave. They must pray to the Lord that neither she nor the baby would come to any harm.

The rest of the congregation was already making for the Trent and the old Roman Causeway at Littleborough, just to the south. It was here that they intended to attempt to cross the river at low tide, over to the Lincolnshire side. Thomas and Dorothy were to meet them there to join the trek, cross-country, to Boston.

Having reached the rendezvous point, the couple dismounted. Thomas did not tether the horse but simply let the reins drop as the sweating, exhausted beast sated its thirst at the river's edge sending clouds of hot breath into the cold still October air. Dorothy immediately thought of dear Comfort and how she was going to miss her friend.

As the two sat on a large fallen tree trunk, they surmised how their comrades must have been praying for the usual thick blanket of mist at this time of year, to cover them as they made their exodus. Instead, the morning was clear and bright making them a sight almost impossible to miss.

Suddenly there was movement from out of the tree line. A spindly figure in a tall black hat emerged awkwardly. It was young Will Bradford, the congregation's adolescent prodigy. He called a greeting in recognition of the couple, and then swiftly another joined him. It was William Brewster. They had broken away from the main party, having reasoned that as Brewster was a wanted man with a price on his head it might be wiser for him to travel separately from the rest. If the worst came to the worst and the congregation were stopped with Brewster not among them, then hopefully they would not be arrested. Besides, two travelling alone had a better chance of avoiding capture. If they came across the Bishop's men first, then Brewster could hide while young Bradford doubled back to warn the rest to spread out and take cover. If the very worst happened and Brewster was caught, they believed young Will would not be arrested, because after all, to the authorities he was only a hapless boy.

After the two Williams had departed, the couple bided until the rest of the raggle-taggle congregation came slowly into sight, desperation etched on every face. United with the congregation, under threatening skies Dorothy and Thomas travelled along the old Roman road heading towards Skellingthorpe. The whole group was all too painfully aware that if they had been spotted earlier and reported to the Bishop's men, this stretch of long, open road was where they were going to be caught. They had no other option though, for there was no way they could travel through the forest. As God's good grace would have it, they saw hardly a soul on the road that day.

Evening found the group making camp in the forest at Skellingthorpe by a little stream. It was cold, so bone chillingly cold. Even with the campfire crackling under a canopy of branches the Separatists found little shelter from the bitter cold wind. The only thing they had to hand in the woods to stave off the cold was brittle, browned fronds of bracken, which they used to cover themselves from the kiss of the cold night air. The women fed the exhausted little ones, making them drink water heated over the flames to warm their insides, then gathered them up to sleep huddled under their own skirts and petticoats for extra warmth. Older children slept tightly in the contours of parents or other siblings, all packed together for warmth. Mary Brewster lay with little Fear snuggled inside her bodice, her shawl drawn up tightly under her chin, praying for her husband, out God knew where.

The murky morning broke too soon. Stiffly they rose on

painful limbs, ate a hurriedly prepared breakfast and were on the run once more. The prospect of the next leg of their journey filled their hearts with dread, for to reach their destination would mean passing close by the City of Lincoln itself. In order to reach Boston they needed to skirt the city down by the south. Rising high above on a rocky outcrop, the menacing glare of both Lincoln's Castle and its awesome Norman Cathedral stared down at them, like Bishop's spies waiting to reach out and snatch them. Lincoln never shied away from its reputation as a hanging city. On the contrary, it set great store by its ability to stage such spectacles from the castle's Lucy Tower, so all and sundry might witness these 'strugglers' play out their gruesome last jig. Each stretched neck only serving to reinforce the fear of the law and God's Bishop. A Bishop, who they feared, could see their every move as they virtually passed by his own back door.

Once they had made their first crossing of the River Witham and climbed up the steep ridge to the heath land, they drew a sigh of deep relief as the Cathedral finally slid from sight. They felt safe on the vast desolate expanse of heath land. If they had been spotted it would be extremely difficult for any pursuer to find them in the failing light, or to second-guess where they intended to emerge from the moor. They had been walking all day and night was drawing in. On and on they struggled on leaden limbs to find some shelter to maker camp, but the moor seemed to stretch on forever. Finally they had no choice but to stop, and the men and the older children set about finding what kindling and brushwood they could for a fire, while the women set about preparing a meal and tending the needs of their little ones.

"Look Dorothy," Thomas whispered tenderly as they settled down to try to sleep for the night. "See how brilliant the stars are above and how they seem to stretch on across the heavens for ever."

The farm girl in Dorothy saw, but it was not their beauty that captured her thoughts. Instead, it was that they were out in the middle of nowhere, when seeing stars up above in a autumn sky, so clear and bright as this one was, could mean only one thing; a severe ground frost. They were in for a freezing night ahead.

Dorothy woke to find Thomas gone from her side. In the flickering light of the death throes of the fire she could just make out that one or two others were missing too. She sat up. She was freezing, her face, fingers and toes biting from the cold. As she looked about further afield, she noticed the shimmering of hoar frost beyond the circle of warmth that had radiated from the campfire. Beyond the mantle of light strange shadows loomed and she wondered what evil might be lurking out there.

Little Patience Brewster began crying and crawled out from under her mother's petticoats with outstretched arms begging to be comforted, just as poor Mary was furiously rubbing little limp blue limbs and battling to breastfeed her chilled baby. Dorothy quickly eased herself up and over to Mary Brewster. She scooped up the little girl and comforted her as she sat down beside Mary, wrapping her own shawl partly around this other woman's shoulders in an effort to help afford a little extra warmth for the infant.

"God help us! " Mary said, with her voice near to breaking. "But I don't think this little one can survive much more of this cold." Dorothy had seen and knew the exhausted mother was probably right.

Suddenly Thomas and the others appeared. Their arms were full of brushwood to rejuvenate the failing fire. It burnt well but not for very long, yet the little extra warmth it radiated for that short time would most likely save young Fear's tiny life, for now.

Morning came like their oppression; bearing down on them like a smothering mass, intent on hampering their every move. The thick billowing mist they had prayed for the morning they started their journey now enveloped them with a vengeance. Already half frozen by the cruel conditions during the night, now with the dawn the damp air clung to them to compound their misery. Progress off the moor was slow and cumbersome, but the inclemency of the weather certainly helped to cover their tracks.

The congregation had come a long way by the time they reached sleepy Billinghay. They dared to allow some confidence to seep into them, making them wonder if perhaps they might have come far enough to have actually got away with it.

After a short discussion it was agreed that a few of the party would risk a reconnaissance mission into the village itself to see if they could find any like minded Christians who might be willing to help them in their plight. For one thing was agreed without debate – to stay one more night out in the open was likely to cost them dear; possibly the lives of the weakest amongst them.

Lots were drawn as to who would walk into the local blacksmiths and engage him in conversation while they employed him to repair one of the broken handcarts and pump him for information that might help their cause. Likewise several others went to the local inn to ask the same sort of tentative questions. The outcome pointed to the same conclusion; the occupants of Tattersall Castle to the east were rumoured to be Separatist supporters. They might just make it before another night fell.

Almost at day's end, in the glow of the fast setting sun, they saw red-bricked Tattersall Castle rising up like a great glowing ember before them. Beyond that, the vast flatness of the fenlands swiftly opened up. This was a mystical, magical sight, yet at the same time an unnerving one, with just the hint of impending menace. If the group were to avoid another night sleeping out at the mercy of the elements, they would have to cross the drawbridge and ask to be let inside. Once they had entered though, they would be at the utter mercy of its occupants, unable to leave of their own volition. Once the drawbridge was raised behind them, they would be as helpless as a rabbit snapped tight in a fox's jaws.

CHAPTER NINE

Tattersall Castle proved a safe sanctuary for the exhausted escapees, who had desperately needed respite for their women and children to recover their strength. Only they dared not tarry for long. As halcyon as their brief stay had been, they were desperate to go, as to remain any longer was a fast fading option. Surely by now the group had been reported as missing to the authorities and a clamour already raised to find them out; the Bishop's bloodhounds could already be hot on their scent.

After leaving a parting gift to their saviours the congregation was away, with the rising sun casting long shadows behind them as they embarked on the final leg of their desperate flight from England. Shortly they would cast their fate to the sea and trust in the fisher of men.

Almost as soon as they left the castle, the outline of an awesome stalagmite of a building swiftly began to climb steadily upwards from out of the flat landscape to pierce the low grey smudge of sky above. Saint Boltoph's church, affectionately known as 'The Stump' to its Bostonian parishioners, stood like a beacon of hope beckoning in the near distance, uplifting their hearts and calling out to their souls to hurry on; salvation was almost in reach.

It was hard going though, across these desolate windswept fenlands of reeds and low sand banks interspersed with vast stretches of impenetrable quagmire. Carts, animals, people, all struggled equally in their effort to churn through this morass in the drizzle of rain that persisted all day. It was the women who were especially hindered by the wet and cloying mud, which clung wretchedly to the hems of their skirts and petticoats, no matter how vigilant their efforts to hitch them, decently, out of the way. Yet the smell of the salt sea breeze and the hearty cries of the black-headed gulls, reeling above, rallied them. It fuelled their appetite to continue eating away at the last few miles and focused their efforts all the more keenly. Then, like some wonderful omen from heaven itself, the afternoon sun broke though briefly with a shaft of glorious golden light. Its overpowering radiance split the gathered gloom asunder, sending a beautiful rainbow arcing up high across the marshland and tailing off right above Boston town.

It was nearing evening when camp was gratefully struck on the outskirts of the town. They had carefully skirted around it to settle, just a little south, in an area bereft of human habitation. Far enough from prying eyes, yet close enough for some of their men to venture in later, on a mission of reconnaissance. Though the weather that night would prove as wretched as any they had experienced out in the open before, the burden of it would bear down all the less heavily because on the morrow they would find a ship.

The congregation set to building a hearty fire with the bundles of firewood gifted from the good folk of Tattersall. As the older women set up their cauldrons and pots to cook a hearty, warming stew of mutton and barley, Dorothy helped keep their little ones amused. Meanwhile the menfolk sat and discussed the final detailed plans for their foray into the port to search for a vessel with a not too fussy Master willing to take on a lucrative cargo to Holland.

"You can't go William!" Mary Brewster was neither shy to make her views known, nor to wear her concern etched deeply on her plump face. "The same goes for you, Dick Clifton and John Robinson," she added, cradling baby Fear close to her breast beneath the warmth of her pale woollen shawl. "The pair of you are both dismissed clergy and as much a sore that the bishop wants cauterising as my man here is! He will be certain to have sent searchers who know you all by sight. If his henchmen are already there in Boston you will be easy game for them, for those seasoned foxes will spot you rabbits by your ears! But answer me this, husband? How are you to know them?"

Brewster typically brushed the warning aside before fully appreciating its implications. Besides, he felt an overwhelming responsibility for the safety of his fellow Separatists. True, Robinson and Clyfton were equally as obnoxious to the Bishop of Lincoln as himself but he knew that he had caused His Grace the most personal offence and affront. The Church owned his home at Scrooby Manor and he'd had the affrontery to allow Christian radicals to meet there in open defiance of this. Not only that, he had become a trumpeting mouthpiece for their cause. However, Mary's words were precisely the same as his own common sense was trying to scream out to him from inside his stubborn skull. He just did not care for the sound of them being spoken aloud, especially by his wife.

"Needs must to find a ship willing to take us aboard," he finally answered.

"But that need does not have to be met by you, William!"

William prodded at the campfire with a blackened branch in an uncharacteristically reticent silence. He knew his wife had a valid point but did not want to admit it.

"Let some of the others go!" she pleaded. "Them that won't be recognized. Safer for you and safer, by far, for us all!"

"Aye, William," old Samuel Cooper said, raking the fire, "listen to your wife, friend, for she makes a sound argument!"

Reluctantly Brewster gave in to reason.

"Then if none of we three are to go, then pray tell me, who will?" asked Richard Clyfton calmly.

There was a long silence. Brewster, Clyfton and Robinson were all natural leaders amongst this autonomous group with the others being well used to looking towards them to make arrangements. The remainder of the men were good, honest, steadfast folk but unaccustomed to being called upon to carry out matters of importance. None felt they had the confidence to carry out the task.

"I will go," piped up William Bradford eventually.

There was again momentary silence.

'Willy Spindleshanks' they affectionately called him. A pale, sick-looking youth of barely seventeen but already a proven and trusted stalwart of the Separatist movement. Mature and worldly wise far beyond his earthly years, he was the only son of a yeoman farmer who had died when Will was just a babe. Before her premature death, Will's mother had remarried and the young boy had been thrust into the care of his grandfather and uncles. They tried hard to make something of him, to form him into a farmer in their own image, but with such sickly makings as he, they were never going to succeed. Instead, by the age of twelve this lad was more interested in reading his treasured Geneva Bible than in tending to the land he would one day inherit from his dead parents. Within a very short time, he had vexed his kin further by becoming an active member of the dubious prayer and discussion group that was then regularly meeting at William Brewster's home in Scrooby. At this point, his family gave up on him. To them he was the runt of the litter, not expected to live to majority and claim his inheritance anyway. Better then, his kin thought, to let him have his own head while he could. At least they would be released of the bother of him. This was how he came to be there on the run with the others. He was following his conscience and evading the authorities with his true family.

"No, Young Will," Brewster shook his head adamantly. "It will be far too dangerous for you!"

"Why me, especially?"

"Because you are just a lad," Brewster replied bluntly.

"Precisely my point. Who is going to be looking for me?"

"True," Brewster had to admit, "but it's still dangerous and I'm not about to let an innocent like you abroad amongst the debauchery of that dockside Sodom and Gomorrah with a full purse to be picked off by the lowlife there!"

"Then I will go with young Spindleshanks and keep an eye on him!" Thomas shuffled up and placed his arm around the young man's shoulders. "If I can survive the playhouses and taverns of London, I can cope with Boston!"

"Aye," added old Samuel Cooper with a toothless grin, "and I will go too then, if only to keep a watchful eye on young Master Thomas here!"

The companions laughed.

"Besides," Samuel added with a glint in his eye, "a pappy and his two 'sons' out on the town are hardly likely to raise a hair of suspicion in any ale house!"

"Then if we are to go, we should go soon!" said young Will, "for while honest folk are in their beds, the inns and taverns will be full of just the shady, dishonest fellows we need to enlist."

"But if they are dishonest, how are we going to know if we can trust them?" asked Thomas.

"We won't!" replied Will putting on his tall, black hat "We will just have to trust in the Lord instead to steer us towards the right one."

So it was agreed.

In under an hour the unlikely trio was scouring the seafarers' haunts of this, the country's second busiest port. Facing east and with the continent but a short way out of the Wash and across the North Sea, Boston was a bustling cosmopolitan, liberal town full of strange contradiction. Ships from all over Europe crammed side by side into her moorings. Here lay at anchor traders from the Holiest of the Holy Roman Catholic States to the staunchest Protestant strongholds, with every shade in between, juxtaposed and harboured away from national rivalries and religious differences. Their crews rubbed shoulders in the nearby taverns and bawdy houses, mostly upholding an unwritten truce dictated by their one common, sovereign lord, the sea.

Amongst the sleazy Godless dockside dens, each of the sacred Ten Commandments were routinely disregarded, violated and broken without so much as a conscience twitching uneasily. Every imaginable facet of shame and debauchery was in turn thrust in the faces of the innocent trio as, foot-wearily they explored its rude streets. This was no place for God fearing, gentle country folk as these to be abroad. It was like stepping into another world. A dark, corrupt world where prostitutes stood beside lightless puke-stained, urine-soaked alleyways beckoning the three to come hither. Painted women with rouged lips and pale faces offering intercourse against the walls amongst the shadows to any sailor with a few ready coins at his disposal to cover the scant cost of the privilege. If these doxies were not to their taste then youths were close by, equally eager to accommodate those needs. This was a realm where gamblers met and cheats prospered, where drunken brawls were hourly events. Violent robbery, murder and mayhem were all just part of the seamier side of the town's daily routine, Samuel, Thomas and William felt, as they wandered in and out of those waterside ale houses, as though they had walked into Hell to hold an interview with the Devil himself in order to find their salvation.

So many vessels, yet which to choose and where to find their skippers? None of the Separatists spoke Dutch and although Thomas spoke fluent French, he swore he was not about to trust their lives to a 'Frenchie'. Eventually, after many enquiries and false starts, they came across the master of a vessel, rumoured to be none too fussy in looking for a cargo to take to the Low Lands. He was a rough Southerner, plying his trade up and down the coasts of Europe wherever he could find a consignment to keep his crew in his pay and himself in his accustomed manner. He was swarthy and rugged with leathery skin deeply tanned and pitted like the rind of an orange. His manners were crude, his words were blunt, yet he was the first they had found willing to hear out the carefully composed overtures that young William played out over a tankard of ale and brandy wine that Samuel obligingly purchased.

The three friends sat with the skipper as he greedily supped and then cautiously they laid their congregation's proposition on the table. The fellow mulled over the matter for some considerable length of time, probably biding until he had sated as much of his thirst as possible at their expense. Then, just at the point where he must have sensed the three were about to get up and leave to trawl in new waters, he suddenly agreed to bargain in earnest. For a handsome price, he would be willing enough to take them.

"Too many prying eyes, hereabouts, to take you on board in secret," he said cautiously, "but I knows just the spot!"

Wetting his finger, he drew out a crude map in the grime on the table.

"Here," he said, pointing to a spot in the river marked just below Boston, "just downstream from where you say you are camped, the Scotia Creek flows into the River Witham before it runs out into The Wash. It's a real lonesome, uninhabited place where we won't be interrupted. I will meet with you there tomorrow, as close to afternoon as the tide permits. That should give you time. Be there," he warned sternly, "for I won't be kept waiting about!"

As a sign of good faith, an agreed down payment was discreetly exchanged beneath the table by way of gold and silver in a pouch Will Bradford had kept carefully hidden beneath his baggy jacket. With that, the three left the tavern and made their way back to camp.

Scotia Creek was a desolate, murky spot, to say the least; made even more sinister by a thick sea fog that had crept stealthily up from the estuary to spill out across the low lying banks this cold bleak day. The Separatists waited patiently there from mid morning on, hoping against hope that the Master would show and not make off with their money. Time passed by painfully slowly and with each passing hour, they began to fear for the worst; that young Will and the others had been duped into parting with a goodly sum in return for a promise as hollow as the dead reeds on the bank all around.

Then, as night was almost upon them, at last the ghostly outline of the three bare masts of a merchantman sliced through the gloom as the longed-for vessel creaked into view from out of the mist. It looked huge against the low blank skyline as it slowly drifted down river towards them. Someone called ashore in a hoarse voice, William Brewster's booming out in clear response and there was a splash as the ship dropped anchor. Presently a party of sailors was ashore to help the congregation aboard with their belongings.

Only once the Separatists were safely boarded did the Master came on deck and greet the group. As he strode purposefully out from his cabin, the crew stepped aside in ominous silence. They looked to be in waiting, waiting in anticipation of something happening. They were a menacing presence, armed with muskets, knives, and all manner of weapons about their persons and all in plain view; in comparison not one of the gentle congregation bore so much as a sharpened tongue.

"I am John Clyfton and greatly pleased to meet you Master," the Separatists' chosen spokesman for that day greeted the skipper and politely asked, "When do we get underway?"

"Underway? Underway where?" the Master replied with a cold stare.

"To Holland," Clyfton replied, "as we arranged".

"Where are your permits?" the Master asked with a sneer.

"We don't have any as well you know!" William Brewster broke in.

"Then you know it's illegal for me to take you."

"But we made a deal!" Thomas shouted. "We paid you!"

"Ah! A deal?" the bilge rat laughed back scornfully. "And what court in the land, do you think, is going to penalize me for not keeping a compact with you criminals? An agreement to commit an illegal act?"

"Then keep the money but let us go on our way!" Clyfton pleaded.

"No! I have plans for you!"

The Master signalled to his waiting cohorts.

"Separate the women and children from the men!" he barked. "Go to it!"

The crew drew their weapons. One half herding the terrified women off to the far end of the deck, like cattle to a market. The remainder restrained their menfolk as they tried vainly to rush to their aid. In the melee, Thomas tried to protect his sweetheart and was soundly struck with a belaying pin. Blood trickled down his face as he sustained a gash on his head for his efforts.

Dorothy cried out his name as she was dragged away from his arms by the scruff of her neck and forced to join the others. Children screamed out in panic as their mothers were roughhoused by the bawdy seamen and threatened and goaded with cudgels when they resisted.

'Shut the brats up or I will turn them into jetsam!" one of these brutes snarled, as another ordered their frightened women to remove their warm, winter outer garments along with any jewellery or trinkets. They were roughly handled and searched for any other possessions of value hidden about their persons. However, the ruffians did show one small measure of Christian decency, by allowing the women to keep their wedding bands.

Meanwhile the men were likewise being mistreated, deprived also of their outer winter garments, purses and personal possessions. With the entire group's goods and chattels now "impounded" by the captain of these cutthroats, the congregation was forced below decks and transported back into Boston harbour. In the morning, bailiffs waiting on the quayside promptly arrested the men. The Separatists were dragged, unceremoniously through the more sedate and genteel streets of the main town to gaol in the town's medieval Guild Hall. Inquisitive Bostonians along the route stopped and stared to see what was going on. Some applauded the sight of these vile dissidents, infected by Lowland theology and openly opposed to the dictates of their lawful sovereign church, being rounded up as criminals. Others though, equally influenced by the wave of new liberalism that had swept in with the traders from Holland, secretly admired the stand that the congregation was making and were appalled at the treatment they were now receiving.

Soon a crowd formed and followed on in rowdy procession. Bailiffs and guards quickly herded the Separatists into The Guild Hall in an effort to get them out of sight, for the mood of the bystanders was getting ugly. The crew of the ship, who had been noisily demanding a just reward for capturing the would be runaways, followed close on the heels of the bailiffs and were jeered and heckled as angry shouts of protest rang out at small children and women being dragged along the cobbles by some of the sailors. Many were enraged even more, when only a little later the bailiffs ejected them forcibly, back out onto the streets to wait in utter abandonment while their menfolk were dealt with.

The last thing the authorities wanted was to risk rioting in the streets. So, the magistrates were swiftly fetched to call an emergency court into session to deal with these transgressors immediately. Yet what should they do? Even these judges could not decide amongst themselves. They had received no warrants for these men so all they had was the word of the Master of the ship that they had tried to bribe him to take the party out of the country. He was a man, they quickly surmised, to be an out and out rogue if ever there was one. Yet, this group of strangers was here in

Boston and not denying being of the Separatist persuasion. It was now imperative that having been brought to the attention of the authorities these men were seen to be dealt with.

Outside the ill feeling of the townspeople was escalating into a tinderbox situation. In order to avoid sparking a riot, the magistrates decided to play for time and defuse the situation quickly by ordering the men to be officially detained until instructions were received from a higher authority outlining the exact nature of any charges to be brought. By higher authority, they of course meant the Bishop of Lincoln. Satisfied with the knowledge that due process of law was correctly being exercised, this judiciary reasoned the crowd would then calm down and go about their business.

Meanwhile Dorothy and the other women waited outside, their noses pressed hard against the leaded glass of the Guild Hall's windows, straining to get even a glimpse of their loved ones inside or hear one word of what was happening. A goodly number of townsfolk were still around and gossiping amongst themselves as they waited for this side show to play out. Some, no doubt, in the black hope that with luck they might be in for a juicy execution at some point soon, if these caged absconders were criminal enough to warrant one. Suddenly and without provocation, a rotund and brutish bailiff manhandled Dorothy out of his way in order to play out some impromptu propaganda to discredit the prisoners within.

"And what are you doing here, my pretty?" he asked her loudly with a leer on his face.

"I am looking for one of the prisoners, sir."

"Are you now? No ring," he said snatching up her hand, "so you are not wed?

"No Sir," Dorothy replied, trying to avoid the burn of his eye and the attention of the throng.

"And we have only gentlemen in there!" he said looking

her up and down, noting her shabby clothes. "Your man can't be amongst them."

"But he is. I know he is!" she protested.

"And what pray does he do, this man of yours?"

"Do?" Dorothy was slow to catch the drift of his question.

"What profession is he? Yeoman Farmer, Innkeeper … defrocked cleric?" he said in an accusing tone.

The crowd hushed with intrigue as they followed this open conversation closely, for this was better than any play.

"No Sir, he is a Tutor," she replied, refusing to be cowed by his suggestion of any impropriety, "and a man of private means."

"Is he now?" the bailiff teased. "And you, my petty, what exactly are you?"

"I am his fiancé," she said firmly.

"Fiancé? Where do you come from? Nottingham?"

"No sir, from here in Lincolnshire. From Gainsborough Old Hall."

"Gainsborough Old Hall? Tell me then," he mocked," you are not a lady of the Manor are you? Only you don't have the look of a gentlewoman, but more the look of a commoner, to me!"

Dorothy began to quiver and falter in the face of this mockery.

"I'm a maidservant, Sir," she answered timidly.

"What was that? Only I couldn't quite make it out!" he taunted her, so he might shame her into repeating it aloud to the crowd to press home his point.

"A maidservant, Sir." She began to quake as a solitary tear trickled down her drawn cheek. "I'm a maidservant."

"A maidservant? Now that's better," he said. " Betrothed to a tutor? A man of means? Huh?"

"Yes Sir".

"Does your Master know you are here?" he demanded.

"No… but…" Dorothy tried to explain but was cut short.

"No!" he said, "I thought as much. Now, tell me truthful

girl. Have you run away with this man?"

Dorothy declined to answer. She knew now exactly what he was trying to do. To attack and slander them all by this vile ruse in any way he could, so that townsfolk looking on would get the worst impression possible of their congregation.

"I see," the bailiff continued, "he is a tutor and a gentleman of means and you are a just a simple serving wench!" he laughed cruelly. "And you believed he would marry with someone so far below his station? And the leaders of your sect? Did they allow and condone you to be brought along knowing your situation?" He turned to the crowd and added, "What sort of Christian men are we dealing with here?"

Somewhere a Bostonian woman shouted out 'shame'. Dreadful memories came rushing in like a wave crashing down and drenching Dorothy with undeserved guilt.

The bailiff turned his attention once more on the young woman in a mock show of concern and continued his exercise in discrediting the captives. "A man like that is only out to use you easy, you little fool! If I were you girl, I would go home straight away and tell your master how you were lured away by this wickedness and beg mercy and forgiveness for this corruption. And in future learn to mix only with your own kind!"

Dorothy turned and ran, sobbing, back to the other women and children. She felt crushed and hurt by this foul slander against Thomas and herself. She knew he truly loved her. He would never do anything to harm her yet that foul-mouthed snake had made the whole affair sound tawdry and sinful.

Suddenly a side door was flung open, just long enough for a solitary figure to be ejected from The Guild Hall, swiftly followed by his hat, which landed in a puddle. It was Willy Bradford. As anticipated, he was not to be detained by virtue of his youth.

Young Spindleshanks retrieved his beloved hat, shook it briskly then replaced on his large head before joining the women and children.

"What's happening?" Mary Brewster was almost beside herself with worry.

"It's alright!" he tried to reassure them and take control of the situation. "The others are all being treated decently."

"But what's going to happen to them?"

"I don't know," he replied, "but Mister Clyfton said you are to all be of good spirit and to pray for them. In the morning the court will meet in full session to hear out our full representation and see if there are any charges to answer."

"What of The Bishop and his men?"

"There don't appear to be any here. Perhaps they expected us to make for the Humber Estuary instead. In any case, there are no other charges being brought just now other than those on the evidence of the Master of our ship. That is what is causing so much confusion for the magistrates. So now it appears to be up to the incumbent of St. Boltoph's to inform his bishop and deal with any church warrants. Yet, bless the man, for I suspect he harbours sympathy for us as he did not seem a willing participant to any of the procedures and may, it seems, delay in his duty. All we can do now is hope and pray, for everything is in the Lord's hands now. He will determine the fate of our brothers."

"Where are they being kept, Will?" Dorothy asked.

"They are being held together in the cells on the ground floor. Later I will be able to show you where you can peek in and just about see them, but not now. Best wait for the townspeople to disperse and the cold to drive the bailiffs inside to their fire. The main thing now is for us to find shelter for the night and I think I know just the place."

Young Will showed his true mettle during that trial in Boston. He took on the mantle of protector of the Separatist women and children. He led them into the porch of the local church despite the protestations of the churchwardens. This, he argued with them, was the house of God and as they were His children, who were these petty officials to deny them His shelter in their hour of dire need? "Suffer the children" he said, shaming them into finding bread and milk for the little ones. Then, as his dependents settled down for the evening, Will donned his hat and went off into the freezing void to knock upon the doors of as many houses as he could in an effort to find sympathizers to help them in their plight until they could be reunited with their menfolk. Will steadfastly held on to the belief that all would come right, even though as the days wore on into weeks, that prospect became increasingly unlikely.

Chapter Ten

Will Bradford's early optimism soon dissipated in the face of delays that saw days stretch into weeks, and still there was no resolution of their plight.

Conditions for detainees in the Guild Hall were far removed from anything these gentle people had experienced before. The tiny cell was only ever intended to physically secure and confine a prisoner until the magistrates could be assembled in the courtroom above to hear the evidence and judge the case. This justice was swift, as was the meting out of any punishment and it was not unusual for the two to be completed on the same day. Imprisonment itself, however, was not one of those punishments; fines, humiliations, mutilations and execution satisfactorily covered the gambit of suitable retribution for all levels of crime. The problems of having to hold so many prisoners at any one time, and for so long, were not occurrences ever envisaged by the town's corporation. Therefore, facilities in this ancient Guild Hall were practically non-existent.

The cell measured a little over six paces in length and four across, barely longer than a grave. Two wooden benches were set into the thick, stone, walls on either side. Windowless, the only source of light filtered in through the tiny square grill set into the heavy oak door that sealed them in like living corpses in their tomb. It was so cramped that the Separatists had no other option than to attempt to sleep sitting up, slumped shoulder to shoulder and knee to knee, whenever they could.. They grew stiff from this enforced idleness, which robbed their bodies of any sort of exercise. There was one mercy at least, from being made to live so tightly packed, their combined body heat saved then from freezing both at night and by day. It was October now and winter had already begun to bite. Day by day it became steadily harder for the men to stave off the bone-chilling numbness settling deep within them. Although there was a huge hearth with its fire constantly lit at the far end of this lower floor, little heat found its way to their cold stone cell. The heavy oak, metal-studded door which kept them in, equally kept out any comforting warmth radiating from the dancing flames; flames whose flickering shadows at night taunted them through the bars of the turnkey's spy hole, making them think of the campfires so recently shared with their wives and children and how very much they missed them.

With each passing day, the realization grew inside them, like some dread cancer, that these brothers might never be going to see the light of day again as free men. The endless hours hung heavily on their minds, with little else to engage them other than to ponder their own impending fate and to agonize over the plight of their women and children left destitute on the outside. Some Separatist prisoners wept quietly at night, when prayer failed to comfort and sleep refused to grant temporary pardon from their troubles, while others cried out in their dreams when it did.

The passing of a stone jar between the men crudely catered for their toileting needs. Defecation was a luxury afforded only by prior appointment with the turnkey, as he had to summon the help of two bailiffs to stand guard while he unlocked the cell door, to lead the prisoner away in chains to use a crude arrangement elsewhere. At least this basic human function offered a few minutes' respite from the claustrophobic conditions inside and one's fellow prisoners. It was a welcome opportunity to readjust sore eyes to the bright light of day, a chance to stretch away stiffness from aching joints and revive impeded circulation in pin stuck limbs. It also offered an escape from the growing stench of stale sweat and urine and an opportunity to gulp down as many lungfuls of the fresher air along the corridor as possible.

Days had long since begun to merge into one another.

Long, endless days marked only by the passage of meals and the marks William Brewster etched onto the stone face of their prison wall with the buckle of his belt. Meals had become a measurement of time and no longer a source of pleasure. It was not that the food was unwholesome; in fact, in the early days the prisoners gratefully received it. Yet, a diet of fish and bread alone can become a sort of torture itself as weeks pass by. That which at first seemed appetizing and novel at the start of their imprisonment quickly staled into but one more facet of the deprivation of their liberty. Added to this, it made them smell. Their clothes, hair, breath and even the pores of their skin, all seemed to ooze the odour of mackerel oil. Within the first fortnight the men had grown foul smelling, uncustomarily unkempt and very close to despairing.

The three principles, Brewster, Clyfton and Robinson tried their best to bolster morale. They were chosen as the natural representatives of the group and as such were regularly summoned to court sessions that tried to remedy the situation. It was a nerve-racking time.

The courtroom was an imposing space. The magistrate's bench stood at one end of the room with the prisoner dock situated beyond a yawning void at the other. On each appearance, the three friends were taken from the cells and made to climb the ten, narrow tightly-spiralled steps up into the courtroom above. Emerging at the summit, they found themselves inside the confines of the tiny dock above which, embedded in the thickly plastered ceiling, was a huge oak timber whose awesome span looked menacingly like the waiting crossbeam of a gallows. It became a sort of life and death balancing act as the three crammed in, shoulder to shoulder, atop the open stairway, trying to put forward, eloquently, their legal and moral arguments as to why they should be released, while at the same time trying to avoid the long drop back into the abyss below.

Along the left hand edge of the courtroom, the public

crush stood, separated only by a wooden rail, heaving with curious onlookers as the scenes played out before them, applauding and jeering in equal measures as the three put forward their submissions to be freed. Once in a while, Brewster or one of the others might cast a glance towards the spectators and pick out the familiar face of a loved one. A hesitant smile may have passed between the free and the bound, but never the opportunity to speak, for the women had been denied any access to their men.

Although the court sat weekly to try to determine the Separatists' fate, they seemed incapable of reaching any agreement amongst themselves as to the best action to take. Some clearly had it in their minds to let the men go on their way, especially as the treacherous captain and his crew had conveniently weighed anchor and disappeared one evening tide, with not only the main source of evidence against the prisoners but also all of the Separatists' worldly goods. There was also evidently growing support for the congregation amongst the local citizens. However, there were those amongst the magistrates who feared for their positions and wanted the prisoners kept until word from the Bishop of Lincoln arrived.

Only one point seemed to unite the bench. All agreed that the cost to the town of keeping these prisoners fed and watered in gaol, fuel for the fire and the extra wages for their jailers and guards, were an ill afforded and unfair drain imposed upon the good citizens of Boston Town for which they would not be reimbursed. Other than this point, the proceedings seemed as securely stuck in the rut of indecision as the Southwell prison cart was that had been previously been dispatched to round them up from their homes in Scrooby. This stalemate seemed set to play on, keeping the Separatists held in uneasy check.

Meanwhile, occasionally the turnkey softened and let Will Bradford in for the odd snatched minute or two with offerings of bread and crumbs of comfort to friends in gaol in the form of much needed reassurance that he was taking care, as best he could, of their precious families.

Will hurriedly passed on messages, his face pressed tight against the grill. "They all miss you terribly and bid me tell you not to worry for their sakes! They are well fed and sheltered thanks to the bounty of The Lord."

"And the baby, Will?" William Brewster jostled Thomas aside to get nearer to the cell door. He had been desolate with guilt at having been instrumental in the placing of so much hardship on his dear wife Mary and his precious newborn daughter. He had to know they were both safe.

"Fear is thriving!" Will reassured his mentor. "Thriving and bonny like her sister!"

Brewster smiled back with relief.

"Kiss her for me, Will," he said. "Her and her dear mother both!"

"Kiss them all, Young Will!" Samuel shouted, unseen, from somewhere deep in the shadows. "Tell them we love them."

Young Spindleshanks had befriended one of the town's blacksmiths who as a sideline to his trade, provided livery for the horses of visitors. The smithy had graciously offered the group shelter in the hayloft of his barn-cum-workshop and use of the facilities, mean as they were. However, there were the hot ashes to cook on at the end of the working day and a hand pump with water in the yard. Although the building was old, rickety and mostly open to the elements throughout the day, and with a draft blowing through it that could slice off legs once its ill-fitting doors were closed to the night, the hay-filled loft was warm and cosy for sleeping in.

Will Bradford proved a very resourceful provider. He canvassed the townspeople, dwelling by dwelling, seeking out those who sympathized with their cause. He begged shamelessly, procuring clothing and blankets, utensils, in fact anything he could lay hands on to help the family survive while they awaited the fate of their men held in gaol. He had also quickly picked up on the fact that being in such close proximity to the sea meant a constant source of free food might be close at hand for the taking. Will organized the older children to watch at the quayside for fishing boats coming in with their catch, to be there waiting to beg for any spoilt fish or trimmings for their communal pot. The fishermen got to know them by sight and sometimes gave them crabs and whatever they could spare. With sea kale and scroungings of beets and barley, or with whatever was to hand, with praise to the Lord their pot never emptied of something warming to eat, though it ran thin at times. For this they were thankful, and indeed, for young Bradford and his sterling efforts but they dearly needed the rest of the men returned to them once more, and soon.

***

Dorothy had been busy setting the little ones to sleep in the small hollows she had made in the hay for each of them to snuggle into. Last, as usual, to succumb to sleep was young Patience Brewster who, supplanted by her baby sister Fear, clung to her like a surrogate mother, just the way dear Lady Frances had. Only after she had been cradled into dreams could the young woman ease the little mite down to rest alongside the others for the night. Now Dorothy sat at the top of the hayloft ladder, perched like a sparrow in the rafters trying to catch some crumb of what was being chewed over amongst the older woman directly below her. Sometimes she thought they ignored her, or maybe it was they simply forgot about her. She had been parted from Thomas just as long as they had from their husbands, yet none of these married women seemed to consider her part in all this; or how she might be feeling. She did not know why. Was it because of her age? In hindsight, and with the maturity that comes after hot headed youth has cooled, Dorothy would come to realize that it was for no other reasons than that they wanted to spare her the dread that pervaded their every waking moment at that time.

Mary Brewster and the others talked in whispers barely audible above the teeth of the gale that snarled outside.

"Winter's closing in for sure. How much longer can we cope with living like this?" Samuel's wife asked as they huddled in conclave, "Scraping by on the handouts of others?"

"As long as it takes," Bridget Robinson replied. "God's will shall prevail. Our loved ones will be freed, of this I am certain." John Robinson's timid wife clung to the remaining straws of her belief that because her husband was a good man following a good cause, God would not let him meet with disaster, optimism must always win out over oppression.

Mary Brewster on the other hand, was a wide-eyed realist acclimatized to a cruel world where the strong often crushed the weak like snails underfoot, simply because they could.

"I am not at all certain of it!" retorted Mary. "I think if they were going to be let out, it would have happened by now."

"But there's been no charges brought, surely that's a good sign," said Mistress Robinson hopefully.

"No, Bridget," Mary Brewster almost snapped. "I believe it's a bad sign. I think it means that the Bishops of Lincoln, York and Southwell are in one accord on this and are merely biding their time. They will want to have a steel trap of a case against my husband and the others to be certain that the only possible verdict will be a guilty one. Either that or they are sending the Southwell prison cart out again to collect them. The roads will be awash with mud and rutted deep after all this early bad weather. Could be it's on its way here, even as we speak. Happen it could arrive at any time and that will be an end to it!"

"God help them then if they are tried at Southwell!" Mistress Cooper exclaimed. "At least the magistrates here seem just and merciful in their dealings so far."

Dorothy could not take anymore. She slipped down from the loft and attempted to join in the conversation.

"What do you think is going to happen to them?" she asked.

"Nothing my dear, don't you worry," Mary Brewster saw the distress in her eyes and tried, a little too late, to reassure the young woman. "They are going to be fine. Just you wait and see."

'Oh, t'is cruelness this denial," Mistress Cooper rebuked Mary. "To lead the girl on with sweet cherry hopes! It looks bad, my dear!" she said speaking plainly. "The longer this goes on then the badder it's beginning to look for them! It's no use any of us denying that any longer! Instead, we should be preparing ourselves for the worst. The next time we might hold our menfolk close is as corpses thrown out into the streets for us to bury! That's if we don't have to go through the horrors of watching them emerge through the door of that wretched gaol, tied to racks, and then driven across the cobbles to the gallows. I do fear that if they were going to set them free they would have done it by now! There you have it! No use in prettying it up into hope. I just pray to God that I am proved wrong, and if I am, then rebuke me harsh and call me fool! For it will be the sweetest name I could hope to hear!" she said, before even she broke down and cried.

"Then come here, Fool, and give your man a kiss!" a familiar voice broke in.

Mistress Cooper looked up in shocked disbelief. It was Samuel. She hurtled forward and flung her arms about him and squeezed so tightly he feared his weary old bones would snap. Within moments the scene was replayed repeatedly as the other men slowly made their way in from out of the cold inhospitable night and into the arms of their loved ones. "Oh Thomas!" Dorothy cried with tears of relief, "I thought I'd never see you again."

"Oh my love!" he said folding her tightly into his arms, "nor I you, my precious. Nor I you!"

The men were quickly comforted with warm food and love from their families, while Mary Brewster, Bridget Robinson and Ann Clyfton stood silently by, almost forgotten in the scenes of rejoicing. Sadly it soon dawned on everyone that Masters Brewster, Clyfton and Smyth remained incarcerated, awaiting the Bishops' pleasure. The joy suddenly seemed hollow when the reality of this sank in amongst those who had regained their men once more.

"Why have you been released?" Mary asked, "and is there any news of our men?"

"As far as we can tell it was a matter of economics to ease the burden of the upkeep of us all. As simple as that. We were proving too big a drain on their resources, so we small fry were thrown back into the sea while they concentrate their efforts on landing only the big fish, I fear!" said Samuel. "But don't you be giving up on the others just yet! They told me to tell you to keep praying hard because they sense a softening in the attitude of the one magistrate that has persisted all along in our continued incarceration until warrants arrived from the Bishop," he explained. "William, in particular thinks this may be a sign that they too are going to walk out of there soon."

Mary wanted to believe. Yet inside she would not allow her hopes to be raised too high, for she feared from there the drop would be all the longer and harder to bear.

That night, in full view of the others, Dorothy fell asleep enfolded in Thomas's arms. Not one of the others raised any objection that these two betrothed, yet unwed young people, should spend the night embraced so and besides, the older women felt the relief of their own men's safe return and could not bring themselves to deny these two this same comfort. Perhaps this was not a good thing after all, as time would tell, for it may have loosened the corner stone that would lead to Thomas's stronghold of abstinence being laid low as his resistance to his baser instincts came to disintegrate into lust.

William's hunch proved right. Within a few days of this majority of the Separatist prisoners being set free, suddenly Brewster, Clyfton and Robinson were unexpectedly and inexplicably released from gaol just before sunset. The magistrates, this time, had met behind closed doors and decided to quietly turn the men loose, on one proviso: that they left Boston Town before sunrise and never tried to return. The three, of course, thanked God and readily agreed.

The congregation made their way back towards Nottinghamshire where they went to ground amongst a familiar landscape. Unknown to them, just as they had made their way out of Boston, warrants arrived from Southwell for their arrest and transportation back to stand trial. Realizing their error of judgment, the Boston magistrates tried desperately to protect themselves against a backlash from the Bishops by implying that the Separatists' release had been completely conditional upon William Brewster handing himself in to Southwell Court within thirty days of release. Because of William Brewster's subsequent absence and construed contempt of court, he was fined a hefty sum of money in addition to being subject to outstanding warrants for practicing Separatism. Further searchers were ordered to scour the countryside around his former home of Scrooby Manor, arrest him on sight and bring him for trial as a subversive activist and traitor to the crown. The penalty for treason would be hanging, drawing, quartering, and burning. Anyone caught trying to hide him could expect grave consequences as well. Therefore it became more imperative than ever that the congregation lie low and plan a second escape attempt. This time, however, they would spare the women and children the suffering inflicted by the first overland attempt by navigating the river network to freedom. They would travel north and try for a ship along the river Humber. For now, this route was frozen but as soon as the spring thaw came they would be on their way again.

***

Whether he sets out to or not, no man passes this way without making enemies. William Brewster was no exception. He was a passionate man, a man not afraid to voice his views and beliefs. Added to this, he was the innkeeper of the crumbling remains of the once magnificent Scrooby Manor, a former royal hunting lodge owned by the Bishop of York, where Brewster ensured that food and a change of horse were always available on this the only road between London and Scotland. Before his dismissal, he had also been Postmaster for that same district, either position could easily give rise to petty grievances. There were those who would gleefully turn him in on sight to the authorities, especially now he had a price on his head. Yet, others loved and admired him for standing up for his faith. Others that were still willing to help him and the congregation, knowing full well that anyone found aiding or abetting them, did so in the knowledge that the Bishop's wrath and punishment would be meted out to them in equal measure too. The searchers were crawling over the East Midlands, intent on rounding up this gang of dissidents who had so embarrassed His Grace by daring to escape his clutches at Boston. These searchers were not about to return to their Lord without the Separatist captives in tow.

Rose Hickman was very glad to have Dorothy back under the Old Hall roof. However, as a known dissident, Thomas dare not return to his post as tutor. He did not wish to repay the lady's kindness by openly visiting the Old Hall and thereby risking implicating the Hickman family as helping the Separatist's cause, for William Hickman's enemies were many and would relish the opportunity to be able to report him for harbouring criminals.

Instead, Thomas came covertly to visit Dorothy as and when it was safest to do so. It became an open secret amongst the loyal Hickman household. Everyone knew the couple were engaged and remained as intent as ever on their plan to hold a Separatist marriage once they reached the safety of Holland. As soon as the first signs of spring arrived, then Dorothy and Thomas would be going on the run once more. For now, though, they would patiently bide the long winter through.

Thomas would slip unseen into the Old Hall grounds from the fields beyond and make his way through the gardens to the unlocked door of the tower. He would wait patiently, as long as it took, until Dorothy returned to Lady Frances' chamber above, or one of the other servants came upon him and let her know he was there. This situation went on for months. Condemned to some hideous half-life, the two were forced to endure long empty hours of separation, just to revel in the few minutes of their next chanced meeting.

These were difficult times for these two young people in love. The clandestine meetings, the tearful passion-filled kisses on parting, coupled with the uncertainty of never knowing if they would meet again or if the chase would be up and Thomas captured. The tension, anxiety and excitement rushed together into a heady mix that led, one night, into an all absorbing intoxication, in the midst of which Thomas lost his precious sense of propriety and, helpless to resist any longer, he gave in to lust instead.

It was Lady Day eve, and the household was gathered in the Great Hall to see in the New Year with revelry. Dorothy too joined in until she suddenly felt a strange certainty that Thomas was awaiting her at their usual meeting place. She slipped quietly away, unnoticed by the throng, up the great stairs, past the Solar and then began the descent down the lonely tower staircase. It was dark and she had no candle, yet she was not afraid to feel her way downwards with her back to the wall, her way lit only by the glance of pale light from the tiny infrequent windows. Yet, before she had reached the last few steps her body was enveloped by eager arms reaching out from the darkness and hot wanting lips pressed hard against her own. Thomas was there, waiting in the depths with his expectations high.

"Oh my darling, how I have missed you!" he said, kissing her longingly.

Although Dorothy could smell strong liquor on his breath, she said nothing, not begrudging him the fortification of Dutch courage that had seen him safely across town and through the searchers' net.

"I just knew you were here," she said softly.

They climbed up the steps together, hand in hand, and paused at the half-open door of the vacant, second floor bedroom. From here they could spoon a while, yet enjoy ample warning of footsteps coming from above or below. Together the pair crept just inside and engaged in amorous play.

"Oh Dorothy! Dorothy! My sweet Dorothy!" Thomas repeated over again and he kissed her soft mouth and then her bare ivory-white shoulders.

Dorothy could not but help notice her fiancé's increasing breathlessness as he partook of this unaccustomed pleasure. In the pit of her stomach she felt a distinct flutter, then a rush of anticipation mixed with a hint of foreboding beginning to rise up to catch at her breath also.

"Curse the bishop for we should be married by now," Thomas panted. "And I so long for us to be married!" he gasped as he delved deeply down into the front of her dress and caressed her soft breast in his hand.

Dorothy's heart raced at his touch, his sweet lovesong in her ear, his manly smell, and sweet-brandied kisses combined and utterly seduced her to bend to his will.

"I want you," he said looking over her shoulder to the naked bed silhouetted against the backdrop of moon-cast shadows. "I need this so badly!"

Before Dorothy could even think she had replied, "I want you too!" and was being lured across the room by her lover's rain of kisses. Thomas was already unbuckling his breeches as he gently laid his love down onto the mattress and lifted up her skirts. Still engaged in kisses and pledging his undying love for her, Thomas started to make love in earnest. As he did, Dorothy suddenly panicked as the past rushed in to taunt her. This was too quick. She had not prepared for this. In her mind she had often envisaged their wedding day; the ceremony and celebration with the long slow build up to those final moments, where alone in their chamber she would be faced with their marriage bed. How she would then enter it, composed, willing and ready to submit to his measured advances - but this? This was too akin to the haste of the rape. Too ardent in its nature and far too suddenly thrust upon her. Dorothy froze. She flinched. She gritted her teeth and spat out his kisses whilst paradoxically her body succumbed far too easily to his advances for her lover's later reflected liking. From somewhere deep within, Thomas's memory cruelly brought back the last words he had heard from his father; final words of disinheritance.

"This is the straw that will break your father's back!" he had screeched at his son in anger. "You marry with this strumpet maidservant of yours and I wash my hands of you for good! A maid savant! A doxy that's probably been laid down and serviced by half the menservants at the Hall before you first laid your foolish hand on her! She does not love you! She's only after a rope to pull her out from her mire!"

Oh but Thomas was aware of this perceived rejection by his partner! Aware yet he was now far beyond the point of

SUE ALLAN

any sound reasoning that might have convinced him to desist. He had aroused some darker base instinct that would not let him, even though somewhere deep inside he knew that he should. He had reached a point where wild horses could not have dragged him off his woman, whether she truly wanted him or not.

Once spent Thomas rushed to his feet as quickly as Dorothy did to hers to straighten her clothing.

"I'm sorry," she said, sensing his deep disappointment. "I'm sorry."

"I'm sorry too," he replied.

"I have to go! Someone might have missed me!" Dorothy said, swiftly making for the door. Thomas followed.

"Good night" she said hesitantly.

Thomas returned the farewell and proffered but a half-hearted kiss as he made his way down the tower stairs and out once more into the night.

Dorothy was close to tears as she reached the Solar landing. She felt so foolish, so ashamed. Not ashamed that she had sinned with Thomas but that she had failed him and his deep love for her. In her mind, she had wanted him as much as he had her, but the past had beguiled her into a defensiveness that must surely have seemed like rejection to her lover. It was not too late though, she told herself. Tomorrow, or the next time they met she would tell him everything. Explain the dreadful truth that she had kept hidden from him thus far. Thomas loved her. He would understand.

CHAPTER ELEVEN

'Ay me, for aught that I could ever read,
Could ever hear by tale or history,
The course of true love never did run smooth...'

Reading Thomas's favourite Shakespeare had bought a little comfort to her. The last six months without so much as a letter from him had been far from easy for her to bear. Rumours had abounded that all the Separatist men had fled the morning after Thomas had last come to visit Dorothy at the Hall. Some had managed, since then, to spirit away their wives and families to the continent to join them, so she lived in the hope that he would send for her soon as well. He was never far from her longing thoughts or yearning heart, for she never doubted that he would come back for her. So daily, as tradition dictated, she had taken to wearing a sprig of willow, tucked into her cap, as an open sign of her remembrance for him. 'For one year and a day, for a true love who had gone away', that's how long folklore dictated, without otherwise receiving word, was a reasonable length of time to live in the expectation that a loved one on his travels would return. After that, he should be given up as dead.

Dorothy broke off from reading aloud to the Lady Rose and young Frances.

"I hear the hour bell ringing, my lady," she said, "Shall I away to the kitchens to fetch the mid morning repast?"

"Yes, Dorothy, go," Lady Rose replied, "for I have such a tickling in my throat that I think some of my favourite chamomile is just the remedy I need."

Dorothy rose from the window bench and carefully put away the copy of 'A Midsummer Night's Dream' and descended the stairs from the Solar. As she made her way slowly through the Great Hall, from the servery she could clearly hear excited snatches of discourse. Then familiar laughs rang forth followed by words like, "Well we all knew it would end in tears," and, "she was absolutely besotted." Then, when Dorothy had turned the corner and was into it, she was painfully aware that the frantic chattering had suddenly stopped dead, mid-sentence. A scattering of her workmates stood gathered, shuffling now in uneasy silence and none would dare to meet her eye.

After an embarrassing moment or two, Mistress Goode approached her and tenderly took her hand.

"Dorothy," she said ashen faced and looking deep into the young woman's eyes, "Master Best here has had news from a friend of a friend concerning your Master Thomas."

"What news? Pray tell me?" she begged.

"He is married, Mistress Dorothy!" Master Best delivered his gift of this news without attempting to wrap it kindly. "He is married and in Holland, these past three months," he blurted out.

"Married! No, you are mistaken!" she cried out. "Not Thomas? Not my Thomas!"

"Yes Dorothy," Comfort chirruped like a spiteful bird. "Married, and no mistake!"

"It is for the best that you know the truth of the matter," added Mistress Goode.

Dorothy reeled in disbelief. How could he have done this? After all they had been through. To leave her, then let her hear of it like this, second hand from the mouths of gossip mongering so-called friends. Dorothy tore the withering sprig of willow from her cap and tossed it aside as she turned and ran, tears streaming down face. Bitter tears that stung like viper's fangs.

She hurried out from the kitchen servants' door, into the garden and toward the tower block. She was crushed, utterly and completely destroyed by the cruelty of this blow. She stopped at the tree, gasped for air but the rush of shock had robbed her of breath. She looked up at the sturdy bare bough above and thought of the gallows. So this must be what it's like, she thought to herself, to be hanged and quartered? Left to dangle for what seems to be an eternity in cruel suspense, begging with the passage of each lingering second for it to be over, to pray for the misery that is choking the life from out of you to end. The light-headed feeling that comes and robs you of all sense of consciousness and sets you apart from this world, until the only reality remaining is the longing for this limbo to finish. Then, when die-hard hope has departed and you think that you are done for, someone one cuts you down and lets you drop. Drop, and you are suddenly, terribly, aware once more. Now comes the cut; the cruel blade that slices you through to the bone. Before you even have time to scream out, it has registered, the excruciating burning pain filling every atom of your being. Then your tormentor, face unseen, thrusts his fist deep inside you and wrenches out your innards with a cruel twist. All that you have kept deep inside is now drawn out for the titillation of the crowd. Then he taunts you, holding up your still beating heart for you to see, like a gruesome trophy, before he callously tosses it aside to the baying crowd. And you? You are, at that instant, still alive - just. Alive, but beyond any mortal help now. Beyond saving. You now know you have no possibility of sustaining life. For you no longer have a heart. You are as good as dead. That man, who has betrayed you, is your executioner. He is a merciless assassin, striking when you are helpless and unable to defend yourself. You have been bound by his deceitful lies. Left in suspense until he deemed fit to strike the deathblow. He shows no mercy in your release and no compassion for your needless suffering. He acts like a cowardly hooded assassin; for he knows you must surely hear of his treachery. He could have told you himself, like a real man, but instead he condemns your love to a miserable death from a distance.

Dorothy ran inside to Lady Frances's empty bedchamber, shut the door and fell sobbing to the floor. She thought about

Thomas, all they had shared together. Every dream in her heart was gone, leaving a gaping void. Inside her head, the words of the Guild Hall bailiff returned with mocking clarity: 'You little fool, you have been done easy.' Now all her friends were mocking her too. Reveling in her undoing. How could she ever face anyone again?

Then, suddenly, she looked up as she heard the oak door that led to the narrow, spiral staircase to the tower creak to. Beyond any conscious thought, she rose to her feet, slipped though the doorway and climbed the forty-five steps to the roof.

Then Dorothy looked down to the gardens below. This was where she and her betrothed had walked and talked about their future together. Amongst the perfume of the summer lavender and the first flush of heady musk roses, Thomas had led her to believe she meant everything to him and that his love for her could never die. She stared hard, directly below to the paving slabs of dismal grey and wondered to herself, would she be dead the instant she hit the ground? Or would she simply be crushed and broken beyond repair. Ebbing away her last few moments but with eyes wide and cognition unimpaired? Would she see her own sin, in vivid scarlet streams? See those who would come running, mouths agape in horror to witness her passage into damnation for this, the ultimate crime?

"And against whom, I wonder, would this be the greater crime? Against God or yourself?"

Lady Rose stood, breathless and leaning heavily against the stairwell wall with her cane in her hand.

"My Lady!" Dorothy turned quickly, curtseyed and rushed forward to steady her mistress. She was shocked that Rose Hickman had so easily read her mind.

"Come, come, my dear," Lady Rose coaxed gently. "Nothing is broken here that the Lord cannot mend. Why don't you help me back down and come pray beside me for a while? A soul can be chilled on even the most glorious autumn morning. I sense a tempest is on the way."

Dorothy meekly obeyed and aided the old lady with her difficult descent.

Lady Rose guided Dorothy to the chapel and led her in prayer. Prayers for comfort and strength in the face of adversity, yet she skirted around the actuality of her encounter up on the roof with this young woman or her suspicions about Dorothy's true intention there.

After this period of meditation, her ladyship rose and spoke gently to Dorothy. It was the first time the two had engaged in conversation of a truly personal nature, yet Dorothy felt completely at ease. Indeed, it was as if her Ladyship was speaking to her as an equal instead of merely a servant.

"I fled to Antwerp during the dreadful purges under Catholic Queen Mary. Before I had though, it was my miserable duty to witness a protestant priest and two of his parishioners burned to death at the stake. The tinder was spoiled, damp most likely for it was after a torrential downpour, but the decree was for the execution to be carried out that day, come what may. The fire spluttered half-hearted then caught but weakly, greatly adding to the suffering of those three wretched souls whose one escape would be at their final consumption by it. What flames there were blackened their hapless victims' clothing and slowly charred the flesh on their lower limbs so that they screamed in their agony. Such screams as I never wish to hear again should I live to be as old as Methuselah. Then all at once, five or six men of that priest's same congregation broke though the jeering crowds with pitchers full of oil and doused the three with it. The flames roared up and burned as hot as a furnace. Within moments, the three were completely engulfed. At first glance, one might think it an act of sheer cruelty to add fuel to the flames that were consuming their friends. In fact it was a mercy. For it quickened their departures from this abject misery cast upon them by others and sped them on their way into a state of grace. Yes, it may seem cruel for those you have lived and worked with all this time to gossip and tittle-tattle behind your back about Master Thomas's treachery. Yet I am sure it's not to injure, but rather to help you see the extent of his villainy and their contempt for the man who used you so easily - so that you might harden your heart to him and get over this deep sorrow the more quickly.

"The reasons why this sadness has come to pass in your life, dear child, we may not be privy to, yet we can be certain of the simple truth that nothing happens by pure chance for all is pre-ordained and part of the Lord's great plan. By trusting and accepting our pain when it comes, we are fulfilling God's plan and working out our purpose for Him. Trust in the Lord, Dorothy. He will never give us more than we can bear. Be as those martyrs. Bless the flame!"

"I thought he loved me," Dorothy said quietly.

"He lied," Lady Rose replied. "From now on, trust truth only, my child".

"Yet how am I ever to know what is truth again and what is lie?"

"Time alone will out the answer to that, Dorothy. Truth stays on the lips forever, while lies fade away. You must live your life forging forward. Never look back and dwell on the past, for a life led looking back is a life that will be forever tripping you up."

It was not easy for Dorothy to resume her life after this but she had at least the courage to try. Although her heart was heavy she tried to be brave, letting the tears flow only in the solitude of the long lonely hours of the night. In time, the memory of that day seemed to fade in the collective minds of her peers as other gossip came and went and lessened the stigma she felt cast upon her. She did not forget, however. The hurt dulled but the recollection of it lingered on to serve as a hard learnt lesson. Men were not for Dorothy. Resolutely she decided never to allow herself to fall in love again. Instead, she would harden her heart and steadfastly devote herself to the service of the Old Hall and the Hickman family. Dorothy would remain a spinster to the end of her days.

***

The place was heaving like carcass full of maggots. Tightly packed, brightly coloured maggots, squirming their way across the Mart Yard and feasting on the myriad of goods on offer. Traders of every kind had pitched their tents and laid out their wares for all to see and sample. The smell of food cooking, fresh tanned leather, wood-shavings, smoke, animal dung and the stale sweat of people permeated the air, yet somehow mellowed in the atmosphere.

There was a wizened looking one-armed monger with a wild salt-and-pepper beard trying to peddle a brace of glassy-eyed, floppy-headed hares hanging down from over one shoulder and a basket of mangy looking chickens at his feet. Next to him, a couple of tinkers sat busily under canvas, with brazier and bellows, hammering and mending broken pots and pans while above them were strung a hundred more, all gleaming new and clanking out a strange cacophonous tune as they swung in the breeze. A tall exotic looking woman with an accent held out strange fruit with brightly coloured skins, no doubt shipped in from the continent, as were many other unusual goods on offer. There were candlestick makers, workers in wood and leather, weavers, spinners, sellers of spices and craftsmen of every discipline all vying for the attention of the throng.

This May Day market was the attraction of the year and it drew of people from all over the surrounding countryside. Many of them were but simple folk who had scraped and saved all year round for this one day. Often entire villages packed up en masse and made their way there, part walking, part riding, to Gainsborough to buy, barter and maybe even sell what little surplus they had to spare.

Both Dorothy and Mistress Goode were about in the crowd that year, with an eye out to purchase items for their employers. Mistress Goode was searching out new threads and bodkins for Her Ladyship's needlework, while a grand stall, weighed down with bolt upon bolt of the finest cloth and trimmings, had attracted Dorothy's attention. She had received instructions for suitable new ribbons and lace to buy to refresh an old gown for Lady Frances. With so many stalls pitched in such close proximity and such a crush clamouring to buy up their wares, little wonder then that, in the mayhem, the old housekeeper and the young maidservant found themselves temporarily separated.

Dorothy was looking about to see where her companion has gone when, suddenly, from amongst the throng a familiar face met her gaze. It was a face she new well from her life before - Judd Lowe.

"Bessie my girl!" he exclaimed in excitement, his face beaming with genuine pleasure, "as I live and breath, it's you!"

Dorothy feigned indifference and stifled any involuntary sign of recognition.

"You are mistaken Sir!" she said politely.

"Bessie, duzzn't you know me? It's me, Judd!" he persisted paying no heed to her denial, "you've grown into a beautiful woman, granted, but I'd know my sweet Bessie anywhere!"

Dorothy bowed her head, uttered some excuses and swiftly made her way back into the anonymity of the crowd. Just as quickly though, Judd caught her up, grasped hold of her forearm and gently persuaded her to stop.

"It's alright lass!" he said, "It's alright! Yous nothing to fear from me. Nor from anyone else come to that!" he added. "If'n I had known where to find you, I would have come and told you as much, sooner."

Dorothy felt torn. She desperately wanted to protect her hard gained new identity and protect herself from the past. Yet, she also wanted to hear Judd out. Perhaps he wanted to talk of her mother. That she was dead or dying? Unless Dorothy took this chance now she might never know what it was Judd seemed desperate to tell her. She might even live one day to regret it. She decided to take a chance.

"Told me what?" Dorothy dropped the pretence.

"That it was all out, lass. That everyone back home knows what a heinous wrong was done you. And that Nathan and Elias are both now dead!"

"Dead?"

"Aye lass. Both punished by Him on high, if you ask me! And not afore time."

"Why? What happened?" she asked.

"There was a lot of nastiness between Nathan and Elias after you left! No one paid it much heed, mind! Why should they have? It being perfectly natural like, to have some vexation and rancour after Elias confessing, like that, about his dallying with you? And a natural despising of him by your lawful guardian was to be expected. Only…" Judd hesitated a moment, "after the stabbing, we suddenly realized we'd only been privy to the half of it."

"What stabbing, Judd?"

"Oh, lass! It happened in the May, almost a year after you left. We was all a–making merry. For what I cannot recall. Nathan and some others were playing cards, all a bit the worse for ale. He was losing badly, Bessie. More than he could bear to lose. And the man who was prospering most from that loss was Elias. He darn nigh cleared us all out that night," Judd laughed. "But Nathan wasn't satisfied that his accursed bad luck was merely down to the turn of the cards. He was certain Elias was cheating him and said so, right to his face. Then it happened, as quickly as you can say jump!" Judd said animatedly, "Nathan reared up like a bull in a rage, clasped his hands about Elias's neck and started a-throttling the life out of him. If only Elias had stopped to think, he should have known he could have trusted to us to pull the mad man off before he could be killed! Only Elias duzzn't think though. He was so afraid of Nat, all fired up, that he took up a knife from the trencher on the table and stabbed your stepfather right in the guts."

Dorothy winced but slightly.

"Nathan's eyes bulged almost out of his head," Judd continued with his grisly account. "Then he sort of grunted and looked down at the knife, stuck up to the hilt, in his fat belly. He pulled it out; all bloody and then just stood there a-looking at it. Then he grabbed hold of his guts, a-holding them in with his hand and staggered off out into the night. Elias was hauled up before the magistrate but, as he was attacked first and in real fear, he got let off for 'acting in self defence'."

"But I thought you said Nathan died?" Dorothy was confused.

"Yes, he did! But not right away, anyhow," Judd went on to explain. "He somehow managed to stagger home to the cottage. Sheer bloody mindedness if you ask me! Anyways, your Mother made a vain attempt to bind him up and heal the wound. But it moldered during the sultry spell we had a-coming, as he lay a-festering on his mattress. There were maggots in the wound but even they couldn't keep apace of the ooze from the blackening gape. Then, inch-by-inch, his own rotting flesh began to poison him. They say the smell was unbearable! That in the end, it even drove the blowflies away that had been attracted by the decay."

Dorothy continued to listen intently, unmoved by the horror of the tale.

"Having suffered such agonies and knowing full well that he was a goner, and with Elias still enjoying his liberty," Judd explained, "Nathan now wanted nothing less than utter revenge upon the man he held solely responsible for his untimely demise. So, he sent your mother out to call for the vicar and summon the Justice of the Peace to come to hear his deathbed confession. So, they came and heard him out of this world. And Nat told them everything, Bessie!

Everything about what was done to you. What they both did to you."

Dorothy looked at his face and knew instantly from his expression that he knew it all.

"He said how he wanted to get it off his chest," Judd continued, "before he went to face his maker. How he was sorry that he had kept quiet about the rape; how he'd known and yet stood by and said nothing, for he was afraid of the consequences and believed that if you were found to be with child, a marriage to Elias would be no bad thing. Then at the wedding, when Elias stood up and said what he did, Nathan said that he panicked, thinking that he might be considered an accessory and taken from your poor mother and hung. He said he thought it was better for you to slip away from the village and that would spare you and her the shame of it all," Judd paused and sighed deeply. "We was all horrified at the way we had treated you, poor dear innocent child! But we all knew too late! Anyhows we suspected Nathan's owning up at that late stage weren't out of any show of remorse. Not from him! Just vengeful spite, that if he was being forced out of this life afore his due time, then he was going to make certain he would drag Elias along into Hell with him. And that he did. He sealed Elias's fate with his last foul breaths!"

"What happened to Elias?" Dorothy needed to know his fate.

"Well, none of us believed it at first!" Judd exclaimed. "And even Elias swore he hadn't done it to begin with. He wanted to save his own hide! But then the vicar took him to one side, and although nobody knows what was said between them, Elias suddenly took it on himself to clear his conscience and set the record straight. He said he could not perjure his soul with a false oath, so he ups and confesses to raping you, saying how he was aided and abetted by Nathan. So, he ended up being taken before Lincoln assizes and they sentenced him to hang."

"And did he hang?"

"Oh yes," said Judd calmly, "from up high on Lucy Tower for the entire city to see. He danced in the air a fine jig for his sins, make no mistake. Yet, before this he was calm, even accepting of the punishment, for he had made his peace with his maker. The vicar was there to comfort him just before and says that the last thing Elias said, up there on the gallows as they put the noose about his neck, was to say how he begged poor Bessie's forgiveness. Though the reverend pleaded and protested after, the authorities refused to allow his body to come home for a Christian burial. So, Elias lies buried in the castle confines, without so much as a marker over his bones.

"And Nathan?"

"The reverend for some good reason, known only to him, wuzzn't about to allow him to be interred in hallowed ground. And, as no one came forward to object, not even your mother, he was buried wrong side of the wall"

Judd looked toward Bessie. He was unnerved by how serenely silent and unmoved she looked. He had expected something else. Some other sort of reaction. Maybe for her to have broken down in tears of joy, thankful that her name had been cleared and her honor restored. Perhaps even moved towards a hint of pity for the soul of repentant Elias. Instead, there seemed to be no response. Nothing. It was as if all Judd had spoken of had happened to somebody else and not the woman that stood before him now.

"Will you come home now?" he tentatively asked. "Home to your mother and me, lass?"

"Why? Are you two…?"

"Married? Yes. Yes, that we are Bess!" he said with a smile. "Well?" he asked a second time, "Bess, will you come home?"

"No, Judd," Dorothy answered without hesitation.

"But what of your Mother, Bessie?" he pleaded. "The lass I knew would not let this come between them. Have you no word for her, at all?"

"Yes, Judd," she said. "Tell her I wish you both well, that you saw me today but that I wouldn't tell you where I bide. That I have a made a new life for myself, Judd, and that I've left my old one too far behind to ever return. Tell her I still love her," she added, "but that I said goodbye."

Dorothy then slipped back into crowd and Judd let her disappear from sight.

"Who was that man?" Mistress Goode had caught up with her.

"What man?" Dorothy said.

"The man I just saw you talking with."

"Oh! That man! No one. Just someone who thought that they knew me."

"And did they?" asked Mistress Goode.

"No," Dorothy replied firmly. "No, they don't know me at all. As I said, they only thought that they did."

CHAPTER TWELVE

Dorothy felt her heart pound with dread anticipation as she approached the Solar door. She knocked once. A familiar voice called out for her to enter. She did, closing the door quietly behind her, then turned to face the bed. Mistress Goode was already stood on the far side of it.

"Good," she said quietly, "you've bought the clean linen. I already have a pitcher of warm water ready steeped with lavender. Shall we begin then?"

Dorothy took a deep breath and nodded 'yes'.

The two women approached from either side of the great canopied bed then stood, reverently for a moment of reflection before setting about this, their last undertaking for their beloved Lady Rose.

Dorothy could still not take in the fact that Rose Hickman was dead. Somehow she had been lulled into the very unrealistic assumption that Her Ladyship would always be there. When Dorothy first entered service at The Hall early in 1604, Rose was already approaching eighty and even at seventy she was deemed to have lived to a ripe old age. It was true that Rose had grown very frail in the later years after Dorothy's arrival, yet she seemed to have plateaued out in decline at around her eightieth year and thereafter remained constant in mind and body until just recently. Then, three months since, the old lady suffered a debilitating palsy, which rendered her paralysed down one side. This reduced her left arm to an unyielding contortion of its former self and her hand into a virtually useless, inflexible claw. Rose could no longer stand or feed herself and suffered with incontinence. It slurred her speech and stole away her lifelong lucidity, took away her ability to while away her hours at her pitifully few remaining pleasures. Last and cruellest blow of all, it had robbed her of her dignity.

Then, just a few days ago the old lady had become rather

withdrawn, indifferent to her food, surroundings and even treasured company. She stopped eating and then steadfastly refused to drink anything other than a few sips of chamomile. Only with her having passed on, could one look back and see that she had made a conscious decision – simply to cease to go on.

Fearing Lady Rose was ailing, Mistress Goode had taken to keeping a vigil these last few nights asleep in a chair by Her Ladyship's side. Meanwhile, Dorothy had been bedding down on a mattress outside on the Solar landing, strategically placed to still be able to attend Lady Frances if she woke in the night, but also on hand should Mistress Goode need her to fetch or carry.

Rose Hickman died just after dawn. She had been awake shortly before and asked for some chamomile, so Dorothy was awoken and went down to the kitchen to make some. Lady Rose was relatively coherent, according to Mistress Goode's later account. Coherent that is, apart from towards the end, when she was asking after the health of Queen Mary Tudor. At which point her devoted servant gently reminded her that Mary was dead and that there was a King now on the throne of this newly united kingdom. Lady Rose sighed deeply and with a renewed look of peaceful serenity replied,

"Oh! Then it is safe for me to go home?"

Without time for Mistress Goode to fetch Sir William or even utter a prayer, Lady Rose slipped quietly out from life.

"Better for the grandchildren to see her at her rest here in her own bed rather than in her box," explained Mistress Goode wiping a tear from her eye with the corner of her apron.

The housekeeper started removing the old lady's jewellery and tying it safely in a linen handkerchief, which she then locked in Her Ladyship's side cupboard with a key from the bunch that she always had at her waist on a battered metal chatelaine. All the jewellery, that is, apart from her mistress's thin, plain gold wedding band, which she had always insisted should be buried with her. Though parted from her beloved Anthony for so many long, lonely, years she wanted to be buried with this visible sign that she had remained his faithful bride to the very last.

Dorothy looked down at the body now lifeless in the bed. For all the importance of the nine decades of Rose Hickman's life there, there now remained barely substance enough to raise a modest mound beneath the burgundy counterpane. Her face was sallow and sunken: her cheeks sucked in with ghastly unnatural pallor. Her eyes, which had been open at the point of death, but quickly closed by Mistress Goode, looked dry and lifeless as they peeked through the not quite met, hooded eyelids. Yet despite this, her deceptively stern visage had been some what softened by death's hand and on her thin, blue tinged lips, lay a serene, peaceful smile.

Dorothy looked on in trepidation as Mistress Goode gently stripped away the outer bedding and neatly laid it at the foot of the bed. Then the old housekeeper began, tenderly, to draw Rose Hickman's fine linen nightdress up her body and towards her head. As she did so, Dorothy broke the hushed atmosphere with an involuntary cry as the wizen corpse of but skin and bones was slowly revealed.

"Help me, Dorothy, with the arms. Ease your one out of the sleeve just as I am doing."

Dorothy hesitated. She knew full well that the palsy had made such manhandling of the limb so distressing for Her Ladyship in life.

"Don't be afraid," Mistress Goode said reassuringly, "you can't hurt her now."

The thin wasted arm was cold and resisted its careful manipulation but Dorothy managed to do as asked. With the shift now eased over the old lady's head and put to one side, her corpse lay completely exposed.

Mistress Goode leaned across and gently rolled Rose onto

her left side.

"Here Dorothy, hold her there why I remove this draw sheet from under her bottom end."

Dorothy did as she was instructed, while her companion started to gather up the large soiled linen pad and replaced it with a clean fresh one up and as far under the body as she could manage. Then the two women tilted the frail body back in the other direction and onto the fresh area of pad. Dorothy then held her there in position while Mistress Goode deftly tugged the remainder of the soiled draw sheet clear and replaced it with the remainder of the new. Then together they gently rolled Rose back down upon the mattress and began the task of cleaning her body.

Dorothy washed and dried the old lady's face with a soft square of muslin soaked in fragrant lavender water, then took up Her Ladyship's carved ivory and silver comb and teased out her wispy white hair. Meanwhile Mistress Goode carefully prepared small wads of clean cheesecloth and discreetly plugged the body's orifices as she went about washing away any remnants of soiling.

The two servants then put Rose into a silk shroud fastened under her chin and crossed her hands in prayer on her chest. Between them, they gently lifted the old lady's head to place some freshly plumped pillows under it, then they laid her gently back down in peaceful repose. Mistress Goode wet her finger and softly ran it across Lady Rose's eyebrows to straighten one or two wispy strays of hair. The women then pulled up the fresh sheets over her and folded them down over the replaced counterpane, which they then smoothed out with their hands. With all the used linen now safety stowed inside a basket it was done. All was now fit and ready for the family and household to pay their last respects.

Within a few short months, Dorothy would be carrying out this last dutiful ritual once more as she instructed another up and coming maid in the art of laying out. After fourteen long and loyal years in the service of the Hickman family, it was from Dorothy's spinster waist that Mistress Goode's coveted chatelaine of keys chinked in authority. She had taken on the mantle of Housekeeper of the Old Hall. It had been a gradual transition from the old order to the new, creeping up on Dorothy's world like a Trent Valley mist rising up to slowly envelope all that is familiar until, suddenly, she was left with the awful realization that all she had known was now lost, along with any sense of previous direction. Within the space of less than a year all those Dorothy had held closest to her heart were gone. Lady Rose and Mistress Goode, both dead within months of each other. Then there had been poor scatterbrain Comfort, late to marry but quick to die in a complicated, protracted childbirth. Gone too was someone Dorothy had not met in life but grieved none the less for in his passing, for throughout those years she had saved all her earnings to buy the imprint of his latest work. The Bard Of Stratford – upon-Avon had died, William Shakespeare, her last treasured link to happier times and her lost love Thomas.

Sir William had taken hard the death of his beloved mother. It was as if life itself had begun to drain from him from that day. The demise of the matriarch left a gaping void that was going to be hard to fill, if ever it could be. He was now in his sixties and becoming increasingly frail himself. Willoughby was growing up fast and already growing into the businessman's shoes. He was astute and soundly grounded in the concepts and strategies of commerce in true Hickman style. The old life was being edged out by a new order, not only at the Hall but across the nation too. A puritan voice now spoke well above a whisper so that its call for reform could be heard. A new world beckoned just beyond the horizon, with the King desperate to exploit it to the full and keep his stake in it safely away from Spanish hands. So desperate was he that he was even willing to pardon murderers from the gallows and criminals from the gaols in order to establish a population there. It was a New World that could offer a fresh beginning to anyone desperate enough to risk the crossing.

CHAPTER THIRTEEN

Flickering sunlight streamed through the open widow, dancing erratically across the brilliant, painted plumage of the peacocks decorating the wall of the garden room. Beneath them, Dorothy and Lady Frances sat engrossed in their embroidering. This was as near as they dare get to sitting in the warmth of the sun outside if they were to maintain their fashionable pale white skins.

Dorothy paused for a moment, tilted her head and arched her back to relieve the stiffness in her neck, then catching in a loose thread with her needle, glanced lovingly across at her beautiful young mistress, sewing away at an intricate piece of featherstitch upon her future trousseau. Lady Frances was now of an eligible age for marriage and Dorothy knew it would only be a matter of time before her beloved 'Sissie' would have flown the companionship of this cosy nest to perch in some other rich man's home. Although love matches amongst members of a peer group were not discouraged in any way, Dorothy felt sad that it would be more likely that any day now some mature member of the landed gentry might make overtures towards Sir William, or even Willoughby, for the hand of this valuable Hickman chattel. Daughters of well-to-do families were always a much sought-after commodity, like brood mares for the elite.

Dorothy knew of many of the family's noble acquaintances who had used up to two, or even three, wives in pursuit of an heir and a spare. More distasteful to her mind, was that the resultant loss of a spouse during childbirth was often made good with almost indecent haste. However, she did appreciate that these arrangements did not usually come about without a welcome benefit to the bride's family too, and therefore were widely acceptable to dutiful daughters. Perhaps better for Frances, Dorothy considered, to marry out of some such arrangement than out of love for a man who would only bring her disappointment.

"Seventeen years?" Dorothy said silently to herself. "Can it really have been seventeen years since I first came to the Old Hall?"

It felt like almost a lifetime. Certainly in Lady Frances's case it was, for Dorothy had been 'in her family' for as long as she could remember. It had been four years since first Lady Rose and then Mistresses Goode had passed over. Where had all the time gone, she wondered to herself? So many years Dorothy had let slip by, yet inside her head were images and memories as vivid as if they had happened only that morning. Memories but not true ones, instead self edited, sanitized, images from her past that had become bearable for her to revisit. However, although Dorothy's past pain and hurt were as tightly corked down as the apple cider in the brown stoneware jar on the cupboard at her side, they could and would be just as keenly felt once more if suddenly found unbottled.

Just then, a rather ungainly serving wench ambled in.

"Mistress!" she said to the housekeeper. "Beg pardon Mistress Dorothy but there was a gentleman caller at the door for you!"

Lady Frances giggled with deep amusement at this and tried to compose herself behind the cover of her embroidery, watching carefully for the older woman's reaction.

"A gentleman caller?" Dorothy raised her eyebrows, frowned and rebuked the young waif with a severe look, yet there was a definite glint of amusement lurking in her eyes as she continued; "I think not young, Nell! A tradesman, perhaps!" she added.

"Did this gentleman caller pass on a name to give?" Lady Frances enquired mischievously.

"Yes, My Lady!" the poor young thing replied in a fluster.

"Well then? "Her Ladyship coaxed.

The maid did not respond, instead she remained blank

faced, as was her usual demeanour.

"This is almost as bad as drawing teeth!" Dorothy exclaimed, trying not to break into laughter. "What is this 'gentleman caller's' name?" she asked.

"I…err…I don't know Mistress!" Nell finally replied. "He did tell I…but I've forgotten!"

"Oh. Nell!" Dorothy exclaimed with an exasperated laugh having failed, miserably, in her valiant attempt to maintain her previously stern expression. Nell so reminded Dorothy of dear Comfort and herself at that age.

"Sometimes," the housekeeper sighed deeply, "I wonder if there is any brain at all under that cap of yours!"

Young Nell stood for a moment, utterly crestfallen, then suddenly her face sparked into animation.

"Master Thomas!" she said firmly, as if to disprove her Mistress's previous aspersions. "He told me his name was Master Thomas something or other, and that he wishes for you to attend him out in the garden. He seemed to know his way around so I allowed him out there already."

The girl registered the immediate change in the housekeeper's face. "Mistress!" she exclaimed, "did I do something wrong?"

Dorothy's face drained of all expression. She looked set to swoon.

"Whatever is the matter?" Lady Frances asked, reaching forward to steady her. "Are you alright, Dorothy? You have lost every trace of colour in your cheeks! What is it? Who is this Thomas?"

Dorothy swiftly composed herself. Valiantly she tried to shrug off the episode.

"I'm so sorry, My Lady, I fear it must be heat," she lied. "I suddenly felt quite faint.'

"And the mystery man, Dorothy"? Lady Frances persisted, as she was by now quite intrigued to discover if staid Mistress Dorothy might have a secret past.

"No one Frances!" she replied, " please do not concern

yourself. It is nobody of importance. Just a slight acquaintance from the past. Come on some trivial matter of unfinished business, I expect. Best I go attend to it directly, for good and all!"

"If you are going to go down to see this man, would you like me to summon one of the grooms to accompany you?"

"No, your Ladyship," Dorothy reassured her mistress. "That will not be necessary. I am certain any outstanding matter can be resolved with few words indeed and that I shall return to you, directly!"

Dorothy rose, curtseyed to Lady Frances and slowly withdrew.

This could not be her Thomas, Dorothy told herself, firmly, as she paced along the corridor. It just could not be. Not after all these years. Dorothy's head and heart began to thump in time as her steps picked up pace and she found herself hurrying out towards the garden. She fairly burst through the heavy oak door with eyes immediately scouring the border pathways, the benches and the arbor in search of the man but he was nowhere to be seen. Dorothy felt sick in the pit of her stomach. It was like some cruel prank being played out on her by mischievous Comfort's ghost.

Suddenly a thought sprang to Dorothy's mind and found voice.

"The Tower!"

Dorothy made her way around the outside of the Old Hall and towards the couple's once favoured rendezvous. She kicked up her heavy skirts, brushing aside the billowing lavender that dared impede her way, sending up a drone of bees her wake. Sure enough, as she turned the corner she found him there, standing with his back to her, under the heavy boughs of the walnut tree beside the tower door.

The split second she saw him, Dorothy felt a jolt. That same exquisite tingling, like in the seconds before a lightning strike, sent the hairs on the back of her neck standing and set a fluttering in her throat. It was the same feeling as ever it was whenever they had met before.

Dorothy paused shortly and placed her hand on her breast, as if to steady her pounding heart before it exploded inside her chest. Quickly she checked the few stray strands of hair back under her lace cap and snatched a long deep breath before continuing sedately over to the object of her attention. He must have heard her footsteps approach, for he turned. Then he smiled. That self-same heart stopping smile, which had always made her melt. Just as she reached him, he thrust her a rose before bowing deeply, in formal respect.

"Mistress Dorothy!" His greeting tripped from his lips mid-stoop.

Dorothy quickly bobbed in polite curtsey.

"Master Thomas!" she replied calmly. Then, catching him on the rise, she gave such a resounding slap around his cheek that it sent him reeling. Having delivered this insult, Dorothy screwed up the bloom in her hand sending its delicate pink petals scattering onto the gravel pathway then, almost immediately, turned and made to walk off back from whence she had come.

A shocked Thomas, still smarting from this unexpected blow, swiftly made after her and caught her by the arm.

"Get your hands off me, Sir!" she hissed like the kitchen cat.

"Alright!" he said, relinquishing his grip and throwing his arms up in resignation, "I deserved that but please! Hear me out!"

"Why should I?" Dorothy paced onwards refusing to even look at him.

"Because you may regret it for the rest of your life if you do not!"

"Regret what?" she snarled.

"Not hearing out the man who loves you."

"The man who loves me? Loves me?" she screeched.

"Loves me by running off and marrying another woman?"

"Please! Stop!" He pleaded tugging at her sleeve once more. "Hear me out! I only arrived back late yesterday. My first time on English soil for over twelve years and you were the only thought on my mind! I rode all night to get here to you. Doesn't that tell you anything at all?"

"Yes!" she retorted, "that you are as deceitful to your wife now as you were to me back then!

"My wife is dead," Thomas said quietly. "She was already dying when I married her."

This throwaway remark took Dorothy aback.

"I am sorry for you," she said, slowing down and letting her tone soften a little. "However, none of this is my concern. Good day to you, Sir."

'Alright! Alright!" Thomas, unrelentingly, pleaded his case as if his life depended upon it. "As I said before, I deserve all of this! I know you must have thoughts about me and that I cannot begin to defend myself, and that I deserve every ounce of vitriol that you can muster. But please Dorothy, please let me explain myself before I leave forever."

Dorothy stopped dead in her tracks. Forever? she thought. As far as she was concerned, he had already gone out of her life, forever. Yet, here he now stood, utterly brazen. How dare he pitch up here after all those empty loveless years? After all the dreamless nights when she had lain awake, in solitude, crying over what might have been, weeping bitterly until she had cried him out from her heart, so she had thought. Now, at the point in her life when she had learned to be lonely, resigned herself completely to a celibate state of spinsterhood, then, suddenly, here he was, swaggering back to add insult to her injury. Was it not bad enough that he'd had the audacity to show himself to her in the first instance, but then to threaten to deliberately hurt her anew by walking away again was more than any woman could be expected to bear! Her mind was screaming out at her to walk on and not even give him the satisfaction of a backward glance, but her heart was fast turning traitor on her. Her emotions burst out of the bottle.

Dorothy turned around to look Thomas full in the face, intent on drenching him with every drop of pent-up anger and humiliation she had been forced to drink in ever since he had abandoned her so publicly. Yet, when she did, she was utterly unprepared for his countenance. Tears pooled in his eyes and were channeling down across the angry raised welt on his cheek where she had struck him so hard a moment or two before. He stood, all atremble with emotion, like a frightened child before a scornful mother. How could she walk away from him now without hearing him out?

"I sail for the New World in a few days' time," he explained, with his words breaking apart. "Don't let me leave your life forever without putting this thing right with you first. Please Dorothy. I beg you to listen to me, take in every last word and hear me out. Only then decide."

Dorothy nodded, reluctantly, and they walked back together to the seat encircling the walnut tree trunk. There she sat and patiently listened.

"Dorothy I've never stopped loving you but...." he sighed. The words were not forming as easily on his lips as they were in his heart. Thomas was overcome by emotion and struggling to make his case in this, the trial of his lifetime and before such a hurt-hardened jury. "The last time we were together...I think the events of that night may have completely clouded my judgment...for the worse I fear!" he said.

"For the worse? I don't understand."

Dorothy's dark eyes narrowed as her lips formed into an irresistible pout. It was an expression Thomas fondly recalled only too well from their many heated discussions together over some learned topic or another that Dorothy might not yet, at that point have grasped. It was a look he had always found endearing and almost impossible not to react to.

"Let me explain to you, first, all that came to pass after that night, then I will come back to reasons why."

Dorothy nodded.

"I returned to my hideout straight after leaving you here that night. It was dark and earlier I had been almost certain that I had been followed part of the way through town. Can you then imagine my anxiety on finding young Spindleshanks, waiting on me there, as I arrived home? He brought me grave news indeed! That those bailiffs had been spotted at Tuxford, again, with a prison cart. The searchers must have sent for them, which in turn could only mean one thing. That they were closing in on us fast." Thomas wiped his eye and continued. "The others had gathered all their belongings together. I already knew the plan we had patched together to get out fast and that it was already well advanced. Will said there was no time for me to come back for you! I had no choice other than to leave with him immediately. He said Brewster would arrange for me to send for you once we were safely settled in Holland. And that, I promise you, was always my intention".

"Then what was it that changed your mind?"

"I will tell you, in a moment," he persisted gently, "but first let me continue? The women were already safely aboard a barge and on the way up the River Trent to the Humber Estuary, to meet up with the Dutch ship that Brewster had already chartered to take us out of the country," Thomas explained "We thought it safer this time, and kinder on the women, to split up. We men would fare better travelling overland, without children and chattels slowing us down. All seemed to be going well, we had got to the creek near Killingholme and how our hearts leapt when we saw the Dutchman laying at rest with its long boat being lowered to take us aboard! Then," Thomas sighed, "as we climb aboard the ship John Robinson suddenly cries out that the women and children aren't there.

The others panic, thinking we had been duped yet again and that something awful was about to befall us. Then, the Master of the vessel hurries over and points to something in the distance, way off up the beach. There they were! The woman and children! Trapped in their boat with a sandbar betwixt them and us and neither able to reach one another until the water should rise up again and float them off towards us. All we could do was to sit it out and watch as we waited for the tide to turn."

"So?"

"Only before we could, soldiers came," Thomas continued. "A dozen or more with searchers and bailiffs, all heading up the beach. The Captain is in such a fit of fear by now, thinking that he is sure to be arrested and his ship impounded, that he weighs anchor and sets sail - without them! I cannot begin to explain, Dorothy, the distress of either Brewster and the others onboard ship or their women and children, screaming for us to help them, as they were dragged from the boat and manhandled away before our eyes. We were helpless to do anything other than escape with our lives!"

"Oh my!" Dorothy exclaimed, "I had no idea!"

"That's not the worst of it!" Thomas continued his tale of woe. "We thought maybe, that after a day or two, we could double back and rescue them. After all, what pleasure did The Bishop stand to gain from holding helpless womenfolk bound to bend to their husband's persuasion? He was bound to turn them loose again by that time. But a storm blew up and snatched us as soon as we cleared the shelter of the estuary and it dragged us out to sea. It was too strong to resist so we resigned ourselves to being forced into making the crossing all the way to Holland without being able to go back for them at all for the time being. Even in rough seas, this crossing should have been simple enough but it soon turned into a nightmare. It should have taken two days at the very most, but instead we were snatched and carried in the teeth of this violent storm hundreds of miles north into icy waters where the maelstrom battered and tossed us for almost a fortnight. The crew and ourselves, we were all utterly convinced we were going to die. When we did not and survived it was nothing short of a miracle. However, I vowed then, that nothing could ever persuade me to cast my fate to the sea again. When we eventually reached Holland, the others immediately drew up plans for a rescue party and made regular forays back to retrieve the families, piecemeal, right out from under the authorities' noses."

"But you didn't send one for me?"

"No Dorothy. I had a lot of time to think about us then. Rightly or wrongly, I let circumstances overcome me and absolve me of the responsibility of making that decision altogether, or so I believed."

'You married?"

"Yes. Dorothy," he replied quietly. "I married one Anna De Kuyper."

"But why? If you loved me?"

"Anna was twenty five. A widow with a beautiful little girl who looked so much like young Lady Frances. Anna was destitute, living on the streets where we men had settled, but she wasn't a wastrel or a vagrant or a woman of easy virtue. Her husband had died and she had simply become too sick to fend for herself and her child. I wanted to help, I could not bear to pass them sleeping on the street as I returned to the warmth of my room. None of her countrymen seemed willing or able to take them in. But I could! I had work and could afford to take her on and care for them both but for decency's sake and for the honour of our group, only if I first married her. So that is what I did…I always loved you Dorothy," he stressed, "I only did what I did out of Christian necessity."

"And she died?"

'Yes, of consumption. About six months later."

'And her child?"

"Dead too the following winter, the poor little mite!"

"I see. So even then," Dorothy noted angrily, "still you did not see fit to send for me?"

"To my eternal shame, no!" Thomas admitted quite openly.

"Then tell me why?" Dorothy asked.

"Because I did not think you truly wanted me".

"Me? Not want you? How could you have thought that?" Dorothy demanded in utter bewilderment.

"Because of what happened that night," Thomas replied, "because of what you did the night we made love."

"What I did?" Dorothy did not understand. "I gave myself up to you before marriage!'" she exclaimed. "That is what I did! Laid down my honor and my body both, for the love of you! You swore you loved me!"

"But," Thomas replied hesitantly, not certain how to put the point tactfully, "I sensed that you had already laid it down before. That I was not the first man to have had knowledge of you! More than this you made it quite clear that you found my advances towards you repulsive, for you grimaced and flinched at my touch when I expected your body to welcome me. It was then that my foolish male pride got the better of me. From that moment onwards I felt rejected and spurned. My friends came to me, over and over again in Holland and pleaded with me to explain why I was deserting you, for they could not understand or hold with my treating you so low. I couldn't explain so in return I gave them all short shrift until they asked no more. Yet still they made certain I had news of you! Made certain that I knew that you were still alive and living in spinsterhood, whenever they came across anyone who had dealings with Sir William Hickman. They all knew that although I remained reticent on the subject, deep inside I still pined for you despite everything."

Thomas paused and after a second of silence there came

the most uncomfortable words that Dorothy had ever had to counter.

"Well, Dorothy. Tell me?" Thomas asked bluntly. "Was I wrong? Had you been with another man?"

Dorothy did not know what to say. Suddenly the tables were turned and it was her turn to feel like the one on trial. Now she must argue her case. She had had no idea up until then that Thomas had felt this way or that he could have determined that this had not been her first act of intercourse. Now she wondered if perhaps she had been at fault, however involuntarily, in their parting on such bad terms as they had.

She summoned up all her courage. Somewhere from the recess of her mind Lady Rose's words came back to her, 'trust truth only'.

"Yes," Dorothy replied candidly. "I was raped," she added looking him straight in the eye. "First I was raped by an unwanted suitor, aided and abetted by my own step-father," she explained, "then I was raped by him as well!" Barely stopping for breath or to gauge Thomas's reaction she continued. "Then, for my sins, I was driven out of my village through shame and that is how I came to be working here, in the Hall, so far away from my family."

Thomas was stunned into silence. It was not, as he had been led to presume by his father's cruel past remarks when first he announced his plans to marry his maid, that she had had a former lover. That would have been one thing, but it was quite another to have been brutally violated against her will. In those few fleeting moments following Dorothy's harrowing confession, he suddenly perceived her in a completely different light. Now he realized the reason for her reaction to him, why she had flinched when he had made love to her. How the horror of her previous ordeal must have come rushing back when he had so shamelessly let lust overtake him that night. He felt ashamed, so very ashamed that he had put her through all this pain because of his shallowness in allowing his worthless pride to be injured. He reached out, pulled Dorothy close and embraced her. Then he kissed her urgently and repeatedly begged her forgiveness.

"Oh my darling," he said tenderly. "Why could you not have told me?"

"I wanted to, many a time I wanted to. Indeed I was determined to tell you everything the next day, but you never came back. I was going to try to prepare myself for our wedding bed but then you came that night and I was not ready. I'm sorry; I see I am to blame now, I should have told you the truth."

"You did tell the truth to me Dorothy. You did not lie for I did not ask the question and sorry is not the word I want to hear from you."

"Then what?"

"I want to hear you admit that you still feel this love of ours, lingering deep within your soul. That it lives still, shifting, stirring and awaiting sweet release?"

"Oh Thomas! I never stopped thinking of you. But it is too late! Too much time has passed by! Look at me! I'm a wizened old spinster, no longer a blushed young thing."

"Still my sweet darling Dorothy," he sighed, "still the woman who moves my spirit and who I want to share the rest of my days with. Please, my sweet Dorothy, tell me that you will marry me! Come away and start a new life with us in The New World."

"The New World!"

"Yes, the rest are waiting for us to join them. We have our own ship now, 'The Speedwell'. They put me ashore off the coast as they made their way down to Southampton."

"Why the New World?"

It seemed so drastic a step for anyone to take.

"Holland is no longer safe," Thomas explained." The King's Ambassador was there looking to arrest Brewster and the others for printing 'seditious pamphlets against the King's Church' or so he tried to accuse in the warrants he kept sending out."

"And is Brewster here with you?"

"Yes! Lying low below deck, no doubt, away from prying eyes! So are many of the others you knew from both Scrooby and here. Holland may well be on the brink of war again with Spain and if that is so, then no protestant is safe there. So, the choice is no choice at all really. Stay in Holland and be embroiled in a war, return to England and be persecuted all over again, or risk striking out to a new world where, if we don't all end up at the bottom of the sea first, we will be free!"

There was so much for Dorothy to consider. The thought of leaving all she had known to flee to Holland with Thomas all those years ago had been a frightening enough proposition, but to go to The Americas! He might as well have been asking her to jump into an abyss!

"Oh Thomas. I don't feel that I can come with you!" she cried.

"Why? If you love me..."

"I do still love you but I think this has come too late!"

"Too late?"

"I am past thirty years of age! I am far too old and far too set in my ways now to cope with change! I have a life here! Responsibilities!" Dorothy replied.

"And what about yourself, Dorothy? Don't you have a responsibility to yourself, right now, after all these years in the service of others, to live out the remainder of your life for yourself? And as for being old, what about William and Mary Brewster? If they are ready to face the challenge...?"

"I'm not sure if it is the real me or some past person, long dead, that you want to come with you. I am not the woman I was and you are not the man I fell in love with either," she explained. 'The years that have passed by since then have shaped and moulded me in ways that you have no way of knowing. I suspect the same is true of you. It's like trying to pick up the rhythm of the dance once the players have ceased playing. We can't hope to step in harmony when neither one of us can hear the music anymore!"

"I hear the music still, Dorothy!" Thomas said boldly. "Listen! It is in the beat of your heart. Every word you speak. The tone of your voice is my lute and the tinkling bells ring out in your laughter. Dorothy, I can hear all the music I need to follow this dance. All I am asking is for you to trust me and let me take the lead. I know we have a long way to go and that we have no way of knowing how we will end up in the future. But once, I was willing to give up everything for you…"

"Give up everything? Give up what for me?" she asked.

"I am sorry. I shouldn't have said that," Thomas replied. "I don't want to sway your opinion one way or the other by going into it just now…but I will…when we are married then I will explain.

Please Dorothy! Please. Consider all I have said. Know that I love you more than life itself and that if you send me away without you then you condemn me to live out the remainder of my life alone. For I will not marry with anyone else if I cannot be with you!"

"I cannot decide. Pray give me time for there is so much to consider," Dorothy pleaded in her turn.

"Time, I am afraid, is something I cannot give, for it is precious and not mine for the giving. Every minute spent on English soil is a minute in which Brewster and the others can be betrayed and arrested. I have to ride south to meet with the others at Southampton. I can only give you until the morning. That is all. Then I must leave ….for good!"

"Then I will sleep on it this night and give you my answer then."

The two parted with a warm adieu and an agreement that Dorothy would give due consideration to all that had been said and would meet with Thomas by the tower door at daybreak. Then she would give her answer.

"You were gone a long time for so sharp a dismissal Mistress Dorothy!" Lady Frances remarked glancing up from her sewing.

She smiled before noticing the deep concern now playing over her friend's features.

"What has passed between you and this man? Tell me, my friend, for I cannot bear to see you so pained."

"I was betrothed to him once, when you were just a little girl."

"Oh the Separatist fellow?" Frances asked casually.

"Then you know?" Dorothy was genuinely surprised that Lady Frances was privy to this most private aspect of her life.

"Yes, sorry. I did not mean to pry, only Mother told me all about it when I was older but bade me never to broach the subject for fear of reopening painful wounds."

"Oh! I did not know it was talked of."

"No, not generally," Lady Frances said reassuringly. "Just the once. What did he want?" she added.

"He came to apologize and to tell me that he is leaving for the New World on the morrow."

"The Americas! How exciting! But what did he want with you?"

"He wants me to go with him."

"To marry?"

"Yes, to marry with him'

"And will you?"

'I don't know. I can't take it all in. It is like some sweet dream, that having materialized appears more like your darkest nightmare. You yearn for someone to return, for so many years, yet when they do and you hear all those sweet words you longed for them to tell you, instead of bringing you joy they fill you with a yawning, dread sickness."

"It's a perfectly natural reaction, I would have thought," Frances observed thoughtfully." You don't want to be hurt again and who can blame you for that?"

"No. I don't think I could bear that again," Dorothy confessed. "I tried to bury him for all these years as I struggled to get on with my life. I have even been happy, yet still I grieved inwardly whenever I heard or saw anything that reminded me of him. Yet, to see this corpse now rise up before me and breathe new vigour into that flicker of a flame that still burns in my soul for him, defies comprehension."

"But Dorothy," Frances pressed. "Do you still love him?"

"Yes," she replied. "I am afraid that I do."

"Enough to go with him to the end of the earth?"

"I don't know. I just do not know!"

"Then," Frances took Dorothy's hand and asked poignantly, "do you love him so little that you can bear to watch him walk out of your life forever, knowing that he loves you?"

"Who loves you?" a male voice demanded to know.

The two women had not heard Willoughby enter.

"Dorothy's betrothed from the past…" Frances answered her brother.

"Ah yes! The Separatist. May the Devil take him for you know he treated you easy! But am I deceived or did I distinctly hear you say 'loves'. Do not tell me the blackguard has returned."

"Yes, brother Willoughby, he has! And he has asked Dorothy to marry with him and go to the Americas!" Frances exclaimed.

"And will you?" Willoughby turned to Dorothy. "Do you plan to go with him?" he asked bluntly.

"I do not know, My Lord. I am quite undecided upon the matter."

"Then pray let me help you. You left with him once before, did you not? Only to skulk back here with your tail between your legs!"

"Willoughby!" Frances jumped to her companion's defence. "That was a long, long time ago! You were only a baby!"

"Yes, when you were only our nursery maid," he added spitefully. "Now you have a position of importance here, graced to you by our family. I hope you will not overlook that duty you hold towards my Father. Not to mention my dear sister here!"

"Well, I for one am in agreement if Dorothy should decide to leave!" Frances warned him. "So pray, dear brother, do not presume to speak on my account for I have a tongue of my own in my head!"

"Maybe so," he replied. "All I want to do is make it crystal clear for dear Mistress Dorothy here, that if she chooses to leave our employ to go with this dubious fellow, then there is no coming back! That is all. I will not allow it and as I am in charge of this estate, de facto, my word is final on that matter."

Willoughby turned to walk away but stopped briefly for one parting shot.

"Be certain, Mistress Dorothy! There will be no second chance for you here if you go with him now!"

"Dorothy go!" Frances urged as soon as Willoughby was gone. "Though it will grieve me sorely to lose you, my dearest friend in all the world, I want you to find true happiness. If this is what is in your heart, then I want you to go. If things do not work out then I will make certain there is always a place for you, as my personal companion, here or wherever I go when I marry. My door will always be open for you."

***

Dorothy tried to sleep that night but in vain. Instead, she lay on her bed on that sultry August night and listened to the bell ringing out at each passing of another restless hour. How often, she thought to herself, had she lain awake and listened to the hours of her life being struck out, one by one? And where was that life leading her now she had finished raising Lady Frances? Mistress Goode had lived and died serving this family as housekeeper before her. She died and the Hall remained. Daily life carried on without her there to oversee it, as if she had never been. Dorothy knew the same would be true of her, whether she remained or left on the morrow. All of her years of service would pale into insignificance with the passing on of the chatelaine chained each day to her waist, for who could recall Mistress Goode now amongst the staff? Who so much as spoke her name? So many had come and gone, with a new order sublimely formed in their waning. Master Willoughby was part of that new order. Though Sir William still lived, Willoughby managed the thriving estate and all of his fathers' affairs until he inherited it, in what could only be a short time. It was true that here she had security and a position in society; respect and a sound roof over her head. No mean feat for the illiterate farm girl who had arrived on the Old Hall's threshold so many years before. How could she be expected to give all of this up for a man who had already betrayed her once before? It was simply beyond sound reason.

CHAPTER FOURTEEN

It was almost twilight. Barely light enough to make out the object of Thomas's excitement.

"Look, Dorothy! Look!" He pointed towards a slender shape at anchor in Southampton water. "That's her! That's our ship, the Speedwell."

There she was, silhouetted against a violet-blushed sky. The crimson sun was fast sinking below the horizon, as if journeying on ahead to scorch out a trail for this ship of dreams to follow. In the dusky glow of lanterns, spilling out from the poop deck and forecastle, the Speedwell was serenely beautiful as she gently bobbed in the wake of the ebbing tide. A ship of dreams indeed, for this was the vessel the congregation had invested so much of their money in to take them across the Atlantic. They badly needed their own ship; not just for immediate passage but to stay with them in America for the future. It was going to be necessary as their lifeline.

If the Speedwell looked as slender and graceful as a fine Arabian stallion, then the companion ship anchored beside her that evening looked like a huge, plodding workhorse. By comparison, it was a monster. A craft of above one hundred and eighty tons, chartered on behalf of the Separatists by the Virginia Trading Company to transport all the congregation's worldly goods and stores to the New World. A hulk of a cargo vessel, it had hauled the burden of tons of wines, furs, cloth and other valuable trading commodities, back and forth, across the seas around Europe for almost forty years. However, she was an old ship, clearly approaching the end of her useful life. Her name was pretty enough though. It was the Mayflower.

"Thomas!" A familiar voice instantly drew Thomas's attention and broke the spell that the Speedwell had cast over the dreamy couple.

"Thomas! You made it then! We were beginning to worry

that you wouldn't get here in time!"

This fresh–faced, flame-haired young man, bearing down on them at quite a pace, obviously knew Thomas well.

"Gilbert!" Thomas replied in joyful recognition.

A firm, friendly handshake quickly passed between them. So firm in fact that this boyish fellow momentarily forgot the small pitcher of milk he was carrying in the other hand and sent it slopping over the filthy cobbles, as it tilted precariously during their friendly exchange.

"And this must be your intended," Gilbert prompted, smiling breathlessly towards Dorothy.

She felt herself blush momentarily. To be addressed as such by this too worldly-wise young fellow who could not be much more than half her age, was to Dorothy just a little embarrassing. Yet she could see that only the kindest of intentions lay behind the remark and in no way was the slightest offence meant. Indeed, on reflection she found it very sweet of Gilbert and completely in keeping with this man she would soon count upon as a friend.

"Yes! This is she," Thomas laughed, and turning to his love added, "Dorothy, I'd like to introduce you to one of the finest of young men, lately of Leyden. Mister Gilbert Winslow."

"Greetings, Sir," Dorothy bobbed in curtsey.

"It's Gilbert, Dorothy!" he commanded with a wide smile, "call me Gilbert, Mistress Dorothy."

Dorothy returned the smile.

"Are you settled in anywhere?" Gilbert enquired excitedly. "When did you get here?"

"About an hour ago," Thomas replied. "And no, we had no way of knowing where you all might be so came here directly to see if we could track you down. I thought if we were to find the Speedwell first, then you must surely be near at hand."

"And you were right!" Gilbert laughed. "We are all lodged, as well as we can at inns close by. They seem pretty packed though, I must warn you," he explained. "But come with me to mine and see if they can fit you in somewhere!"

Thomas and Dorothy walked with Gilbert along the narrow, dingy, dockside lanes. As they did the couple listened intently as Gilbert recounted all the trials and tribulations that had befallen the congregation since the Speedwell had put Thomas ashore off the Lincolnshire coast. The most worrying events it turned out, had only occurred during the past day or so and both were to do with the backers of the venture.

The congregation's appointed business spokesman, John Carver, had apparently had hot words with one Thomas Weston. Weston was a financier, and an avaricious one at that. The obvious desperation of this group of people, apparently headed by Carver, to get away from England aroused his cupidity. Acting as one of the backers of the Virginia venture, he had already agreed terms with John Carver and extremely extortionate terms they were at that. However, on the congregation's arrival in Southampton, greedy Weston had the audacity to approach John Carver yet again, in an attempt to renegotiate the terms at an even more outrageous rate.

"What did John Carver say to that?" Thomas asked worriedly.

"Turned him down flat," Gilbert replied bluntly. "Told Weston he'd rather go to Hell in a handcart!"

Thomas gasped in disbelief momentarily, before breaking out into a chuckle.

Dorothy had not yet had the pleasure of meeting John Carver. He was not among the many Separatists whom she had come to know from their various visits to the Old Hall. Later though, once she had, she would come to realize how under-handed Weston's overture must have been that day for John to reply as angrily as he did. He was usually so courteous and considerate: always sober and even-tempered in his business dealings. And careful; Carver was never a man to take an uncalculated risk. He had not become such a wealthy merchant down in Kent by being reckless.

"So what happened? Did Weston back down?" Thomas asked.

"No, he didn't," Gilbert, sighed wearily. "In fact he was so angry at John's refusal that he withdrew his financial backing altogether!"

"Sweet Heaven!" Thomas exclaimed. "Wasn't Weston's finance crucial to the whole project?"

"It's alright! "Gilbert lightened up and reassured his friend. "It has all been sorted out. True, we were forced to sell off a fair proportion of our stores," he explained, "and all of us handed over whatever we could spare from our own belongings to be auctioned off to make up the shortfall. I tell you Thomas," he added with a wink, "none of these money men can boast a father amongst them!"

Thomas laughed heartily.

"But that wasn't the half of it!" Gilbert continued. "The Virginia Company had deliberately doubled-booked our passenger places upon our chartered cargo ship to a bunch of some pretty dire, private settlers and get-rich-quick merchant adventurers, also bound for Virginia. There's not a thing we can do about it!" he fumed. "That Company has taken advantage of us all along, knowing full well that we had come so far with our plans that there was no going back for us!"

The three had reached a typically dubious dockside establishment. Light blazed out from diamond-leaded windows, burning a pathway to its door from the street; the reverberation of revelry from within shattering the end of day silence.

Dorothy paused briefly to look up at its half-timbered, black and white facade. A crudely painted, weatherworn sign swung slightly from a metal bar on the overhang outside. On it was depicted a flaxen-haired, half–woman, half-fish sea creature, complete with a shell comb in hand, reclining on a rock surrounded by stylised white-tipped waves. They had reached The Mermaid Inn.

"This is it!" Gilbert exclaimed. "My brother Edward, his wife and myself, along with my little brood, are all crammed into one tiny room up there!" he said, pointing towards the second storey. "It is rough lodgings but everywhere else is full."

They went in and Gilbert turned to go towards a narrow side corridor.

"If you'll excuse me," he explained, "I must go up to my children and take them this milk. It was hard enough to find and I have been away far too long. I bet they have given me up for dead!" he joked. "Ask inside if there is any room left for you to stay. It will only be for the night as we plan to set sail tomorrow, if the weather and the Company allow us to at last!"

"Oh!" Dorothy exclaimed, once Gilbert had disappeared upstairs and was out of earshot. "He's so very young to have children and he didn't mention a wife. Is the poor man a widower?"

"No, my dear," Thomas explained. "His children are three orphan siblings from amongst our congregation. He has taken then in until suitable families can be found to take them on from him. He is like a mother hen with them! Such a saint!"

Dorothy smiled in agreement.

The inn was brim full with a curious mix of seasoned, often blasphemous sailors and members of the mild-mannered, God-fearing Separatist congregation. The old salts were rowdily making the most of their last remnants of shore leave, for only God knew how long it would be before they could return. The others, quiet and reflective, knew they would never be coming home again.

Thomas and Dorothy elbowed their way through the throng inside and made their way across the sawdust-strewn floor to a grubby looking, heavily stained dark-wood table. The air inside was thick with the smell of burning wood from the open log fire that spluttered and spat almost as furiously as the seamen themselves. The odour of stale beer, with overtones of vomit and sweat also permeated the atmosphere but none of these could compete with the unmistakable aroma of tobacco. Smoking was a sailor's habit; the small white clay pipes cupped to their ruddy salt-tanned faces almost an obligatory badge amongst them.

A surly looking serving wench, running the gauntlet of vulgar whispered suggestions in her ear and the molestation of hands upon her body, made her way over to the table. During the most cursory of conversations, Thomas managed to order food and enquire about a room for the night. There were none.

So, after a supper of pork boiled with cabbage and onions, accompanied by bread and a badly chipped beaker of small beer, Dorothy and Thomas spent their last night ashore together, sitting side by side in the corner of a rowdy alehouse. All their worldly belongings were at their feet, stuffed beneath the rough wooden table on which they then pillowed their heavy heads in their arms and tried to get some sleep.

Come morning, they gathered on the quayside with the rest of their congregation. Like most dreams faced with the scrutiny of the cold light of day, Dorothy's first impressions of The Speedwell and The Mayflower were quickly shattered. Even to her untrained eye, neither vessel inspired confidence as being particularly seaworthy. Indeed Thomas had overheard a conversation between members of the hired crew upon these very same lines on the way over from Holland, but had dismissed their concerns about the ship's list toward port as probable exaggeration. After all, it had made the voyage from Delfshaven with little incident, unlike his previous storm battered crossing to Antwerp some twelve years before.

Dorothy scanned the others milling about waiting to be

given permission to embark, trying to pick out familiar faces from across the years. She immediately recognized the well-built frame of William Brewster, still blessed with his undiminished flamboyant dress sense. With his violet coat and green breeches, his clothing was almost as bright as his disposition that morning. The only real difference she could see in him from the passage of years was that perhaps he was little heavier, certainly much greyer, and that he was now sporting a Dutch beard that suited him rather well. His ever-homely wife Mary, despite being in her middle age had not been worn down by the years. She appeared as calm and peaceful as ever, which was surprising to Dorothy who quickly noted that Mistress Brewster had lately been blessed with two more offspring since last they had met. The Brewsters' older children, in particular Fear, who had only been an infant when the group had first left for exile, were not among the congregation. At first Dorothy dare not ask after them as she assumed they must have died. However, when during the course of conversation, Mary volunteered information about them, Dorothy was comforted to hear that they were alive and well and would be following on to the New World once a new homestead had been established. In fact, she quickly learnt that this was the case with many on the venture. Entire families had been cloven apart, sacrificed in the short term in order to gain future freedoms.

Dorothy also recalled many others there. One man looked so familiar to her yet, on her life, she could not put a name to him or even remember where they had met.

"Oh Dorothy! Shame on you!" Thomas teased. "That's William! Spindleshanks William Bradford!"

"William Bradford?" Dorothy could not believe her ears. How could this tall, dark handsome, healthy looking man possibly be the same pallid, sickly looking youth she had known from just twelve years before?

"He has matured out of all recognition," Dorothy

remarked in amazement. "God must surely have smiled on him all these years!"

The other man who caught her attention was the man she thought must be John Carver. He was very different to how Dorothy had pictured him in her mind's eye when Thomas and Giles had spoken of him the night before. Despite his middle-age spread, stocky built and balding hair, he cut rather a smart figure. He was well groomed and his very strong chin was closely shaven. He was the sort of man who inspired confidence just by his appearance. His wife, Katherine, dressed in a low cut saffron gown with wide white collar and deeply cuffed sleeves, stood at his side, Not a pretty lady, with overly pointed features and heavily-pitted skin, but nonetheless a pure-spirited, happy, kind woman. Upon their introduction, Dorothy instantly warmed to the Carvers, and she felt that they returned the warmth.

Then the realization dawned on Dorothy that many past friends, made during the first failed attempt to from Boston, were missing. Samuel Cooper and his wife she learned, had both passed on through old age as had Richard Clyfton. Younger, yet still taken by consumption had been John Smyth. John Robinson had selflessly volunteered to remain in Holland to care for the remainder of their flock, either too young or too old to take this monumental journey into the unknown.

After quite some period of uncertainty and inaction on the quayside, a message suddenly appeared and was handed to John Carver. Finally, he was in a position to call the congregation to attention. At last, they were going to depart on the next tide and so all had to be allocated their places for the voyage, split between the two ships. None were too keen to be billeted upon the Mayflower in the company of 'strangers' so a simple ballot was held. However William Brewster himself, volunteered to go on the strangers' craft to help ensure the well being of their own brethren

Despite Dorothy's personal misgivings, she and Thomas were soon aboard and the Speedwell was ready to up anchor and depart. They watched as the crew of the Mayflower swarmed, like ants, up the rigging and unfurled her six sails. On high, from the lateen yard the red ensign fluttered, while the flag of King James flew from the main mast. Soon her canvas sheets billowed out and filled as she caught a lively late summer breeze and headed down the Solent. Within minutes, the Speedwell was soon under sail too.

Holding fast to her cap, Dorothy swayed unsteadily as the Speedwell's timbers lurched beneath her. Unlike the others aboard, this was her first experience of being on the sea and she quickly felt queasy.

"It's alright, my dear," Thomas said reassuringly as he led her towards the deck side, "you will feel better once you've got your sea legs. Here, try to fix your eye upon the horizon. It will help you adjust to the motion of the ship. And never stare at a swinging object!" he warned.

Dorothy did as Thomas advised but soon suffered sickness. However, after a while she did seem to throw this off and felt a little better. The couple stayed on deck as long as possible to admire the view as they hugged the coast shadowing the Mayflower. Yet even at this point, the Speedwell appeared to belie her name and struggled to keep pace with her larger, much more powerful companion.

For the others aboard, the novelty of being at sea had already worn thin and the bluster of the chill wind on deck made below seem positively inviting. Soon Dorothy and Thomas too retreated below to settle into their sack-curtained-off spaces. There was just room enough to stretch out and arrange their belongings around them. The ships of these times were never designed with the thought in mind that they might some day be pressed into service to carry so many passengers, let alone women and children,

SUE ALLAN

nor on a voyage of thousands of miles either.

The gloominess and dampness of the craft was tolerable but what Dorothy found especially hard to contend with at first, was the overwhelming feeling of claustrophobia. After all, she had spent almost half her life until then living in the lofty space of Gainsborough Old Hall and the headroom below deck never exceeded five and a half feet. Not quite so bad for her as she stood hardly above five feet tall, but it proved a greater discomfort to Thomas and many of the other menfolk who had to be forever ducking and stooping to avoid cracking their heads on the heavy oak beams. It was no wonder that whenever possible she, like most of the others aboard, made for the deck and the open sky above

However it became all too soon apparent that the Speedwell was fast taking on water. In no time the old girl began to list heavily, as her bilges lost the struggle to pump out the unrelenting seawater seeping in through her rotten hull. Frantic signaling passed between the two sister ships. There was a real fear that the Speedwell might even be in danger of sinking, so there was no choice other than for the two vessels, reluctantly, to put into port again. This time at Dartmouth.

Once there it transpired that it would take up to a week before the shipwrights could complete re-corking and tarring the affected areas on the Speedwell in an attempt to remedy the leaks. Again the Separatists would be forced to make hard decisions as to which of their precious commodities they could afford to sell off to meet the cost of both these repairs and yet more harbour dues, before they could contemplate making ready to set sail again.

Yet it is an ill wind indeed that blows no one any good, for during that brief respite, with time spare for properly renewing their past acquaintance, the bond between Dorothy and Thomas strengthened. With summer all but spent, love blossomed all over again. So, in a borrowed blue

196

gown from Katherine Carver and with the gift of a lace-trimmed cap and collar from Mary Brewster, Dorothy and Thomas were quietly married.

CHAPTER FIFTEEN

All seemed to be going well upon the Speedwell as she left Dartmouth and skirted along the coast. Then the Captain followed the Mayflower's lead, altered her degree heading towards landfall at Virginia and turned to catch full advantage of the wind. The plucky old girl willingly rose up to meet the command and with sails billowing headed out to the open Atlantic.

It was just off the Isles of Scilly, as the Speedwell tasted her first turbulent seas, that Dorothy became aware that something was terribly amiss with their increasingly creaking vessel. Seawater, leeching its way in at first, suddenly began to stream through the planking as it groaned and stretched then started to split apart.

"It's too much for her!" Thomas cried out in alarm. "Get above, Dorothy! Quickly! We may have to abandon ship!"

Dorothy shook with terror as they scrambled up the ladder. She had swum before, in the beck as a small girl, but this expanse of water looked so vast and unforgiving. Besides, there were her heavy skirts. Once they had become sodden, surely the weight would drag her under like a stone.

Likewise, the same thought had struck many others. The result was utter pandemonium on the deck as passengers panicked and the ship's bell frantically rang out a warning of the Speedwell's imminent demise. Almost immediately, the Mayflower made about and lumbered back towards her wounded sister, ready to pick up survivors as soon as the order to abandon ship was given or else she broke up completely, whichever came first. Meanwhile as the Mayflower struggled to catch up, the badly listing Speedwell fought valiantly to limp back to the mainland. She succeeded, but only barely, in making Plymouth harbour. The venture for her was now at an end for good and along with her, much precious investment was lost.

There remained no choice left open to the Separatist congregation as to what course of action to follow. They were tied and bound so tightly by the contract they had made with the Virginia Company that they just had to go on somehow. In any case, to stay behind in England would certainly mean the arrest of Brewster and many of the others, with all the horrors that that would entail. Also everything they owned, everything they had ever achieved in exile, was stowed below in the hold of the Mayflower. Their goods, chattels and above all, the most powerful weapon they had ever owned in their struggle for reforming the established church, William Brewster's printing press. Therefore, it was decided that this plucky old cargo ship, at least, would go on across the Atlantic alone.

The port of Plymouth was Sir Francis Drake country. Almost as southwesterly a port as you could find on the mainland of the recently united kingdom of King James, which was capable of handling this newly found trade in transatlantic shipping. These Devonshire people were stubbornly resistant to change. There was no Protestant stronghold close to these shores. Not like the continental lowlands that traded so freely with the ports on the Humber or at Boston, or along the coasts and tidal waters of the Separatists' East Midlands homeland. The Devon locals did not take so kindly to the passengers of the Speedwell once they heard whispers that they were possibly naught but a party of anarchist state-church dissenters. A latent hostility, barely tangible at first but nonetheless present, was bubbling away just below the surface of the town from the moment the Mayflower and the Speedwell dropped anchor in the harbour. The Separatists were a metaphorical spark waiting to set Plymouth's tinder alight.

Dorothy realised that hard choices were about to be made by their group, choices that for many would make the difference between life and death. Whether, after this dreadful near catastrophe with the Speedwell, they should travel on to Virginia in the Mayflower or to take their chances by remaining in England. Either way, one thing was blatantly clear, without the Speedwell there was no way the congregation could fit aboard the surviving vessel.

Some had already made up their minds. They had had their fill of the tempestuous sea and were too terrified to contemplate going on. Instead, they gave up their places and retrieved their goods from the ship's hold. Others, like Brewster, had no such compulsion to remain. They had to go on, regardless. As for Dorothy, she cast aside her trepidation and like a good and loyal wife, placed her trust once more in Thomas, who was adamant they should go.

Names were struck off the Mayflower passenger list and others reallocated the now vacant places, by a mixture of negotiation and ballot. While this process took place, many ventured ashore to make use of this last unexpected opportunity to do so. Having successfully secured passage for both himself and Dorothy, Thomas was among those who risked one last foray into town. He had in mind to buy a special purchase for his beloved new bride, so he went off alone. However, he failed to return either later that day or the next morning. The Mayflower was by then, ready to sail but Thomas was still unaccounted for. A worried John Carver mustered a search party to go ashore to seek their friend out. However, late that evening they were to return with grim news.

"Dorothy you must be brave." Mary Brewster and Katherine Carver had volunteered to break the news to a desperately worried Dorothy.

She knew instantly that something dreadful must have happened the moment the others came near. She could read it in their faces, almost reach out and feel the cruel edge of the words that would cut into her heart within seconds.

"Brave? No!" She recoiled from them in horror. "Not Thomas! Not my Thomas!"

Mary sprang forward to grasp the distraught woman in

her arms. How she hated to be the bearer of such news, knowing all that these two had gone through to be married at last.

"Yes!" Katherine Carver eased Mary's burden by taking from her the grim task. "We are so sorry but a man answering to Thomas' description was killed last night," she said as gently as she could, "during some sort of altercation in the town, within hours of him leaving. The man died where he fell, they said, from a single blow to his skull. He wouldn't have known anything, my dear," she tried to reassure Dorothy. "After that, his assailants apparently just cut his purse and fled."

"I must go to him!" Dorothy cried hysterically.

"It's too late for that, I'm afraid," Katherine said. "With all this heat and the body unclaimed, the magistrate has already given orders for the corpse to be buried. Most likely, dear Thomas is already laid to his rest."

"Then I must at least go to his family and explain what has happened to their son," Dorothy countered, calming down in acceptance of the situation.

"I would not venture there my dear," Mary warned her, "for they would not suffer you amongst them or thank you for your trouble."

"Not suffer me? But why? I have not even met them!" she exclaimed.

"And that is why," Mary explained. "Surely Thomas told you?"

"Told me what?"

"Oh my dear! I am sorry to say that Thomas' parents disowned him as soon as he told them he wanted to marry a maid."

"Disowned him?"

"Yes, before he left for Holland. His father cut him off without a penny because he told them he was set on marrying you."

"Then that is what he meant when he came to me and

said he had given up everything for me! And I never knew! He was going to tell me but he never had the chance. Oh my God!" she cried, "What am I to do? What am I to do without my Thomas?" She broke down completely as the two women tried to console her, but they too gave in to tears.

"Come with us," Mary Brewster pleaded. "God has work for you upon this voyage, I can feel it. There are so many little ones we will need a hand with, especially as three of their mothers are heavy with child. Who knows when they might be called to their labours?"

"Thomas would have wanted you to be amongst friends," Katherine Carver added. "And besides, you will still share in any entitlements."

"But I may not come!' Dorothy countered. "For have not the Company forbidden unaccompanied women aboard this venture?"

"Yes," Katherine confirmed, "but my maid has run off and is already counted. She was terrified of drowning when the Speedwell began to take on water and refused to go on with us. Take her place Dorothy. I shall have much need of reliable help on the other side. We will care and support you, my dear, and help you build a new life there. You belong with us!" she said. "We are your family now. There is nothing here for you now in England!"

Dorothy knew Mistress Carver was right. Without a husband, she had no position in society in her own right. With no close family and Willoughby's dire warning still fresh in her mind she knew that there was nothing to hold her in this old world. Maybe this had been God's will for her all along, to serve some purpose on this great voyage.

So finally, on September the sixth, in the year of Our Lord sixteen hundred and twenty, Dorothy left England as the Mayflower set sail from Plymouth.

At the bark of Ship's Master Jones's orders, the crew braced the yards and let go her sails. The Mayflower shuddered,

as if somehow she knew that every voyage she had
undertaken up until that time was naught but a rehearsal
for this one monumental role in history. Cupping a breath
of light breeze in her sails, she groaned, and swaying gently
began to move. Heading west-southwest out of Plymouth
Harbour, with Drake's Island astern, she was quickly on
her way to join the Channel. White foam danced in her
wake, and on high seagulls screeched out as if in a sad
lament.

Dorothy watched for as long as she could up on deck,
her shawl clasped tight around her shoulder to shield
herself against the offshore wind. Bitter tears burnt her face
as she remembered but a few fleeting days before, how
Thomas had steadied her as together they departed
Dartmouth on the Speedwell. Now he was dead and the
Speedwell lost. Yet, through some cruel trick Dorothy
fancied that somewhere on the shore she could sense
Thomas looking out to sea. Then far too quickly, the soft
contours of the land began to disappear from sight and she
sensed him no more. It felt to her as if Thomas had broken
his word to her, turned his back on her once more, leaving
her cast adrift to ride out whatever course fate planned to
set her upon. Resigned now to following its flow, Dorothy
looked on as a misty haze set about swallowing up all she
had ever known and loved.

Others, also, stood on deck, many weeping as their
England faded and slipped gently over the horizon. Then
cold reality hit like the driving hail now smiting,
unexpectedly, from on high. There was no realistic hope
for the majority of ever going home again. Never would
they revisit the old familiar haunts and landscapes of their
youth, nor would their hearts leap to hear the first cuckoo
call in May. Suddenly deprived of the comfort of the land
of their birth, they felt like orphaned, motherless waifs on
the sea.

From the start of the journey, all were encouraged to some

extent by the favourable wind and the Mayflower's progress out to sea and of her early effort to break free from the jaws of the Channel. Dorothy soon became accustomed to the below deck confinement and the pungent smell of wood, canvas and rope. They were fortunate to have pressed this, of all cargo ships, into passenger use. As the Mayflower was accustomed to carrying wine, any spillage from this had seeped down into the bilges where it had neutralized the odours from the filth her crew were used to discarding there when the weather was too rough to reach the beak. Thus, she was aptly described as being 'a sweet ship'.

Overall, Dorothy adapted admirably to the inherent difficulties of life living on board a ship. She settled quite quickly into a pattern of cooking and tending to her new family's needs. The only aspect Dorothy found almost unbearable was the use of the ship's crude sanitary arrangement. To use them meant her having to hoist her skirts to climb onto the forecastle and then down into the 'beak', where a square of planking had been cut away to expose the sea below. Unease at the lack of privacy, and the sight of the sea opening up beneath her, was only heightened for Dorothy by the seemingly habitual presence of one lewd sailor in particular. He seemed to haunt the mizzenmast and its shrouds whenever she approached the forecastle to use the beak. It was as if he was deliberately making an effort to spy on her. Then, as other women came forward with the same complaint, this swiftly pressed them into making their own arrangements, behind curtains below, for themselves and their children.

With the sea quite calm and the weather set fair, as it was this early on in the voyage, the ship's motion was more pitch than roll, which Dorothy found quite soothing, although many other passengers felt quite queasy. In fact, one or two individuals seemed to Dorothy, perpetually trapped between decks, poised in readiness to hurry up the companionway to seek the side of the deck. Indeed many, including Dorothy, found comfort in being on deck for as much of they day as they could manage.

Dorothy deliberately busied herself. It was the only way she knew to try to staunch her flow of grief over the cruel loss of her husband. If she kept busy then she did not have time to think and besides, it gave her great comfort to be entrusted with much of the care of the little ones on board. She diverted all of her spare love and attention towards them, while usefully easing the burden of their mothers or guardians, for while there were many parents who had taken the unenviable decision to leave some, or all of their children behind for the present, there were many youngsters aboard without any parent at all. Amongst these were the four little More siblings, whom Thomas had described as 'orphans" in Gilbert Winslow's care when first Dorothy had been introduced at Southampton. The four children had by now, been 'farmed out' amongst willing members of the congregation. The youngest pair, placid Richard at six and clingy, straight haired, stern-faced little Mary, barely four, were now entrusted to the tender arms of seasoned 'Mother Brewster'. Boisterous Jasper plugged the childless void in the Carvers' life while the oldest, loud and bubbly eight-year-old Ellen, remained the much-indulged ward of all three Winslows.

The thought of four such tender children being orphaned so young deeply touched Dorothy, even more so when she discovered the truth about their coming to be upon this dangerous voyage. To her utter horror, she was to learn that these little ones had not been orphaned at all. In fact both natural parents were still living. Their mother, Katherine, had entered into and endured a very unhappy arranged marriage to her cousin Samuel. At some point unknown, Katherine had been discovered having an affair with another man whom she loved deeply. On discovering that he had been cuckolded, and maybe even deceived into accepting this other man's offspring as his own, an enraged

SUE ALLAN

Samuel More divorced their Mother without further ado.
As a proven adulteress and a divorced woman, Katherine
lost all legal claim to her children and was utterly powerless
to prevent her vengeful husband from then 'disposing ' of
them as he thought fit.

So it was that the four innocents had been wrenched from
their mother and ended up being sent to the New World to
whatever fate awaited them. The four motherless waifs
easily won over Dorothy's affection and, unbegrudged,
occupied most of her time.

To start with the Mayflower made decent headway as
the kindly wind blew and sped them onwards. Although
they had already sailed across the North Sea from Holland
and along the southern coast, and were now clear of Land's
End and out on the more tempestuous Atlantic seas, many
more passengers quickly succumbed to seasickness before
losing their landlubber legs and innards.

During that time, one of the hired hands made those who
were ill already suffer to the limit through his unremittingly
cruel and wicked taunts. He seemed to have taken a
particular hatred to the children on board and seized every
opportunity to make them cry with his dreadful taunts.

"God forgive me!"

Dorothy came across Mary on deck as she sighed.

"I wish no living being harm, but that man, I swear, is the
Devil's own spawn!" she said.

"What is he about now?' Katherine Carver asked
despairingly.

"I found my son Love in a terrible state after that wretch
told him that where we were going, in Virginia, there are
giant cockroaches as big as a man's fist that crawl out of the
ground at night to feed on sleeping children. And, if that
were not bad enough, that there are maggots as big as
earthworms crawling in the sacks of flour in our stores and,
that if Love looked, he would find them baked in his bread
at supper!"

"Oh the wicked man!" Katherine recoiled in horror.

The object of loathing then appeared and Mary took him to task.

"Shame on you!" she exclaimed. "Scaring the little ones out of their wits and making them afraid to eat good food!"

"If you ask me, it ain't worth the bother of feeding these ankle biters at all," he hissed back in a London twang through his rot-blackened teeth. "None of them is gonna to make it to the other side, alive anyway!"

For once Mary Brewster was stunned speechless as the lout continued his abuse.

"Can't you shut that brat up?" He picked next on Sarah Eaton, who was trying to calm her small baby after the shouting had made him cry. "Give it 'ere and I will smother it for you! That should do the trick!" London taunted.

"See me?" he added smugly, turning to the women. "Me, I'm going 'ome again but you lot ain't! Women shouldn't even be on a ship! You're a jinx! And yer men ain't cut out for the sea neither! You's all on a one way trip!" he laughed in their faces. "You's all gonna to die! Might as well pitch the lot of you over the side right now and save the stores! We're casting lots already, me and the lads to see who gets what once you lot 'ave snuffed it." With that, London calmly swaggered off leaving the women silenced in disbelief at his heartlessness.

However, the sailors were not the only thorn in the gentle congregation's side. There were strangers that the Separatists had been duped into sharing the Mayflower with. Most were southerners, merchants and fortune seekers who ridiculed their gentle fellow voyagers for their singsong Midland way of speech and godly manners. Many of the more nobly born of these 'strangers' were every bit as rude and uncouth towards the congregation as the lowest, foul-mouthed crewman, openly mocking the Separatists' style and manner of worship and trying to goad them into open conflict.

Soon the weather began to change and in the following sea, the Mayflower raised a little more fuss as her speed increased.

A leak had sprung in the tiller flat between decks, but the Master assured Carver that there was no need for concern, so long as the weeping stayed at just that. Because of the time lost in Dartmouth and then in Plymouth, the Mayflower was entering the season for storms in the Atlantic and it was not long before she got the full taste of one.

The wind began to freshen from when Dorothy had been up on deck early one morning and the sea had begun to rise. The white caps on the waves had become numerous and some of the crew were starting on plugging the base of the capstan with tallow and caulking to try to stop water getting down between the decks as the weather steadily worsened. By afternoon a heavy swell had started washing over the scuppers and curling the gunwales, and the Master had ordered all passengers below as the gale struck in earnest and started to throw the ship around. The helmsman found it increasingly difficult to hold the ship on course with the sea coming in on her beam. Thankfully, after the lateen yard was lowered and made fast with the topsails taken in, the Mayflower began to settle a little.

However, the sea was heavy and quartering for most of the next three days resulting in a terrible pitching and rolling of the ship. All Dorothy and the others could do was huddle together and pray between bouts of nausea, as they sat out the storm in the gloomy confinement below. This meant that Dorothy could not cook as conditions were too dangerous to use the fireboxes. Besides, many had no appetite for food at all, as no sooner had they consumed it than motion sickness sent it spewing forth again. Instead, bodily needs were sustained by the passing around of platters of dried biscuit and cold, sliced meat.

As many of the Speedwell's stores as it had been possible

to transport between the ships had been squeezed into every conceivable nook of the Mayflower. Therefore standing or walking about during such stormy weather was for safety's sake kept to a minimum, especially after one of the strangers was thrown off his feet by the shift of some crates and knocked senseless after striking his head on a beam. The blood from his scalp wound streamed scarlet ribbons for hours, serving as a grim warning for others to stay put. Space for this human cargo was at a premium, barely six square feet, per family, being the average allocation.

So it was that the pattern for the rest of the voyage for Dorothy and the Separatists was set. Once the first storm had abated there was hardly a day in which the ship was becalmed and there were only brief periods of relatively comfortable weather when Dorothy could snatch a lungful of fresh air up above on deck to sustain her through the dark stretches trapped below as further storms broke over them. Sometimes exceeding a week in duration, these storms caused them to huddle like sheep in their enforced confinement, trying as best as they might to pass the time with the help of prayer and talk of the fine plots of verdant farmland promised them at landfall in Virginia. The thought of this was the prime factor spurring many of them on. The scene was going to be beautiful, so the Virginia Company had assured them. The rich soil of the shires of Lincoln and Nottingham were poor in comparison to that which awaited cultivation on the other side for them. So rich was it, the propaganda claimed, that every seed a man planted there sprang up almost overnight and grew into a magnificent crop, which was a wonder to behold. There were forests with the best standing timber one could hope for, teeming with all kind of game for the taking. The rivers and creeks were awash with good fish, as were the seas off its coast. The living was going to be easy and better than they had ever known, so the test of the transatlantic crossing should be regarded, they agreed, as a small price to pay for such future bounty. Thus they resolutely agreed to endure all that the sea could throw at them, for they trusted in the Lord to see that they would prosper despite their present tribulation.

Mid-morning one day, after the ship had experienced some thirty –six hours of near calm, Dorothy and the others were unexpectedly asked to assemble on deck. The first death of the voyage had occurred and the funeral at sea was about to take place. It had happened very early. The Master had given the order for the main tack to be let down and one of the hands eagerly threw off the starboard clew garnet, sending the turning rope flying into the air. Unbeknown to either Master or hand, at the time, an already ill 'London' was 'at rest' in the coils and it caught him about the neck and strangled the remaining life out of him before he could be cut free.

It was a nasty end to a nasty fellow, Dorothy could not help thinking as the body neatly sewn into its canvas shroud slipped, un-mourned, from its board to be swallowed up by the waiting gape of the cold sea below.

A few days later, when the Master judged them to be about half way across the Atlantic's span, the Mayflower fell foul of the mother of all storms, swaying and pitching, switch-backing up and down the swell and rolling so much that even the most hardened sailors were sick, and again the reluctant passengers were shut in below decks to ride it out. As the mighty sea slammed into the ship, she was viciously shaken to her limit. Then, suddenly Dorothy heard a terrifying, soul- churning crack from somewhere above her. Within minutes, the Mayflower began to take on water in earnest. She watched the commotion going on all around her, followed by a surge of dread as the bo's'un ominously called out for Carver and Brewster to come immediately atop to parley with the Master.

They soon returned, ashen faced and headed straight for the cargo hold. As Carver opened up the trap, rats scurried out from below and ran about the passenger deck sending a frenzy of screams up from the terrified children. In Dorothy's mind there could be no doubt. The Mayflower was sinking...

CHAPTER SIXTEEN

Quickly gathering him up in her arms, Jasper More's tiny fingertips clung like cold limpets to Dorothy's neck as his whimpering siblings, Mary and Richard, grasped at her bedraggled skirts, cowering in fear. Terror, however, soon rendered them mute as the last of the ship's few lanterns were hurriedly snatched away, plunging them into darkness. Vainly Dorothy tried to keep the little ones clutched to her and out of the reach of the freezing fingers of sea slipping through the planks from above. It was impossible. Water was pouring in from every direction as if the ocean was clawing its way in to claim them. With each new sickening heave of the ship, Dorothy and the children were tossed about like limp rag dolls, slithering this way and that across the slippery planking. Each slam of the furious waves groaned and reverberated around the ship until she was certain that the end of life for them all was close by. Yet, strangely unlike those gripped by hysteria around her, she remained remarkably calm. The thought of being drowned no longer harboured any fear. Instead, Dorothy found the prospect strangely liberating, as then this whole dreadful ordeal would be over and she would be reunited with Thomas.

The heart-stopping crack that Dorothy had heard at the height of the latest pounding had been the full force of a colossal wave powering down upon the Mayflower. It had split her main beam asunder. The awful result was that at the forecastle, the most vulnerable part of the ship, there were now unsupported deck planks sagging under the torrent of water that was gushing into the passenger deck and rapidly seeping below. Unless the ship's carpenter could somehow repair this, there was nothing to stop the Mayflower from sinking. If she did, then they would all be drowned like a knotted sack full of blind kittens.

Clawing the children up close to her, Dorothy somehow

managed to brace herself against an upright and then, with her feet, to wedge herself between that and the hull. Thus she was able to witness the drama unfold.

It was a desperate situation, yet, in the midst of that desperation, William Brewster had been struck with a revelation for their salvation.

In the faint arc of light, wildly swinging from across the passenger deck, Dorothy could see his strong broad frame astride the open hatch.

"Quickly!" Brewster called out frantically. "I need volunteers to help me and John below! The screw, men!" he explained, "we can use the screw from my Press!"

Lateral thinking had told Brewster that the giant screw from his beloved, but now dismantled printing press, could be used to jack up the massive beam and buy the carpenter precious time to try to make good a repair. If only they could find it!

Peering down into the blackness Brewster could not possibly have been able to see anything, yet he must have realised that there was precious little time to waste as he and John Carver jumped in.

Without hesitation, Francis Eaton, Miles Standish and William Bradford quickly came forward in response to Brewster's plea. Knowing none of them could swim, Dorothy flinched as she watched them pitch bravely down through the hatch and disappear out of sight.

While the bo's'un and his mate swayed aloft wielding the flickering lanterns, trying to throw down enough precious light to cut through the murk, Dorothy could picture these five men bravely plumbing the cold depths below in a desperate search for Brewster's press. She could hear the clunk and thud from beneath, as now floating barrels in the hold were being thrown together with each lurch of the ship. This continuing shift of the cargo would only serve to make it all the more hazardous to locate the dismantled components. Dorothy's imagination sketched in the fine detail of the commotion coming from below. She could picture this courageous handful floundering in the shadows like beached fish, flipping their arms this way and that, feeling their way through the flooded hold in a frantic fingertip search for the screw. All the while, heavy butts and barrels clashed together, threatening to crush the skull of any man caught betwixt them like a cobnut in a vice. Dorothy sat and watched, suddenly realising that all about her the earlier cries of panic had now hushed into an eerie whisper as the rest of the ship prayed for their lives.

Finally, after what had seemed an age, a shout resounded. "We have it!"

Dorothy saw the hefty screw hauled up from out of the hold and manhandled aft into position beneath the broken oak beam. With hardly a moment to consider success or failure, Brewster set about expanding the screw to jack up the broken beam. As he did so, the Mayflower moaned out loud as the great gaping wound began to close up and the torrent of water to subside. With the beam now supported, but in almost impossible conditions, the ship's carpenter, aided by Frances Eaton, somehow managed to firm it up again with a new supporting post beneath and ad -hoc reinforcements hammered in at either side. To everyone's utter relief it appeared to have worked! For the present, the imminent danger of sinking looked to be past. As for the dislodged decking above, for now it still let some water in but the crew could set about re-caulking it, as best as they could, as soon the storm began to wind down. The question now in everyone's mind was would the repair hold?

Over the coming twelve hours as the storm abated, battered and bruised, the passengers began to recover from their ordeal. Unfortunately, faith in the Mayflower had been sorely tested. Mumblings of concern and misgiving soon cankered their way through the sailors, worm-holing confidence in the ship and her ability to complete the voyage. A few days later they mustered themselves and approached both the Master and Ship's Governor, Carver, to argue that the Mayflower was now un-seaworthy. Forcefully they pressed Master Jones to turn about for England. Dorothy quickly joined with the passengers as the remaining crew too gathered to hang on every word of the heated debate that followed.

"We don t like it Cap'n!" the mouthpiece of the mariners piped up.

"Tell me your grievances," the Master said dispassionately, "and I will hear them out! I promise to give due consideration to whatever anyone has to say before I make my decision firm and commit to the course of action to take."

Dorothy had grown to learn that Master Jones could indeed be expected to do just that. He was a fair and even-tempered man, and she believed he was not about to risk their safety on a whim. She was not alone amongst the passengers on this assumption.

"With all due respect, Cap'n," the seaman continued, "we think we durnst risk going on! For pity's sake, go back Sir! We aren't afeard to work honest for all that our wages demand, but we are afeared now that we be recklessly hazarding our lives by proceeding with a craft so much depleted in its seaworthiness!"

A undertone of agreement droned forth from his cohorts.

"Her's never gonna be able to perform as well! Not after all this! And her's a cow to sail at the best of times!" shouted one of his more vocal supporters from the disgruntled rank.

"I understand your concerns," the Master replied, "and I am likewise not willing to put my life, nor my craft, at peril for the sake of a wage!"

The crew cheered, believing they had won their point, but the decision was not to go their way.

"However,' Master Jones briskly continued, "if I break this contract and on inspection, the Virginia Company deem that we have acted too rashly in turning back, then we can all kiss our wages goodbye. We will have earned nothing and all this hardship will have been suffered for naught!" he warned solemnly.

And what of the congregation, Dorothy thought to herself? Where would that leave them if the ship turned about? Therefore, it was with the deepest reservations that she followed the rest of the argument intently.

"But the caulking won't hold if her timbers move again!' another crewman protested loudly in response.

"Perhaps not, for I too expect her to spring leaks where her planking was stretched if we hit inclement waters once more! But t'will be only superficial, I am certain, and can be much prevented if we do not press the old girl with too much sail!"

The Master's Mate, Robert Coppin, a much-respected mariner of the Atlantic, stepped forward and asked permission to speak.

"Down below," he told the gathering, "I have inspected the ship and I swear to you that she is sound!"

"And surely," Master Jones interjected, "that is what really matters! Not that she may weep at a storm, for she's only a female after all!" he joked reassuringly. "The bilge pumps will soon shift the water from her petticoats!"

These words seemed to settle his men down again, for if Master Jones owned but one thing of value above all else, it was the respect of his men; they knew him to be a fair man and a good, honest Ship's Master.

"Having taken full review of the repairs, "Master Jones continued, "and in consideration of our being near half way over the Atlantic, I am of sound persuasion that this ship is well capable of continuing on to the New World and with no greater risk than in turning back. I propose we go on, unless of course," he turned towards John Carver, "the Governor here presses me also to turn back. For then I will be absolved of my obligation to the contract."

Dorothy thought it a well-put proposal by the Master and

was relieved that both Separatists and Strangers alike rallied behind Carver, unanimously agreeing with him that the Mayflower should continue to make her way over to Virginia.

***

Dorothy and the others grew to realise that Master Jones's faith in the Mayflower was well placed, for although they did pass through several more bouts of truculent weather, the courageous craft held her own. Some of the gales lasted several days and were so bad that Master Jones saw fit to lower the sails and let the ship drift with the will of the waves. She found these the hardest times of all. Able to do little more than to sit in her allotted space and try not to be sick, time cruelly taunted her. She came to dread these voids, when bleak thoughts and regrets filled her mind. She soon found grief welling up again and threatening to drown her in sorrow. Although she was so newly widowed and this was when she needed it most, the comfort of seeing Thomas's face once more, if only in her mind's eye, cruelly eluded her. It was as if he was slipping away from her daily by degrees, just as the Mayflower was from her course. Then at other times, she found herself wallowing in deep remorse at her own shortcomings. Ashamed, Dorothy looked at the children and realised how selfish she had been in wishing that the ship should have sunk. At over thirty, she had had a life, but they? They had hardly begun to live. What right had she to have tried to wish it away from them? Slowly but surely, she resolved she was not to give in to this depression. Instead, she would fight for survival.

Having narrowly escaped sinking, shut in below in near darkness, battered from all sides with their fate firmly cast to the sea, Dorothy thought circumstances incapable of throwing up any further situation more desperate than those they had already faced up to. How wrong she would prove to be.

"Lord have mercy on us!" Mary Brewster picked her way across the deck on hands and knees to the Carvers' berth. "Katherine!" she cried agitatedly, "it's Lizzie Hopkins! Lord help us, but she's gone into labour!"

"But she can't be," Katherine Carver replied. "She said January! That's more than two months away!"

"Well you try telling that to her baby!" Mary replied. "Her husband says she had such a griping upon her and sickness that he thought it only down to the motion of the ship. But then, when she begged him to come get another woman to her aid, he came and fetched me. Her bedding is soaked, and the stench of ammonia is everywhere! It's her waters gone, I am certain! After so many children of my own, I'd recognize that smell anywhere!"

"What can I do?" Katherine asked apprehensively, for she had no stomach for this herself.

Mary turned and looked towards the Carvers' maidservant.

"Let me take Dorothy for a while?" she pleaded. "There's naught but silly girls spare, else! You know yourself, what a good nurse she is!"

Katherine nodded in agreement.

"Dorothy, will you come? Help me assist with the birth?"

"Of course I will!" Dorothy replied.

The two women scrabbled back across the floor, weaving in and out of prostrate bodies and splayed limbs, crawling through filth and mess to reach the meanly curtained off nook where Lizzie was well advanced towards giving birth.

"Let us see how far along you are, my duck!" Mary knelt in front of propped up Lizzie, carefully lifted her skirts and gestured to her to part her knees."

"It wont be long, Lizzie!" she reported. "You are well on the way to being open and I can just about see the crown of the little one's head!"

"But it hurts so!" Elizabeth Hopkins gasped, "so much more than the first time!"

"Oh. I know dear," Mary reassured her, "but no two labours are ever the same! Believe me! Mayhap," Mary suggested, "this baby is just a bit bigger than the last. Perhaps it's a little brother for darling Damaris here!" she said, smiling at the babe blissfully asleep at her side in the capable arms of Lizzie's stepdaughter, Constance.

"Maybe it's time now," Mary tactfully suggested, "for her father to take her away from here for a bit. Eh Stephen? This is no place for a man to be now, is it?"

Steven Hopkins leaned over, kissed his wife tenderly and took Constance and the baby to wait out the delivery with a nearby family.

Elizabeth's contractions continued apace, ever strengthening but with apparently little passage of the baby. Dorothy noted Mistress Brewster's growing concern and so went to the sailors and managed to beg a ship's lantern. She placed it close so Mary could inspect Lizzie, below, once more.

"Oh my!" mother Brewster whispered quietly to her companion so as not to frighten their patient. "I see what the matter is now! Look!" she said. "Dorothy, look at the head."

Dorothy leaned in toward Lizzie and peered carefully. "I can see it, "she said "but it's very smooth. Shouldn't it have some hair, at least?"

"Exactly what I was thinking?" Mary replied. "In fact I don't think that's its head at all, more like his rump or a shoulder!"

Just then, Lizzie was gripped by another contraction.

"Don't push my dear," Mary warned."Pant my darling, but whatever you do, don't push, Make her pant Dorothy, while I fetch surgeon Fuller! Make her pant through the pain like this - Huh! Huh! Huh!" she huffed. "I will be as quick as I can!"

With that, Mary scrambled away to fetch Doctor Fuller.

"It's alright," Dorothy said, squeezing Elizabeth's hand

tightly. "Pant! Come on, good girl. Pant with me. Huh! Huh!"

A bewildered Lizzie complied.

Thankfully, Samuel Fuller was close by.

"Ah!" he said with genuine concern, "you are right, my dear ladies! The child is a bad breech and cannot be delivered like this!"

"What can we do?" Mary exclaimed with concern.

"Very little I fear. Normally in a case like this I would consider, as a last resort, cutting the perineum, here," he said making an incision-like gesture with his pointed finger. "But in this light and with the pitching of the ship? I dare not!"

"Then what?" Mary Brewster asked worriedly.

"There's very little, I am afraid, that I can do, "he sighed, "except to pray that the baby turns itself about!"

"Wait," Dorothy said. "Can we not turn the baby? I know the same happened with Lady Hickman at The Old Hall and her child was delivered safely!"

"Turn it? Yes, that is certainly a possibility! But it's a difficult manoeuvre and my hands are too big to assist internally."

"And mine too arthritic," said Mary quickly.

"But I could try," said Dorothy. "I wasn't there myself as her Ladyship's son was delivered, but I heard every minute detail of it from another maid who was. She told me how one of the midwives pushed the child back up into the birth passage and eased it across with the tips of her fingers, while the other cajoled it to move from the outside, with her hands pressed firmly on the mother's belly."

Lizzie shrieked loudly as another strong contraction started to grip her. Her face grimaced in fear as she realized how serious her predicament now was.

"Yes," Doctor Fuller said, looking at the desperate mother. "It's worth a try! Let's do it! If you try to move it across from below, I can try assisting with my hands on her abdomen.

We have nothing to lose! Be brave Mistress Hopkins," he urged. "This may be very painful indeed but we will do everything we can for you and the baby!"

"But which direction?" Dorothy pressed with renewed urgency, "which way should I turn it?"

"To your right," he replied, "we should both try to persuade it to the right and hope that this moves the head downwards and not his feet. But in any case we need to get the mite out one way or another, or lose it and the mother, else!"

Dorothy kept calm and did exactly as he directed, while Mary tried as best she could to comfort Lizzie through her ordeal.

After what seemed a dozen or so more contractions and with the mother totally exhausted, Doctor Fuller suddenly recoiled in delight as the mother's swollen abdomen surged with a frenzied rippling of activity as the outline of limbs clearly moved below the skin. Then Dorothy suddenly felt a mat of warm hair wet against her hand.

"It's here, I am certain this is the head!"

Samuel Fuller quickly checked.

"Yes! Yes! Thank the Lord, you are right!"

"You hear that Lizzie, do you hear?" Mary Brewster urged the weakened woman on. "You must try now my dear and push with all your might as soon as the next contraction comes."

Somehow Elizabeth rallied and within moments it was all over. A small baby boy, later named Oceanus, was delivered into this world alive.

During these hours while attending Mistress Hopkins, Dorothy was to learn that another desperate episode had been played out, unnoticed, up above their heads. The Carvers' young manservant, John Howland, had finally been completely overwhelmed by the claustrophobic conditions there. As fear and tension fast became too much for him to endure, he lost his senses and became resolved that somehow he had to escape from it all. Even if it meant risking his life.

Apparently, he rushed past the mariners, also holed up below for the duration, and made for the open deck. On seeing him, a couple of mindful sailors made after him, only to witness the ship suddenly pitch and watch helplessly as the youth was swept overboard by a wave and swallowed up by the yawning sea. However, by some unfathomable fluke, Howland had managed to grab hold of the topsail halyards as they too ran out overboard and disappeared under the water. He continued to hang on to them as, unimaginably, he resurfaced with the next surge of the waves and the sailors managed then to haul him back on board with boat hooks and drag the sodden wretch back down below decks.

"How he was not drowned, Lord knows!' Katherine related the tale. "Though my husband jested that mayhap he was so useless a servant that even the sea didn't want him!"

Yet despite this episode of good fortune, Dorothy still found herself fearing for the worst and so she was not surprised when fate finally claimed its price. The good doctor's own manservant, the mischievous youth, William Butten, fell ill beyond his master's skill and died. Up until that point, all things considered, it seemed the price for the passengers had been set remarkably cheap.

**

At daybreak a few days later, a watery sun struggled forth from the bleak November night to herald a sunrise that would never dim from their memories. Dawn broke to an unrestrained chorus of shouts of joy and relief, as high land was spotted just above the misty horizon. Quickly the passengers and crew scurried on deck to get the first glimpse of this beautiful sight. The Mayflower had reached the New World at last!

However, Dorothy soon noted a great deliberation amongst the crew as to where exactly they were now. They knew, certainly, they must be off their intended course by some margin after all the turbulent weather of late. After much discourse between Master Jones and Hopkins and those mariners who had previously crossed the Atlantic, it was conceded they were probably lying well north of their intention and lying off a place known as Cape Cod, with the mouth of the great Hudson River lying somewhere to the south.

With the weather being fairish, the Master decided to tack the Mayflower about, with the intent of heading on into the mouth of the Hudson and up it until they found a good place fit for habitation. Yet, after struggling for more than half a day against an impossibly strong headwind, dangerous shallows and roaring breakers, Jones and his crew reluctantly abandoned this attempt and instead headed into safer waters before nightfall. Finally they lay at anchor and in relative peace and that night they praised their God for their deliverance from sixty –five days on the sea, knowing the worst for them was now over.

As the following morning broke in Cape Harbour, Dorothy saw the joyous mood of the company soon sober as they gathered on deck and realized they were pitched up on an inhospitable looking coastline, far beyond any friendly habitation. This was not what they had bargained for. This was not Virginia. After such a perilous journey, there was no one to greet them, to offer them shelter or help tide them over until they could become established. Worse still, they were without the Speedwell, which they had originally purchased with the intention of sending out to reconnoitre for other settlements should this very situation have happened.

Though Dorothy and the other women had chivvied each other along throughout the most despondent days of their voyage with thoughts of how all would be well once land was sighted, now it had been, it offered them little consolation. The landscape they were now forlornly looking out on was windswept, poor and inhospitable. This savage, winter-ravaged panorama was far removed from the verdant land they had been promised in this, their newly gained Eden.

"Oh Thomas!" Dorothy cried to herself. "Is this it? Is this what you gave up our lives for?"

Her peasant- born eye saw in an instant, that this was no land fit for farming. Thickets, though bountiful, would not see a single starving belly through the icy mantle of winter already closing in around them. There was no great forest to provide the timber for the building of homesteads; no sight of the promised sweeps of game running wild to either feed or benefit them from the lucrative trading of their fur. Though there were sea birds aplenty.

Although their menfolk addressed the situation with cheerful bravado and bold talk of expeditions to be made inland, they could not dispel the utter, wretched disappointment now haunting every woman aboard. They had trusted their menfolk; they had followed faithfully and in return been led to this. Deeply dissillusioned, Dorothy now stood huddled with her sisters as they openly wept, grieving for the homes, lives and the loved ones they had left so far behind.

However, it soon became clear to Dorothy that this disillusionment was not confined to the women alone. She noted disconcertedly that men too were soon taking to shedding tears, seemingly stricken down by some all-enveloping melancholia, which far exceeded anything any aboard had ever experienced before. To Dorothy it was as if some sinister, alien entity had been eating its way through each and every soul. She did not know how close she was to the truth, for a deadly, unnamed and as yet unrecognised enemy was festering away, unchecked within them all.

Uncharacteristically, Master Jones, who Dorothy liked and

had witnessed being so even-handed in his dealings up until now, was suddenly pressing as fiercely as his crew for the passengers to be put ashore as quickly as possible with their belongings, so that the Mayflower could be gone and on her way home.

"I have had to put up with far more than I bargained for!" Dorothy heard him snarl during an animated discourse with Governor Carver and William Brewster. "I have had much to suffer too, and I fear delaying in this accursed place for a moment longer than I can help it!"

She thought how unlike him his present demeanour was.

Carver was sympathetic to the fact that Jones had taken on the contract to bring out the Mayflower on the strict understanding that there would be a lucrative cargo to bring home for a profit and plentiful stores to re-supply the ship. However, both sides could plainly see neither for him here. Jones and his men would be lucky to find fresh water ashore to fill the barrels and maybe catch some fish to supplement the crew's meagre supplies; otherwise, they would have to face the mercy of the sea on the homeward voyage with only the reserves they had put aside out of the remaining limited stores.

From her regular cooking duties, Dorothy knew only too well the state of the rations. The original provisioning at Southampton in the summer should have been more than enough to last out the voyage and well beyond. Besides, they had intended to make land long before winter set in. However, there had been the unforeseen delays with trying to patch up the Speedwell and then the much longer crossing than expected. There had been too little fresh fruit and much of the fresh vegetables had either been consumed or had perished before they had even left Plymouth. The green cabbages, though brightly leafed when brought aboard, had not bulked up to maturity by then and soon yellowed and slimed to an inedible state. The turnips, parsnips and onions from the root store were mostly last season's with those from this current year, again being wanting in maturity. They had purchased plenty of cheese and butter, smoked beef and pork but also a good proportion of these and other more 'popular' foodstuffs had been sold off again to pay for the extra harbour duties and repairs. In short, what they had was running out and mostly past its best.

The longer the passengers now remained here, then the less food there would be to go round. In all, it would appear a sorry prospect and Dorothy could see Master Jones's point.

"You press us Master Jones!" William Brewster vehemently argued their case, "knowing, full well, we have nothing and no one ashore to sustain us?"

John Carver stepped in to staunch the flow of hot words he suspected were about to flood out between the two men.

"Master Jones," he said calmly. "I fully understand your predicament, but I beseech you to look about and appreciate ours! The winter here is already biting, and without proper shelter if you cast us ashore then none of us hold much hope for survival. Would the Company condone such an action that condemned their heavy investment in us to death? None of this is either of our making or yours, but fate's alone. Now the cards are dealt and the die is cast, we have no other choice, surely, than to try to make the best hand for us all."

My God! Dorothy thought to herself, surely Master Jones is not seriously proposing to put us all ashore.

"Of course I won't leave you to die!" Master Jones replied coolly. "But what of my responsibility to my men? We cannot stay here, at anchor, indefinitely! Neither can we survive very long on the scant victuals left aboard. Some progress has to be made, and made soon, or I may indeed be forced into that which I would rather not contemplate."

"Nor do we plan to sit idle!" John Carver assured him. "We are agreed on a plan to make a foray ashore, just as soon as our shallop can be bought up from the hold to be reassembled and trimmed for our safe use. Then we will find a suitable site for a settlement as quickly as God will allow and be, at one stroke, out of your care and into His!"

Dorothy could not understand the Master's increasing hostility; however she still knew that John Carver would be as good as his word. But although he set the carpenters immediately to the task of readying the Separatists' modest craft for exploration ashore, it was still not quick enough for an increasingly impatient and unreasonable Jones. So, without waiting for the shallop to be ready and with the Mayflower in as shallow water as she dare, sixteen volunteers made their way ashore though the freezing water on a reconnaissance mission, by land instead. Although well armed and under the able leadership of their own seasoned military man, Miles Standish, Dorothy and the others realised just how dangerous a foray this could be. Especially if it were discovered that these shores were not as deserted as they first thought.

***

Dorothy sat and occupied sickly young Jasper, listening quietly as John Carver related his experience ashore to his wife.

"What are they, husband?" Katherine Carver asked, rolling the strange kernels in the palm of her hand and noting their hardness, "are they some kind of beads?"

"No! They are a kind of corn, so Steven Hopkins informs us," John Carver explained, "grown by the savages here about. Luckily Hopkins has been to the Americas before and is quite knowledgeable of them."

"Savages?" Katherine seemed quite surprised.

"Yes, there are the native peoples here. We came across some not long after wading ashore. Five or six of them, tall fellows coming towards us with a dog, but when they got near enough to make us out as strangers to this land, they ran off."

"Did you go after them?" she asked.

"Yes, but we lost them," John replied exasperatedly. "We kept trying to track them but they were like roe deer, once spooked they scattered to the woodland and were as good as invisible."

"And this corn? How did you come upon this?" Dorothy's mistress asked.

"It was when we returned to our original plan to investigate this so called river we had spotted. We found a fresh water pond and a large area of land cleared and recently cultivated. There were fields where a crop of sorts had been harvested and when we excavated a trench of newly dug sand we found a cache of this corn buried there in baskets."

"Is it a good place for us too?"

"It's a start, my dear. We found good harbourage for our shallop, but that is all for we dared not stay any longer this trip. We need our boat repaired before we dare return for another reconnaissance. But how have things been here?"

"Bearable, husband, but that is as far as I can say. Dorothy here, has been a godsend as usual, not only to us and with the care of the children but to poor Mistress Bradford too."

"Why, what has been the matter with her?"

"Oh, I really do not know but both Dorothy and I are deeply concerned for her state of mind. It seems more than just homesickness and a pining for her child left behind. I fear it is a deep depression that is crushing her mind and her health is in spiralling decline too. She has bruises and bleeds in her hair when Dorothy brushes it out, and she has taken to such bouts of crying as is so distressing for any of us here that try to comfort her. Perhaps she will be a little better now William is aboard again. They seem so happy together."

"Yes, pray God that he sets her poor troubled heart to rest!" John replied with deep concern.

"Yet, husband," Katherine continued, "there is a strange

atmosphere aboard nowadays, not just confined to Dorothy-May Bradford! Such an aura of foreboding is about this ship of late, and I cannot quite lay my finger upon what lies at its root of it all! I have the deepest misgivings that something is amiss in the minds of many around us. So many are complaining of lameness and sores and unexplained injuries similar to Dorothy-May. And I have an ulcer in my mouth that sore vexes me whenever I attempt to eat."

"Well, perhaps some of this might help," John said drawing, a crumpled spray of wilting vegetation from inside his leather pouch and giving it to his wife. "It is grass for an infusion!" he explained. "Both Steven Hopkins and Robert Coppin are seasoned mariners and have journeyed to America before. Both swear by it as a restorative after a long sea voyage, so we have all been supping it ashore and I have to admit, I feel much the better for it! We all need to get away from this ship," he added, "and into homes ashore as quickly as possible. If the weather holds out that's exactly what we intend to do, so don't worry, my dear! All will be well."

Dorothy was much relieved to hear John Carver pledge to his wife that an expedition would again shortly go ashore, and not return this time without having first found a firm site for a permanent settlement.

***

Waves gently lapping against the hull of the ship had long since lulled all below into an impenetrable slumber several nights later. All, that is, apart from one restless soul.

Dorothy had seen Mistress Bradford get up and make towards the steps up to the open deck above, and assumed that the sleepless woman was heading up to use the beak. She will catch her death, Dorothy thought, going aloft in just her frock! Pulling her wool blanket up about her shoulders, Dorothy slipped on her shoes and crept over to

Mistress Bradford's bed. She snatched the young woman's heavy shawl and followed her up the steps to find her.

Atop, it was cold. Eerily cold and silent, with the sky draped above like an ebony blanket sewn with a million bright diamonds. Amid them, the moon shone out like a candle flame shrouded in delicate gauze. Crystals of glistening ice had stiffened the furled sheets and silenced them to the bare, skeletal masts. The solitary figure of Dorothy-May Bradford stood like a pale, willowy spectre, alone in the moonlight, high up on the forecastle.

"Mistress Bradford!" Dorothy called out softly.

There came no reply. Instead Dorothy-May just stood motionless, with the cold air biting at her delicate face. Her staring eyes appeared fixed somewhere in the far distance.

Dorothy called out her name again as she approached up the steps.

This time Dorothy-May turned and looked her full in the face.

"Why! You are half frozen!" Dorothy exclaimed as she rubbed Mistress Bradford's corpse-cold hands. Then quickly she threw the shawl around her delicate shoulders and snugly wrapped it round her body. Dorothy-May seemed strangely oblivious to this kindness. Oblivious even to the fact that she was so dreadfully cold.

"Try as I might," she then explained quite calmly to Dorothy. "I struggle in vain each day to picture my little boy's smile!"

Dorothy soon realised that Mistress Bradford's thoughts were drawn, as was her face, to her little boy so far across the distant ocean.

"On a good day I can almost smell his soft curls and taste his baby sweet skin," she sighed, "but I just can't see his face anymore."

Dorothy felt for her. She knew what this was like.

A muted cry in the distance scarcely broke the silence, yet instantly drew Dorothy's attention. It was the drawn out, muffled howl of some tortured creature upon the savage shore. Dorothy thought of William Bradford and the rest of the party on land searching for the right place to settle. She stopped and prayed, silently, for their safety. Prayed that they lay secure behind some crudely-fashioned shelter, with a bright fire and God posted as their sentinel.

Dorothy shivered.

"Mistress, it's so cold!" she said. "Can we not make our way down and out of this bitterness?"

Dorothy–May nodded in agreement and seemed to be following Dorothy's lead back down the steps and across the deeply iced deck. Only, as Dorothy turned her back to walk on, she suddenly heard an ominous splash. Then….silence.

The shore party returned in triumph next day, relieved and excited to report that they had at last found a site to start building their new lives. The jubilation however was cut cruelly short.

Dorothy could not bear it when William Bradford was told how Dorothy-May had been found dead; face down in the bitter water, after having come so far with him on God's journey.

"Why me, Lord? Why me?" he cried out in anguish. For him there seemed no rhyme or reason, no justice in why his beloved should be taken now. Yet no loss truly comes without a reason, for all is part of a greater plan. Perhaps had he not been tempered by this early grief now visited upon him, in the cruel weeks and months that followed he might have equally cried, "Why not me?"

Shortly he would find the roles reversed. The unenviable task of trying to give succour and comfort over the loss of a loved one would soon fall to him. Many of those now gathered around him offering their deepest condolences would shortly themselves be in mourning. For while William had just lost his loved one, others were about to lose theirs...

Chapter Seventeen

'The plague of the sea' and the 'spoyle of mariners' is how it had come to be called.

It usually started to raise its ugly head after a month or two at sea, by inflicting nothing more sinister than a loss of appetite for food. Hardly surprising, one might think, after the fresh stores have dwindled down and the monotony of an unappetizing ship's diet takes hold. Then, one has to take into account the circumstances in which one is made accustomed to dine. Sat crossed legged, down on the floor, with head and shoulders stooped over a slopping bowl of something barely recognizable as a meal, while above and around the storm howls and all is in shift, especially the intestines of others.

After being shut in below for days on end in the dank and dark, then who would pay much heed to the fact that many of their companions were beginning to suffer with peevishness, or that tempers became short and some turned on each other at the slightest excuse. So many symptoms lost in the general day-to-day struggle of survival had simply become part of life for the Mayflower passengers to endure. Even the bouts of feverishness when they came, and the pain, the tenderness and swelling in the long bones that many now suffered, were all blamed on long cramped hours of restricted movement and lack of real exercise. Who could expect to feel less? Besides, nobody doubted that once arrived in Virginia and able to walk abroad in the sunlight once more on firm green land, then all these bone aches and ailments would quickly disappear of their own accord.

A little more difficult to explain though, were the rashes of bruises, the haemorrhaging and over bleeding from the slightest knocks or cuts. Then there was the plague of teeth that unexpectedly loosened or fell out. Yet again, on reflection, the decks were cramped with goods and personal belongings stored wherever they could be shoehorned in.

In the storms they fell, or shifted and almost everyone aboard had suffered some sort of tripping, falling, or bumping accident at some point or another. It was a minute-by-minute hazard!

Then again there were those curious niggling nuisances, reported mainly by the women and girls aboard, of bleeding scabs at the roots of their hair that streaked their brush bristles red each night as they teased out tangles and knots. Nagging irritation from itchy patches of rough red skin and cotton spots blemishing their pale faces. Chapped, angry looking washday hands that actually longed for the luxury of being able to soak in some laundry now.

Later in the voyage, coughs began to take hold and lungs wheezed trying to snatch in short choking breaths of the already putrid air. Eyes became uncomfortably dry and mouths cracked or ulcerated.

At the very same time as the scourge of this unseen visitation was increasing in severity, so too were the conditions aboard this aging hulk deteriorating. Sleeping on bedding damp from the leaks brought about by the storms could not be good for anyone's health, so when the little ones started with feverish coughs and colds their lethargy was met with motherly concern but not alarm.

Yet Katherine Carver, as almost a throwaway remark during that one simple discourse with her husband John over the corn had almost set her finger on it, for she had momentarily glimpsed the overview, astutely observed the change of the mood on board and raised her concerns for poor Dorothy-May's state of mind, only to let it then slip away. If only she had known how important those observations might have proved to be.

Yet, as the men regularly formed into work parties ashore, and often returned with newfound vigour, the false assumption that this must hold the sole explanation for their ills gained credence. Then surely this was all it could be. If so, then once also ashore, the rest of the passengers could be expected to soon pick up too.

In the meantime, for the majority, overwhelmingly women and children, their confinement aboard ship was entering into its fourth month. It was around this time that the terrible toll in death began to steadily rise. For if no one on board the Mayflower had recognized the dreadful ill that was already at large and seriously undermining their health, how could they understand its cause, let alone be expected to affect a cure? Scurvy, at best leaves one weakened to other infections coming in. At worst, if left untreated, it is fatal.

***

The Mayflower had shifted position several times since her first arrival in Cape Cod. Finally, she now lay at anchor more than a nautical mile out to sea. It was as close to shore as she dare get for fear of a lack of depth for her draught, but the Separatists' shallop proved ideal to explore the shallow bays and inlets where this ex-cargo ship could not go. Instead, the Mayflower lay up in tender watch like a mother duck anxiously watching her brood explore.

On a morning four and a half months after they had made landfall, Dorothy huddled her body under a tarpaulin in the little open boat, but with her wide-eyed face open to the elements, droplets of sea spray soon ran down her cheeks like fine morning dew. It was a sight like no other Dorothy had ever seen. The shallows were one large, heaving, frenzy of bird life, both on the water and sweeping across the low mackerel grey sky above. As the shallop's bow struggled to cut a swathe through the countless thousands of seafowl bobbing on the surface of the waves, Dorothy felt an almost irresistible urge to lean over the side and pluck one from the water, simply because she could. Fast approaching the shore, she could smell the overpowering fusion of every minute essence that combines to make up firm land. The New World smelt so good.

The shoreline here was so different to that other desolate one with its rolling dunes that had saddened their weary eyes at first. Beyond the beach, dense, dark forest towered with tall cedars, pines, spruce, maples, elms, ashes and oaks. There would be no shortage of building timber here or of dead wood for fuelling fires. Many of the trees looked very familiar to Dorothy, yet the tree line was not quite the same as any forest she had ever seen in England. In fact, Dorothy soon discovered that this would set the pattern for life ashore; there would be so many familiar looking things, yet none of them quite the same as their equivalents back home. These subtle differences at times served as comforters to ease the settlers' homesickness while at others it made them keenly aware that they were in unfamiliar territory and so pine for England even more.

As the boat drew nearer, Dorothy saw this forest was not as impenetrable as she had first assumed. For here and there were a few open patches that had obviously been laboriously cleared by someone before and used for cultivation.

"Indians?" Dorothy thought. "We are building our new settlement on some one else's hard–gained farmstead. Surely that can't be right?"

Once arrived, the men seemed so absorbed in the melee of getting weapons, tools and supplies ashore, that they seemed almost to have forgotten about the three women aboard. As Dorothy and the others pushed aside their protective covering and made to disembark themselves, Miles Standish, gallant as ever, stepped in to lend a hand. Standing upon a flat stone in the shallows that the men had already adopted as a mid-tide landing stage, he scooped Dorothy out of the boat and waded ashore with her safe in his arms.

"Welcome to America!" he said warmly, as he stood her down on the sand.

Dorothy immediately swayed unsteadily. Her legs felt as

thought they were no longer part of her own body and were about to give way.

"There, Mistress Dorothy!" Miles proffered a steadying hand and added with a weary yet still rakish smile, "hold still for a moment until you get a feel for it again! You will soon become reacquainted with terra firma, I assure you!" he laughed.

Although quite short in stature, Dorothy could readily understand why Captain Standish had courted such admiration amongst the women on board, although he was not always so popular with the shore party now working to construct a settlement under his leadership. Standish liked things done in a military fashion and on the occasions when he forgot he was no longer in command of soldiers but instead men of free will, hot words sometimes flared from the ranks.

Miles was right though about adapting quickly from so long a time at sea, although Dorothy could not refrain from walking with a pronounced starboard tilt for quite a little time after.

"Odd feeling, isn't it?" exclaimed a rather plump Alice Mullins, as she too was ferried ashore in an equally gentlemanly fashion, "to be here on dry land again after all this time?"

"Yes!" Dorothy replied with a smile, "but it's a very nice feeling all the same."

The two seasoned women cast their eyes about the foreshore as they waited for Alice's adolescent daughter, Pricilla, to be bought from the shallop. The beach looked relatively flat and was growing all the time as the placid waves steadily retreated. Above, as the higher ground rose away inland, much progress looked to have been made in the weeks since the men had started building in earnest, even though the weather had been quite inclement at times with a fall of snow that mercifully had not lingered. In fact, the temperature seemed warmer than she had been used to in Lincolnshire for that time of year. However, despite their sterling efforts, the men had faced a cruel setback and suffered a fire in the partly built common house, which had destroyed its thatched roof. Thankfully, though, it had been spotted quickly and the burning thatching tossed off with pitchforks before the whole building was wrecked.

"It don't look so bad as it does from the ship, do it?" Alice remarked with an air of optimism. "Not so inhospitable looking once you are actually here! Mind you, that wind is surely chilly!"

Alice was right to Dorothy's way of thinking; it looked a lot more inviting close up.

"It's winter! Winter always makes things look bleaker than they really are,' she noted thoughtfully. "I expect this place is quite different come the summer."

Two of the hired hands proceeded to haul three huge canvas bundles of laundry ashore, for this was no pleasure trip for the women, indeed not for anyone taking up precious space upon the little boat on its trips ashore. There was far too much to be done to be indulging in such trifles as mere sightseeing. The three were here to work.

Under the watchful gaze of an armed sentinel, Dorothy and her companions soon set about untying the bundles of soiled bedding and such and then sorting them out into piles on the beach. Just a little higher up one of these same hands had set to, helpfully rigging up lines for the women to dry their laundry on.

"Ooh, the stench from this," young Pricilla shrieked, recoiling in disgust as the second bundle was opened upon the ground.

It was indeed overpowering, unpleasant, yet someone able bodied had to attend to this odious task for those too desperately ill to 'do for themselves' on board.

"Oh don't take on so!" her mother said, trying to make light in an effort to lift the grim task along, "be thankful it's not you who has been taken so ill!"

"Yes, thank God!" Dorothy thought silently to herself.

Dorothy found Alice Mullins a relatively easy woman to get along with, although she got the impression that as a southerner and a 'Stranger', she sometimes looked down a little on Dorothy and her Separatist companions as 'yokels'. She was somewhere in her forties and although her husband had worked his way up in the world to a position of comparative wealth, Alice Mullins remained very down to earth in her manners. Her daughter Pricilla, despite her reaction was very much like her mother in temperament. In all, quite a level-headed girl for almost eighteen years old.

Then again, Dorothy had observed, the ordeals of this voyage had brought about a certain enforced maturity to many of the young girls aboard. It could not have been easy for them to have embarked upon this adventure along with their fit, healthy young peers, fired with such youthful hopes and excited anticipation and then in so short a passage of time, to find themselves as helpless witnesses as many of these same bright things were condemned to the darkness, snuffed out like wax candles in their midst.

The three women discreetly discarded their woollen stockings and gathering up the hems of their heavy outer skirts, hitched them securely at either side of their waists. Then they were down to work, carrying the first pile of less heavily soiled bedding across to a small rock pool to wash through. The water looked freezing and indeed was a shock to the senses, but they soon warmed to the task in hand and shaking off the cold, in no time at all they had worked their way through the first bundle and were carrying the wet bedding up to the lines to hang up in the breeze to dry.

The more badly soiled of the blankets had been cast aside to form another pile. For these, the women decided the best course of action would be to drag them down into the sea and weigh them down with heavy boulders. Then they could let the action of the waves break down the heavy particles stubbornly adhered to the rough woollen weave. While the sea did its work, this left their red-chapped hands free to continue with the next 'load'.

Alice's cold-numbed fingers fiddled at the knots on the third bundle as Dorothy and Pricilla pegged out the last of the blankets from the rock pool to dry. Just as they came over to help, it fell open, sending clothing tumbling out over the sand. The women stared down in silent contemplation as the fragility of their situation struck home once more. Much of it was instantly recognizable as having once belonged to many of the souls who had already died aboard ship.

Glancing up towards Dorothy, Mistress Mullins said mournfully, "Do you think the worst of it is over now? The deaths, I mean? Do you think this is it now?"

Dorothy hesitated before answering.

"I don't know,' she replied a little unconvincingly. She wanted to be truthful but dared not give vent aloud to the grave fears she harboured about their true situation. "There are still one or two who are giving cause for concern. Still some very weak and with little sign of improvement yet."

As Dorothy spoke, Alice came across a small pair of green breeches entangled with a child's kerchief. Dorothy knew them in a heartbeat and tried hard not to break down into tears. A lump rose in her throat and she stifled her anguish as she remembered watching helplessly, as little Jasper More slipped away in a distraught Katherine Carver's arms. It had been Dorothy who had gently eased off his clothes after death. She who had lovingly performed the last offices of washing down and laying out his little emaciated body. Just as it had been she who had attended to the stillborn baby that had slithered, lifeless, from Mary Allerton's labour and she who had tenderly 'dealt with' the tiny corpse after.

"Some of the children look so thin and drawn," Alice ploughed on with the conversation without even considering the deep furrow cut through Dorothy's emotions. "Especially the three little Mores since that brother of theirs passed away. It's always hard when little ones pass, "she sighed. "Don't seem right somehow does it, that they should be the ones to get cut down, so often afore they've even had time to sprout?"

Alice paused for a scant moment's reflection then continued.

"My husband overheard Doctor Fuller saying how it must be all the bad miasma aboard that's to blame for so many different ailments. For he says it is curious how the men who have been ashore are much improved in their general condition. That's why I volunteered to be on laundry duty. I said to my man, 'I don't mind washing sick people's filth just so long as I can get ashore so I don't take ill as well!' So I am certain I shall not succumb to it now, yet I do feel sorry for those too weak to come too. Those who cannot get up and do for themselves. Still," she said, sighing yet again, "I suppose I should be thankful for that or I wouldn't be here myself ashore. I expect the worst is over now as it seems to have taken the weak, which is only to be expected in any winter."

Dorothy picked over the remnants of Alice's words. Jasper certainly was only a child, who though spirited always appeared less than robust in health. James Chilton had been the oldest man aboard and might well have been expected to succumb to winter illness whether here on the Mayflower or back in the old country, but that didn't explain the others. Certainly they were sorely weakened by the final stages of whatever it was that had ailed them, but even before this recent illness, Richard Britteridge, Edward Thompson, Degory Priest, Christopher Martin and his stepson, Solomon Prower had all seemed robust enough to Dorothy's eye. Whatever this sickness was, it seemed capable of claiming whoever it chose as far as she could see! She sincerely hoped that Alice was right and that the sickness would burn itself out without inflicting any further fatalities.

She'd had her fill of dealing with corpses, yet inside she very much doubted that Death had had his.

"Why are we washing these anyway?" Pricilla asked naively as she rejoined her Mother. "It's not as if they will be needing them now!" she added with the tactlessness of youth.

"No," Alice replied, "but there are other young ones coming along and God only knows where we are to get new clothes from for them? We need to take good care of whatever we have already and make it last, for who knows when we might get our next supplies. That's why we are here in the first place!" Alice went on, turning to Dorothy. "A golden business opportunity, my William said. 'Where Alice', he says to me, 'where do you think all these settlers will get new boots?' So, that is how we came to be here. Mister Mullins sold up his leather business and brought his entire stock of shoes and boots and cobbling tools here. 'Like horses, people will always need shoeing!' that is what he says, 'and I intend to do it!'"

Alice looked once more at Jasper's breeches and continued, 'I expect these will go into the common store until needed!"

Dorothy quickly pretended to be engrossed by the activity of the men as they worked diligently apace to erect the first buildings. Anything to distract her thoughts away from that poor child and his miserable death.

"They are coming along very well!" she remarked. "I don't think it will be long before we will all be here and off the ship for good."

Alice seemed reluctant to be drawn from the subject of illness until Dorothy made a suggestion.

"Shall we break for some refreshment? Before we attend to those bits still in the water? I see smoke up there," Dorothy directed their gaze, "there's a fire near to where the men are working. Shall we go and get warmed up for a while? I could brew us some warming pine needle tea or I have spotted some rosehips close by."

Alice and Pricilla accepted the suggestion of stopping by the fire to chase out the cold, but declined the offer of the tea.

"Not for us, thank you," Alice commented politely, "we have not the liking for its taste! But some small beer would suffice."

The three reached the construction site and thankfully approached the watch fire. There was no beer, so the mother and daughter made the best of hot water. Dorothy brewed and then sipped her tea and had to admit to herself that it tasted far better with honey. Then she wondered for a moment if she would ever taste honey again. Were there any bees in the New World? At least on board, Mary Brewster was always on hand to offer a little malt to temper the brew in its stead.

"Mistress Dorothy!" One of the men approached.

"Mister Hopkins!" Dorothy acknowledged him.

"Come to cook for us then?"

"I hadn't," she replied, "but I would if you have need of me to!"

"Please do," he said with a grin, "for 'tis awful when the task falls to me, as it has today! Captain Standish complains I give him belly ache!" He laughed heartily. "I can provide well enough for the pot but when it comes to cooking it. Well..."

Dorothy rose to his well-thought-out bait.

"Very well," she responded with a smile. "What do you have? Some game from the woods?"

"Sadly not. We have been in with the dogs several times to see what we can flush out, but without much luck so far. You see, it's very dense forest in there," he explained. "The trees are very mature and with such a canopy above, there's very little undergrowth below for browsing animals to crop."

"Then what do we have for the makings?" she asked

despondently.

'Well, we have some dried split peas and ground Indian corn," he said with a grin, "and I know where to lay my hand on a passable substitute for cabbage over yonder." Then he stopped.

Dorothy smiled a little smile of disbelief. Surely there were more ingredients than just these.

Hopkins gave in to the sight of her pained expression.

"Oh," he continued, "and there's whatever we can find underfoot here!" He stretched out his arms in a gesture to encompass an empty stretch of beach ahead of them.

Dorothy and the Mullins women just stared in blank astonishment and amusement.

"Here?" Dorothy said. "But there is nothing here!"

"Ah, but there is, Mistress Dorothy," he assured her. "Like the best things in life, you just have to go in search of it for a bit! Come hunting with me, Mistress," he said, "and let me show you the bounty of the sea."

Dorothy turned towards her companions.

"Are you coming, then?"

"No," Alice replied. "You go! Me and Pricilla here will sit a spell and dry out a bit before we finish off the wash! Besides," she added, "you are going to be busy enough cooking for all of these men! I just hope you know what you've let yourself in for!"

Dorothy left her two companions to warm by the fire while Stephen Hopkins picked up a wooden pail, handed it to her and proceeded to lead her up along the beach a little way.

Stephen Hopkins was a good man; well travelled and respected for his knowledge and experience gained at sea, due to having been to America before.

"I wanted to thank you Mistress Dorothy," Stephen said as they walked, "for saving my wife's and baby's lives."

"Why? I did nothing!" she protested. "It's Doctor Fuller you should be thanking."

"I have," he explained, "but both the good doctor and my wife, Lizzie, told me how marvellous you had been. Only I haven't had the opportunity, until now, to thank you properly."

Dorothy smiled.

"They are most precious to me," he continued. "I have already lost one wife that I loved most dearly, and I know that you must have an understanding of how great such a loss can be to go through once, let alone face the prospect for a second time."

Dorothy knew he was referring to her Thomas and her eyes dropped away with that memory.

"I am sorry," Dorothy apologized. "I had no idea you had lost a wife."

"Don't be," he said. "It was a long time ago and I have been made to feel so much sorrow over it, that there really is no need for you to feel sorrow as well."

Stephen grabbed at his leather cap just as the wind was about to snatch it. Smoothing down his receding red hair, he replaced it, firmly back on his head.

"I was away from her, you see, for far too long," he said, picking up his tale. "Then when I finally came home again, they told me she was already dead and buried. But my daughter lived. It was then I made a vow that if I ever married again, I would never go to sea again without taking my family with me."

"So, you were a sailor before?"

"No. Not exactly. I was a minister's clerk on the Sea Venture, bound for Jamestown, Virginia back in 1609."

"To Virginia? So, you've been here before?"

"No, we are too far north for Virginia. Besides, I never did get directly to Virginia that time either. You see, I was shipwrecked in the Bermudas. At a God awful place called the 'Isle of Devils'."

"Shipwrecked?"

"Yes. We were stranded on an island for more than ten

months before we were rescued."

"How did you survive? Was it inhabited?"

"No. It was not and surviving was hard. We hunted wild boar, birds, turtles, anything we could lay our hands on to eat. Then we were picked up and transported on to Virginia. I wanted to get home to Mary and my little girl, Constance, but I couldn't. You see I was held in the Jamestown Prison."

Experience had taught Dorothy that guilty men were usually fined or hanged. Imprisonment was often no more than a cowardly ploy used to subjugate those whom the judiciary knew in their hearts were innocent of any real crime, but whom the state deemed it desirable to have snatched out of public circulation without arousing possible public sympathy caused by an unjust execution.

'It's alright. I paid my dues and am grateful for that chance. You see, I spoke out against those in rightful authority over us, as we lay shipwrecked on that island. I was accused of mutiny, so I am lucky not to have hung. Only by the time I got released and worked my passage home, my wife had passed on." He sighed but seemed relieved that Dorothy was smiling sympathetically.

"The Lord spares me my life on one side of the world but takes my wife's on the other. I wished he taken me though and spared her sweet soul! But as I say, I've sorrowed mightily over that and learnt a hard lesson from it. Now I cherish the ones I love and, if I can help it, won't be parted from them again."

By now the two had walked quite a way out towards the turning tide. Dorothy regarded the fat looking ducks feeding in the frothy strand. Surely, she wondered, Hopkins didn't intend that they try catching one of these armed only with a bucket!

'Well, this it!" Stephen suddenly said, stopping beside a rather unlikely looking rock pool scattered with stones and strands of fine seaweed. Putting aside the bucket, he sat down and started casually to remove his boots and roll down his woollen stockings.

Dorothy looked about in amazement, wondering what exactly Steven was about. She was a country girl, and had never seen the sea until she had made her way to Boston with the congregation a dozen years before. Then she had not encountered it again until after she had reached Southampton with Thomas.

"What are you doing?" she exclaimed. "This is no time to be washing your feet!"

Stephen laughed heartily.

"Wait and see," he said, "and prepare to be astounded!"

For a moment Dorothy's mind shot back to the Old Hall gardens, a smile rippling across her cold face as she remembered Thomas and the bats on that balmy evening so long ago.

Stephen meanwhile, stepped boldly into the water. Seemingly undeterred by the icy cold he proceeded to paddle, feeling his way as he went, across the ridged bars of sand left in the wake of the retreating tide. He was obvious probing for something beneath the surface with his toes and the soles of his bare feet. For what, Dorothy was at a loss to know.

After just a handful of paces, he stopped and called out.

"Aha," he exclaimed, stooping down. He scrabbled about in the sand, furiously, with his fingertips. Then he seized upon something with glee and snatched it up to show it off.

"There!" he said proudly. "Isn't that a beauty?"

Hopkins opened his fist to reveal something round and smooth inside. At first Dorothy took it to be no more than a pebble. Then she suddenly realized it must have been some sort of sea creature.

"It's a quahog!" he explained. "They are very good eating!"

"A 'co' what?" Dorothy said, clearly amused.

"Quahog!" Stephen repeated.

"And pray tell, how are we going to cook that?" she frowned

"Easily! Let's pop him in the bucket and gather up a few more of his brothers and see if we can't have a veritable feast!" he laughed.

Dorothy laughed back, for although she was impressed that Hopkins had found the creature she did hold out much hope of finding enough for a feast!

As Stephen continued his hunt, they chatted and scooted from pool to pool in between the tide lines. Dorothy's thoroughly tousled hair, now unleashed from beneath her cap, whipped wildly about her rosy cheeks as she clasped the ever-increasing pickings tightly in her freezing hands. The hems of her skirts were sodden and encrusted with wet sand, yet despite this and the raw wind she was thoroughly enjoying herself. It was so good to be able to let go, if only for a fleeting while, and forget the dire times they were living through just now.

Soon they had a whole pail of weird and wonderful shellfish to add to the quahogs, so Stephen donned his stockings and boots, and once more they headed back up the beach. On the way Hopkins stopped and showed Dorothy where he collected his 'sea cabbage' from and several other useful plants he knew.

While he returned to work, Dorothy set the seafood, as he had instructed, to steep in fresh water. There was only an hour or two of precious daylight left and so the men would be fussing for their supper by five. In the meanwhile, she set the large cauldron of water over the fire to cook the dried peas. As she waited for it to come to the boil, she busied herself making up a stiff dough with the corn meal and water, shaping it into cake-like patties and 'baking them off' on a large greased skillet set over the red hot embers. Alice and Pricilla were by now, setting the last blankets to drip from the line. Then, having finished their allotted work, they joined Dorothy to dry themselves off by the fire.

Dorothy showed her companions all the other things she had gathered from the beach with Stephen. She had handfuls of various pretty seashells she had collected with a mind to taking back for the children on board. She also had a variety of stalks and leaves from different plants carefully wrapped in a linen square to protect them from getting gritty bits in amongst them.

"This looks very much like the 'sweet breath' we get back home," Dorothy explained, tearing off a wilting sprig of leaves and showing them to Alice and Pricilla. "We used to pluck sweet breath leaves all the time, from the Old Hall physic garden and chew them," she added. "It freshens the mouth and is good for ulcers in the mouth too. Alice, would you care to try some?"

She declined, although Dorothy knew she had complained of sores in her mouth earlier that day.

"Don't seem natural to me!" she said. "We don't go in for it much in Dorking. A bit of ash on your finger to clean the teeth has always done for me and mine," she exclaimed, "besides, doesn't it turn your teeth green?"

"Only for a minute or two!" Dorothy replied.

"How do you know it's not poison then, if it's not quite the same as at home?" Pricilla added suspiciously.

"Oh, Mister Hopkins told me!" Dorothy explained. "He is very knowledgeable about the native plants and creatures in this New World. Besides, he says if you can see where some of the leaves seem to have been nibbled by an animal, then it's more than probably safe enough for us to eat too!"

"Nibbled by animals?" added Pricilla, screwing up her nose in disgust, "then I definitely don't want any, thank you very much!"

Stephen Hopkins returned and showed Dorothy how to prepare the shellfish and make certain they were 'safe' to eat by discarding any that gaped open in steep, or did not once they were steamed. Dorothy's initial uncertainty over their 'catch' evaporated as she discovered how appetizing they smelt and tasted to her ship-jaded palate. While Stephen helped separate off the shells, Dorothy shredded the sea cabbage and added it to the gently simmering soup of dried peas before adding the seafood to the pot with some ground pepper. Accompanied by the Indian cornmeal biscuits she made and cooked earlier, the menfolk declared it 'a meal fit for King James himself' and gratefully devoured it all. As Dorothy watched, a troubled thought struck her. This sea's bounty, as Stephen had described it, was indeed wholesome and plentiful, yet she wondered to herself how long would it remain so good once the whole company was ashore and this bounty was being plundered every day.

After the meal, the women gathered in all the washing that was dry enough, leaving the remainder to drip at will.

"What if it rains overnight?" Pricilla asked.

"Then the Lord sees fit to give it a second rinse!" Alice laughed.

As they returned to the fire, the men relieved them of their wet shoes and thoughtfully filled them with hot sand to gently dry out the leather for morning. After building up the fire to deter wolves and posting armed sentinels at their palisade, they all retired to the shelter of the common house.

Bedded down snugly for the night, as she drifted into sleep Dorothy smiled quietly to herself at the thought of being greeted in the morning by blankets, as stiff as boards, hanging from the drying lines.

Dorothy woke with a start. It was pitch black and in the confusion of the moment she almost forgot where she was. Figures darted about in the darkness amid a cacophony of shouts and barking dogs, a calamitous collection of black silhouettes rushing through the doorway and slipping out into the moonlight. As her eyes swiftly adjusted, she realized they were all carrying weapons and had their boots in their hands, as they scrambled to get outside quickly.

Alice sat bolt upright and screamed out.

"Are we sinking?"

"No! No! We are ashore! Remember?" Dorothy reached out to try reassuring her.

Then the Mullins girl woke up beside her mother and started crying in sheer terror.

"What is it, then?" Alice shouted.

"Indians!' Dorothy replied. 'I very much think there are Indians out there."

"Savages?" Alice was horrified. "Good Lord, are we come all this way to be murdered in our beds by savages!"

"Alice!" Dorothy rebuked her harshly. "Have a mind for your daughter! They are probably just curious." Dorothy threw her arms around the hysterical girl and tried to calm her down, "That is all, I am certain. No one is going to harm us..."

CHAPTER EIGHTEEN

Climbing back aboard the Mayflower, a dismal sight greeted Dorothy and her companions. Under the sullen grey sky above, several pitiful bodies, of which one was a child, were laid out in a row on deck. Each was neatly sewn into a heavy canvas shroud. Dorothy tried not to dwell on them, but a cold sickly feeling rose up in her as she anticipated, with dread, discovering shortly whose familiar face would no longer be waiting below.

Unnervingly for her, some of the children were also up on deck. They were noisily making the most of the fine but chill day, boisterously playing with a fraying quoit fashioned from a hank of old rope. They laughed and shrieked as children do. It was as if they were somehow oblivious to the fact that one of their usual playmates was no longer among them; that he was unable to join in with their laughter now as he lay silenced under the canvas close by. Dorothy found this stark juxtaposition of life and death almost surreal and utterly abhorrent to her sensibilities. Had it come to this, Dorothy wondered, that death was losing its bitter sting? Had these innocents suddenly become so callous as to be indifferent to the demise of their peers around them? Or could it be that they were simply at play, expressing themselves in the only way they knew how in some desperate attempt to try to neutralize the macabre happenings around them?

On seeing Dorothy, the little More sisters ran hand in hand towards her in exuberant greeting. Brother Richard followed on closely. For the first time, Dorothy found herself recoiling from their touch. She hated herself for it. It was exactly the same response she has witnessed a dozen times before between those sickening below and some others, who miraculously seemed to have been passed over by this harbinger of death. As an awful premonition crushed in on her, Dorothy realized instinctively that she needed to let go of these dear children. Somehow, she had to learn to detach, or at least distance herself if she was going to continue to be useful to those around her. That is if she was going to survive.

Dorothy forced a brief smile. Then watching their darkly-ringed eyes sunken into cadaver-pale faces suddenly brighten, she no longer begrudged these little ones taking their play where they might. She handed over the bundle of shells she had collected and hurriedly left the Mores to excitedly divide out their spoils as she made her way down to the passenger deck.

The Mayflower had taken on a curious odour these past few weeks. As overpowering as it was, strangely those who had remained on board seemed completely oblivious to it. It was the smell of death. Only now, as Dorothy returned to the ship and descended the last few steps below, it caught the back of her throat and made her gag and retch. She quickly realized that far from the sickness abating, it appeared instead to be taking a firmer hold on those snared in its grip. A morbid thought crossed Dorothy's mind. She sincerely hoped she was not stepping back down into her own grave.

Breaking away from attending to a ghastly-looking Mary Allerton, Mother Brewster glanced up and a wave of relief visibly rippled across her care-worn face to see Dorothy return.

"I will be back in a moment or two, my dear," she said soothingly to her patient. "I just need to fetch you a nice clean blanket and have a word with young Dorothy here."

Mistress Allerton raised her head, stretched out her blackened fingers and murmured something weakly, before collapsing back down onto her pillow. She had been such a beautiful, lively young mother-to-be but now the sickness had rendered her almost unrecognizable.

"Truly a sight for sore eyes, Dorothy!" Mary exclaimed, wiping her troubled brow. Directing her eyes towards the sick woman, a perturbed Dorothy inquired barely above a whisper, "How is she?"

Mary Brewster's eyes said it all. She bit her lip and nodded that it was not good at all.

Dorothy heaved an uneasy sigh. Then, casting her gaze upwards towards the deck above, she gestured discreetly and mouthed but one word towards the older woman. "Who?"

Glancing back across her shoulder to check Mistress Allerton was settled peacefully, Mary briskly strode the few paces across the floor to Dorothy. Slipping her strong caring arm about her young friend's shoulder, Mother Brewster hugged her firmly, then guided her back towards the now vacant stern of the passenger ship so they might pass a few words in confidence.

"It's Thomas Tinker's wife and boy," she said, "only I dursn't tell him," she explained. "He is so weak himself that I'm afraid the shock will kill him."

Dorothy found this bitter news to take. The Tinkers were such a pleasant family. She could clearly picture the boy in her mind on the day she and Thomas had watched him waiting on the quayside in Southampton, lining up excitedly with a huge cloth bundle over one shoulder waiting to board the Speedwell with his friends. He was always such a bright, amiable and helpful lad and should have had all his life before him still.

"Oh no!" Dorothy tried to stifle a whimper of despair and take on board her newfound conviction to harden her heart, but it was so difficult to go against her true nature.

"He was such a lovely boy, only thirteen or so, wasn't he?"

Mary nodded.

Dorothy allowed herself to brood for a moment on death's utter contempt for youth before finally asking.

"Who are the other two, then?"

"Crew," Mary replied abruptly.

"Oh!" Dorothy blurted in surprise.

The sailors had been lucky up until then, relatively unscathed by illness. So much so that they had taken great pleasure in pointing out this fact, squarely placing the blame for all the ills on the sufferers themselves. Making out that it was punishment for the unnatural act of bringing women aboard a ship.

"Yes," Mary added, "that certainly took the wind out of their sails!"

"Perhaps now they are beginning to lose some of their own, they will be a little more compassionate towards us," Dorothy commented a little bitterly.

Mary looked at her and raised her eyebrows.

"I doubt it, though Master Jones does seem to be coming round by degrees now that it is also obvious that the sickness cannot be down to having to drink the water. Today he has even rescinded his previous orders and said how he would allow us passengers access to beer once more."

"That will cheer up Willy Spindleshanks!" Dorothy remarked with a glimmer of a smile, "he was feeling really down the other day and craving just a small mug of beer. Stephen Hopkins told me that when he approached Master Jones to ask if some might be spared for William, he firmly declined! Stephen says that Jones swore at him and said that even if William Bradford had been his own father, he still wouldn't give him any!"

"There's a fine Christian gesture for you, then. And how is Will now?"

"He is slowly recovering. Still weak and a little lame but up and about and in good spirits, thank goodness! In fact, you can see for yourself, presently! Confidentially, he has come back to discuss with Master Jones the prospect of taking a cannon ashore or such."

"Well, that's a blessing, Praise God!" Mary replied, unruffled by Dorothy's last remark. "Much as it has grieved and sorrowed us to lose any of our dear brethren, and each one will be sorely missed, if we were to lose that man it would be like losing our right arm!" she declared. "As for the crew, well the Lord has given them his judgment now. For as meanly as they have treated us and blamed us for their ills, it seems this visitation is set equally on them! Only now, even some of these sailors are changing their tune since Doctor Fuller has been in deep conference this past night with Mister Heale, the ship's surgeon."

"And?"

"They think they may know what all this ill is about."

"What?" Dorothy clamoured to know. "What is it, Mary?"

"Well, Doctor Heale has never seen a case of it before and neither has our Samuel Fuller. But one of the Master's Mates says he has seen and heard of a similar affliction before," Mother Brewster explained. "You see he has travelled by sea extensively - to Jamestown even. But he was captured by the Spanish and dragged off to Cuba and then all the way back to Spain for inquisition. He thinks it's some kind of mariner's disease- the scurvy."

"What? All this sickness, which is afflicting us now is the scurvy?"

"Most likely for the greater part, though I do not doubt we have also our fair share of the usual diverse winter ills upon us too. It was the terrible rotting gums, blackened skin and the stench that made the Mate suspicious that it be the scurvy though," Mary grimaced. "He heard tell how the Spanish have reported suffering the same symptoms amongst their crews ever since they started exploring the Americas and the Pacific. He heard that on some long trips as many as half the mariners died on the voyage or very soon after returning. And they didn't have any women aboard," she added. "So much then for these sailors cursing at us for being a jinx!"

"Then he knows how to cure it?" Dorothy surmised hopefully.

"No! Now there's the thing. They don't rightly know what

causes it, only that once it gets real bad in the mouth and on the skin..." Mary did not finish. There was no need for her to expand upon this for Dorothy, as the two women had already begun to associate the acrid stench of rotting gums and blackened feet with having reached a point of no recovery. For many of the adults who, having bravely struggled through the whole gamut of the other horrific symptoms this disease imparted on the way to death, it often proved the final insult.

"Doctor Fuller is certain of one thing," Mary continued, "for some reason it appears to occur at sea and he says we need to disembark from the Mayflower just as soon as we can. We have got to get the shelter ashore completed as quickly as possible and get everyone off this floating coffin!"

"And until then? " Dorothy pressed, "what does he intend for us to do until then?"

"To carry on as best we can," Mary replied placidly.

"Is that it?" Dorothy was clearly agitated. "No cure, no remedy?"

"He says that there is nothing more to be done than we are already doing. And that's little enough for most of these poor souls," Mary sighed,

"But then why are some of us not getting ill at all? That is what I want to know." Dorothy struggled to try to make some sense of it, "There must be some reason or rhyme to it!"

"Well I've thought of that too, but I can't see no pattern to it," Mary replied, "other than it is simply God's will."

"God's will?" Dorothy expressed her deep-seated doubt. "To let us die like this? Do you really believe that, Mary? That God would lead so many of us here. So many who had given up everything to obey his command only to let them die like this? Little children? Just because it is His will? Is this the kind of compassionate God we have learnt to read about in our Bibles?"

"Dorothy! You are upset!" Mary was visibly shaken by

Dorothy's outburst.

"Upset?" Dorothy quaked as she replied. "Upset is when you kick over the pail after milking and spill the milk. I am not upset!" she cried. "I am destroyed inside. I feel like a blind beggar stumbling in some dark alley after being set upon by robbers. No sooner do I rise up from one body blow than I am sent reeling by the next. I can't defend myself anymore and I can't stop the onslaught of the hurt or the pain. I don't even know if I have the will to get up anymore, or if maybe it would be a blessed mercy to lie down on the floor and give in!"

"Do you think I am not affected by all this?" Mary retorted. "That I don't care? Or that I am somehow hardened to it all? Because I am not!"

"But you still have your man, Mary!" Dorothy sobbed hysterically. "I do not! I have lost everything. And for what Mary? Because, please God, if you know the reason why, then for pity's sake tell me! Tell those little ones up on deck that I have just passed by. Tell them why they are dying! Because I do not know Mary. I do not know anything anymore! Only that I hurt inside and the grief I am carrying is more than I can bear and is choking the will to live from me."

Mary's strong arms crowded around the sobbing woman and enfolded her with soothing warmth.

"Oh, my poor darling. Come here!" Mary cried.

Dorothy let her head droop down upon her confidante's willing shoulder where she wept her heart out.

"How do you think I feel watching these people sicken and die?" Mary whispered in her ear as she grappled to hold back her own tears. "People I have known for years and years. How do you think I find the strength to face them, after watching them lose children, husbands and wives, knowing that none of my family has fallen to this? Don't you think I feel guilty? Or that I am not equally terrified that any day now one of them will get ill and die?"

Mary tenderly stroked Dorothy's hair like a mother with her child. "Or, that I don't realize that but for my William, most of our congregation would probably not be here in the first place? Do you think I have not lain awake at night wondering if all this is a punishment from God for going against the established Church of our King and country? Or that my husband or Will Bradford has not been equally tortured by these very same thoughts? Dorothy," she implored, "this is the one time, if ever there was, when we dare not lose our nerve and our faith!"

Dorothy looked up and into Mary's beautiful homely eyes.

"Dorothy," she pleaded, "I know you are still deep in mourning for your husband Thomas and that there must seem no dawn to this grisly night. But," she added, "you must not think like this! If you do... if I do... then we are all lost. What has happened...what is happening to us is dreadful. There is no escaping that! But we have to accept that not all desires can come to be. Just as not all babies are born, nor all plans seen through to fruition. We have to hold tight to our belief that there is a reason to all of this suffering, and that one day it may become clear. Meanwhile, we need to trust in God. For if we do not cleave together now in that, then what is there to stop us from being cloven asunder? I do believe this is a trial, Dorothy. A test of our resolve to do God's bidding. Just as Moses was destined to reach yet never enter the Promised Land, we too have to accept that some of us were never meant to enter this New World either. Yet through this sacrifice, this obedience and faith to follow God's calling, to sow the seeds of reform, I believe that many more will come after, through the example of those who answered His call without seeing the harvest home. I believe that we will, one day, grow a nation from the seeds of their devotion. Nothing is wasted here, Dorothy. Nothing worthwhile is ever gained without sacrifice along the way."

Dorothy listened and was comforted by Mary Brewster's

quiet wisdom, yet deep inside, her turbulent soul remained only partly appeased by her friend's argument, however sincerely felt. What Dorothy really craved, as did many among that sorry ship's complement, was one irrefutable sign from God Himself for them to cling on to.

As Dorothy composed herself, it was only then that she truly noticed Mary's condition. She looked haggard, utterly exhausted by her labours and in dire need of rest herself .Dorothy regarded this middle-aged woman now with deep concern and wondered how much longer Mother Brewster could go on without falling ill herself. Yet when she suggested that Mary take a break, she would not hear a word of it. Instead, she went over to a canvas bundle as it dropped, with a thud, unceremoniously through the hatchway above and immediately started to pick out an armful of clean linen to distribute amongst the neediest cases.

"There's too many very near to the end, I fear," she said gravely. "I can't just stand by and let them slip away uncomforted."

Dorothy threw aside her doubts along with her shawl, rolled up her sleeves and began to help.

'Why don't you see to the little ones and their mams, my lovely," Mary Brewster suggested gently. "There are so many ill I just don't know how we will manage if any more mothers die!"

Dorothy knew she was right. There were many children and with Mary Allerton obviously moribund, there would soon be her three little ones without a mother as well. She shepherded as many of the children as she could coax away to the stern and instructed the older ones in some diversion for the infants while she slipped away to the firebox and boiled up some water. She brewed up a mess of tonic beverage with the fresh basket of bright, wind-desiccated rosehips she had found sprawling across a fallen tree ashore. She then set about persuading the children to sip a little.

SUE ALLAN

Then after this she started to distribute the brew amongst the others on board.

At the far end of the passenger deck Dorothy came across Pricilla and Alice, once more in some state of dismay. In their absence ashore, Mister Mullins had been taken poorly.

"William was all right before we left,' Alice explained to Dorothy. "He was complaining a bit about his bone ache, but he always gets that in the winter. Now look at him, though! He can't even stand and he looks awful!"

"Now, now woman, don't take on so," William protested. "I will be all right. There is no need to worry. Just see. I will come right again."

"Here," Dorothy suggested, "take a little of this to warm you." She proffered him a mug of the hot infusion.

"I'd rather have a little beer," he replied, "if there's any to be had?"

"Yes," Dorothy replied, "I hear from Mary that it is to be rationed out again to us. Perhaps Pricilla...."

With out further mention Pricilla went away to procure some for her father.

"I was telling my William about the savages ashore. Quite scary, wasn't it?" Alice said excitedly.

"I don't think there was anything to be too alarmed at." Dorothy tried not to be drawn into any conversation that might give rise to further concern amongst the already ailing company.

"Only I hear they are taking some of the ship's ordnance ashore later to defend the settlement against native attack!" Alice added.

Dorothy marvelled that Alice seemed to have an unrivalled knack for gleaning information from snippets of conversation she so often unintentionally listened in to.

"I had not heard," Dorothy replied, "but I expect it's more to do with precaution, Alice, don't you? Besides..." she added, "there were no Indians the other night we spent ashore. It was only wolves howling that set the dogs off so!"

"But there were Indians, before..." Alice would not let it lie. She was like a terrier at a rat hole.

"Yes Ladies, there is no need for alarm!" A gaunt looking William Bradford stooped under the beam overhead and steadied himself with his makeshift crutch. "Mistress Dorothy is right. The Indians have ventured out from the woods but they probably won't come any closer. We have encountered them before but they have so far shied away from us. I suspect they are indeed curious about us and may even be afraid, though they do appear to becoming bolder as time goes by."

"So we are still all set to come ashore?" Mister Mullins asked.

"Yes we are, my friend," William Bradford tried to reassure him. "Just as soon as we can get the houses built! So you just concentrate on getting fit again for we will have sore need of a boot shop when we are done!"

"If you will excuse me," Dorothy said politely, "there really are lots of sick to attend to." With that, she withdrew and went about her calling.

***

A week or more passed by and a bitter wind howled in through the gaps around the closed deck hatch. Below, it cut its way through, like a cold-toothed saw, deep into a stooped Dorothy's already aching bones. Regardless she carried on, busily bundling up the next batch of soiled bed linen to be taken ashore for washing whenever the weather next broke. Someone had to do it and Dorothy was amongst a handful who had not succumbed to the full effect of the dreadful scurvy.

The relentless task of trying to nurse all the sick who needed attention had at times become utterly exhausting. So many were now ill that with so few able enough to care for them, Dorothy seemed to labour every minute of the day that the good Lord gave her. The only saving grace that Dorothy could see, and which in turn saved her and the others still standing from becoming utterly overwhelmed, was that so many had now passed out of life that they at least gave up time and space for the care of the living.

"Well it's a blessing that Master Jones has at last changed his tune!" Mary Brewster whispered to Dorothy as she hobbled up and dumped yet another armful of foul smelling laundry onto the already festering heap. "Thank goodness he is no more a-pestering us to get ashore so he can be off and back to England!"

"Goodness has nothing to do with it!" Dorothy retorted sharply "It is not that he doesn't want to leave but t'is more of a case that he daren't."

Dorothy was right. With so many of the passengers now sick, for him to strand them there without adequate supplies and shelter in the heart of winter would be condemned as an act little short of criminal.

"I suppose that is right, especially with so many of his mariners now dead or ailing too!" Mary reconsidered. "Still," she went on, "I would like to think it is because he has recovered his senses at last! At least he seems more vital and of his old self since he's been putting ashore with John and the others, from time to time."

"Yes, that does certainly seem borne out of late!" Dorothy replied, "and it could only be construed as madness for him to contemplate putting out to sea just yet. Perhaps he and his crew now realise that we are all very much in the same boat. All we can do is try to make the best of the situation and to pull together, if we are going to reach spring alive."

Mary and Dorothy were not the only ones come to realise of late that reaching spring alive for any of them was fast becoming a distinct improbability. Food was a worrying issue, with the stores on ship running low and in desperate need of supplementing. Pressure was on to build substantial dwellings ashore as sickness continued to run rife upon the Mayflower. The general consensus was that unless the settlers were got off the vessel fast then the death toll would just keep on mounting. At the very same time though there were many hungry mouths to be fed, yet the vast majority were helpless to find extra food for themselves. With so few ablebodied men now available, hard decisions had to be made as to how best to deploy this valuable and limited resource. Should they build or should they hunt? As a result, soon the strain for providing for the many was placed upon just a few to forage for whatever they could find.

Master Jones and his men took to fishing and had some success. On one day they even managed to catch three seals, but only the hardened mariners could stomach the most palatable part – the livers. Others tried to eat but retched. The sailors did however catch some a good-sized codfish most days, which Dorothy, occasionally helped by Pricilla when she was able, made a hearty stew of, but even so it proved a nigh impossible burden for the mariners to catch enough to feed everyone sufficiently, even for one scant meal.

John Carver was aboard one evening, having returned with the shallop earlier that afternoon to bring much needed supplies of fresh water, shellfish, eels and a brace or two of fowl. Dorothy thought of all the duck and geese that she had seen offshore and the same consideration had also crossed Mistress Carver's mind.

"Cannot your hunters take more wildfowl?" Katherine asked John as he crouched over his meagre meal.

Her husband explained that catching these was not so easy a task as it might first appear. Once a few had been clubbed and taken by sticks, the remainder soon fought shy of even the sight of the men.

"Can you not just shoot them?" Katherine persisted.

True, most of the huntsmen had muskets and flintlocks

and had shot quite a bit of game, yet they did so only frugally.

"How many fowl would you think sufficient to feed us all for one good meal, Dorothy?" John asked.

Dorothy thought for a moment before replying that she thought that fifty would supply sufficient meat after plucking and drawing.

"So our handful of hunters need shoot at least fifty good birds each day to provide for just one substantial meal for the company as a whole?" he said quietly. "Even without missing a single bird, that would mean us expending fifty rounds of shot and powder every day. Although the game birds are seemingly infinite, I am afraid our hunters are acutely aware that their ammunition most definitely is not! You understand our plight?" he stressed. "Whatever powder and shot we have now must last us until a supply ship can return and that could take more than half a year! That is, always assuming that the Mayflower makes it back to England safely and can then tell the Virginia Company where, exactly, we windblown settlers have landed up!"

Suddenly Dorothy understood.

"And we need to conserve our shot and powder in case of attack by Indians?" she said calmly.

Attack was something the leaders of the Separatists had been warned of by the Virginia Company, yet had played down to a certain extend so as not to cause unnecessary fear amongst their families. Carver and the others had been told about an earlier Virginia settlement that had been brutally massacred to the last man, woman and child. They had not kept these reports to themselves out of any wish to mislead or play down the inherent dangers of their present incursion into a new, yet already populated land. It was more to do with their reasoning that having learned a hard lesson from the events, and perhaps the mishandling of certain situations between those settler and their eventual murderers, the leaders of this expedition were intent on not repeating such fatal errors.

"That is why Standish has already summoned the cannon from the ship to be positioned up on the hill above the settlement," Carver explained. "That is also why there has been extra delay in building the accommodation ashore. Out of prudence, our attention has been diverted away from erecting houses and instead to fortifications in case of such attack. For this reason above all others, we need to make certain we have plenty of powder set aside to defend ourselves. This need is paramount, including hunting. It is a trade off, you understand? Our safety, against the need for food. We may go a little hungry now, but we are not starving yet!" he added. "Better lean and alive than full and dead."

***

Shortly after this conversation came one day of particular note.

"Dorothy, Dorothy! Quickly! " Mary Brewster's unmistakeable tone boomed out unexpectedly and excitedly across the passenger deck from the bottom of the hatch stairway.

Dorothy dropped what she was doing and hurried towards her friend's call to see what the hullabaloo was all about. Only, when she reached the steps, she found that Mary was gone and the hatch above was open to the bright blue sky. Dorothy scrambled up to where she could hear a loud commotion. As she approached the side of the ship where others stood craning their necks out to sea, she was amazed by the spectacle that met her eyes. There, in the water, a huge humpback whale had suddenly appeared from out of nowhere to frolic, tantalizingly close to the Mayflower. As he spewed up water from his blowhole he circled the ship repeatedly, as if mesmerized by it. He looked like a lovelorn suitor engaged in some hopeless ritual courtship with this unobtainable mate.

The whale was like manna being offered up by the sea. Accordingly, Master Jones and his crew were of a mind to pursue the great creature, but then were reluctantly forced to think better of it. They had neither the equipment, nor more importantly, the manpower to capture the beast or do service to the resulting carcass. Furthermore, if they were unable kill it, they were fearful that such a huge creature if merely wounded could easily turn upon its tormentors and pound the Mayflower to driftwood. So instead, all they could do was watch from above as the great creature continued to sweep by the ship majestically. The amount of whale meat it would have provided, not to mention oil, blubber and bone, did not bear thinking about. It kept the Mayflower company for the best part of that day before at dusk it headed off out into the open sea.

. By January's end, Dorothy had tallied some fifteen souls in total from amongst the passengers that had died since setting out from the Old World to this. With the passing of February, there were more than that number again, and March looked likely to carry forward this awful trend. Mercifully, winter broke early with the coming of March. The wind turned south and soon the woods on shore were ringing with the sweet sound of birdsong and heavy hearts began to lighten a little.

Amongst the rising toll of death, Dorothy tried to comfort the orphans it made, like Pricilla Mullins and Elizabeth Tilley, who were left to face the New World alone without their treasured parents. Dorothy saw whole families, like the Tinkers and the Turners, wiped away entirely. Others she witnessed simply had the hearts torn out of them with grief.

Mary Allerton never recovered after the stillbirth of her child, while Susanna White was delivered of a healthy son, Peregrine, only to have her husband cruelly taken within days. Sarah Eaton and Mistress Fuller both passed over leaving inconsolable husbands in their wake. Most heart-wrenching of all for Dorothy, was the loss of angelic, irrepressible Ellen More and her little frown–faced sister Mary. The girls died within hours of each other, leaving Richard as the sole survivor of this ill-fated brood. Perhaps it was the death of these little ones, above all others, that profoundly touched and scarred gentle twenty-year-old, Gilbert Winslow's heart. That and struggling to help his distraught brother, Edward, adjust to losing his young wife, Elizabeth. Gilbert endured the trauma of seeing his cherished 'children' die as well as many of his peer group around him. Maybe it was this entire trauma, this heartache, which would lead him in later life never to risk marriage and fatherhood for himself so he might never have to face such pain again. Then there was brave Captain Standish. While not experiencing a single day's sickness himself, Miles had to face up to the anguish of losing his beloved wife Rose. He coped with his grief by striving relentlessly, like a man possessed, to get the settlement ashore secure and completed as quickly as possible to receive the dwindling number of settlers still left alive. Each man, woman and child carried on with living as best they could, though not a one would be left untouched by the devastating loss all about them.

Dorothy regularly heard snippets of news from ashore. Especially of how the men there were growing increasingly accustomed to sighting Indians who persistently skulked about on the peripheries of their encampment.

"We have seen them often before," John Carver told Katherine and Dorothy one early march evening, "but only for the briefest of time before they dart back into the cover of the tree line, like frightened rabbits. Yet, just of late, they grow bolder. More often now, they take to standing out in the open for quite a few minutes at time. They stand defiantly and in full view of our sentries."

"What are they like, John?" Katherine asked.

"They are powerful, tall and muscular," he said. "Clearly

they are seasoned warriors for they pose for us, showing off that they are well armed and have bows and arrows. Then they turn slowly and wander away once more to wherever it is they have come from. It is as if they are toying with us. After dark is the hardest part. We hear them; their shouts and cries moan on the breeze to us and so pierce our sleep that we find it difficult ever to be truly at rest. I am afraid they are shattering our dreams of a peaceful co-existence with them."

Then, to their horror, John Carver told the women that some of these Indians had actually gone so far as to dare to sneak right up to the construction site itself and had stolen precious tools right out from under their noses as the settlers broke away from work for their dinner.

"If this is so then it can only mean one thing," Dorothy interrupted. "To do this means they must have lost their previous fear of you! If so, what is there now to stop them attacking us and taking back their land?"

"Precisely," Carver replied gravely. "That is why Captain Standish gave the order that no more of our dead be disposed of by daylight. For he feared that the Indians might be keeping a reckoning of our strength and are therefore alerted of our greatly weakened force."

"What are we to do, John?" Katherine was deeply shaken by this disclosure.

"Nothing more than we are doing, my dear," he replied. "All we can do now is to wait and trust in the Lord for our deliverance!"

Then, as William Bradford wrote in his journal, on the sixteenth of March a stupendously unexpected thing happened. One of these Native American Indians walked right into the settlement, alone. With lion like courage, he strode up to the dumbfounded men where they were busy at work, then unflinchingly stood his ground, tall, upright and noble as the astounded settlers gathered around him.

On hearing of the account, Dorothy found it hard to decide

whether it was this audacious show of boldness that stunned the Englishmen most, or the fact that this fellow then proceeded to address them in corrupted yet clearly discernible English. In all the wilderness that threatened to smother them from every side, with unknown numbers of hostile Indians apparently holding hatred towards all white men, that this one native American should stand amongst them now speaking to their grateful ears in their own language was unbelievable. The exhausted pilgrims concluded that this, at long last, could only be a sign from their God.

CHAPTER NINETEEN

Being Governor of the new colony was an unenviable task. For John Carver, trying to hold together the moral fabric of this fledging society was like sitting at a loom weaving with a mischievous youngster by your side, quietly snipping away at the supporting threads in order to unravel all that you have striven to achieve. Not motivated by either the Spirit or morality, but instead purely by the pursuit of mammon, there was a persistent minority amongst the 'Strangers' that if left to their own devices could prove the downfall of them all. In order to keep order, the letter of the law would need to be vigorously upheld in plain sight of all.

There was also the question of how to handle the native incursions. Although up until then no serious exchanges had come about, having heard lurid tales of massacres of earlier settlers, some of the ' Strangers' had been vehemently in favour of attack on sight as a means of defence. John Carver, on the other hand, ever God's diplomat was determined to settle in peace with the indigenous population if possible.

Miles Standish was also of this persuasion, although due more to matters military than for any overriding reason of Christian sensitivity towards these people. Besides, unlike many amongst his number, Miles did not underestimate the military prowess of these natives simply because their weapons and methods seemed primitive. He too hoped a peaceful understanding might be arrived at between the two parties. The idea of waging war against an enemy of undetermined strength, in unfamiliar territory, with his tiny 'army' of sickly and untrained men was something that he did not savour. There was nowhere to retreat to and no hope of reinforcements if things went wrong. Therefore, it made perfectly good sense to bide their time until the next shipload of settlers arrived while also gathering military intelligence in case of further need. Standish recognized that these natives were probably every bit as much seasoned soldiers as was he, and therefore deduced that they would form very similar strategies to his own. This, to his way of thinking, may well have been the primary reason behind risking one of their number by sending him into their camp in the first place. They too needed to judge their possible adversaries' strengths and possible weaknesses.

Dorothy soon learned that the Algonquin Indian who had come amongst the men that day, was named Samoset, and that after an extended parley in which he was offered gifts and hospitality, he had left but come again later with others to return the stolen tools.

Katherine and Dorothy were also privy to all the details of the week that had followed, as John Carver recounted how Samoset had arranged to return with the local Indian Great Chief, Saakimaawa Massasoit, and a host of warriors for further 'discussion'.

As it turned out, it was to be an occasion when Steven Hopkins' gleaned knowledge of Indian etiquette would come into its own and prove an invaluable asset.

"Hopkins and Bradford received Chief Massasoit and his men most graciously. They were led into one of our barely completed houses, where they were then invited to sit in comfort and await my arrival," John Carver explained.

"Ah!" Katherine exclaimed. "I see why you sent for my green rug and best cushions now."

"Then," John continued with a sheepish grin, "as a recognized sign of respect, I, in my capacity of Great Chief of our colony, immediately came to join him. Heralded by a non-too-tuneful fanfare of drum and trumpet, in a grand entrance I sallied forth, accompanied by a few of my own 'token' but heavily armed 'braves'! I think Massasoit was suitably impressed, especially by Miles Standish who had polished his body armour to an uncommon brilliance and had marched in with a cutlass, two daggers and seven, if you please, assorted muskets strapped about his person!"

The two women giggled as they tried to picture the scene.

"The meeting was extremely cordial," John went on, "with the kissing of hands, and exchanging of gifts as if he were the King of France and I our sovereign James! The entire proceedings were quite extraordinary to say the least!"

Dorothy went on to learn that amongst Chief Massasoit's entourage there was another curious fellow named Squanto, who had acted as interpreter for the greetings and speeches that flew between the two parties. Not only did he speak near perfect English, but he agreed to stay on after the Chief's departure to assist the settlers.

"Most importantly of all," John added, "before this momentous meeting was finally concluded, we agreed a treaty of peace between Chief Massasoit and ourselves. Which means that we now consider it safe enough to start moving the rest of the company ashore in earnest."

This was tremendous news for those who had been left stranded upon the Mayflower for so many months, with only sketchy reports of the new land waiting to sustain them ashore.

"Perhaps now at last," Dorothy thought aloud, "we might shake off this dreadful sickness."

Having a native living amongst them seemed very strange at first to the English, but after a surprisingly short time Squanto became an accepted part of daily life. With his expertise, especially of how to coax the best crop and yield from this famished soil, the settlers now stood not only a better chance of thriving in their new surroundings but of also repaying the Virginia Company backers.

Although he insisted on building his own modest traditional dwelling close by, Squanto soon became a part of the Carver household. Often he would seem to have just upped and disappeared only to return bearing a string of game casually slung across his broad muscular shoulders. Always, as a sign of respect, he would hang something for the pot on a hook by the Governor's threshold, but the bulk of his catch he would take to those households where the young children were.

"The children are the future," he said to Dorothy as they worked alongside each other clearing ground to make way for a planting of corn. "Though you and I are still alive, we belong with the past. We have had our time, but the children...," he seemed hesitant, "they must go on or all who have lived and died before have done so for nought."

Though he simply continued, sickle in hand, to cut away at the stubborn scrub, Dorothy could not help but notice the tinge of sadness in Squanto's eyes and the tremble in his voice as he spoke to her of these things. As they laboured on and their conversation progressed, she came to realise why; why he had seemed so unwilling at first to help the settlers tear down the abandoned native dwellings left to the mercy of the encroaching undergrowth, the same houses which now needed to be cleared to build new English homesteads for the fast expanding settlement of Plymouth. Most importantly she found out where to hunt and fish, where to trap valuable beaver for their fur was so very good.

"I once lived in this very place," he told her, "but I was seized from the shore more than six years ago by an English sea captain, who had it in mind to sell me into Spanish slavery."

Dorothy was horrified and at the same time, deeply ashamed on behalf of her countrymen. Squanto, however, seemed not to make this connection or, if he did, he covered it well.

"Yet luck fell with me and I escaped in England," he continued. "I was taken up by a wealthy merchant and much later fell in with another ship's captain. Then, about four years after I was taken, I realised that this vessel was now lying off a coastline I recognised. So, I jumped ship and made my way back here."

Dorothy's heart went out to him when she heard him

relate how he had eagerly returned to his village only to discover that his tribe were all dead, wiped out by a wicked pestilence just the year before. Now she understood his reluctance to help tear down the crumbling remains of the native dwellings. He was being asked to wipe out the last remnants of his lost friends and family. Yet, amazingly to Dorothy, Squanto appeared to bear not an ounce of malice towards these English settlers, although he knew only too well that they were kinsmen to those who had been the instruments of his own past sadness. More than this, he became their helpmate and continued to live amongst them at Plymouth until his death.

By the time the Mayflower eventually departed on April 5th 1621, half of Master Jones's original crew was dead and the remainder barely well enough to handle the ship, and of the original company of Mayflower passengers, there remained less than twenty-five men, seven women and twenty-four children.

***

Dorothy bided in with Governor John Carver, his wife Katherine, manservant, John Howland and houseboy, Billy. Also lodged in with the household was the young daughter of two Leyden members who themselves were not a part this venture. Her name was Desire Minter.

"I swear that girl is neither use nor ornament!" Katherine Carver complained bitterly to her husband. "Dorothy and I work in the fields while she takes her leisure!"

"Then it must be made perfectly clear to the child that if she refuses to work, then she will be put upon the next ship back to her relatives in disgrace!" John Carver said calmly, with little time to look up from planting corn with Squanto.

"It's not that she refuses outright to work, John," she said with an air of utter exasperation. "In fact she never declines to undertake any chore set her! But either she does the thing so badly that Dorothy or Howland have to follow on her heels to put it right, or she feigns illness! I am certain she cannot at one time be sickening yet put away as much as she does at the table. And as for being a child! I fear she is far too forward for her years, especially in the distraction she causes our man Howland!"

Stooping beside the carefully prepared trench Dorothy smiled to herself as she listened to the discourse between Katherine and her husband. She knew too well how cunningly this Desire contrived her laziness and how unseemly her conduct was for a fifteen year old girl in the company of the men. She was but an accident in the making as far as Dorothy could see, and she agreed wholeheartedly that it might be best for all concerned to remove this spark completely from causing havoc amongst the ample spare tinder. Better that than have this now tightly knit community ruined by one up-and-coming loose woman.

"As I said my dear. It must be made plain and clear that those who are of an age to earn their bread here must do so or depart! I will talk to her on this matter later myself if you wish, but for now I must press on with getting this crop in the ground or none of us will have bread come winter!"

Katherine returned to the house with her face flushed, but not as red as her husband's. He was not angry, but Dorothy suspected the combination of the stresses of governing the Plymouth colony, toiling so hard at manual labour coupled with, although he would quickly deny it, advancing age, were beginning to take their toll on his health. She noticed the increasingly high colour in his face, which she put down to working out in the fresh air. True, he was first to be out working the fields and last to be away, yet on top of this he was also carrying the burden of worry for running the settlement and trying desperately to turn in a profit of sorts to pacify the greedy backers of the venture far behind in England.

Dorothy and Billy continued with their labour, mirroring

exactly John Carver and Squanto as they too toiled in the warm spring sunshine. Billy filled the trench at set intervals with the flyblown fish heads and trimming fertilizer from his handcart, while Dorothy all but crawled in the dirt behind, sewing the precious seeds and covering them over with her hands. It was hard, dirty, smelly work but so necessary if they were going to have a harvest to look forward to.

A little while later John Carver was called on again to settle a dispute in his role as Governor. John Billington was causing trouble by arguing with Captain Standish over a beaver pelt that he was trying to keep for his own profit instead of putting it to the common good as agreed.

"This Billington will be the death of me!" he muttered as he left the field.

It was just the latest in a long line of petty theft and misdemeanours on this troublesome family's part, and although the matter was quickly settled once he arrived, it meant John Carver having to work on even longer in the field to make up for lost time.

Dorothy and Billy, having finished off their allocated work went to offer their assistance to John Carver and Squanto, but their help was graciously declined in favour of them returning to the house to assist Katherine in preparing the supper. Governor Carver adding laughingly, that he thought he was beginning to feel so hungry that he might take to eating the fertilizer if supper were not ready for him on the table by his return.

Dorothy thought fleetingly of suggesting that he leave the rest of the planting for the next day, but she did not. Instead, she smiled and obediently gave way to his wishes.

About an hour or so later the door to the cottage opened and a worried looking Squanto helped John Carver in. The Governor's hand was pressed hard against his right temple and he was complaining bitterly about having a blinding headache. Squanto and Dorothy helped him up to his bed, while Katherine prepared a cold compress. He thanked her and closed his eyes, saying that he would lie a while for it to ease before he ate. Only when Katherine went to rouse him to tell him the meal was plated up, she was horrified to find that his face was palsied and he could not speak or move properly. Dorothy kept watch, hoping against hope that this illness would not end the same way Lady Rose's last one had. Sadly, it would. John Carver died a few days later.

The colony found the loss of their deeply respected Governor almost as hard to bear as his wife Katherine did his funeral. Throughout his burial and the respectful volley of shots fired by those who had arms, she had to be supported heavily by Dorothy. After this, it was as if she simply lost interest in life around her and took to her bed.

"Do the best you can to get her to eat something, Dorothy," Doctor Fuller instructed her. "She has always been of a weak constitution and I fear now, without John as her strength, she may simply pine away."

Dorothy tried but with now having to run the household, work the fields and keep a wary eye on Desire Minter's flirtatiousness, she felt torn and she could not lavish enough time and attention upon John Carver's grieving widow. Perhaps if she had, Dorothy cursed herself later, Katherine might have survived instead of dying from heartbreak a few weeks later. Then again, perhaps Katherine was not the weak woman Samuel Fuller assumed, for it takes enormous strength for a woman to will herself out of this life to be with the one she loves. Just as much, in fact, as it takes a body to struggle against a seemingly inevitable death for the very same reason.

On the deaths of both Katherine and John Carver, Dorothy's future was thrown into uncertainly. With the coming of the next ship from England, it had already been decided prudent for the well being of all concerned to return the under-aged Desire upon it.

"There will be no doubt be more settlers coming with it," Mary Brewster warned, "and they will all be in sore want of accommodation. It is only right that the Carvers' house be passed on to another family, my dear. Besides," she tried to add tactfully, "once Desire has gone, it won't be proper for you stay on there Dorothy, to be alone under the same roof as that lusty young Howland."

"But where shall I go?" Dorothy asked worriedly.

"That I can't say, "she replied. "Our cottage is bursting at the seams already and I have more family to come out to us yet!"

However, events overtook Dorothy and settled the problem for her. Late in the year, just as the England-bound ship left Plymouth with Desire safely stowed aboard, another near tragedy struck carpenter Francis Eaton. His young motherless son, Samuel, was laid dangerously low with a wretched illness.

"Please, Mistress Dorothy," a frantic Francis had practically begged, "Doctor Fuller sends his respects and asks if you might be persuaded to nurse my poor boy?"

Dorothy did not hesitate. She went with Francis to the child and immediately knew the illness to be the croup. However, after spending several un-chaperoned nights tending the child under the same roof as the young widower, some cruel shot of slander let off by the wretched Billington family was sent ricocheting around the settlement and finally back to Francis Eaton's ears. With that, he immediately did the only honorable thing he could under the circumstances. Despite their obvious age difference and with no romantic attachment, he asked her to marry him. So, out of necessity and on a certain understanding, Dorothy did.

As many months passed by in this arrangement, Francis watched his new wife with an ever-growing admiration. Quietly he looked on, amazed by her industriousness and humbled by her utter unselfishness in all her everyday dealings. The tenderness Dorothy showed towards his own young child naturally only served to endear this new 'wife' to him also. Therefore, it was not unexpected that Francis should find his feelings naturally progressing towards a love for this woman. A wife with whom he lay down each night, yet never with the touch of a husband. Francis was a man of his word. He treasured Dorothy's commitment to be a wife to him in all other respects and understood her wish to retain fidelity towards her lost Thomas. Yet, even so, Francis would lie awake and watch her asleep in the moonlight; faithful to the word of his agreement yet dreaming that one day, Dorothy might fall in love with him.

***

The weather that spring of 1623 was warm and so very welcome. The crop was in the ground early and putting on so much growth as to make Dorothy smile with contentment each day as she tended the fields. However, this early joy soon faded, as did any sign of the rain. From the third week in May it became clear that a drought had set in, and unless it broke they would starve come autumn. Dorothy was at first hopeful that the fish fertilizer buried under the corn would retain enough moisture, as well as nourishment, for the planting to survive.

However, as spring ran into summer still the rain failed to come. It remained dry and the weather became increasingly hot. No matter how much of the day Dorothy and Francis struggled with yoke and pails to ferry water to the thirsting corn from the stream, it was never enough to quench the thirst of the cracked, dry earth. Even with Squanto's help, in the naturally drier ground on their plot, the parched crop withered into looking more like hay and was far beyond reviving. Instead, Dorothy and her husband now concentrated their efforts on trying to save the healthiest looking of their languishing crop. It was no mean effort and the heat and grinding toil began to take a terrible toll on Dorothy's previously robust constitution. The drought finally broke by mid July, but Dorothy's health did as well.

It was more than mere exhaustion, though Dorothy had tried to shrug it off as such. She was tired and lethargic, completely ground down by her efforts to save the corn. Then one Sunday and quite out of character, Dorothy suddenly took to her bed. For several days, she complained of a racking pain in her limbs and she suffered 'the shivers' badly. Yet, after these passed off, for a short while she seemed recovered and much her old self again. However, Francis noticed that there was now a hitherto unseen fragility about his wife.

The following Saturday, Francis arrived home late. It had been a glorious summer's day and he had been working the fields until noon before going over to lend Stephen Hopkins a neighbourly hand. Francis had quite lost track of time and fearing that supper would be spoiling on his account, hurried to the hollowed log trough set outside his cottage to clean himself up before going in. As he did so, unusually he found there was no bucket of water waiting to be used. Instead, he went indoors fully expecting to find his family there but was met only by silence and with no evidence of a meal in progress. Suddenly realising that the yoke and pails were missing Francis then presumed that Dorothy too, late in realising the hour, was away with young Samuel fetching water from the stream. However, as time passed by and with evening drawing in, he decided to go and look for her.

Outside the sky was blanketing down with dark raggedy–edged clouds. Francis could smell the sweet rain in prospect as he skirted the field to pick up the track he knew Dorothy usually took to the stream. As he did so a breeze whipped over the tops of the corn, sending a wave rippling out across the rustling sea of gold.

Just as a summer shower began Francis followed the path

as it meandered into the cover of some trees, he paused and listened a moment, half certain he could hear something other than the pattering of raindrops on the canopy all about him. Then, just a little further on and approaching the stream by now, Francis heard the unmistakable whimpering of a small child. Drawing nearer to the sound, he suddenly came across his distraught son crouched upon the ground beneath the wizened branch of an old oak tree. He was crying, holding his stepmother's hand in his as she lay slumped motionless, face down in the dirt. Close by Dorothy's fallen body, a sad pool of water spilt from the upturned pails, trickled its way like a tear back towards the stream.

Francis quickly bent down and eased Dorothy over. Fearing the worst, he checked for signs of life and was deeply relieved as his wife responded with a slight sigh. Scooping her up in his arms, Francis ran towards home with the child scampering after. Nearing the cottage and within hailing distance of the lane, Francis began to yell out frantically for someone, anyone, to run and fetch Doctor Fuller. As luck would have it, Squanto was at that moment on his way back from a day's hunting and answered his plea for help.

Over the following days, the fever ferociously tightened its grip on her and her husband slipped deeper into despair as his wife began to ramble incoherently, insisting that her name was not Dorothy.

"It is delirium, Francis!" Doctor Samuel Fuller tried his best to comfort him. "It is naught but the fever talking! There, there," Samuel soothed Dorothy, taking the cloth from his patient's forehead and replacing it gently with a new one that had been set to soak in a bowl nearby, "try to rest, Dorothy."

With this, Dorothy rose up a little from the pillows and her eyes finally fluttered open. Fleetingly they fixed, staring beyond that simple cabin interior to some distant point that may even have transcended life itself. Laboured, yet clearly audible, she gasped but five words, "Bessie', my name is Bessie!" before gently falling back and into a deep, peaceful repose.

Francis was still deeply perplexed.

"But why say she is someone else? Why should she insist her name is Bessie?"

"Who can truly understand the working of the human mind?" Doctor Fuller answered, "let alone when tormented with such a fever as Dorothy has had to endure these past days. Mayhap she is dreaming of someone from her past. Who can say? I doubt that even she could tell you if you could raise her to full consciousness now. So, do not worry, Francis," he smiled, "take comfort that for now, at least, she seems to be at peace!"

Doctor Fuller closed the catch on his small oakwood medicine chest, picked up his black hat and made for the door.

"I will be back soon, Francis," he said, lifting the latch.

As he opened it, a streak of lightning shocked its way across the ghostly sky, followed by a low rumble of thunder from somewhere far out across the harbour.

"Looks like a storm's rolling in!" Francis said, as a scattering of gust-blown leaves rustled in across the threshold.

Doctor Fuller shuddered.

"Yes, I am afraid it does!" he replied. "Something unpleasant in the offing, I would not be surprised. Still," he turned and smiled genially, "I could do with being away to my own bed for a while and there is little more I can do here anyway".

No sooner had he arrived at his own cottage and was getting settled to sleep than a frantic rapping hammered Fuller's door. He opened up to find a fraught-faced William Brewster there.

"Excuse my intrusion," Brewster apologized profusely.

"William! What is it man? Not someone else fallen ill I hope!"

"No Samuel. None that I know of anyhow. How is Mistress Dorothy? Is she...?" Brewster hazarded to ask.

"Still very much touch and go, my friend, I am afraid to say," the doctor replied cautiously "But she is still holding her own, so we must not give up hope completely that she will make a recovery."

William looked strangely disappointed.

"What is it William? Something has happened, hasn't it? Something to do with Dorothy?"

William Brewster refused to be drawn.

"Samuel, you will be told in due course. But for now I have been asked to see if you can be spared from your duties for a short while to meet with Governor Bradford. I am certain that he will give you an explanation directly."

Samuel Fuller lost no time. He pulled back on his boots, donned his hat and left with William Brewster.

"What is all the mystery then?" Samuel asked.

"I dursn't say," Brewster replied. "Not until we reached the privacy of Bradford's house. If news of this gets out.........well."

Samuel was intrigued.

"Is this something to do with Mistress Eaton?"

"No," William replied abruptly. "I would say it's more to do with another man's wife. But more of that later..." He broke off from conversation as they continued down the lane and passed Susanna Winslow.

"Looks like a storm, Mistress Winslow," Samuel lifted his hat in greeting.

"Yes, Doctor. Mister Brewster," she tipped her head in greeting as she snatched her clean washing from the clothesline. "How is poor Dorothy today?" she asked with deep concern.

"No better, I am afraid to report," he replied gravely.

Susanna sighed with a knowing resignation, then quickly

changing the subject added, "Is it true," she asked hurriedly, " that there is a shallop come ashore? Is it a supply ship already, do you know?"

A shallop? It was the first Samuel had heard of it.

"No," Brewster replied. "It's but a survey ship, up from Virginia. Re-mapping the Cape so I believe. A small detachment is ashore seeking out victuals and water from the Governor, and such a loutish bunch that he thought best they not roam the settlement at large."

"Oh," she replied, "I was hoping for news from England. Never mind.........It can't be long now," she said as the heavens opened and sent her scurrying into the house with her infant in tow.

A mapping ship? Samuel's curiosity was running as wild as his footsteps as they hurried the last few yards to Governor Bradford's house. For a usually self-possessed man his imagination was fired. What could a mapping ship have to do with Dorothy?

William Bradford was ushering the two men into his house before their shadows had even hit the threshold.

Like a dog fresh from a stream, Samuel shook the rain from his hat and coat. Only then did he notice that William Bradford had not been alone whilst waiting for him. There was a stranger standing with him. A swarthy looking, heavily-bearded unkempt fellow. A sailor by the looks of him.

"Good morning, sir!" Samuel greeted him politely.

"Good Morning Samuel!" the stranger replied.

"I am sorry sir. You appear to have the advantage of me," the doctor exclaimed in surprise.

"Indeed I do for once," the stranger replied, only this time Samuel Fuller suddenly had the measure of his man.

"My God! Thomas! Can it really be you? I thought you were dead!"

"Yes it is and I almost was!" he replied. "Almost buried too! But at the last was discovered breathing, though my health and memory took months to recover, I am here as you see very much alive! But enough of this. Please! Someone! Will you kindly take me to my wife?"

***

The storm had driven workers home early from the fields and children scampered in from the lane. Soon the only signs of life in Plymouth were smoke swirls from cottage chimney pots mingling with the gathering black above as the settlers sheltered safely indoors behind shuttered windows. The thunder growled on like a wild cat snarling in the heavens as lightning glanced the forest treetops beyond.

Nonetheless, they had waited until dark to be certain no one witnessed the four silent figures stride purposefully along the empty, rain-sodden lane towards the Eaton's cottage. Once secreted inside, Francis dragged the only chairs he owned up to the battered oak table and bade these unwelcome intruders into his private life to sit down. Meantime, he took to the rickety stool that his wife regularly tipped upside down and pressed into use for 'dripping' her delicate soft cheese in its fine muslin cloth.

Perhaps it was a blessing that little Samuel Eaton was too young to understand the gravity of the anguished look on his father's face, or to remember the tortured words that passed between him, his friends and the stranger that night. The child peered down for a little while from the loft above, with his little face puzzled by the frantic yet muted exchanged below. Soon bored and with the sound of the thunder growing louder and the wind buffeting at the window shutters and door, he crawled away to seek out familiar warmth and comfort, by lying down beside his sick stepmother.

Meanwhile Dorothy was caught up in a swirling stream of near consciousness from which she would begin to rise up momentarily, only to be dragged back down into the depths where once again she was Bessie, a young, carefree girl skipping along the leafy lanes near her village, with the sun on her neck and a warm breeze licking at her face. As she happily gambled on, she heard Judd Lowe's friendly voice call out from the fields in greeting. Then, as she heard an even more familiar voice from close quarters call out in reply, she was suddenly aware that someone's hand was tightly holding hers. Squinting up against the strong sunlight in her eyes, Bessie smiled up at her father walking beside her.

"This is real nice, my girlie," he said smiling back. "A real beauty of a day to be alive."

"Yes," she replied, then hesitating a moment added, "but what is all that whispering I can hear?"

"Whispering?"

"Yes Daddy! Whispering. I can hear men's voices but as if they are ever so far away."

"Ah!" her father replied. "T'aint nothing to be afeard of then," he reassured her in his usual calming way. "T'aint nothing but some moanings on the breeze. Some folk do say how it's echoes from the past, or mayhap even snatches from the future. Can you hear what they are a-saying child?"

"No. I cannot make out the words."

"Then it don't matter! It's just voices," he said. "If you canst make out them words then maybe they are not meant for you to hear. Don't let it concern you, my lovely. Just you and I enjoy the stroll now, for it canst last forever."

The pair walked on, father and child clasping each other hand in hand, but as they did the voices became clearer and the little girl was able to make out some of the words...

"What a nightmare! What do we do?" Francis exclaimed still unable to comprehend Thomas's sudden re-emergence from the grave. "Until now, I feared losing my wife," he exclaimed with deep anguish. "Now I find I never had her! Oh God, what do we do? Why can't you just go away, Thomas?"

"Nay!" Thomas was adamant. "I will never do that! Dorothy is my wife! I shall never leave. Not unless the words come from her own mouth!"

"Yet, even if he did go," William Brewster cut in, "it would not be the end of it! Dorothy is and would continue to be legally married to Thomas. It is a fact duly registered in England and cannot be undone. You have to face up to it, Francis, your union with her as husband and wife is null and void in the eyes of the law. And that will not go away, even if Thomas chose to! Which brings us to the crux of the matter..." William's face turned hard as stone. Combing through his grey-peppered beard with his fingers, he teased out the ragged bush as he did the tangled strands of his argument. "As it stands, Francis," he said, "at best you are as equal with Dorothy, guilty of the crime of adultery and therefore punishable as the Law of England dictates."

Francis was appalled by the prospect. Back in England, adultery was regarded as a serious crime against the teachings of the scriptures. Though technically punishable by death, adulterers were traditionally branded with a hot iron bearing the letter 'A' pressed into their forehead, then whipped through the streets for all to see. It was a terrible stigma to bear. Even more so if one had unwittingly transgressed.

"But we believed...we all believed Thomas was dead!" Francis protested. "We did not do this thing deliberately! It was a mistake. A dreadful, dreadful mistake!"

Brewster's expression remained unmoved.

"Yes, but it has happened," Brewster pressed on. "Though neither you nor we were in possession of the facts at the time, in the eyes of the law it changes nothing. You are guilty of adultery, Francis, and subject to punishment for the same!"

Francis fell silent for a moment. His head fell and his demeanour changed to that of a man with a guilty secret to unburden. Then, bravely looking up, he faced the others with a confession they had not expected.

"There has been no act of adultery," he said with obvious regret. "Although I have come to love her more than anything, by mutual agreement our union has never been consummated."

Thomas received these words with thankful relief.

Brewster however did not.

"Even if the authorities chose to believe that," he warned coldly, "for Dorothy, there are far worse consequences to face than just that of adultery."

"Worse?" Thomas did not understand Brewster's drift.

"Yes, for she stands not only guilty of adultery but the far more serious offence of bigamy too. And the church will exact the most severe of punishments for that."

"The Church.... The Law.... It sounds like you who condemn her out of hand, William!"

Doctor Fuller sprang to Dorothy's defence. "This is no low harlot we talk of! This is our Dorothy! Your wife's friend! The same Dorothy who nursed our sick and dying and lovingly laid out the bodies of the dead! Yet you make her sound like a wanton jezebel."

"That is not my intention," William Brewster now defended himself vehemently, "and of course I do not see her like that! I am simply acting here as the Devil's advocate. Somebody has to! For this is how others will attack her, us and any ill founded decision, we make!"

"Oh my god!" the Doctor gasped, now realizing what Brewster was getting at.

"But," Thomas seemed puzzled, "if she married Francis in a civil ceremony here, as I understand you have adopted from the Netherlands, then surely she cannot be deemed guilty of breaking Church law? Can she?"

"Maybe we could argue that case, but then," Will Bradford entered the fray, " by following that line, we leave ourselves open for the authorities in England not to recognize any of the marriages carried out in that manner already amongst our congregation. That, I fear, could make bastards of half the children here and throw the question of property arrangements and inheritance into complete disarray! Although we have been promised self-determination by patent, with no codified law of our own, we are therefore bound to comply with the wisdom of those of our most dread sovereign King James. We have got to try her under English Law!"

"But why?" Samuel Fuller demanded. "Have we not paid lip service to both the sovereign and bishop's laws on many occasions? Why is this different? Why not just pass this quietly over?"

"Do you really think we can pass this matter quietly over?" Brewster asked in all honesty. "Do you really think that we can keep this situation at bay here? How shall it sound to the authorities in England? That the Plymouth settlement condones bigamy and adultery? How long do you think it might take the patents here to be revoked and our leave to stay rescinded?"

No one answered so Brewster continued his onslaught.

"And what of the effect that turning a blind eye to a case, however misguided, of adultery and bigamy might have upon those low-moral 'strangers' that we have amongst us? We already struggle daily with them to check against any possible outbreak of lawlessness. If we are seen to then disregard the law ourselves.... You see the grave quandary we have here?"

Indeed they now did.

"Then what do you suggest?" Francis dared ask.

"I think the only option we have to defend the honour and standing of Plymouth, is to return Mistress Dorothy to England and lay her case open to the mercy of the authorities there," Brewster sighed.

"Mercy?" Thomas sneered. "Do you really think they will show her any mercy? The Bishops will hang her as an example, especially when the details of the civil marriage here mark her out plain as a Separatist dissenter! No!" Thomas retorted, "I cannot let you do that! I will go, and go now! I love her! I won't stand by and let you send her to her death. If I leave now, it can be as if I were never here. As if I am truly dead to you all!"

Thomas rose to his feet only to be restrained by Will Bradford's loving hand.

"No Thomas," he said with compassion. "It can never be as it was. You see, we know. We cannot stand by and watch Dorothy remain under the same roof as Francis now. For with every day that then passed we would be guilty of watching them both live out a lie in a fraudulent union. We may not stand by, in good conscience, and condone that. Openly or privately."

"Then what do we do?" Doctor Fuller demanded. "For to settle this matter will take the wisdom of Solomon himself!"

Suddenly upstairs, as if dredged up from the depths of storm tossed ocean, Dorothy surfaced again briefly into consciousness and called out above the turbulence of the weather. Francis Eaton quickly sprang to his feet with the intention of going to her aid. Thomas stood up too. For an agonizing moment, there was a silent impasse with each man glaring at the other.

"May I go to my wife, please, Francis?" Thomas not so much asked as insisted.

Turning, hoping for support from his friends, Francis caught the full meaning of Samuel Fuller's sideways glance. Reluctantly, a shaking Eaton nodded and then biting his lip resumed his seat. Thomas made his way over to the loft ladder, and started to climb the steps. As he did, an uneasy silence fell upon the company sitting below. William Bradford sat with his head in his hands in deep contemplation. As governor, the ultimate decision lay with him. Then, after long and careful consideration, he looked up and gravely gave his verdict.

"Better, perhaps for all", he said calmly, "that Mistress Dorothy does not recover from this fever."

Thomas ascended in search of his past heaven to find a slumbering cherub, arms outstretched, embracing the waist of his own lost angel. With the autumn tints in her hair picked out by soft lamplight and her pale translucent skin radiating serenity, to Thomas's artist's eye Dorothy looked every inch like a Tiziano Vecellio Madonna. He knelt silently at her side in awestruck adoration until she stirred and softly murmured once more.

Deep in some recess of her mind, Dorothy still languished within the walls of Gainsborough Old Hall. At cockcrow she had risen, gathered up her bundle of possessions and made her way down the dark stone tower stair and out into the still gloomy garden beyond. There, in eager anticipation, she had sheltered beneath the leafy boughs of the walnut tree, her worldly goods on the ground at her side, waiting for her true love to arrive. Her heart raced but her thoughts had been calm and crystal clear. She was going to accept Thomas's proposal of marriage and go away with him to the New World.

Beyond the ancient garden wall, high up somewhere in branch of a churchyard yew, a lone blackbird had begun to sing out its heavenly solo in greeting for the new day. The faint eastern glow steadily intensified, spilling across the garden and melting away the shadows in its path as it gently bathed the garden in light. Another cock crowed. A second blackbird then sang out in reply to the first; a song thrush and sparrows joined in and soon birds had begun to sing from every nook and cranny.

Still Dorothy had waited. Then she saw him, a lone figure striding across dew-spangled lawn towards her. Dorothy had run to him and thrown herself into his outstretched arms. He in return had held her tightly. So very, very tightly, as if terrified of ever letting go.

"I dared not let myself believe that you would be here!"

he cried breathlessly.

"And I was afraid that you would not come!" she sobbed back.

"I had to come. Even if it meant my returning here every day for the rest of my life, I could never leave for good without you. I know I can never bear to be parted from you again, my love."

"Nor I from you!"

"Are you certain, Dorothy?" he said, smothering her cheeks with his joyful kisses. "Are you certain that you can leave this life and come away with me forever?"

"Oh yes, Thomas," she said, finding his lips with hers. "I would ransom the chance to live a hundred years more in this place in return for just a few minutes with you."

Thomas lifted up his wife's slender hand and pressing her cold fingertips to his lips, he tenderly kissed each one in turn, as he had done so many times before in the past. With that gentle familiarity, Dorothy's eyes fluttered open and glimmered with instant recognition. For a few fleeting moments it was as if the world had stopped turning. As Dorothy lifted her head up a little, such a beautiful, love-filled smile lit up her pallid face. She gazed longingly into Thomas's face as he did into hers. Then, an almighty gust of wind rushed at the shutters sending the whole house a-trembling. Upstairs the lamplight flickered furiously and was all but snuffed out before settling once more. With that, Dorothy gently closed her eyes and slipped peacefully back onto her pillows.

The savage gales raged on for several more days before supplies and fresh water could be negotiated aboard the shallop and taken back to the mapping ship in the bay. As anonymously as he had arrived, Thomas departed with it. He did not stay to witness the sparsely attended ceremony where a plain coffin was respectfully lowered into the sodden New England earth, nor did the slender, cloaked figure who accompanied him when he left. Instead, he was on his way back with the surveying vessel to Virginia. It is said that that is where he made his fortune, before eventually returning to England with his wife, Bessie.

The Mayflower Maid- Epilogue

Why write the Mayflower Maid?

Roger writes:

It all started when Sue and I were working towards the
end of our second novel together. Having spent some time
in Maryland the previous spring discovering America 'first
hand', she invited me, in return, to visit with her in the fall.
I was not at all sure that I wanted to go. I was also uncertain
how to express this to my co-writer without causing offence.
It wasn't that I did not want to go England; indeed, it had
been my dearest wish to return there since I was in London
in the early sixties while in the U.S. Army. It was just that I
did not want to visit her 'neighborhood' – Lincolnshire.
There was nothing there as far as I could see! To back up
my fears my trusty American 'traveler's bible', an extremely
well respected tourist guide, said so! So, over the following
month or so, whenever we spoke and the question of 'when
are you coming over' arose I tried to wriggle out of giving
a firm refusal to this kind offer of hospitality until I could
wriggle no more. One day she insisted, rather forcefully,
that I give a firm answer and I finally had to be up front
about to my 'reservations' and tentatively read her the
relevant passages from the travel guide.

"Nothing here?" she exclaimed in a colorful way only
Sue could get away with. "Forget the book! Trust me!" she
said, so I did.

I cannot recollect much of my journey to Lincolnshire from
the airport. It had been a long overnight flight and I was so
tired I slept most the way back and only really surfaced
again a few miles from her home.

The sight of open, green, rolling countryside greeted me.
It was beautifully scenic but as I had suspected, with nothing
much of interest to fire the imagination. Her house though

did live up to my American expectation of the quintessential quaint English country cottage, with low ceilings and black painted oak beams in abundance. However, as I gratefully settled down to sleep in the pleasant floral surrounds of my guestroom, I could not help but think that the ensuing five weeks of my stay there were going to be terribly disappointing from a sight seeing point of view. Boy, I couldn't have been more wrong!

After resting for a day or so and getting my bearings in the tiny village that was to be my home for the next month, Sue took me to a small unpromising-looking town called Gainsborough some twelve miles away on the River Trent near the border with Nottinghamshire and Yorkshire. After leaving the parking lot, we meandered through some side streets that suddenly opened up into a residential square. There, slap in the middle of it was the most awesome and unexpected sight I could have imagined - Gainsborough Old Hall. It was just suddenly there, a magnificent jewel of a medieval manor house sitting on its emerald green cushion of lawns among the surrounding streets of ordinary houses. I could sense almost immediately that the townsfolk must treasure this building like a well-loved favorite old Aunt at a family gathering. Just standing out front of its black and white half -timbered facade blew me away.

Sue gave me the full tour as I snapped away furiously with my camera trying to capture the awe I felt inside me as I wandered from room to room. As I walked into the Great Hall itself, I was dumbstruck. It was like the set of a Hollywood movie come to life before my eyes. It was incredible enough to be inside a house dating from around 1460, but even more so to discover its huge medieval kitchens were perfectly preserved and dressed as if their cooks had just walked away for a break from work These were kitchens in which I learned, lavish banquets had been prepared for such notable visitors as King Richard III and Henry VIII.

There were very few visitors that day and as we walked unhurriedly from room to room, it felt as though we had the whole house to ourselves. Yet the strangest thing of all that day was the total serenity of the place and the strange feeling of belonging that I, as a 'foreigner', felt in the Old Hall. It was as if it was trying to speak to me, to tell me about my roots. It was then and there it first hit me, how wonderful a part of the world this was.

Finally, as we were reaching the end of our tour, I found myself suddenly ushered into a small exhibition area. It was all about the Pilgrim Fathers, the Mayflower and the Separatist movement in England at the time. I was puzzled as to what it was doing here. I just reeled in utter bewilderment as I read the information boards. I consider myself a regular guy with a university education. How could it be then, that I did not know any of the stuff I was now reading?

"Your Pilgrim Fathers came from around here!" Sue said. "See, I've brought you home!" .

For almost six decades of my life, I had thought that the Pilgrim Fathers had come from a place called Plymouth, hundreds of miles from where I was now. How could it be that my friends and family back home were probably also clinging to the same misguided notion? Sue quickly realized this, and so during the rest of my stay took great pride in taking me out to tour all the places related to the Pilgrim Fathers that she could think of.

The Town of Boston, some sixty odd miles to the south was another place I had not realized existed. It boasts not only the medieval Guild Hall Jail and 'The Stump' as depicted in the novel but also just downstream near Fishtoft is a memorial marking the place where William Brewster and the Separatists made their first attempt to escape to Holland by ship. Standing by it and gazing across the rugged windswept fenland towards the water, I soon realized what a truly desolate spot this must have been at the time and how desperate these people were. Tattershall Castle, that sheltered them briefly, also survives, in part, to the north west of Boston and is open to the public.

Nearer to Gainsborough where my enlightenment by my friend's gentle hands began there are, unfortunately, other Pilgrim sites, still in existence, yet out of the public domain. At Austerfield the Norman church of St. Helena where William Bradford was baptized still stands. So does his former home and at nearby Scrooby, William Brewster's Scrooby Manor still exists but again is in private hands and not accessible to visitors. We did however get to tread some of the very same lanes William Brewster and William Bradford must have walked along in their daily lives here and glimpse their ancient homes, from a distance through roadside hedges.

I was at once heartened and disheartened to hear Sue explain that a local charity, the Pilgrim Heritage Trust, had been set up with the prime aim of acquiring, preserving, restoring and making available for viewing historic buildings, ancient sites and artefacts associated with the Pilgrim Fathers but that the present state of affairs was giving cause for concern. A lack of financial support for their efforts meant that many of these would inevitably be lost for all time. It was then I realized that somehow, some way, we must try to ensure that this was not allowed to simply happen. Then Sue said, quite matter of factly, "Why don't we write a book bringing the English and American parts of the story together and try to raise awareness that way? If it took off, then we would be able to finance some of the work too."

"What a brilliant idea!" I replied. Then I thought to myself, "How on earth was Sue ever going to work out a plot to make the Pilgrim Fathers sound interesting? The story had just been allowed to become so dull over the years!

***

SUSAN WRITES –

Having established that we wanted to write a novel to tie together the story of the Separatists'of England and the Pilgrim Fathers of America, as authors, we found we needed a thread free enough to be drawn through the events of the time to help embroider all these patches of historical fact together into one blanket story. All of the main players in the Pilgrim story left behind extracts or accounts of events of the time, most notably William Bradford's 'Of Plymouth Plantation' which is widely known already and used as a valuable research tool. Therefore, we did not see the point of simply rewriting these into a novel. Besides, they do not delve far enough into the background of the social and political climate of that time as they are writings very much of their time and take for granted that the reader will already be familiar with a religious backdrop of a persecution which has long since disappeared from memory.

To do the story full justice, we needed our thread to be free to weave in and out of the known historical facts from the early days of this Separatist group of Brewster and Bradford's and continue right into the founding of the new colony at Plymouth in the New World. Therefore, our main character for the novel also had to have been aboard the Mayflower. Yet they also needed to have led a life so scantily documented as to allow us to use them freely within the plot. As we intended to fictionalize this person's life we decided it was more fitting if this someone had also left behind no descendants.

Some of the more obvious choices we might have seized on, were the numerous children who were on board and who did not, unfortunately go on to survive. However, events using one of these as our protagonist would have incurred many unacceptable limitations for us as writers, not least of all being the short time span one of these children's lives could offer. Then there was also the fact that events of such a monumental nature could never be realistically portrayed through such young eyes and remain plausible to any discerning reader. As we started to research in earnest into the fine detail of the backgrounds of the fully documented list of passengers aboard the Mayflower, it soon transpired there were very few who might suit our very demanding brief. Then, as I examined a very graining looking download from the Internet of a section of the hand written passenger list from Bradford's time, one entry aroused my curiosity immediately. It was of one person who was listed, yet inexplicably left completely unnamed and therefore totally anonymous. Amongst John Carver's extended household, in which menservants, a bond boy and various children 'put to him' were all fully named, one line simply reads 'a maid servant'. Not only had I found the character needed for the purpose of the novel, but my ever-enquiring mind was left pondering as to why the personal details of this maid were omitted by William Bradford in his otherwise meticulously detailed account. Why, with many opportunities to amend this error over the years in which he kept up and added retrospectively to his notes, did Bradford leave this maidservant so mysteriously anonymous? In entering up, for example, his notes on the 'increasing and decreasing' of Plymouth (presumably in 1650) with such precision, when he recounts the fate of this maid servant he simply states that 'His (Carver's) maidservant married and died a year or two after, here in this place' Is it not very strange that he fails to state even here, either her name or whom she married, though he must have surely known.

Francis Eaton married a certain 'Dorothy' in those very early days of the Plymouth colony, who therefore must have come across on the Mayflower. By a process of elimination, this Dorothy could only have been this maidservant. More curiously, as it is very likely that these early marriages were not religious in nature, Bradford himself as Governor must surely have attended, if not presided over it himself.

This would not be the only notable omission on William Bradford's part, as he also fails to mention the death by drowning of his first wife in the harbour shortly after arrival. Professor Samuel Elliot Morrison mentions in his introduction to 'Of Plymouth Plantation' that many believe Dorothy Bradford's death may have been suicide. In the light of this, I must ask why the identity of John Carver's maidservant remains so sketchy. However, both authors have no doubts in their minds at all that William Bradford was a deeply devout, honourable man who would have followed his conscience in all his dealings to act, as he believed his God willed.

All of the main characters in the novel, with the exception of Master Thomas, existed in real life and events from their lives (such as we know them) have been faithfully portrayed in amongst the fictionalisation of the life of the Mayflower Maid. Extensive research has been carried out to make the scenes in this novel as authentic as possible and where able, passages have been written in situ at various locations in the novel where they would have played out in order to bring about a sense of realism to the book, so often missing from non–fiction accounts of the time. The result, we sincerely hope has been an enjoyable yet informative novel bringing the reader a fresh perspective on the lives of the Pilgrim Fathers and perhaps inspire them to delve a little deeper into the history for themselves.